# HART *of* ROUNDSTONE

## DEBBIE TAYLOR

WESTBOW
PRESS®
A DIVISION OF THOMAS NELSON
& ZONDERVAN

Scripture taken from the New King James Version. Copyright © 1979, 1980, 1982 by Thomas Nelson, Inc. Used by permission. All rights reserved.

This is a work of fiction. All of the characters, names, incidents, organizations, and dialogue in this novel are either the products of the author's imagination or are used fictitiously.

WestBow Press books may be ordered through booksellers or by contacting:

WestBow Press
A Division of Thomas Nelson & Zondervan
1663 Liberty Drive
Bloomington, IN 47403
www.westbowpress.com
1 (866) 928-1240

ISBN: 978-1-5127-3812-4 (sc)
ISBN: 978-1-5127-3813-1 (hc)
ISBN: 978-1-5127-3811-7 (e)

Library of Congress Control Number: 2016906167

Print information available on the last page.

WestBow Press rev. date: 05/31/2016

# Contents

# Acknowledgment

To my lovely granddaughter,
Emili Trousdale
who created the beautiful cover for *Hart of Roundstone.*
I thank you!
You caught the essence of Nellie as well as God's blessings at the
Hart of Roundstone!

*For though we have never yet seen God,*
*when we love each other God lives in us*
*and His love within us grows ever stronger.*
1 John 4:12

# Author's Note

In July of 2012, with shovel in hand, I began to dig in my backyard to place a fish pond form. I found and dug up the rock that I now call the Hart of Roundstone. The limestone rock came out of the ground just as it is in the picture. I feel the rock was sculpted by Charles Cosby, owner of Roundstone in the 1800s. (Charles is Thomas in book. Names have been changed.) The rock was sculpted by Charles for a tombstone for his first wife. Historical records show that Charles' first wife was killed by a tree falling on her. Their oldest son drown in Roundstone Creek, and he is buried on the Roundstone property. Charles Cosby later remarried Martha who is Mary in the book.

Charles Cosby owned 4,000 acres in the Roundstone/Upton area. At one time there were three mills on the Cosby place. Charles Cosby was a businessman and played a critical part in the history of the Civil War.

I hope you enjoy the adventures of the Cosby family. There are many characters in this first book, many of whom will appear in subsequent books. In the next book, Nellie, Mike, and Tommie leave Roundstone as they are separated for their calling.

Upton Baptist Church is mentioned many times in *Hart of Roundstone*, and it is modeled from the real church which my family attends today. I hope you will be blessed by the love the characters show for one another. Family, community, and church are all built on Christian values and a heart like His.

Debbie Taylor

# Dedication

I dedicate this book to my mother-in-law,
**Oleta Catherine Money,**
who has been an inspiration for this book.
Oleta's exemplary life as a Christian has been a blessing in many ways.
As I developed the character of Katherine Cosby, I
thought about what Oleta would say and do.
Of course, even though the character of Katherine
Cosby is fictional, I am sure there were
many matriarchs of the families in the 1800s who
nurtured their families through God's love.

## SPECIAL DEDICATION

In June of 2014, just before this book was to go to
print, a tragedy occurred to our family.
Brianna Taylor was killed in an automobile accident.
Less than two weeks later Brianna's brother,
Brice, was killed in an accident.
Parents, David and Tanya Taylor had to bury their only two children.
Because Brianna and Brice were such dedicated
Christians, their family grieved
but rejoiced in the hope that they would one day see their loved ones.
Both Brianna and Brice
had been witnesses for Christ and both had been an inspiration to
their friends, family, teachers, coaches and many others.
I dedicate the characters in this book to the memory of
**Brianna and Brice Taylor**
and their love of their
Lord and Savior.

# Prologue

She was young and foolish with a heart for the young man.
She had a plan.
The young man loved the Lord and was on a mission.
He had a calling.
On a warm spring day, the plan, like a spider's web, awaited the victim.
Planting corn in a creek bottom, the young man
works as he dreams of life in ministry.
Daring, the young girl wades downstream through the cold creek water
until she gets to the field.
His field.
Splashing and laughter.
Curiosity leads him to the snare.
Beautiful, she appears slightly embarrassed from being discovered.
He should run away, instead he lingers.
He throws her his shirt, as she asked.
He helps her up the steep creek bank.
She convinces him to walk upstream to her clothes to return his shirt.
As they walked together, feelings intensify.
He retrieves her clothes hanging from a grapevine.
She removes the borrowed shirt.
Under the boughs of a huge oak tree, lives were changed.
Forever.

# Chapter 1

# The Wedding

Nellie balanced the wedding cake, nestled in a dishpan, as the buckboard bounced through a mud puddle. Her thumb poked through the side of the cake coating it with the delicious icing. As Nellie licked her thumb of the sweet, brown caramel icing, she thought how it was a shame to waste such good cake on a wedding. The wedding, which she had protested for so long, would take place today, despite her efforts. Within a few hours, her father would be married to Miss Mary Reynolds and the cake would be devoured. To Nellie, her father and the cake were both meeting their demise.

Granma Katherine gripped the worn leather reins to Ol' Dan while six-year-old Renie cuddled beside her with her doll, Ella. Katherine was determined to be a blessing to everyone, especially the children, today, the day of her son's wedding. Thomas, Katherine's oldest and only son, was getting married, despite how she and the children objected. Now, resigned to her son's wishes, Katherine had to be a good example for the children, regardless of her uneasy feelings.

Tommie, on the rear buckboard seat, hugged a huge, brown pottery bowl of new boiled, red potatoes covered with a kitchen towel. With a free hand, he wiped sweat from his forehead and loosened the collar on his shirt. Tommie was uncomfortable being forced to wear his Sunday-best clothing on this hot afternoon in July. Although Tommie was usually well-mannered, he had already shared his miseries and objections with the family several times.

"You know, Gran, I could use these new potatoes," Tommie said rather cunningly.

"What? Tommie, what are you up to?" Katherine asked as she glanced behind her.

"Just thinking how fast they would soar with my slingshot." Tommie chuckled as he expressively described his plan.

"I'll just hide and when Mary least expects it...splat!" In a quick-witted manner so typical of Tommie, he began his poetic verse.

> "A bride, Miss Mary wanted to be,
> But she hadn't planned on shrewd Tom E!
> For he had a plan to prevent a wedding,
> a day his father was actually dreading.
> Tommie, girded with slingshot and red spud,
> while Mary screamed as she felt the thud!
> (Using his best dainty voice)
> Oh no! Thomas please make him stop,
> for this wedding will be a flop!'"

Katherine interrupted the rhyme with an obvious rebuke.

> "And his grandmother scolded and gave him a warning.
> You better be good or regret it by morning."

Nellie giggled at the vision of red skinned potatoes smashed on Miss Mary's face and dress. Turning to Tommie, Nellie gave her brother an approving wink.

Although a year younger than sister Nellie, Tommie appeared older as he seemed to have grown up fast over the last two years. He was a brawny, sandy-haired boy for his fourteen years and as dependable as the July heat. Tommie was not at all like older brother Johnny, the oldest child of the family. Johnny, Jonathan Wilson Cosby, had been named after his mother's grandfather. Johnny was much like Grandpa Wilson as he was a fearless young man. However, Tommie was the intelligent, philosophical member of the family.

However, things had changed two years ago, spurring a multitude of sorrows. First, Johnny drowned in the creek while rescuing Goldie's pups. Goldie, the family's old yellow dog, had chosen to have her puppies just across the creek, close to the mill. A sudden overnight spring rain had brought the creek flooding over the bridge.

Planning on an early morning arrowhead search, Johnny was the first to get up that morning. As Johnny stepped out on the large porch, he realized Goldie and her puppies would be in danger from the high waters. Without letting the family know what he was going to do, Johnny headed to the rushing water.

When Johnny did not return for breakfast Thomas became worried. Goldie, anxious to have someone take notice, was barking and running back and forth on the creek bank. As soon as Thomas' saw the raging creek, he feared the worse.

Roundstone Creek begins at the Cosby place. When the springs fill with rain, the creek rises quickly. That awful morning, Johnny had tried to swim across to rescue Goldie's pups, but the depth and the power of the creek's whirlpool proved too strong.

Johnny's body was retrieved in a log dam on the creek. Rissa, his mother, was so overcome with grief she would never be the same. Unfortunately, the Thomas Cosby family suffered through two deaths within a year, leaving suspicious minds, particularly Katherine's.

"Nellie, are you paying attention to that cake? That cake took a lot of my time, and I don't want to see it bouncing off onto the road," Granma Katherine advised, with a little more nerves and desperation than concern about the cake.

Katherine said a silent prayer that she could push back the disturbing dream for at least today. All her life, Katherine had dealt with dreams and visions and she prayed they would stop. Yet, she knew they were a "gift," one that had brought blessings and sorrows.

Katherine Cosby had come to live with her son's family after the death of Thomas's wife, Rissa. Katherine had a home and farm in Upton, but she felt she was needed with her son and his family. Thankfully, she was able to leave everything with her farm managers, the Highbaugh family, who were dependable, trustworthy people and members of the local church. However, Katherine continued her beloved job as the local midwife, which she had enjoyed since she was seventeen.

"I'm careful, Gran. But what are we going to do if Ollie's wife goes into labor? I want to be there to help. You think the baby might come today?" Nellie asked as she swatted a horse fly from her arm. "I don't want to go to the stupid wedding anyway," she mumbled.

Katherine forced a patient smile. "Don't worry about it, sweetie. Everything will be good. God will work things according to His plan. And, Nellie, it is not a 'stupid' wedding. Your father is marrying someone he loves, and we have to respect his wishes. Your father has prayed about marrying Mary, and he feels it is God's will." Katherine tried to keep her voice from showing any signs of tense feelings, but in her heart, she held a suspicion she had not shared with anyone. The dreams and suspicions clouded Katherine's happiness for her son's wedding.

Nellie wanted to ask if it was God's will that both her brother and her mother had died and left their family to miss them so much. It seemed to Nellie that Thomas had been able to get over his grief and get on with his life, while the children had suffered so much after the double loss. Something just didn't seem right to Nellie; maybe she was a little jealous of Miss Mary. Still, Nellie, her brother and sister had lost not only their brother but the mother they knew and loved.

Rissa, Thomas wife and mother of his four children, had grieved for months over Johnny's death, but seemed to be getting better. The family would never forget that day. Miss Mary and Katherine had come to cheer Rissa. The visitors had helped with lunch and decided to stay awhile to spend time with the family.

At the table, Thomas explained that he and Paul would be cutting trees on the south side of the farm and everyone should keep a safe distance away. The two men, who were skilled at timbering, discussed the process of bringing down, or felling, a tree.

Katherine commented on the dangerous the job. Thomas laughed at his mother's loving concern. He assured her that the tree was always secured by the huge rope which he had left at the barn. The rope, Thomas had explained, kept the chopped tree from spinning the wrong way. Still, Katherine urged Thomas and Paul to use extreme caution while bringing down the trees.

Katherine wiped her brow with her handkerchief as she recalled the events of that terrible morning. Miss Mary had excused herself while everyone was having blackberry cobbler. When Mary returned, she encouraged Rissa to accompany her outside to pick blackberries.

"I just saw a beautiful bunch of blackberries beside the barn. We really should go pick some more berries, maybe for jam."

Katherine had suggested the two young women be on their way, and she would take care of the dishes. Rissa and Miss Mary had carried their buckets to the barn and picked there awhile. Miss Mary told Rissa she would go back and get a hoe from the shed to help hold the blackberry vines back as they picked.

Rissa, in her excitement, wandered from the barn to a lush patch of blackberries. Preoccupied with the business of berry-picking, she did not think about her dangerous location.

Meanwhile, the men were diligently swinging their axes into a large sycamore which was a good distance from the barn's blackberry vines. Thomas had secured the tree with the strong rope to make the tree fall to the south. Then, a freak accident, a horrible accident! The tree spun as it was about to fall, and broke the rope that directed it southward.

Rissa had assumed she was well out of the way, but the top of the tree struck her head. She lived for two days but Doc Routt said her brain had swollen with blood and eventually brought her to an untimely death. Rissa was thirty-eight when she died; way too soon to leave her family. The three children and Thomas had loved her so much, and their grief had been almost unbearable.

Katherine had relived the tragic day Rissa was killed many times. Even now there were questions unanswered. Mary had told the others about Rissa moving down the fence row picking berries. But what had caused the strong rope to break causing the tree to fall on Rissa? Katherine was suspicious that someone had meant for the rope to snap. She shuddered as she remembered the dream about Rissa with the menacing objects. The tree like the one that had fallen, Thomas' rope, and something else, something shiny and sharp.

However, today Thomas was marrying Miss Mary, the teacher at Roundstone School. Nellie and Tommie agreed Miss Mary was a good teacher, but their new mother? No way!

Miss Mary had wedged her way into their family when she came to pay a visit after Johnny died. She had befriended Rissa Cosby, and helped her deal with the grief. Today, Miss Mary Reynolds would become Mrs. Mary Cosby and their new mother.

Well, Nellie vowed, she might be my father's new wife, but she will never be my mother! Nellie knew she had to temper her feelings. After all she was at church, a holy place. She began to concentrate on the sanctity and the beauty of the church.

The church pews were decorated with red roses and white and red ribbons. A wide, red ribbon was curled and strung across the front of the primitive pine-log church. Nellie had never seen the church so festive, even at Christmas when Sister Kay decorated with pine cones and candles.

Guests arrived at the small country church with food, gifts, and smiles. Katherine greeted everyone with her blessings and inquiries about each family. The ladies wore their finest frocks and bonnets, and the men wore their Sunday best. Gifts and food were placed outside on the massive pine tables. Thomas Cosby and a couple of the deacons had built tables on the church grounds which were used every Sunday and on special occasions like today.

The handsome groom eagerly entered the crowded church. Thomas Cosby had won the respect of the community by being a successful businessman and deacon of the church as well as a good friend and neighbor to many. There were only a few people who did not come to the wedding; they felt Thomas was marrying too soon. Rissa Cosby had not been laid to rest very long before Thomas began courting Miss Mary.

As Thomas walked by the church pew his family occupied, he glanced at them with a warm smile. Nellie wanted to be happy for her father. She wanted to be agreeable because she loved him, but she could not deny the hurt and the feeling of unfaithfulness toward her mother.

The Cosby family watched as Miss Mary enthusiastically strolled down the aisle clutching a bouquet of white hydrangeas and red roses. Mary wore a dark pink silk dress with a full gathered skirt. The dress had a plunging sweetheart neckline which would only be acceptable for a wedding. With Mary's blond hair up in curls that accented her dainty face, Miss Mary was almost pretty. Local folk figured Miss Mary would be an old maid school teacher the rest of her life. She was thirty-eight and Thomas was forty-one. Miss Mary was short, petite, and was the opposite of Rissa Cosby.

Mary was thrilled for she truly loved Thomas and had loved him for longer than she cared to admit. Today she felt exceedingly happy, and besides the bit of guilt that she hid deep in her heart, Mary was excited she was becoming Mrs. Thomas Cosby.

Pastor Ship said a short message from 1 Corinthians in which he challenged the bride and groom to love each other above all else. Mary said her vows as she looked affectionately into Thomas's eyes. Thomas, in turn, said his vows. *And I will betroth thee unto me forever; yea, I will betroth thee unto me in righteousness and in judgment, in loving kindness and in mercies.*

Beautiful vows, Katherine thought as she watched her son and new daughter-in-law. Thomas' vows, I have read them somewhere...? She was drawn back to the wedding as the two exchanged rings. No matter how Katherine felt, the ceremony was lovely.

After a brief, but beautiful ceremony, the crowd poured out of the church and quickly assembled around the rough picnic table. The table was laden with chicken, ham, and fresh vegetables. Several people had brought cakes, along with Nellie's white cake with caramel icing.

Nellie was glad that her Granma had let her decorate the cake by herself. She used edible flowers, nasturtiums and lilies, along with some wild roses, which made the cake look like a small flower garden. Nellie was proud of the cake, but certainly not proud of the wedding and her father's decision to marry Miss Mary Reynolds.

Men, women, and children brought their own tableware and filled their plates with the array of country foods which were offered. Nellie filled her plate, and her sister Renie's plate, with fried chicken, potatoes, and wedding cake. She guided Renie toward their usual picnic spot where Granma Katherine had spread an old wedding-ring quilt under a large maple tree.

Renie had been barely four years old when their mother died, and when she first saw the angels. Nellie had been thirteen and Tommie twelve. The children were too young to understand death and how it could happen twice—Johnny and their mother in less than a year. Both bodies were buried close to the house as though the family wanted them as close as possible even in death.

Since then, Nellie and Granma Katherine promised they would fill the void of mother for six-year-old Renie and for fourteen-year-old Tommie. Katherine had assured Thomas she would stay and help raise the children as long as he and the children needed her. Yet, Thomas had to change their plans, plans of a happy family living together, grieving together. Nellie felt that accepting Mary as a mother would be disloyal to her mother, and truthfully, she felt ashamed of her father.

Renie sat on the quilt with her crispy-fried chicken leg and wedding cake and began to eat. Nellie watched her little sister and thought about how much she looked like their mother. Renie's hair, a beautiful shade of auburn, curled around her delicate face. Mother and daughter even had the same skin tone, a light porcelain complexion. Renie wore a kelly green flowered frock with a yellow apron, which Rissa had made for Nellie. Like most of Nellie's clothes, the dress became Renie's in the hand-me-down collection.

Katherine had bought material and made Nellie a lovely blue muslin dress with a fitted bodice, which accented the fifteen-year-old female figure. Nellie had embroidered a yellow morning glory vine around the neckline. Katherine sighed as she watched Nellie and Renie, both growing so fast.

All the Cosby children were different. Johnny, the oldest, had been a dark-haired, dark-eyed young man with a vivacious personality. He was the kid who would impress others with his tales of adventure and dangerous escapades. Johnny looked more like his father, Thomas Cosby, than any of the children. George Thomas, who preferred to be called Tommie, was the quiet one of the family, the reader, the student, a young man with intellectual and spiritual insights.

Nellie, a dark-haired, dark-eyed, lovely, fifteen-year-old girl was as good as she was beautiful. Having to grow up early to meet the family demands, Nellie had not had time for much of anything except her chores and the piano. However, she had developed a most unusual skill for a fifteen-year old, helping Katherine, her grandmother, deliver babies. Nellie loved her job, loved the babies. She dreamed someday she would follow in her grandmother's footsteps.

The wedding party lasted all afternoon. Guests enjoyed the food and fellowship while Thomas and Mary shook hands and talked with everyone. Soon the party began moving down the road to Deacon Gorin's barn, which had been prepared for dancing. Katherine gathered the children and edged in between Thomas and his new bride.

"Thomas, I insist you stay at my place for a couple days, be sort of a honeymoon for you and Mary. There are all kinds of foods there, so you shouldn't need anything. Don't forget about the cellar, lots of things you like! I'm going to take the kids home and don't you worry about anything. We will manage just fine. God bless you kids," Katherine said as she hugged and kissed both of them. Katherine had a way of telling her family what to do, and they didn't argue.

On the way home Katherine took the reins and began to talk about her wedding to Parson Cosby, Nellie's grandfather. They had gotten married when Katherine Avery was only seventeen, in 1800. Her father had claimed a piece of land in 1775. When Katherine and Parson got married, her parents had given them part of the land for their own. Before the wedding, the Avery family built a small cabin for the couple. Katherine reflected on how rich they felt at their wedding, full of hopes and dreams. They wanted children, several children.

Most of all, the couple declared to serve the Lord which was their most important goal. Katherine blinked back the tears and bragged on how handsome Parson had looked in his new white shirt and brown trousers on that day so long ago.

"What did Mama wear for her wedding dress?" Nellie asked her Grandmother. "Did she look beautiful?"

Katherine's voice was filled with love and pride as she talked about Thomas and Rissa on their wedding day. "Your Mama was beautiful, tall, and slender, and had that beautiful auburn hair and porcelain skin. She wore a dark green, or was it a dark red, umm, well anyway, she was the most beautiful bride I ever saw, Nellie," Katherine reflected.

"Rissa's family had a big wedding and reception for the kids in Boston at her Grandmother's church. You know it still amazes me how they met. It was as though God brought them together. Both of them had gone to a Baptist Convention in Boston and it was love at first sight. Thomas did not return home that summer and instead worked at the harbor on the docks until fall. On September 22, 1820, Thomas and Rissa got married and traveled back here to make their home at Roundstone," Katherine said.

"Do you think Mama liked living here, in the country in a log cabin? There had to be a lot of change for her."

"Change? I'll say there was change! You know your mother lived with her Grandmother Wilson, but her parents made sure she had all she wanted and more. She had the best of everything; and then she came to Hart County to live on a farm with a mill--not the same. But, she never acted like she regretted it. She loved your Daddy so much." Katherine stopped to wipe a tear away.

"I'll never forget the day the wagon came to Roundstone with Rissa's piano. Took four men to get it off the wagon and into the house. That Chickering grand piano is very heavy and it took up every spare inch of the little log cabin. But your dad loved her so much, and he told her he would build her a house and she would have plenty of room for her piano, which he did. Thomas loved your mother so much, Nellie, and you never forget that."

"She loved her piano. Some of my best memories were listening to her play. Was she different than women around here? Did they like her?" Nellie asked.

"Your mom was like a rose in an onion patch. Being from Boston, she had polish and charm with perfect grammar and speech. But, although the other women may have been a little jealous, she managed to fit in. The ladies

9

admired her for everything she was and often they asked her opinion on matters. The one thing that your mother was very unyielding on was that you children be brought up with good social skills, being able to talk well to others, without using the country slangs.

"You know, she was the reason the school was built here at Roundstone. Her very valid argument was that the children would not be able to read the Bible if not educated. That point helped her get the influence she needed from county officials. Rissa insisted on all children getting a good education even in rural Kentucky."

"I wish Mama hadn't died, Gran. I miss her so much, and I hate Miss Mary for marrying Dad. He had no right to marry so soon. We could have made it just fine without her; you know we could have. It's all her fault," Nellie fussed.

"Nellie, there is nothing we can do about it. They are married. Now, get used to the idea! The less time and energy you spend fussing over the wedding, the more time and energy you will have to enjoy things you love! I want you and Tommie to try to like her and welcome her when she comes home," Katherine scolded Nellie.

Nellie needed to lighten her mood, to forget about Miss Mary for a while. She began to dream about her own wedding day: what she would wear, how she would do her hair, all the things a young girl dreams of for her own wedding day. Nellie knew who she would marry, no question. Nellie was fifteen, would be sixteen on her birthday on September first. Mike would be seventeen on November 29. If Miss Mary thought she would take over, then Nellie would run away and get married. Now that would show her father her hurt and humiliation!

In the back of the wagon, Tommie and Renie lay curled up on the quilts asleep. As Nellie looked at them, she knew they were completely unconcerned with the events of the day. However, Katherine and Nellie realized the day had been a wound in the flesh for all the family; one that would change their lives forever.

# Chapter 2

# Picking Tomatoes

As Nellie dangled her feet over the edge of the deep feather bed, she inhaled the mouth-watering smells wafting from the kitchen. Peering into the kitchen, Nellie watched as Gran fried bacon, rolled biscuit dough and talked with Renie. Elbows on the large oak kitchen table, Renie rolled her snake, shaping and reshaping her small piece of biscuit dough.

Nellie bowed beside her bed and gave thanks for another day. Both mother and grandmother had mentored her with her daily devotions. There was a time when prayers had been meaningless to Nellie, until last year when she could not stand the pain of grief any longer. Nellie had knelt in prayer and had given all of her grief over to the Lord. She poured out her heart and asked forgiveness of her sins. Then, a marvelous thing happened—a Holy Spirit experience so intense and powerful she knew she was loved beyond all earthly expectations.

Nellie changed into her worn, calico work dress and boots, greeted Gran and Renie, and headed toward the barn with her buckets. Father would be home in a couple days with his bride and Nellie knew she would be expected to make Mary feel welcome. Well, she would not go out of her way to do anything for Miss Mary.

Tommie had the cows in the barn and was feeding the horses. The smell of fresh manure mingled with the smell of newly cut hay. Tommie emptied a bucket of crushed corn feed in the last trough and ushered the five goats into the shed.

"About time, Nellie. You're moving about as fast as cold molasses. Reckon you could help me with the hay since Dad won't be here? I've already fed the goats and the horses, so you can feed the chickens and gather the eggs." Tommie started repairing a trough, hammering, upsetting the barn swallows.

"Hope they aren't trying to set again." The White leghorns and speckled domineckers had been hiding in the grass to make a nest which made it difficult to find their eggs. "You're gonna have to quit that pecking. Bessie and Berthie won't give any milk with that commotion going on!"

Lifting the three-legged milk stool from the peg, Nellie returned to the stalls. "Gran has a lot for me to do today too, gathering in the vegetables, and other chores she is sure to imagine. Maybe Miss Mary will be able to help by the first of next week," Nellie said sarcastically. Nellie figured Mary would be too busy telling everyone else what to do, especially her father.

Nellie pulled the cow's udders, shooting a stream of warm milk into the bucket. Often, she would play with the kittens while milking, squirting milk in their mouths as they tried to catch it with their paws. She filled the first frothy bucket from Bessie, their old Jersey cow, and started milking Berthie, another Jersey with soft, big, brown eyes. Nellie didn't mind milking the cows. The cows' gentle disposition along with the way they batted their long eyelashes was endearing. She considered the two cows her best friends, at least at the barn. Nellie often whispered her deepest secrets as she rested her head on the cow's warm, velvety-soft stomach as she milked.

Nellie carried one full bucket at a time down the hill to the spring house. She strained the milk through a clean muslin cloth into the creamery bucket. Nellie would clean the floor after the next bucket was strained. Gran always said the floor in the spring house should be clean enough to eat on. Keeping the table, buckets and floor especially clean meant the flies and critters would stay away, hopefully.

After Nellie had completed the routine with the creamy milk, she collected a bucket of water from the spring to clean the floor. A few good swishes with the handmade broom and she would be finished. Nellie picked up a creamer full of cold milk to carry up the hill. Gran's fluffy buttermilk biscuits, bacon, and eggs were summoning her empty stomach.

Nellie gave Gran the milk and a kiss as she prepared to wash her face and hands. "Renie, you will have to come to the barn today. Patch's new kittens are just so cute! Just like you, Renie!" Nellie teased Renie who was already sipping her cold cup of milk at the breakfast table.

"Yeah," Tommie added, "but they don't get as much milk on their mouth and whiskers as Renie."

"Renie, Renie, lips so creamy!
With eyes so lyrical and dreamy,
Because of her cup of sweet milk,
she has skin like Chinese silk.
Auburn curls emulate a crown,
with freckles across the nose of our clown.
Cream mustaches and whiskers compare!
Kittens beware! Renie doesn't share!"

Everyone laughed for it was true. Renie loved the rich cream on top of the milk and could hardly wait for Granma Katherine to skim the cream and add a spoonful to her cup of milk. She had a cream mustache every morning.

At the table, Katherine said grace and talked about the day's chores. "Nellie, do you think you could get the tomatoes picked this morning? I will start on the hickory cane sweet corn, and we can get it put up today. Think I will make ripe tomato catsup for the smaller cellar crock. We will slice cucumbers tonight to put in the large crock. A lot of vegetables to be put up; we have been blessed. Tommie, I guess you are going to work in the hay?"

Tommie replied, "Yes, Mam, I'll get the south field of orchard grass up and in the shed today. Can you spare Nellie a little while? It would really help for her to take Ol' Dan with the wagon while I pick up the hay stacks. Or, she can fork the hay, and I'll drive Ol' Dan."

Katherine shook her warning finger at Tommie, but agreed that Nellie could help as soon as she was finished with her chores. "Sorry, children, I was just thinking about how much we have to do. We lost a bunch of tomatoes Thursday because I didn't have time to put them up...preparing for the wedding."

Katherine had promised herself she would not show resentment toward the wedding or Mary. Yet, her feelings were more transparent to the children than she could help. Again, Katherine had dreamed about Rissa's death. She wished she could accept Mary with no suspicions.

Nellie enjoyed a hearty breakfast of a biscuit with bacon and eggs and a biscuit with fresh blackberry jam which tasted especially good that morning.

Nellie relished the morning when the smells of breakfast filled the entire cabin. As Nellie finished the last of her biscuit she considered the house that would soon be Miss Mary's house. The kitchen on the north side, a large living area in the middle, and a fireplace on the west side of the house made the cabin feel cozy. Nellie's mother had a couple of rocking chairs made, one for her and one for Thomas. She had made several braided rugs and all of the curtains, which made the house look better than any home Nellie had visited. The entire large kitchen/living room area was designed by Rissa who had made the log cabin a comfortable home for her family. Nellie wondered just how quickly Miss Mary would start changing things. Oh, then, Nellie would really be upset with her!

As soon as the family had finished breakfast, Katherine took the family Bible from the fireplace mantle as she sat in a rocker. Nellie could see from the look on Tommie's face that he wished Gran would just skip this part for he had so much work to do. However, the family devotion had been a morning and evening ritual as long as Nellie could remember.

Katherine read one of Nellie's favorite stories from the book of Daniel about Daniel's friends and the fiery furnace. She explained how everyone needs to practice having faith every day. She explained how reading the Bible, along with prayer, and worship increases faith. Katherine asked the children how their faith made them stronger individuals.

Nellie and Tommie thought for a while, and Renie answered.

"I believe God has something good for us because I dreamed about Mary being a good mama to us."

Tommie and Nellie looked each other, wanted to make a negative remark, or at least have Gran see them smirk, but they did not get the chance. Katherine had already stopped the discussion.

Katherine finished with a prayer and said, "Now, children, scoot! We have a lot to do today, and there may be a treat for Saturday if you work hard today!"

Renie exclaimed, "A treat? What is it, is it an adventure like Johnny went on?" Renie thought for a moment, then asked with more of a determination. "Or is it a visit to Aunt Annie's?" With a smile of pretend sweetness, Renie pleaded, "Gran, what is it?"

Katherine shook her head and realized she should not have mentioned the surprise. For the older two it was an incentive, but Renie would not let it go. Renie had not been old enough to remember all the adventures Johnny had been on before he died, but she had heard the many stories told by the family. Katherine calmed Renie by telling her she had to start her chores, or she would not be included in the treat, which was one of Johnny's favorite things to do.

Johnny had been the firstborn grandson and had a special place in Katherine's heart. He had been a very unusual young man with unique interests. If Johnny had any free time, he would be exploring somewhere, in one of the three surrounding counties. He would always take a paper, pencil and a slingshot stuffed in his pockets.

"Nellie, you and Renie can get started on the tomatoes and I will do the breakfast dishes. We want to get those beautiful tomatoes collected before the sun scalds them."

Katherine reminded Renie to get her bonnet and Nellie to take the strong baskets from the wall on the porch. Nellie chose a few of the baskets her mother had made. Rissa's basketwork was everywhere. She had made the baskets from the white oak on the farm. Nellie had helped her with a little of the basket-making, but Rissa was an artist at making beautiful baskets from the white oak tree.

Rissa had learned basketry from her grandmother in Boston. She had made egg baskets, pie baskets, garden baskets, and picnic baskets, and she often gave them to couples as wedding gifts. Nellie thought her mother was so talented. Proof was everywhere that her mother could do anything.

Washing the dishes, Katherine thought about Renie's dream. Renie had shown evidence of the gift after her mother died. Since then, Renie had talked to Katherine many times about her dreams and visions.

Katherine's grandmother had confided to her that one female in every other generation would have the gift of dreams and visions. Sometimes, the dreams and visions seemed to be a curse, not a blessing at all. Frightening dreams about the day Rissa died had bothered Katherine, and her suspicion of Mary was unrelenting, even though she had prayed for peace.

———◆———

The girls made their way along the garden path discussing Granma's surprise. Suddenly, Nellie saw Goldie jump back as if frightened by something. The family's big, yellow dog had obviously seen something in the tall grass. Then, Nellie saw it, a huge orange and brown snake! Nellie screamed and grabbed for Renie's hand. Yelping, Goldie put her tail between her legs and ran away.

Nellie felt frozen in her tracks. The snake was holding ten inches of its body off the ground with its hood spread. It looked like it could strike any moment and Nellie was so frightened she did not know what to do. She began to pull Renie backwards as Tommy appeared beside her with a hoe. Cautiously, he moved closer and the snake lunged forward, striking close to Tommie's trousers. Tommy poked the snake with his hoe, causing the snake to react with strikes at the hoe. Soon the snake started crawling away while Tommie was able to attack. With a few swift chops of the hoe, Tommie had succeeded to chop off the head of the snake.

"Oh, Tommie! That was the scariest ever! I hate snakes!" Nellie shivered in relief.

"Aw, it's just a hognose snake," Tommie said as he lifted the snake with his hoe and showed the girls. "They rear up like that and spread their head when they feel threatened. It wouldn't have fought if Goldie hadn't scared it." He picked up the head with his bare hands. "See, Nellie, it has round eyes, and it is harmless as a lamb," Tommy said, sounding much older and braver than his fourteen years.

Renie teased, "Nellie, was scared, I wasn't scared, just a snake that's all!'

"Renie, please, have a decent fear of snakes. There are lots of copperheads around here. The next one might not be so friendly," Nellie pleaded. "Now, I will have nightmares about snakes. Snakes and Mary, or both! Well, I guess they are pretty much alike anyway."

Still shaken by the horrific scare, Nellie pulled Renie along through the garden to the rows of tomatoes. Thankfully, she had kept the garden clean of tall horseweeds and menacing grasses, so she was able to detect any snakes that lay waiting for the unsuspecting tomato gatherers. Even though the tomatoes had been picked a few days ago, they were hanging ripe from the vines.

Realizing Renie had left the house without her bonnet, Nellie became impatient with her and scolded. "Renie, you know you will redden in this sun, you will burn in no time. Go get your bonnet and get back here to help me."

As Nellie picked the tomatoes she daydreamed about the garden that she and Mike would have someday. Perhaps she would invite Mike over for supper one night soon. Ugh! Miss Mary would be there in a few days, sitting at the table all smug, acting like she owned the place. Nellie picked up a rock and pounded a clod of dirt, pretending it was Miss Mary's face.

Renie was soon back by her side. Her little hands pulled at the tomato vines, and broke a few as she went. "Nellie, why did Daddy get married?"

"Well, Renie, a man needs a wife, especially if he has a family like us." Nellie was not in the mood to explain, and her patience with Renie was stretched. Still, Renie needed to talk.

"Yeah, but Daddy had Mama. He loved her, I know he did. He loved our Mama because she was an angel...." Renie began to cry.

Nellie realized with all the business of the crops, the mill, and the wedding, possibly no one had taken time to help Renie understand. "Dad loved Mama very much, Renie. She was the love of his life. No one can ever compare to Mama. But Mama is gone and we have to help Dad be happy now. And he thinks Miss Mary will make him happy.

"You know, you look so much like Mama. Mama was the most beautiful woman in the world. Everybody said so. Gran said she could have stayed in Boston and married anybody she wanted," Nellie explained.

"Then, why didn't she? She might still be alive," Renie whined.

"Yes, but she wouldn't have had you, and Johnny and Tommie and me. And she would not have been married to our father."

"I know, but I miss her," Renie said squishing a small tomato in her hand.

"I do too, Renie, but we will always have her in our hearts. Daddy says, 'To be absent from the body, and to be present with the Lord.' So we know Mama is in heaven being one of God's most beautiful angels."

Renie started trying to catch a frog and Nellie hurried up her pace of picking tomatoes. A lot to do, and there would be a special surprise if the work was completed. Wonder what it is, Nellie thought.

As Nellie carried the heavy baskets of tomatoes she saw Tommie coming from the hayfield. "What are you doing back so early? You finished already?"

"No, thought I would bring Gran something to fix for supper. Look here!" Tommie dangled two young gray squirrels by the tail. "Shot both of 'em with my slingshot," Tommie bragged.

Johnny had been so proud to be a big brother and to teach Tommie many boyish trades, one being how to use the indispensable sling shot. The brothers joined together as they hunted with their slingshots and brought home their rewards. Though there were six years between them, Johnny had been a good big brother. He had played with Tommie and taught him about nature until he died and left Tommie without his best friend.

Johnny had also taught Tommie about arrowheads and other Indian relics. Once they had found a large cache in a cave on the creek. Johnny's big arrowhead collection had been passed on to Tommie along with his sure-fire sling shot.

"Well, Tommie, can you get this other basket of tomatoes? Renie is more interested in catching frogs for supper!" Nellie teased.

Renie had already moved on to another activity, her favorite, swinging from her own swing. Thomas had made swings for the children in the maple tree, and all the children loved swinging over the edge of the cliff.

As Nellie carried her tomato treasures to the house, she gazed, once more, at the large oak tree behind their log cabin. There, a few feet from the gnarly oak were the gravestones of her brother and mother.

Nellie had watched her father chip away on the large limestone for weeks until he could labor no more, physically and emotionally. When the family placed the huge stone they noticed that there was a perfect round hole on one side of the stone, the heart. The hole was smooth and appeared to have been there for years, although everyone agreed that it was not there before that day. Nellie was the first to explain that the hole in the limestone heart represented the hole left in their own hearts when Rissa Cosby died.

Thomas Cosby called the large, heart-shaped rock *The Hart of Roundstone* because his wife, Rissa Cosby, had been the heart of his life, his family, and of course of Hart County, Kentucky.

# Chapter 3

# The Visitor

Katherine pinched a bit of salt from the salt cellar and tossed it into the Kentucky wonder green beans as Nellie watched. "Gran, you made all this food just for us?"

"Well, of course, you kids are my joy. And, Nellie, you know I love to do things for people I love."

Along with all of her other jobs, Katherine had prepared squirrel with dumplings, fresh green beans, and a crusty, bubbly, rhubarb cobbler. The bowl of sliced red and yellow tomatoes in the middle of the table served as a colorful centerpiece. Another bowl held fresh cucumbers in salty vinegar water. Nellie was hungry and could hardly resist sneaking a cucumber out of the salty brine.

As Nellie lifted the heavy, brown pottery plates she reminded Renie to wash her face and hands for supper. Placing the plates around the table Nellie remembered the pride that her mother communicated when she used the dishes. Nellie's Boston grandparents had purchased the dishes as a wedding gift. Nellie's mother, Rissa, had loved the way the table looked and said they were grand enough for royalty. Nellie wondered just how long they would be used now that Miss Mary would be taking control of the table setting.

"Mmmm, something smells good," Nellie said as she lifted the top of the big, black pot on the stove. Nellie saw the two squirrel heads in the pot and gasped, "Ugh, wish I hadn't looked. But, it does smell wonderful."

With a dishcloth, Katherine playfully swatted Nellie on the butt and reminded her, "That 'ugh' is our supper, and we do not diminish the food that your brother provided for us. Well, your brother and the Lord. We can never be thankful enough for the food we have on our table. God gave man dominion over animals, so he could use them as needed. But, God never meant for people to kill just for the sake of killing. So, when we cook, we use the entire animal, no wasted parts!" Katherine said emphatically.

Renie heard the discussion and wanted to talk about the snake. "Tommie killed a snake. Was that bad, Gran, because we didn't eat it?"

Katherine quickly replied, "Snakes are different. Glad Tommie killed it."

Nellie could not resist the opportunity to reply, "Yeah, it looked like Miss Mary, as it slithered its way into our family. You know, Tommie, they are quite alike, a snake and Miss Mary." Nellie and Tommie shared a laugh as Katherine pretended not to hear.

After a well appreciated meal, Katherine picked up the Bible and relaxed in the oak rocker. The three children sprawled on the cool, oak plank floor. Katherine read "Matthew 16:24, Then Jesus said to His disciples, 'Whoever wants to be my disciple must deny themselves and take up their cross and follow me'."

Katherine explained how we must have the courage and strength to follow Jesus, no matter what happens, despite the chance of being persecuted. "We must be able to deny ourselves for the benefit of others. Can you children think of a time when you denied yourself so that someone else was able to receive something that they needed?"

Tommie mentioned he had shared his lunch with another boy at school.

Nellie suggested Granma had denied herself when she came to live with them, to take care of her son and three grandchildren. "You didn't have to come live with us and help us, but you saw a need, so you came to help. It would have been much easier for you to have stayed in Upton and you wouldn't have to work so hard. Isn't that the same thing as being a disciple for Jesus?" Nellie asked.

Katherine fixed her eyes on the fireplace as she thought for a minute. "Well, in a way, I suppose it is. If I had known you needed me, and I hadn't come to help, I don't think Jesus would be happy with me. So, we learn from this verse we have to forget about ourselves and think about what Jesus would want us to do. A serving attitude and a heart for missions should be important for our lives."

After devotion, Nellie and Tommie prepared for the barn. Renie played on the porch with Callie, her three year-old calico cat. Katherine started cleaning the kitchen and putting away the leftovers so she could begin work on the cucumbers. Occasionally, she had Renie help with the dishes, but actually Katherine wanted to preserve Renie's innocence and youth as long as she could. Renie already had the weight of her gift which was a challenge for someone so young.

Katherine started slicing cucumbers in the large crock for the lime pickles she made every year. After each layer of pickles in the crock, Katherine sprinkled agricultural lime which caused the pickles to become brittle. The pickles would stay in lime water for a few hours, rinse, and place in a vinegar, and honey spice solution. Finally, the sliced cucumbers would be stored in the crock in the cellar, alongside many other crocks with pickled vegetables.

As Katherine threw away the damaged cucumbers, she thought about the pickling process. If she put bad cucumbers in the crock, they might ruin the entire crock. Katherine hoped her family would never allow the bad cucumbers, or sin, to enter into the family. She knew that Rissa had been such a good Christian wife and mother. Katherine had her doubts about Mary.

———◦———

Swinging both buckets with one hand, Nellie tossed a stick for Goldie. As usual, Tommie was already in the barn with the horses. Nellie heard voices.

"What?" Nellie turned and yelled back at the house.

When she didn't hear anything, Nellie resumed her trip to the barn, but stopped when she heard the voices again. Goldie heard the sound. Her ears perked up as she barked and growled. Both Nellie and Goldie had heard voices from around the mill. Hurriedly, Nellie called for Goldie to follow her into the barn.

"Tommie, I hear someone at the creek. I think someone may be at the mill," Nellie exclaimed.

Tommie froze for a second, and then suddenly threw the pitchfork down. He picked up a few rocks he had gathered that afternoon and headed out of the barn.

"Nellie, you stay here. I don't want..."

"No, I am going with you. Dad would want me to," Nellie replied. "But wait, let's lock Goldie in Dan's stall." Giving Goldie her favorite leather strap to chew on, Nellie whispered, "Sorry, Goldie, you need to be quiet in here and we will be back soon."

The kids knew just how to get to the mill without anyone seeing them. Staying on the high ridge around the creek, the children watched from a ledge over the mill. There, they saw someone at the back door of the mill store. A strange man was talking to someone, but they could not see the other person.

"I'm going to get closer. You stay here," Tommie whispered. Tommie cautiously made his way off the ledge down the fifty foot hill. Fortunately, the path was clear of leaves and branches since the kids took this path to slide down the hill. A large, triple trunk sycamore tree served as a hiding place for Tommie as he aimed his slingshot at the strange man.

"Oh, what the....Ow! Did you do that? Ow! That hurts! What's going on?" The man shouted as he recoiled from the third hit of Tommie's slingshot.

"What is it pa? What's wrong?" cried a child.

"Aw, come on let's get out of here." The stranger took the child and pulled him along as they headed to the other side of the road. In a minute they were gone and out of sight.

"Did you get a good look at him, Nellie?" Tommie asked as he ran up the hill to Nellie.

"I think so; I think I saw him in town when we were at Riders. He was with his wife, and son, I guess, and a little girl. Gran talked to them, like she does everyone, so she may know them. Let's go tell her," Nellie said, brushing the leaves, dirt and twigs off her dress, as she rose from her hiding place.

"No, Nellie, we can't tell Gran! You know what Dad said about me using the slingshot," Tommie pleaded. Tommie grabbed Nellie's wrist and stopped her from starting up the hill.

"But I am sure he would understand."

"No, Dad made me promise never to aim my slingshot at a person. He said it could hurt someone, put out an eye or even kill someone. So, if they know what I did, Dad would take away my slingshot. Please Nellie, don't tell Gran."

Nellie pulled her wrist loose and began to hurry up the hill, "Okay. I promise I won't tell; I'll let you do that."

Still excited from the slingshot shooting, Nellie and Tommie speculated on the attempted break-in. Tommie mentioned there was never much money in the mill, but there were a few sacks of meal and flour. Whatever the man had wanted, he probably wouldn't be back for a while.

———•———

After the work had been finished on Saturday morning, Katherine revealed the surprise for the day. "Sweet ones, we are having a picnic at the creek for this afternoon."

When Johnny had drowned in the creek, everyone thought they would never again play in the clear, cold creek water. Thomas had reminded the family that fear should not keep people from doing the things they enjoy, as long as it is in God's will. The creek was not only the power source for the mill, and for fresh water, but also the trout hole. Once again, the creek had become a playground for the children while everyone respected the blessings the creek provided.

Katherine brought a maple leaf quilt and spread it under an oak tree by the creek. The children waded cautiously into the chilly water. The clear creek water came from the twelve springs which bubbled up from the ground at a cold fifty-seven degrees, winter through summer. Yet with one of the hottest days of summer, the cold water felt good as the children played and splashed one another.

Taking advantage of the free time, Katherine began her crocheting. A yellow baby hat was one of Katherine's favorite items to make. As she made a double crochet stitch she said a prayer for Thomas and Mary. Katherine knew, all too well, even in the best of situations that family relations could be difficult. Mary had explained that she wanted to go back to school with the children until another teacher could be found. Katherine agreed. Thomas said it would be a good idea since this would be Renie's first year at school, and possibly the children would accept her more as teacher and mother.

All three children loved getting in the water, and searching through the sand bars for any rocks, flints or quartz that washed up from the last rain. After a couple hours of wading and swimming in the creek, Katherine finally managed to harangue the children out of the creek and on their way back to the cabin. She reminded the children that today was weekly bath day, after their chores were finished.

"Gran, do you think things will be the same when Daddy and Miss Mary get home? Renie asked as she dramatically whined and started up the hill.

"No, honey, I don't think our family will ever be the same again, but that is something we will take one day at a time, and you know, Renie, it could be even better than before," Katherine replied.

Tommie and Nellie couldn't help but react to the statement.

"No," Nellie replied, "it could never be better!" Nellie said with a furious stamp of her foot.

Tommie chimed in, "Never be better than when Mama was here. I will never accept Mary as my mother! She is Dad's new wife, but not my mother!"

Katherine stopped the children and pulled them to her, "I am sorry, I didn't mean it would be better, it will never be better than when your mother was here, I agree. What I meant was it might be better than just me being here with you children. I just hope you will give Mary a chance. Promise me you will try to be nice, okay?"

Tommie and Nellie agreed to Katherine's request, even though they did not want to. The children could not say 'no' to their grandmother.

Nellie stopped to pick an occasional wildflower. She had to keep an eye on Renie because Renie would often pick a handful and leave them on a rock or strewn along the path. Nellie had explained to Renie that the wildflowers should stay so they could reseed.

However, Nellie picked a flower specimen each season and put them in her journal, the journal that had belonged to her mother. Rissa Cosby had divided the journal into seasonal sections which described each flower with the color, stem type, number of petals and leaves. Nellie had been collecting flowers since she received the journal, following the example set by her mother.

Nellie picked a purplish bergamot which her grandmother told her was an herb used by the Indians for colds, headaches, and fevers. Next, Nellie picked a couple white flowers from the Indian tobacco plant. The old folks had told her the Indians had smoked this plant. Spying flowers off the path, Nellie found a pink swamp rose and spotted knapweed.

Katherine saw Nellie pick the knapweed and grabbed Nellie's hand. "You know the story about this flower?" Katherine smiled and as she held the pink/purple flower to her nose, and explained.

"The folklore about the spotted knapweed is that if a young girl hides one of these flowers under her apron, she will be assured of having the man of her choice. Maybe that would even work for an old girl like me." Katherine laughed and hugged Nellie.

Nellie didn't believe the folklore was true, yet it was fun to think about the story and Mike, of course.

As soon as Nellie got to the house, she pulled the journal from the dresser drawer. Adding the new flowers to the journal, Nellie used her best penmanship to record her observations. As she worked Nellie felt as though her mother was with her.

Preparing for the evening chores, Nellie and Tommie walked to the barn together. "Do you think Miss Mary is going to make us call her Mother?" Nellie asked.

"I think she had better not, I only have one mother and Gran. She better stay out of my way at home, as far as a fox out of a henhouse. I'll listen to her at school, but not at home."

Both Nellie and Tommie began their chores, feeling like comrades by their distaste for their new stepmother. Bessie and Berthie were ready for Nellie to spend some quality time with them as they chewed their feed and swished the flies.

Tommie finished feeding the horses and goats and excitedly jumped into Bessie's stall with Nellie. "Look, Nellie, I found this beautiful flower, thought you might like it. And, you know it taste really good, a minty flavor." Tommie breathed in through his teeth as though the flower gave a fresh taste. "Here, you want some?"

Nellie looked at Tommie then at the flower, "Tommie, you didn't really eat this flower did you? You surely know better," Nellie said, trying to see if Tommie was telling the truth.

"Yeah, Nellie, it's good. Here, try some," Tommie exclaimed, handing her one of the flowers.

"Tommie that is water hemlock and it is poisonous! Just one mouthful can kill you. If you ate it … well, we need to get you to the house and let Gran know." Nellie was becoming frantic as she put the bucket aside to leave.

Tommie chuckled. "Just kidding you, Nellie! You believed it! Don't you think I know what it is? You are so gullible, Nellie."

"And you just made me stop what I was doing for your immature joke!" Nellie said. "I will get you back, Tommie Cosby, just wait and see. And get that flower out of here, the cats could eat it!"

"Hey, now. Don't get your feathers all ruffled." Tommie was leaving the barn as he shouted back, "Just your dignity a little bruised."

Oh, he is so aggravating! Nellie thought. Guess Tommie is more like Johnny than we realized. Nellie imagined Johnny pulling the same trick. Johnny had so often played tricks on Mom and Dad. As Nellie thought about her two brothers, she had pangs of grief for her brother and her mother.

Her family had been hurt and had grieved for so long after Johnny's death and then her mother's death. Now, Miss Mary would be adding to their grief. Surely she wouldn't be her teacher when school started! She could not handle that. Guess she would have to leave before that happened, run away, or get married. Anything would be better than living here with Miss Mary taking her mother's place.

Nellie grumbled, feeling a little sorry for herself. Having to milk the cows, do her chores, be the big sister, and now accept a stepmother, was too much. Then, Gran's warning that she had to be nice to Miss Mary and she had to promise!

Even though Tommie's prank was just a harmless joke, Nellie felt betrayed by Tommie and her father and Gran! Feeling as though nothing she did was appreciated, Nellie began to sob. She brushed the tears on Bessie's soft, warm belly and dabbed at her eyes with her apron.

Then she heard the Lord whisper to her, "Nellie, whatever you do, do it well for me!"

"Even milking the cows, Lord?" Nellie asked between her sobs.

"Even milking the cows and being the best you can be, for I have great plans for you, my child."

# Chapter 4

# Ollie's Family

Tommie, Nellie, and Renie were squeezed together on the front pew of the log cabin country church with their grandmother. Katherine reminded the children of Thomas' usual petition, 'Eyes and ears open to the Word.'

As the first hymn began, the congregation stood, eager to worship through song. Quickly the attention turned to the door as everyone looked to see who was a little late for church. Mary Cosby had a firm grip on her new husband's arm as he escorted her to their pew. Mr. and Mrs. Thomas Cosby took a seat just behind the rest of the Cosby family.

Katherine was proud of her son. She had told them to stay on their honeymoon until Monday, but she knew Thomas would not miss church. He was a good man that Thomas, so much like his father, Parson Thomas Cosby.

The preacher had started reading the scripture when someone entered. The guest noisily opened the double pine doors and rushed halfway up the aisle. A man in overalls, with a crimped, stained hat, had hurried in and clearly was not looking for a seat. He stood shifting nervously, waiting for the preacher to let him speak. Finally, he took a step forward and cleared his throat. Katherine motioned to the man to remove his hat.

"I'm sorry, real sorry, Pastor, sir, but I need Ms. Katherine real bad. My Lyssa's having a baby. I need her to come with me if she will." The man beckoned to Katherine, turning his hat around in his hands. "Will you please, Mrs. Katherine?" The man pleaded with Katherine.

"Sure will, Ollie," Katherine said as she stood and walked toward the front of the church. "But before I go, let's have a word of prayer."

"Ms. Katherine, I'm much obliged, but I don't know we got time. She told me to hurry," Ollie said urgently.

"Ollie, a prayer is the best help she can have right now. Pastor Ship, would you lead us as we say a prayer for Ollie's wife who is having a baby?"

Pastor Ship and the entire congregation gathered at the mourner's bench for prayer. For about five anxious minutes, Ollie waited as the swell of voices rose in a cacophony of praises and amens. He listened, and when he thought he could not wait a second longer, the prayer ended.

Katherine motioned to Nellie to come with her as she left the building with Ollie. "I'll take my own wagon and follow you," Katherine said hurriedly.

The rough ride to Ollie's place took almost thirty minutes. Katherine was praying all the way, between giving Nellie a list of preparations and reminders. "Remember, Nellie, the first thing is to put water on to boil, you may have to even draw water from the spring. Just do it quickly. I should have checked on her yesterday instead of piddling." Katherine was worried.

As Katherine's wagon pulled into the yard, a young boy ran to meet them. "Please help my Ma. She's having a baby," the child said, peeking from his overgrown locks.

Anticipating Lyssa's delivery, Katherine had put the bag of clean rags in the wagon. She grabbed the bag and jumped down. "Ollie, I need plenty of water drawn. Do you have extra buckets to fill?"

"Yes, ma'am, I got buckets 'ready full of water. You let me know, and I'll shore help." Ollie was anxious for his wife, wringing his hands and fidgeting with his hat. "When my boy was born, Lyssa had no trouble, but this time's different, Ms. Katherine. Lyssa, well, she's said more 'n once, that this time's been a hurtin' might near ever day fir the past month.

"Now, Ms. Katherine, I got Oliver and me and him will be about. We'll take care of yer horses. Jist u call if 'n need me and I'll come runnin."

Katherine and Nellie rushed into the house without a moment to waste. "Lyssa, I am going to examine you. Do you know how far apart your contractions are?"

Katherine spoke soothingly to Lyssa, trying to keep her calm and as relaxed as possible. After washing her hands, Katherine examined Lyssa. Fortunately, Lyssa was not ready to have the baby right away. However, the baby appeared to be coming butt and feet first.

Katherine remembered the last time she had a case similar to Lyssa's. She had help from an older woman who was there for the delivery. They had lost the child and almost lost the mother, but Katherine had learned from the experience.

"Lyssa, the baby is coming breach. Its butt and knees are folded together and that is the way it wants to make its arrival. I'm going to try to turn the baby. You try to remain calm. Everything is going to be fine."

Ollie sneaked back into the small cabin to check on Lyssa, leaving Oliver outside. Nervous, Ollie towered over Katherine asking questions. "Is she gonna be alright, Ms. Katherine? How long before the baby? What can I do? You wanna me go get Dr. Routt?" Ollie whispered.

"Doc Routt is out of town." Katherine hugged Ollie to assure him as well as herself. "She will be fine, Ollie. We are here, and God is with us. This baby isn't the first baby to be born, you know. Now, you get out of here and let us do our women's work," Katherine said as she messaged Lyssa's stomach.

After an hour of Katherine's efforts with Lyssa, the baby was in the right position. Katherine would not leave Lyssa's side, as she rubbed Lyssa's back and feet and tried to keep her comfortable. Soon, the young woman's contractions were coming closer and stronger.

Katherine carried a bottle of moonshine to give to her delivering mothers to ease their pain. "Lyssa, it won't be much longer now. If you raise up, I will give you some of this moonshine. I have a cup here with some of the nasty stuff. Just enough to help with your pain."

With the contractions becoming more severe, Lyssa was eager to take the pain-numbing liquid.

"Gran, I have the muslin catch-pad ready. Do you want it now?" Nellie could see that the first pad was soaked since Lyssa's water had broken.

The two worked with Lyssa to get the catch pads in place.

"Nellie, you know the routine. As soon as I catch the baby, and cut the cord, I will give it to you, so you need to have your supplies ready."

Before long a baby was screaming and Katherine was in her glory, delivering a baby into the world, praising God and giving thanks for another miracle of birth. Katherine cut the cord and Nellie took the baby.

Nellie grasped the baby firmly and carried her to a large dishpan filled with warm water. "Hello, Baby Girl! Welcome to the Booker family home. You have a wonderful mommy and daddy and even a big brother. God loves you, Baby Girl."

This part, the bathing and cuddling of a newborn was Nellie's favorite part of the delivery. Nellie cooed to the baby girl as she washed her tiny body. "Now, Baby Girl we are going to pat you dry and put on your first gown that your mama made for you." Nellie finished dressing the baby and swaddled her in a small quilt Lyssa had made for the baby.

Katherine always had a routine for the delivery. Before the delivery, she would put a few layers of soft muslin under the laboring mother. After the birth, Nellie took care of the baby while Katherine helped the mother as she expelled the after-birth. Katherine then wrapped the afterbirth in muslin and had the husband either bury it, or burn it in a fire outside.

Caring for Lyssa, Katherine cleaned as much as possible. "Ollie, could you please come in now?"

Ollie was beside her before she could finish her sentence.

"Ollie, you are the father of a beautiful baby girl. Mother and daughter are doing fine. Just one thing, before you get to see them. Remember the instructions for the afterbirth? You must dig a hole and bury it or burn it. After that, you can come in and visit your new family member." Katherine handed Ollie the muslin package and he hurried outside.

Anxious to be back in the house with Lyssa and the baby, Ollie dug a deep hole, placed the bag of afterbirth in the hole, and filled the hole with dirt. He placed a large rock on top for assurance that nothing could dig it up.

"Baby Girl Booker, meet your mommy." As Nellie handed the baby to her mother, she sighed a prayer of thankfulness. Nellie always enjoyed watching the eyes of the mother as she held her baby for the first time.

Lyssa's eyes sparkled as she admired her baby girl. "She's so beautiful! I want to see her, all of her." Lyssa started unwinding the quilt that Nellie had patiently tucked around the baby, as she examined the baby's fingers and toes. "She is so perfect."

Nellie smiled because all mothers did the same thing. They would look at the baby, and then unwrap to make sure the baby had ten fingers and toes.

"Lyssa, if you are feeling up to it, we will help you to the chamber pot while I quickly work on your bed. Or you can sit in the rocker, if you had rather. That is if you can give up the baby for a few minutes."

Katherine removed the sheets and cleaned the bed. She flipped the mattress and fluffed it on both sides. Nellie helped Lyssa relax in a rocking chair while she put her feet up on a small wooden stool. Katherine and Nellie worked as a team taking care of Lyssa, the baby and the cleaning.

Ollie rushed in the cabin, eager to see his wife and baby. He watched as Lyssa cuddled their baby girl. Ollie kissed Lyssa's forehead as a tear ran down his cheek. Katherine smiled as she watched Ollie's gentleness with his wife and baby. Big brother Oliver stood beside his tired mother. What a beautiful little family, Nellie thought.

Katherine sighed and put her arm around Nellie's shoulders, "Child, you should go home and get some rest. I will stay here so I can help Lyssa for a day or so. She is going to need some food cooked and all of these rags and her sheets will have to be washed and boiled. And Nellie, please gather some baskets of vegetables and bring them back tomorrow. Maybe your dad could send us some trout. Anyway, I've got plenty to do for the next couple days, and you need to get some rest tonight."

———✦———

Nellie was glad Ollie had taken care of Ol' Dan, giving him hay and water. She hitched the horse to the wagon again and guided the old horse toward home. Since it was Nellie's first breech birth, she planned to write about the birth in her journal. However, there were many things she wanted to do, like spend time with her father and possibly make a gown for the baby. Most of all she just wanted to avoid Miss Mary.

"Whew!" Katherine said as she sighed softly. Lyssa's rocker was inviting her to sit and relax and she certainly would take the opportunity. Katherine was exhausted when she finally allowed herself to stop for a while.

Sunday morning seemed so long ago. Katherine had gotten up early on Sunday morning and killed a young rooster to fry. The molasses apple cake was an afterthought which rushed her to finish. The cake was Thomas' favorite and she trusted he and Mary would be at church to help eat it. Thanks to Nellie, she had brought the food into Lyssa's kitchen while waiting on the birth.

Katherine put the food out and called the little family to the table. Ollie helped his wife to the table, anticipating her every need. After the family had taken their places, Oliver started to eat a chicken leg.

"First, let's join hands and hearts in prayer to our Lord and Savior," Katherine said as she winked at Oliver.

After the prayer Katherine explained the food. "On Sundays, everyone brings food and stays after church. Members, families, friends and neighbors eat, pray, fellowship, and study the Word. Usually, everyone stays until milking time. When people leave they feel more loved, more close to Jesus. They also feel like they have kept the commandment, to keep the Sabbath holy. Deuteronomy 5:12 says, 'Observe the Sabbath day, to keep it holy, as the LORD your God commanded you'."

Later Katherine delivered a devotion from the Ten Commandments. She explained that now we have Jesus Christ and salvation through grace.

As Katherine rocked she felt so at home in the Booker cabin. Ollie and Lyssa's log cabin was average size, but every inch was made functional. The kitchen, on the left, had a couple of big windows for light. Lyssa had hung sprigs of dried herbs and flowers in the windows and a few bundles around the ceiling beams. On one side of the kitchen was a stove with a stone chimney. Beside the backdoor was a wood box which held the firewood. In the back of the house was a fireplace made of large stones taken from around the home place.

Ollie had made the few chairs and stools placed around the fireplace. On the other side sat the bed, a chest, and a trunk for the couple. Oliver had a room upstairs in the loft. The little cabin was simple, yet a loving spirit prevailed. Lyssa had sewn ruffled curtains, colorful quilts, and made a braided rug for the floor. Ollie had hung the horns from a buck he had killed over the fireplace. Every nook and cranny was clean. Lyssa and Ollie definitely had talent to create a warm, inviting home for their family.

Katherine was so filled with God's love she began to hum a hymn. As she sat there in the quiet of the night, she reflected on her marriage and her own babies. Thomas had been born first, then Annie. Parson and Katherine had wanted more children, but Katherine assumed God wanted her to have children in a different way, to bring these children into the world and love their families. She certainly felt a connection to this family; they had won her heart.

With the baby and Lyssa napping, Ollie pulled a chair up beside Katherine. "Katherine, I really thank you fir your taking care of my Lyssa and our baby. You shore know what you are doing. How did you learn to birth them babies?"

Katherine explained as she rocked. "Dr. Routt and his wife, Melissa, taught me most everything I know. When they moved to the community as young people, the Routts lived with our family over a year. Meanwhile, they taught me and my sister many medical skills, including delivering babies."

"Yea, Doc Routt, he's still a good 'n," Ollie said, bringing Katherine a cup of coffee.

"Well, Ollie, I have been lucky because my Papa and Mama were a good example for me and Kenneth, Rowena, Delo and the whole family. They always put God first in their lives, along with church, family, friends, and hard work. They always prayed that all of their children would meet a good Christian person to marry, which has certainly happened for us kids."

"I admire that kind of family, Ms. Katherine. That's how I want to raise my kids. Now, why don't you get some shut-eye whilst I do some chores."

Katherine thought to herself, planting seeds, harvesting later.

Ollie went outside to bring in some fresh water when the baby started crying. Katherine helped Lyssa sit up and encouraged her to drink more water. Lyssa's baby was hungry and clearly wanted to nurse. After several trying moments, the baby was sucking and happy. Oliver, asleep in the loft, was unconcerned about the commotion.

After the baby finished nursing, Lyssa gently placed the baby girl in Ollie's arms. "While you are holding your daughter, think of a name for her. I have to go to pee, and you need to get to know your baby girl."

Ollie looked at the baby with such pride as he said, "I been a thinking. I want her to have a good name, a Bible name too. Ms. Katherine, what is your middle name?"

Katherine was shocked, but pleased. "Well actually my middle name is Katherine but my first name is Oleta. I would be happy to have her named after me. I don't think there are any Oletas around here. What about Sarah Oleta or Mary Oleta, or Rebecca Oleta?" she suggested.

Lyssa heard the discussion and remarked she liked the name Oleta. "I know about Mary but I don't know about Sarah or Rebecca."

Katherine replied, "It's late, why don't you get back in bed while the baby is sleeping and I will tell you about the women in the morning?"

# Chapter 5

# Recruiting

Since Nellie and Katherine had left the church for Ollie's house, Renie and Tommie stayed with Thomas and Mary for the remainder of the day. Renie quickly latched onto Mary's hand and wouldn't let go.

Thomas led the prayer at the benediction of the Sabbath Day activities and quickly made his way to see a few visitors. As the men gathered around their buggies and buckboards, most were discussing their crops and livestock. Thomas had noticed there were a few new faces at the services. He wanted to make sure he introduced himself and learn a little about the visiting worshipers. Meanwhile, Tommie offered to help with the clean-up, shoveling of the horse poo, off the church grounds.

"Hello, I'm Thomas Cosby…how are you today? I meant to get over to talk to you earlier but have not had the chance," Thomas said as he extended his hand.

"Pete Goodwin, and this is my wife, Andrea. We enjoyed the church service. Enjoyed the people and the fellowship. You don't get this feeling of the Holy Spirit just anywhere, you know," Pete answered.

"Well, that is good to hear, Pete. You and Andrea are invited every Sunday. We always need young people. Are you kids staying around awhile, or just up for a visit?"

"Actually, Andrea felt she needed to be closer to her sister and her husband after the loss of their two children last year," Pete said as he looked sympathetically at Andrea.

Andrea looked at Thomas, "My sister is Tammy Taylor…if you remember?"

"Yes, very sad about their children. I know she will be glad to have you. So are you staying awhile?" Thomas asked.

"I think so. We are looking for work in one of the three counties, Hart, Hardin or LaRue. You don't know of a job, do you?" Pete asked.

"Well, what kind of skills do you have? Where have you worked before?"

"Andrea and I went to school together and she is qualified to teach, but not many of those jobs available. I have been trained in building. In fact, I built our little house in Haywill. But jobs are just not plentiful right now." Pete's horse was anxious to leave, so the conversation was coming to an end.

"Pete, you may have just come to the right place. I don't talk business on Sundays, but if you can come to my house tomorrow morning about nine o'clock, I can talk to you about what I am proposing to do. And Andrea, I believe my wife will have something to talk to you about. We live at the Roundstone. Your father-in-law can give you directions. Okay?"

"That sounds good," Pete answered. "See you tomorrow."

Thomas was about to get in his buggy when he heard someone calling him.

"Hey, Thomas, hold up. Meant to say something to you earlier. A man and his family came looking for a house to live in, no money, and they needed a place. I told him about the old Bimbi house. He said he was looking for a job, and whenever he found a job, he could get something better." Ben Logsdon looked down as he was talking, as though he was thinking about saying more.

"Okay, I will run back there and check on them. See if there is anything I can do."

Ben took off his hat and scratched his head. "Well, you can make up your own mind, but, Thomas, I don't know about that guy, a little concerned about his attitude." Thomas shook hands with Ben and assured him it was alright. "I will go by the Bimbi place and check it out."

Tommie heard the conversation and wondered if the man Ben was talking about could be the same man who was at the mill yesterday.

"Mary, I think we will go back to the Bimbi place on our way home. We'll see if there is anything we can do for the family," Thomas said as he picked up the reins.

"I think that is a good idea, don't you Renie? We can see if they have any children," Mary smiled as she hugged Renie. Renie had insisted on sitting between Mary and Thomas.

On the way to the Bimbi house Renie told about everything they had missed. "And you should have seen the snake Tommie killed. It was huge! Nellie was scared, but I wasn't. Gran took us to the creek yesterday and we had so much fun. Why don't we go when we get home? Don't you think you would like to get in the creek and splash, Mary?" Renie rattled on, craving the adults' attention.

Mary laughed at the exuberance of the six-year old as she thought if only all the family was as welcoming as Renie! Thomas gave Mary a wink which seemed to say that everything was going to work out with her new family.

Thomas pulled the buggy into the Bimbi place and saw someone come from the back of the house. "Hello, there!" Thomas jumped down from the buggy and met up with the stranger. "I'm Thomas Cosby. Saw Ben Logsdon at church and he told me you needed a place to stay."

"Yeah, my wife and kids, well, we came over this way looking for work, needed a place to stay. You own this property?" The man seemed to be either unfriendly or afraid of Thomas.

Thomas felt the needed to put the man at ease so he immediately put his hand out to shake hands and the other hand on the man's shoulder. "Yes, that's fine. Glad you found the house." As Thomas chatted with the man, he prayed God would lead him to help this young man and his family.

"I'm John Dales and me and my family was looking for a place to stay, couldn't find a place. They said you were getting married and wouldn't be around."

Thomas shook his head, and explained he had been gone, but his family was at home. "You are welcome to stay here, but this place is falling down."

"Well, I'm kind of handy with a saw and hammer and I fixed up what I could when we moved in. Just needed somewhere to stay. The wife has cleaned the place and stuffed up the holes so the snakes and mice can't get in. But, if you want us to get out, we can."

Thomas assured him he need not move, that it was fine for his family to stay as long as he wanted. Before Thomas could stop himself, he was asking John if he needed a job. He explained he did not talk business on Sunday, but if he was interested he could come to his place tomorrow morning at nine o'clock.

"Sure," John replied, "I'll be there. I need a job. Oh, by the way. Me and my boy went to your place yesterday. Thought maybe the mill might be open so we could get some cornmeal. We didn't have any flour or meal, and I thought about going in. But, something hit me on the shoulder three or four times, so I figured something was telling me that I needed to move on. Thought I better tell you what happened."

"I'm sorry, John, sorry that I wasn't there to help you out. You can come over now and get a bag of meal, or get it in the morning. Have a good evening, and I guess I will see you in the morning, if not sooner."

The two men shook hands and John seemed much more at ease than their first handshake. Somehow, Thomas felt that John and his family had been placed in his path.

Thomas explained to his family what he had just done. "I may have made a mistake, but I invited John to come in the morning to talk about a job. I have to admit, I am not feeling good about this, but maybe it will work out. He needed a job and I need another worker."

---

Nellie was glad to get home after the long afternoon at Ollie's. She explained to Thomas what had happened as she unhitched the horse from the wagon. Tommie joined the two of them to take the horse to the barn.

"I'm going to take a couple baskets of vegetables to Ollie's in the morning. Looks like they didn't have much of a garden, this year. Gran suggested maybe you might want to catch some trout and I could take them to Ollie's in the morning."

Tommie heard the request. "Yeah, Dad. Let's so fishing. We haven't been fishing in a long time. We can have some for supper and send some to Ollie's family." Tommie actually wanted more time with his dad without having to share him with Miss Mary.

"Good way to spend about an hour, Tommie. Then we will have to do the chores."

"Yeah, let's go Dad. I found a good place for worms the other day. If you get the poles, I'll get the worms," Tommie said excitedly.

"I'll just let Mary know where we are headed. Meet you at the bend in the creek."

Trout flourished in the cold water of the creek. Thomas had taught Johnny how to fish in the creek and Johnny had taught Tommie. Johnny was a little too impatient for fishing, but Tommie loved it. He would often be found by himself with a fishing pole if he had free time.

The two guys sat on the huge roots of the old river birch. The ancient tree looked like it was losing its grip on the creek bank, slowly sliding into the creek. Today, it provided a great place for Thomas and Tommie to sit and throw their lines into the creek. The guys didn't have to wait long for a bite. Unfortunately, the first two bites were crawfish. Tearing them apart and using them for bait, Thomas began to tell Tommie about John's visit to the mill.

"He said that he was hit on the shoulder three or four times. Tommie, you wouldn't know anything about that, would you?"

Tommie shifted his pole and looked down, trying to think of a way to explain. "Well, I thought he was going in the mill. I was just trying to scare him away. I just hit him on the shoulder."

"I understand, Tommie, you were just trying to protect our property. But the thing you have to remember is no property is worth killing someone. You could have hit him in the head or he could have turned and you could have hit him in the eye. And what about the little boy? You see, he wasn't going in to get money, just a sack of meal for a hungry family. Next time, Tommie, let me handle the situation."

"Dad...I practice a lot! I use a variety of projectiles and angles. I have studied the rate of propulsion in relation to the wind velocity and I never miss."

Thomas pulled up his pole with a trout flopping from the hook. "Tommie, you amaze me. How do you know this stuff?" Removing the trout, Thomas started talking about Tommie's art project. "How are you coming on the house project you had started in the spring? Do you need any help? Removing the trout, Thomas started talking about Tommie's art project. "How are you coming on the house project you had started in the spring? Do you need any help?"

"Well I haven't gotten much done lately, but it is almost finished. I have some questions about a few things. It is so big! How are you ever going to get it level?" Tommie asked.

"I think leveling won't be difficult if I can find strong backs. The biggest problem for me now is figuring out who is going to be the best to help me and where I can get my supplies, the kind of supplies I want."

Tommie pulled another feisty trout in. "Dad, I can help you. You know I don't have to go to school, least not every day. I'm smart and I can stay home to help, especially if Miss Mary, or Mary, what do I call her anyway?"

Thomas was trying to pull in another trout caught under a beaver's dam. "You can call her Mary at home and Miss Mary at school. Eventually, I hope you kids will call her mom, she would like that. Of course, you know she may not be your teacher come school time in September."

Tommie grimaced at the thought of calling Miss Mary 'mom'. No way, that wasn't about to happen. "You think we will have a new teacher?" Tommie questioned.

"Could be, don't know yet. Okay, I have two, you have three. We will have three for us tonight, and send the two big ones to Ollie's. You ready?" Thomas asked.

"Well, I love trout, but I ate a lot of that country ham today and apple pie, and I'm still full. What I was really looking forward to was Gran's molasses apple cake. She made fried chicken and the cake but she took it to Ollie's after church."

Thomas laughed at his son. Growing boys were always hungry. "I am sure that the chicken and the cake were appreciated, probably more than you would have enjoyed it."

---

On the porch, Nellie took a deep breath before going in, fearing the changes that were sure to take place. Sure enough, Mary and Renie were unpacking some of Mary's belongings. Tears welled up in Nellie's eyes as she watched Mary putting her things in her mother's cedar chest. How she would like to swipe everything onto the floor and tell Mary that she didn't belong here. When Mary and Renie saw her, they stopped unpacking and asked about Lyssa and the baby.

Giving a quick reply, Nellie started outside. She couldn't stand being in the house with Mary another minute. Nellie yelled back at Renie. "Renie, come out and watch the men clean the fish. You need to learn how!" Reluctantly, Renie left Mary's side to be with her sister.

The girls were outside on the swings when Thomas and Tommie brought the fish to clean. "Did anyone gather the eggs today?" Nellie asked, knowing the job probably hadn't been done.

Thomas confessed, "No we haven't, Nellie. Would you and Renie care to do that while we clean the fish?"

"Sure," Renie said. "I like gathering the eggs. Mary said she would make us some custard tomorrow if we found a lot of eggs. I like custard."

"We don't need to use the eggs for custard, Renie. That is just for a special occasion. Mary needs to learn that we don't waste eggs," Nellie replied rather sharply.

Renie stopped and stared at Nellie with tears in her eyes. "Why are you so mean, Nellie?"

A stab of guilt and shame hit Nellie's heart as she hugged her little sister and apologized. "I'm sorry, Renie. I just don't like for Miss Mary to come in and take over, try to take Mama's place. Let's find those eggs for your custard, sweetie."

Nellie and Renie checked the chicken house first. Nellie reached in the nests, making perfectly sure there wasn't something else in the nest, like a snake. Nellie shared with Renie about the time she had been gathering eggs and she heard a hissing sound.

"Luckily, the hissing startled me enough to keep me from plunging my hand into the deep nest full of straw…and snake. Mama said it was just a chicken snake and sometimes they like to suck eggs. Thankfully, I haven't seen or heard from it since. Mama said it probably would have scared the snake worse than me, but I really doubt that," Nellie explained to Renie as she tried to get a laugh from the six-year old.

Since Nellie couldn't find a couple of the chickens, she looked in the tall orchard grass areas where she had found the chickens before. Sure enough, there were a couple of chickens that had laid eggs and were trying to set on them. Nellie explained to the chickens that it was not the right time of year for baby chicks. Next spring would be a great time, and no one would stop them from setting on their eggs.

Nellie let Renie take the egg basket with the large, brown, speckled eggs to Mary. Renie was excited and reminded Mary what she had promised to do with the eggs.

"How about I make some for Ollie's family, too? Would you be able to take some to them tomorrow, Nellie?" Mary asked.

"Sure," Nellie replied, trying to sound as uninvolved with Mary as possible. Nellie turned to Thomas, "Dad, I heard that the Millers have some sheep to sell. Could I buy two or three before school starts? I have a spot picked out for them and I can do so much with them… like using their wool to make yarn and to knit with," Nellie pleaded.

"I don't know if this is a good time. You know we have a big project to begin soon. We are going to start building the new house, for our growing family. We are cramped in this house, and each of you kids need a room, along with a room for Mom and guests when they visit," Thomas explained.

Mary looked worried, "Now, Thomas, you don't have to go building a new house for me. I want things to stay the same as much as possible for this family. And we still don't know if I will be teaching, I don't know about the young lady who is coming tomorrow."

"Well, Mary, you can decide tomorrow. You can recommend her or not based on what you see and hear. And, of course, I'm talking with the two young men tomorrow about helping on the house. They will be here at nine o'clock in the morning. In fact, we have to get up early enough to get chores done, breakfast over and vegetables picked for Nellie to take to Ollie's place. And don't forget Nellie, to take the fish. It is cleaned and salted in the cellar."

Mary prepared the trout with a few fried potatoes and sliced tomatoes. Nellie did not offer to help and looked through her fabric stash for gown material. When the meal was ready, Nellie picked at her food, but didn't eat much.

"Nellie, you go relax, you have had a hard day. I'll do the dishes. You might want to work on the gown, so you just do what you need to get done." Mary smiled at Nellie as she waved her away from the kitchen.

Nellie was glad to get out of helping Mary, but that meant that Miss Mary had done a favor for her and she did not want any favors from her! Nellie caught Tommie watching Mary with a look of disdain. Mary was removing the old metal utensils from the cabinet. Nellie realized that this was Mary's way of taking over the kitchen, claiming it for her own.

Thomas gathered the family for the evening devotion. The scripture was from the book of Job. Thomas compared his life to Job's life. "I have lost my wife and son, while you children have lost your mother and a brother. But God has brought many good things in our life." He praised God, because he had Mary. They would be a family and be closer to God because of the hardships the Cosby family had endured.

Nellie and Tommie listened to the devotion, but looked at each other with disdain. Mary did not see them, but Thomas did.

Thomas reflected on the last few days as he said, "God has a plan for this family. When things look impossible, look up and God will prove faithful."

Thomas realized Nellie and Tommie missed their mother, but they would adjust to Mary and love her one day. He prayed for the Lord to help his family embrace each other. Thomas felt the letter hidden away in his pocket. He and

Mary had been married one day when he received the letter that would cause a major change in his family.

The Lord whispered to Thomas, "To much that is given, much is expected."

I guess, Lord, you are telling me I should take care of those in need. Mary would surely be upset. However, Thy will be done.

# Chapter 6

# Mary

Mary awoke, a difficult night, the first night spent in the Cosby home. Due to the hot and humid air, Mary threw kindling in the outside stove. Maybe the house didn't need any more heat, Mary thought. There had been friction between the children and herself the night before, which she had not really anticipated. Thomas had given the children the look which she had seen many times before when the children were out of line.

The outside kitchen which Thomas had designed was ingenious. He had used large limestone rocks to make a floor approximately twenty by twenty square. A large red cedar which Thomas had milled in his saw mill served for a counter. The fireplace was a simple fire pit made with large limestone rocks and was built into a three by three square stove with a grate on top. The stove had a lower grate which could be used for baking. As Mary put the old metal coffee pot on the grate, she thought about last night's surprise.

Just before bedtime, Thomas had shared the contents of the mysterious letter he had received. One day after Thomas and Mary had wed, Thomas had received a letter from Rissa's parents, the Pattersons, saying they were coming to visit in the spring. The fact that Rissa's parents had not been invited and were actually forcing their visit was still not as bad as the last surprise. The Pattersons had hinted that they might move in permanently.

"Of course," Thomas had explained, "I cannot possibly tell Rissa's parents they can't come." Mary asked why Thomas thought the Pattersons would stay longer. Thomas sighed and seemed reluctant to tell her but he admitted what he had learned.

Thomas had read between the lines of the letter penned by Trigg Patterson, Rissa's father. Trigg had alluded to business problems at the bank in the letter. As main loan officer of his bank, Trigg had loaned money to a Utopian community in Boston. The commune had boasted of many big names, even well-known authors. Therefore, Patterson had figured the community would be a good investment.

Thomas had read in the newspapers that the commune had undergone several changes in its philosophy. The indebtedness of the commune's farm and school had been bad enough. To make matters even worse, a fire which took down most of the buildings, resulted in bankruptcy and the closing of the farm. "I imagine that the deal with the community caused Trigg to lose his job," Thomas explained to Mary.

Mary asked Thomas about the Pattersons' faith in God. He explained that Rissa was brought up by her grandmother, a devout Christian. He admitted that he thought the Pattersons did not go to church at all. These people, her husband's in-laws, were coming to her home in the spring.

The entire situation seemed unbelievable! However, she was Mrs. Thomas Cosby now, and that was all that mattered. She was a wife, a stepmother, a daughter-in-law and now a…step daughter-in-law? Mary had heard the Cosby family had accumulated a lot of wealth. Thomas Cosby had bought 4,000 acres in the Roundstone area which had brought him success. Neighbors said whatever Thomas touched turned to gold. However, Mary knew Thomas was a fair and honest man. Before they were married Thomas had told her he would always give at least ten percent tithe and he had charities and families he helped in time of need. Mary felt in the dark about finances. How could Thomas afford such a luxurious house as he was proposing? She would have to draw on her courage to ask Thomas about the finances because now it was *their* finances.

Mary reminded herself of her own secrets, the guilt and shame. Trying to keep a secret from Thomas and his family would be difficult but she had to think of herself. After all, she could lose a lot if, well, if things didn't go as well as she had planned.

Mary had returned to Roundstone to teach four years ago, two years before Johnny had died. Mary shuddered when she recalled her mistakes, the guilt she couldn't escape. If she could turn back the clock and do things over, people wouldn't have been hurt, she would not have… she didn't want to think about it.

This morning, Mary would talk with Andrea Goodwin about the teaching job. Thomas had said Andrea was anxious to get a teaching job. Mary had to admit, at least to herself, she would like to keep her job. She loved the children so much, and education had been her life for almost twenty years. Each year, the students made progress in their studies and, for her, their progress was her greatest achievement. Her joy was seeing the students learn.

Now, she was married, with three stepchildren, a live-in mother-in-law and more house guests to come in the spring. Maybe wanting to go back to school was her way of getting away from the situation. After all, how many wives have to take in her husband's in-laws?

While starting breakfast, Mary prepared a checklist for Andrea. As she prepared breakfast, she made a few extra bacon biscuits in case someone was hungry. Mary thought about her own kitchen utensils and her lovely rose-pattern china. She longed to get her own belongings unpacked to make the house feel more like her home. Mary needed her things to help disguise Rissa's handprint everywhere.

Family fed and chores completed, Mary helped Nellie pack the food and gifts for Ollie's family. Giving the floors a good sweeping, Mary shook out the rugs and put them back on the oak plank floors. As Mary carried a bucket of water from the well she saw Goldie racing up the road. A horse and buggy followed by a horse and rider were meandering down the hill.

Punctual, the Cosby guests, Pete and Andrea Goodwin, and John Dales, eagerly walked to the house. Greetings and introductions over, Thomas invited the group to gather around the table to enjoy Mary's bacon biscuits and coffee.

Thomas wasted no time as he explained his business proposal, the building of a large, two-story home. He stated that his family would be having house guests in the spring who may be staying permanently. As he spoke of the situation, he looked to Mary with a look of empathy.

Mary took the opportunity to invite Andrea to the porch to talk. Andrea complimented Mary on the beautiful log cabin and the comfortable porch with the magnificent view of the creek. Mary had to agree the first time she saw the cabin she was enamored with the beauty and the design. The cabin's four large windows in the front along with a long porch and rocking chairs made the home look relaxed yet sophisticated. Of course, the house was built especially for Rissa Cosby, a sophisticated lady.

Mary had to control the old jealousy of Rissa that so frequently reminded her of past sins. After all, Thomas was hers before Rissa, before his trip to

Boston. Had Thomas not left for Boston and met Rissa, her life would have been so different.

Mary had to bring herself back to the conversation with Andrea. While the women talked about a variety of topics on the porch, the men at the kitchen table talked about house construction.

Both of the two younger men were apprehensive about building such a large house, and had plenty of questions for Thomas. John was concerned about the removal of the large rocks in the proposed site of the house. Pete asked about blueprints.

"No, I don't have blueprints yet, but my son has a talent for that sort of thing and he has managed to draw a picture of the proposal. He has even made the picture to scale. I will take the picture to Elizabethtown to an architect I know who will draw up the blueprints. I realize my architect may take longer than I would like to develop the blueprints, but we do have a couple small projects until then." Thomas passed the plate of bacon biscuits as he tried to make his guests feel welcome.

Tommie fastened the drawing to the wall for everyone to see. He pointed out the outside divisions of the house, the portico, the verandas, the placements of bedrooms, and outside kitchens and a shed. "This is the lay-out of the bedrooms and the water closets in each. My mother's grandparents and parents are from Boston. I heard about the water closets from my grandmother Wilson because Boston has the first hotel with indoor plumbing. A brilliant architect, Isaiah Rogers came up with this idea." Tommie could not hold back his enthusiasm. "Yeah, I want to be an architect someday and build innovative buildings."

On the porch, the two ladies talked about everything; their marriages, their families, and the church. Finally, Mary discussed the position available at Roundstone School. Andrea was excited about a teaching job at Roundstone. She shared with Mary some of her ideas on curriculum classroom design in regard to multi-levels. Both ladies were excited with the prospects of a new school year. Mary explained she would be glad to help out for a while, until Andrea felt comfortable with the classroom. Reluctantly, Mary suggested they join the men inside.

Mary poured another cup of coffee for her guests. After making small talk for a few minutes, Mary was anxious to make her announcement. "Andrea and I have discussed the teaching position at Roundstone."

Mary paused, took a deep breath and smiled at Andrea. "I am recommending Andrea for the teacher of Roundstone School. Andrea said she and Pete will pray again about the decision, but she feels good about it."

"Congratulations, Andrea, I feel sure the Board will take Mary's recommendation. I have to admit I want Mary at home this year to help with the building of this house, and the building of our family," Thomas added.

Getting back to the business at hand, Thomas couldn't hold back his enthusiasm, "The lumber has been milled here at my mill. Some of the lumber has been drying out for the past year in the barn. However, before we start on the Cosby home, we have other projects. I want to share with you some of my ideas.

John, the Bimbi place needs a lot of work. You can fix it up with the lumber we mill, or we can build another cabin closer to our place for your convenience. Pete, the same goes for you. We can have a log cabin structure up within a month. You can have the house we build, if you want to stay on and work for me. There's always plenty of work to be done here. I will pay you weekly as we work on the Cosby home."

Thomas continued, "We have plans to build another mill downstream, upon completion of the house. After these two projects, the house and mill, there will be a bigger project, which I am not at liberty to discuss at this time. So, gentlemen, what do you think?"

Pete extended his hand across the table and gave Thomas a hearty handshake. "I think I would love to work for you. I don't know if I am really knowledgeable of such a project, but I am more than willing to learn."

"Good, good! I think you will learn, as we all will." Thomas looked at John, "So, what about it John? Do you think you would like to work for me, and build a big house?"

John was much more reserved than Pete. "Well, don't know yet. Never really planned on staying in this part of the country. I'll talk with the wife and let you know something. I'm not good at blueprints, never learned to read very good." Looking up, John continued.

"Sallye likes the location of the house, with the spring so close and there are plenty of wildflowers close to the house. We noticed that the house is close to the school which will be good for little Everett."

"That's great, John. We will make sure that Everett makes friends at school," Mary added.

Thomas reminded John that he could get the lumber he needed from the mill at any time. "We will be glad to load a wagon of lumber and bring it and help build what you need. And, Pete, the same goes for you and Andrea."

Pete thanked Thomas for the offer. "We appreciate the offer, but Andrea's family has assured us that we could use their little cabin for as long as we need it."

"Right now, the cabin is all we need and we are close to the family, which enables me to help mom and dad, plus my sister," Andrea added.

Thomas thought of one more thing he wanted to tell the young men. Getting the Bible from the small table, Thomas respectfully placed it on the kitchen table. "I would like to encourage both of you to come to church regularly. I believe people who worship together, work even better together."

John looked stunned. "So, are you saying if I don't go to your church, you won't hire me?"

Lost for words, Thomas looked at the two men before his reply. "If you work for me, I would like for you to attend church, but perhaps that is my job, to witness to you about how the Lord has been so good to me."

John immediately got up from the table and thanked Mary for the breakfast. He put his hat on his head and started out the door, ignoring Thomas' outstretched hand. "I'll think about your offer."

Thomas followed John out on the porch. "John, I really want you to work for me. I think the Lord led you this way."

John avoided eye contact with Thomas. He was not going to be forced into anything. John wanted to talk to Sallye, they made decisions together and he did not know how she would feel about the church.

As Thomas rejoined Pete, Andrea, and Mary, he studied his coffee cup for a minute. He wanted to discuss John, but thought he better not.

"I want to read from I Chronicles Chapter 28-29. This chapter talks about David giving the job of building the temple to Solomon. He placed his trust in Solomon, he would follow the Lord's commands and do his best."

After Thomas had read the scripture, the two couples had prayer and shook hands. "This is the beginning of a long journey with a team of God's workers. With prayer, patience, and respect for one another, the Cosby home project will come to completion by the end of spring." Thomas and Mary walked the Goodwin's to their buggy.

Mary felt a bit of relief as she warily returned to the kitchen clean-up. "The new house is going to be built sooner than we thought," Mary mumbled to herself. Thomas had told her that if there was anything she wanted in the house, she needed to include it in the plans. Mary couldn't think of anything Thomas hadn't already thought of, except maybe…

One of the most important things would be an adequate cellar under the house. Turning Thomas' notes over, Mary scribbled in some thoughts, "large cellar." She knew a large cellar would be difficult because of the many huge limestone rock at the proposed location of the house, but with a growing family they would need it.

Mary recalled the dirt walls and floor of the cellar in her parent's home. It was a large cellar, dark and scary, where the family stored fruits and vegetables. However, she remembered that when she was only six, the family had used the cellar to hide away. It was during the war of 1812 and her father had seen some men with guns headed toward the house. The concealed trap door in the kitchen floor was covered by a rug that hid the entrance to the family cellar. Her father had quickly gathered his family and hid with them in the cellar. The weary soldiers came in the house, took what they wanted, and eventually left. Mary shuddered to think what might have happened had the family been upstairs in the house. Rumors of the soldiers raping and ravaging the women caused fear among the settlers. Soon after, her father built a store and the family lived over it, but they always had a cellar.

Mary remembered how she had nightmares of being in the dark cellar hiding from men with guns. At the end of the dream, the soldiers had found her and were pulling her out of the cellar. She would wake sitting up in bed, terrified and trembling.

Mary talked to herself, "Why had God punished me with the nightmares? I had been scared as a child, and now as a woman, I still have fears, guilt, and shame. Why hasn't God helped me when I needed it?"

Mary's parents would not go to local churches, insisting that their church was the only way to worship. When the family had moved from New England to Kentucky, they did not find the European Anglican Church, so they did not go at all. When Mary's older brother was ten years old, he became ill and died within two weeks. Mary's father had insisted that his faith was the only way and he would not allow anyone from the local churches to come visit. Both parents had vowed to never allow a Bible with a New Testament in their home.

Mary had never gone to church until she came to Roundstone a few years ago. She had told everyone that she had been saved, baptized and belonged to a church up north. Truth was Mary's father had kicked her out of their home as a teenager and told her he never wanted to see her again. The most difficult years of her life followed and who was there for her? Nobody! Mary laughed to herself as she recalled how she had had told everyone at church the story of her "Christian upbringing" because she would have never been hired to teach or even to marry Thomas without the false endorsement.

Looking at Thomas' notes, Mary tried to envision the house with her suggestions. Mary recalled Aunt Lizzie's two story home in Bardstown. The upstairs had a secret wall which was hidden behind a large bookshelf. In front of the massive bookshelf was a chair with a table and candle, looking very obscure. One day when she and her cousins were playing, they found a button inside the bookshelf. One of the children pressed it, and when he did, the bookshelf moved forward as if on a spring. The children went in the small narrow room that was dark and fairly empty, a great hiding place. The secret room had a passage through the house. A small stairway which led to the first floor and on to a cellar was entirely hidden. She and her cousins had a great time afterward because they were either playing in the secret passage or they were looking for other secret hiding places in the house.

Scary hiding places and fun ones! Mary thought. Picking up a piece of paper, Mary began to write

> Must have:
> Large cellar with a hidden door,
> Long porch with swings, large porch pillars,
> secret room upstairs.

Now, Thomas would laugh about the secret room and the cellar. Oh, well, there may be children in the house someday who would love the excitement of a secret room or passage through the house. What an exciting way to build a house, with a little mystery and a change from the usual log cabin. Secrets in her life and secrets in her home, she had to laugh. Yet, Mary felt, there seemed be another reason the house would someday need the secret room.

# Chapter 7

# Ollie and Lyssa

Lyssa cuddled Baby Oleta as they enjoyed a quiet time of rocking while the men chopped wood. Lyssa was grateful to Katherine and Nellie as they had done so much for her family; especially their thoughtfulness of nursing her through the birth of her baby. *I was sick and you looked after me.* Katherine had delivered her baby, cooked, cleaned, washed clothes, and even groomed her family.

Lyssa had remarked to Ollie just that morning, "Katherine and Nellie went above and beyond anyone's expectations and they did everything with love."

Katherine had read from the Bible and prayed with Lyssa and Ollie. Lyssa told Ollie she felt something in her heart she had never experienced. It was as though the Holy Spirit was drawing her near. As Lyssa rocked Baby Oleta, she thought about the words Katherine had read to them about God's love. Never had she known anyone to explain the Bible to her so plainly. Lyssa discussed with Ollie the verses that Katherine had read to them. She confided with Ollie, "There seems to be so many verses assuring God's love which includes everyone, even me with my sinful past."

Lyssa shuddered when she thought about her past. She had lived a life of sin; and she hadn't cared about anything or anyone until Ollie rescued her. Ollie had given her a good home and children.

Katherine had read the story of Boaz and Ruth to the couple while she had been staying with them. Lyssa felt a kindred spirit with Ruth. She even compared the situation of Boaz and Ruth to herself and Ollie.

Lyssa wanted to know, no, she *needed* to know more about Jesus. She had promised God that she would take Katherine's advice and go to church on Sunday to learn about Him.

Lyssa studied the face of her baby as she talked softly to her Sarah Oleta. "You know, Little Oleta, you have to thank Katherine and Nellie for everything they did for you and your mama. Nellie made you a cute, pink gown. On Monday, Nellie brought two baskets of vegetables with trout and a jug of custard." *I was hungry and you fed me.* Lyssa smiled as she thought. She even brought Oliver a pair of Tommie's pants he had outgrown and Katherine took up a pair of Thomas' pants to fit Ollie. What good friends!

Lyssa moved the baby to the other shoulder as she rocked and hummed one of the songs that she had learned from Katherine. Lyssa looked at the dress, hanging on the wall that she would wear to church on Sunday. Nellie had been so sweet when she presented her with a dress. She had dug into the chest containing her mother's dresses and had chosen a lovely, pink print dress along with a hat. *I was naked and you clothed me.* Lyssa realized that Katherine and Nellie had done so many loving and kind things for her and her family, she could never repay them.

Lyssa confided to Baby Oleta, "You know, I don't know much about prayer, only what I've heard Katherine and Nellie say when they were with us. Perhaps, I can say a simple prayer, like Katherine suggested."

Lyssa put Baby Oleta across her lap and said, *"Forgive me of my sins and thank you, Lord Jesus, Amen."*

Lyssa longed for a Bible, for she knew how to read and would read to Ollie and Oliver for their family devotions. She couldn't wait for Sunday to go to church and learn more about Jesus. Lyssa wanted to tell everyone what she had learned and felt in her heart. Katherine told her that was called "witnessing" to others about how she felt. Lyssa hoped she would be strong enough to witness when the time came.

At the woodpile, Ollie stopped chopping wood and wiped his brow. Little Oliver struggled at picking up the larger pieces. "Oliver, Son, just get the smaller ones, I'll get the big pieces."

"I hear something, Papa!" Oliver said excitedly, pointing to the path across from the house. "It's over there. Looks like a horse and a rider."

Soon Ollie saw the horse and rider. "Hey, there!" called Ollie. A little louder, he called again, "Hey, there!"

The rider, a gangly man, dressed in black, replied, "Heard you the first time. Howdy, Son, I'm a Circuit Rider, and I'm headed toward Elizabethtown. Thought I would take a short cut and save some time. Am I close to the road now?"

Ollie shook his head, "Yes, sir, there's a good road not too far from here on the east of the old shack straight ahead." Ollie felt he needed to befriend the stranger. "Would you want to come in for a drink and something to eat maybe?"

"God bless you, young man. Yes, yes, I would. Haven't had anything to eat for a good while and just ran out of water a little ways back. I would most appreciate it." The eager man hurriedly dismounted and tied his horse to the house railing. Before walking away, he pulled a Bible from his saddlebags.

Ollie stuck his head in the cabin first and announced, "Lyssa, we have company."

Lyssa and Baby Oleta greeted the men at the door. "Come in, please."

Ollie started to introduce the man, but realized he did not know his name. "Now, what do we call you?"

"Most people call me Reverend Morgan. I live at Rowletts when I am at home with my wife and four children. I have a ministry, First Baptist Church in Rowletts, but I ride circuits and do revivals everywhere."

"Well, Reverend Morgan, My name is Ollie Booker and this here's my wife Lyssa. She just had a baby Sunday, Baby Oleta. This here's my boy, Oliver."

"Glad to meet you. Please have a seat and rest. How about a cup of coffee?" Lyssa asked.

Ollie pulled out a chair for the Reverend at the large pine table. The men scooted their chairs up to the table while Lyssa poured a cup of coffee for everyone.

"Well, young lady, that coffee smells great," the Reverend answered. Being on a mission to witness to others, the Reverend didn't waste any time. Placing his well-worn Bible beside him on the table the Reverend asked, "So, are you and your husband Christians?"

Lyssa explained to the Reverend, "I don't think we are Christians. But we have learned about the Bible and we certainly want to learn more."

Ollie explained how Katherine and Nellie had ministered to their needs. The three of them talked about families, babies, and being a Christian. Ollie and Lyssa enjoyed listening to the Reverend with his knowledge of the Bible.

Lyssa began to prepare the evening meal. She took special care setting the table, using her best tablecloth, making sure the table looked lovely for her respected guest. Placing the food on the table, Lyssa offered the very best of her cooking. Lyssa remembered to ask the Reverend to bless the food. As Reverend Morgan ate he kept telling the family how much he enjoyed the food. Lyssa felt good that she was able to do something for someone else. She recalled what Katherine had said, she was 'ministering to another's needs.'

After the meal, the Reverend picked up the dishes, carried them to the dishpan, "Well, young family, it has been nice but I must be on my way. I thank you for your hospitality."

"Do you have to leave? We would love to talk more about the Bible," Lyssa urged.

"I would love to stay a little longer, but the sun is setting and I need to get to the road before it gets dark," the Reverend replied.

"Well, you could stay the night. We have an extra bed up in the loft, with Oliver. You probably need a good night's rest. We have a few eggs and some bacon to make breakfast in the morning. Why not stay the night? That is, if that is okay with Lyssa," Ollie pleaded.

Lyssa agreed with Ollie and urged the Reverend to stay. As soon as the Reverend accepted the offer, Lyssa climbed to the loft while Baby Oleta was sleeping. She felt humbled to have a man of God to spend the night at their home.

With particular care, Lyssa made the bed for the Reverend, making sure the mattress was stuffed with plenty of corn shucks. She used a flower embroidered pillowcase on the one extra pillow she had recently made. She placed a nine-square quilt at the bottom, just in case. The clean pee pot was in reach, along with fresh drinking water from the pitcher and bowl on Oliver's trunk. Lyssa had never entertained a man so honorable, so close to God and she wanted to make sure the little space was worthy.

When Lyssa returned to the men, the Reverend opened his Bible and began to talk about Jesus. He read and explained the first few chapters of John. Ollie and Lyssa had questions while Lyssa swaddled Baby Oleta. The three of them talked into the night with questions and praises.

When Reverend Morgan asked if they were ready to pray for salvation, Lyssa sighed and began to cry. "You don't know my past. You do not know what I have done. God could never accept me and forgive my sins. I have done too many things. Believe me, there is nothing I want more, but my sins are too black for God."

Reverend turned to the New Testament and read, "First Timothy 1:13, Although I was formerly a blasphemer, a persecutor, and an insolent man; but I obtained mercy because I did it ignorantly in unbelief." The Reverend closed the Bible and gazed at the couple. "You see, Paul, the writer of several books of the Bible was the one who threatened Christians, put them in jail and even murdered them. Yet, Paul was saved by the grace of God, by the blood of the cross.

"David, in the Old Testament, was guilty of adultery and murder, but God forgave him and blessed him. Rahab was a prostitute, but God blessed her, and in fact, she is in the lineage of Jesus. In First John 1:9 we read, If we confess our sins, He is faithful and just to forgive us our sins and to cleanse us from all unrighteousness. In Romans 3:23 we read, for all have sinned and fall short of the glory of God.

"You see, Lyssa, Ollie, none of us are righteous enough, but God loves us and wants to give us life everlasting."

Reverend Morgan asked, "My children, do you want everlasting salvation? Do you believe that Jesus is God's son? Do you believe he died for your sins? Do you believe he can be your personal savior? If you do, we will pray that Jesus will forgive your sins and come into your heart tonight."

All three, the Reverend, Ollie, and Lyssa knelt in prayer. Both Lyssa and Ollie were wiping tears and sobbing as they stood up and hugged each other. Katherine had planted the seed in their lives and Reverend Morgan had led them to Christ.

Although they could have stayed up all night singing praises to God, they eventually had to go to bed after Baby Oleta was fed. A night of grace had brightened the little log cabin with Jesus' love.

The next morning the Reverend ate breakfast with the little family and gave them some advice. "You kids need to go to church regularly and you need to read the Word every day. Since you said you don't have a Bible, I am giving you this one for your family Bible. I knew there was a reason the Lord was leading me toward your cabin yesterday, but I didn't know why. Now we all know, it was simply God's will."

Tears streaked Lyssa's face as she thanked the reverend for the gift. "I wanted a Bible so much, I know the Lord heard my request and He sent you. If there's anything we can ever do for you, please let us know. We do not have money but we will remember you in our prayers."

Ollie saw Reverend Morgan to his horse and thanked him again for everything. He and Oliver waved until the reverend was out of sight.

Now, Ollie thought, Lyssa could read to the family every night. He was so proud of Lyssa. She had come a long way since he met her.

Ollie had been in Louisville when he met Lyssa. He had gone to purchase supplies for the wagon shop when he saw her. She was sprawled in an alley, listless and half beaten to death, she smelled like liquor. She was a mess, but he fell in love with her at that moment. He put her in his wagon and took her to a doctor. The doctor told him she was not worth saving, a prostitute, an alcoholic, the scum of the earth. Ollie told him she was a human being and one worth saving. He would take her home with him and hopefully, she would marry him someday.

At first Lyssa wanted to go back to Louisville. She wanted alcohol and often screamed at Ollie because she wanted it so bad. Ollie had no alcohol and really didn't have anywhere to get it, or that was what he told her. He had to go to the wagon shop every day to work. Ollie was afraid she might be gone when he got back, but she had stayed. Slowly, she began to regain her strength, and before long she was thanking Ollie for what he had done.

During the cold winter months, Ollie and Lyssa built their love for one another. They made love and made baby Oliver. As soon as the weather cleared, the couple went to the justice of the peace and was married. Lyssa said it was the best day of her life. Ollie knew it was the best for him, married to the prettiest girl in Hart County. He was so proud and would work hard to be the best husband ever to Lyssa.

Lyssa and Ollie talked about their salvation. They prayed together, read the Bible together, and worshipped together. However, both of them felt they needed more and they were going to find a way they could lead others to Christ.

"Lyssa, what is your dream for your future, if you could do anything you wanted?" Ollie asked. "Do you have anything God has put on your heart to do?"

Lyssa smiled, realizing how good Ollie was to her, "I think someday I would like to open a shop in Upton. I could have a line of fabrics, and soon the new sewing machines will be available to sell. I think I would like witnessing to the women and families as they come in the store."

Ollie was happy for Lyssa as he said, "That's a great idea, and 'fore long Baby Oleta will be helpin' sell. I've dreamed about having a hardware shop, tools, wagon needs, you know. Everybody has to have that stuff sooner or later. Maybe we could put the stores together."

"But Ollie, we don't have the money for that kind of dreaming. And with the baby, I would need help, cheap help. I guess we just have to be happy with what the Lord has given us."

Determined to give hope to Lyssa, Ollie added. "What if we found help? Someone who could help us start the store?"

Lyssa looked at Ollie with a new-found hope. "You could be right. You know, the best thing is that we could have a place to witness to people as they come in the store. We can spread the love of God with our neighbors and friends, and most of all to strangers."

Both Lyssa and Ollie were giddy with excitement. They kept adding to the list of things they could do. Lyssa suggested, "We could live over the store which would make it easier on our family."

Grabbing Ollie's hands to her chest, Lyssa whispered, almost afraid to say the words. "But, Ollie, do you think we are smart enough to do something like this? Having a business is a lot of hard work and I would think you have to be really smart to make it," Lyssa admitted.

"Anything, *anything* is possible with the Lord. Remember the verse that Katherine read to us? 'I can do all things through Christ who strengthens me.' I think it was from Philippians. So if we pray about it, and this is God's will, He will make it happen," Ollie added as he lifted Lyssa's chin and kissed her.

"And I know He will. He has already done so much for us," Lyssa said as she smiled broadly.

The couple said a prayer, thanking God for everything He had done for them already. They asked that if it be the Lord's will, He would provide the money, the place and the help for the business, and in return, they would be a witness to those around them. Ollie and Lyssa held hands and made their pledge to God: they would be faithful servants with or without the business. "If the Lord directs us along the path of the store, or whatever path he leads us, we will always remember this moment of our lives," Lyssa whispered.

Lyssa looked down at Baby Oleta who was getting fretful and hungry, "I just can't get over the fact Jesus would save me knowing what a sinner I have been, knowing I have not read the Bible and been to church like other women my age. I have to admit it is hard to believe He could ever love me."

Ollie put his arm around Lyssa and watched Baby Oleta nurse. "Would you stop loving our little Oleta if she disappointed you someday, if she did something sinful?"

"I would never stop loving my children, never. I want to give them the best I can so they will know God's love too. But I would never stop loving her. I think I understand, I guess that's why Katherine keeps saying, 'God is love'."

# Chapter 8

# Tommie and Thomas

Tommie had actually impressed himself on his presentation of the house plans. He had noticed his father seemed proud of him when he presented the drawing to Pete and John. Even Pete had commented, "Tommie, looks like you know what you are doing!"

However, it was Thomas' approval Tommie craved. Tommie loved his father, but more than that, he admired his father and he wanted to be just like him. Well, except marrying Miss Mary! He could not understand how his father could forget his mother so quickly and marry that woman.

Tommie's bookshelf bulged with the books that Thomas had given him, the books Thomas had read as a young man. Thomas had encouraged his children to read the Bible, but also to read about other Christians so they could learn from others.

Jonathan Edwards, an early pastor and theologian, was one of Tommie's favorite examples, someone who he would emulate. Edwards was only thirteen when he went to Yale, obviously a very intelligent young man, one whom Tommie admired. Tommie had read the resolutions of Jonathan Edwards, copied them on pieces of paper and posted them over his bed. His father had suggested he review the resolutions often and pick out some favorites to live by. Aloud, Tommie repeated his favorite resolution, *"Resolved never to do anything but duty."*

Flipping through his Bible, Tommie read, "Ephesians 6:6-8, not with eye service, as men-pleasers, but as bondservants of Christ, doing the will of God from the heart, with goodwill doing service, as to the Lord and not to men, knowing that whatever good anyone does, he will receive the same from the Lord, whether he is a slave or free."

Tommie thought about the influences in his life, his father, the church, the people in the books and Johnny. How much he missed Johnny, who was not only his older brother, but his best friend. Johnny had taught him so much as they enjoyed their time working and playing together. Yet, the two boys were so different. Tommie loved to read, study, draw, and work hard on the farm. Although he loved nature, he did not have the tenacity Johnny had for entreating every living thing.

Johnny loved being out discovering new things, seeing nature, and investigating caves. Tommie picked up the journal that Johnny had used to record the habits of the birds, lizards, snakes, rabbits, deer, and everything he thought interesting. As he flipped through the pages, Tommie recalled how excited Johnny would be when he came home with some of his collection of feathers, bugs, snake skins, snails...everything he found, he studied.

> As Tommie held the journal, he said a prayer. "Father God, please give me answers to my troubled mind. Johnnie left me with a mystery to solve. 'Two Cosby sons will add another.' He died before we could solve the mystery and I think he really wanted us to know something. Lord, if it be your will, help me. Amen."

Tommie put the journal on the shelf in the bookcase and pulled out another book. The book he held, *Birds of America* had become Johnny's favorite. Their father had been in Lexington on business when he found the perfect book for Johnny. The book, by John James Audubon, had been Johnny's favorite resource as he identified the red tail hawk, the nuthatch, goldfinch, sparrows, the red headed Indian hen, the yellow breasted sap sucker, along with the crows and ravens. He was able to identify feeding times and mating periods. One of his favorite shows was the blue jay races up and down the creek. Tommie recalled the first show they had watched together.

Tommie picked up Johnny's box of Indian relics and fingered some of the largest arrowheads. Johnny had a passion for the Cherokee Indians who once lived less than seventy years ago in the Roundstone area. Johnny would dig along the creek bed and after a rain he would scout the wet weather springs for arrowheads.

One spring day, Tommie and Johnny explored the creek ledges. Fear seized Tommie as he saw Johnny running from the barn with a rope, harness and a pulley. Tommie knew that Johnny had another one of his wild ideas.

"Tommie," Johnny had gushed, "this is going to be very simple. I just need you to hold on to this end of the rope. When I get this harness rope wrapped around me, I want you to pull on the rope. It will pull through the pulley on that tree. I can swing up to the ledge over there. See, Tommie, there's something in the crevice of the ledge that I have to get. You can do it, Tommie, just hold on to the rope."

"Okay, but I'm scared. What if the rope breaks or you fall? You could break your legs!" Tommie argued, trying to get Johnny to change his mind.

"Hey," Johnny retorted. "Just listen to your big brother and you'll be fine."

Tommie felt very uncomfortable about being in on this scheme, and he figured Dad would be furious with both of them. However, he would trust Johnny this time and follow his direction.

Tommie pulled on the rope and let it go, giving it slack, as Johnny directed. Johnny made several attempts at pushing away from the tree before he could reach the ledge. Soon, Johnny was able to grab hold of the ledge. He held to the side of the crevice and pulled out the contents of the rock's pocket. Johnny yelled at Tommie to be careful and let the slack from the rope.

Tommy had gently let the rope slip, then the rope suddenly spun out of his hand and Johnny landed on the sandy bottom of the ravine. With his heart in his throat, Tommie ran to the bottom of the ravine, sliding down the hill.

Johnny was pale and moaning, but he was alive.

"Johnny, Johnny, are you okay?" It took what seemed like forever to get down from the ledge, run, and slide down to Johnny. By the time Tommie got there, Johnny was sitting up looking at his newest discovery.

"Look, Tommie, it's a real Cherokee bow and here's the quiver of arrows. This here's what they call a warrior headdress! And look! This bag inside the quiver has arrowheads, best ones ever! Look Tommie, here is a scraper, a dove tail, a turkey tail, and a clovis!"

The excitement and the thrill of the adventure was worth it for both boys until Dad learned how the mission was accomplished. As an upset father, Thomas warned Johnny he took too many chances and he should never involve his little brother in something so dangerous.

Secretly, Thomas was amazed at what Johnny had found. He too had seen the small patch of red, the feathers, but figured there would be no way to ever retrieve them. Of course, Johnny's curiosity and determination was part of his character.

Tommie pondered the Indian collection which now belonged to him. To think, this area was the home of Indians at one time. They worked, played, and raised their families' right here on this creek. It was all so intriguing for a boy who had learned a healthy respect for the Kentucky Indians, Indians who were no more in the area. Perhaps someday he would learn even more about the Indians who had lived right here at Roundstone. After Johnny's death, Tommie promised that one day he would meet some of the Cherokee people and ask them about their ancestors' stories of living in Kentucky.

Thomas shouted upstairs, "Tommie, are you ready? We need to go help Paul awhile. It looks like we have several wagons waiting for their grain to be ground."

We really need that second mill, Thomas thought. We also need to get someone permanently to help Paul. He works too hard, and he seems depressed. I have a feeling he feels bad because he often grabs his thigh and grimaces when I talk with him. I am not going to have time to help him before long. I'll see if I can find someone to help Paul.

Thomas had so many projects he wanted to do that occasionally God had to show him he needed to slow down and enjoy what he had, to appreciate his family, his friends, and his church. After Johnny and Rissa had died, Thomas promised the Lord he would not let work and his ambition get ahead of the Lord's will for his life. The grief Thomas had felt was the hardest thing anyone should have to go through. Anger at God, for letting this happen, was difficult for Thomas. Thomas was reminded God also lost His son, his only son. God had given His only son for the propitiation of our sins. Thomas had given his anger, his hurt and his grief to the Lord and asked for forgiveness and comfort.

When Rissa had been killed, Thomas had felt guilty, guilty of neglect and more. Had he stopped his work and helped Rissa pick the berries, he could have gotten her safely out of the way. Had he given her his time, his Rissa, the love of his life, would be with him today. Thomas had learned repentance of sin, grief and guilt through all the tragedy. Instead of turning away from the Lord, Thomas had been drawn to the Lord for comfort. Thomas remembered his favorite comforting scripture: Romans 14:8 *For if we live, we live to the Lord; and if we die, we die to the Lord: Therefore, whether we live, or die, we are the Lord's.*

At the mill, Paul kept the grinder fed while the Cosby men helped unload and load the wagons. Some families came to the mill weekly, others came monthly. Yet, there were a few wagons each day, Monday through Friday, some months on Saturdays. Often children would get out and play in the shallow springs at the head of the creek. The clean, cold, clear springs provided a drink of water which was much appreciated on a hot summer day.

The last wagon had left the mill when the men walked to the saw mill on downstream. After the early spring tree cutting, there were many stacks of trees which needed work. Their job that day was to take an inventory of what the workers would need for the construction. Hauling the logs would be a job for all the men.

"Tommie, it looks like we may need to go to town and order some of our materials. We can get some of the supplies today. Let's see if the girls want anything or if they would like to go with us."

"Aww, do they have to go with us? They are too much trouble and we will have to wait for them to doll-up. Let's leave them and go."

"Tommie, that's not a good attitude. You know the girls would like to go. In fact, why don't you go ask them if they want to go?"

Out of breath from running to the house, Tommie blurted, "Dad said to ask you girls if you would like to go to town with us. We are in a hurry, so if you don't want to go, we will get on the road." Tommie tried to get out the door before they decided to take him up on the offer.

"Oh, how nice of you to ask, Tommie, Yes, I would love to go. There are a few things I need to get at the mercantile store." Mary gave Tommie a delightful smile as she put away her sewing.

Nellie tried to say she and Renie would stay home, but Renie begged to go with Mary. Frustrated, Nellie decided she might as well go along with the family and perhaps find some material for a dress for Baby Oleta.

On their trek to Upton, Thomas talked about the new house and Mary's suggestions. Nellie and Tommie sat quietly behind the adults making faces at Mary and whispering sarcastic remarks.

Upton's stores, mercantile, hardware, grocery stores were close together along with the bank and post office. While Thomas and his son went to the hardware store, the girls went to the domestic's area of the mercantile store.

"They don't have many fabrics here, Nellie. We will have to go to Elizabethtown to get what we need for your sewing projects." Mary hoped to encourage Nellie to share with her as she had in school when she was teacher and Nellie was student. "Look, Nellie, this is an ad for the new sewing machines that will soon be for sale. What do you think about sewing on a machine?" Mary asked Nellie.

Nellie shrugged because she had no idea. "I suppose I could learn. Mama could have sewn on a machine. She was really clever like that." Nellie meant to frustrate Mary, and it appeared she had succeeded. Meanwhile, the men had met up with them, carrying their purchases.

"Thomas, what about a shopping trip to Elizabethtown? We need some material for a new dress for Nellie and Renie for the first day of school. I am sure Tommie could use a couple new school shirts. We could take Katherine with us," Mary suggested as she smiled at Thomas ever so sweetly.

"Well, Mom will be back on Wednesday so we could plan on a trip on Thursday. It would give me a chance to get everything I need to start the building next week. I can't think of a better way to spend the day, than with my family. We can even go eat at one of those fancy restaurants," Thomas agreed.

Renie clapped her hands at the prospect of shopping and eating at a restaurant. She had heard of people eating at a restaurant with tablecloths and fine dishes, and the stories sounded magnificent.

Mary enjoyed being with Thomas and his family even with the barbs that Nellie and Tommie had thrown her way. She had to be patient with the two older children, and soon she would have them eating out of her hand. Mary took every opportunity to make eye contact with each child and smile lovingly on their way home.

After the chores, the family ate a simple meal of bacon, tomatoes, and fried hickory cane corn. Thomas read the devotion from Psalm 103:17. As he cleared his throat, Thomas glanced at all the children to make sure they were paying attention. "But the mercy of the LORD is from everlasting to everlasting on those who fear Him and His righteousness to children's children."

As Thomas talked about the importance of family, he remembered the journal. After a few minutes of scratching through the old family trunk, he found what he was looking for. "I want to read you a couple pages my grandfather wrote in his journal many years ago.

March 15, 1775

We were able to stake our claims. Everyone wants their own place, no matter how much they fear the Indians. Me and my boy are cutting trees and clearing for our house. Sarah and Rachael have been working hard. We have prayed unceasingly these first few days. There are neighbors on down the path, but they are a good distance away. Unfortunately, all of us are too busy to help each other.

March 24, 1775

A late snow caused us to get behind, but we managed to put up a temporary cabin. We have enough dried meat for a while and we had roasted squirrel today. We have grain and we make corn cakes on the fire. Our prayers are that God will watch over us. Today we cleared the garden spot and we have seed potatoes to plant soon.

April 5, 1775

We have been sick with something, a bit of colds. Potatoes are planted and the soil is so rich it looks like it could grow anything. Indians came by today. Gave them Sarah's shawl and they were happy. We pray for God's everlasting blessings.

April 17, 1775

Logs are going up on cabin, everyone helps. Sarah and Rachael are a big help and of course I couldn't do without Daniel. Hope to have cabin up by the end of next month, if rains don't delay us. Praying unceasingly for our family. God is good.

April 30, 1775

God has answered our prayers and we thank Him and give Him all the glory and the honor. Our Indian friends came by this week and helped us with the cabin. They were great and we couldn't have done it without them. We gave them another trinket, Sarah's hand bell, but it was worth it. We worship our Lord who gives us such great gifts and we thank Him for sending the Indians to be our friends.

May 6, 1775

Garden is planted, beans, corn, beets, cucumbers, and squash. The potatoes planted last month are breaking through the dirt. Our family has worked hard and God has provided our every need.

Through all the work we have always had our daily Bible reading, morning and night. My hope and prayer is that my children, and their children will always give the Lord their love, and they will read from the Word every day, twice a day and they will pray unceasingly.

### May 15, 1775

Working hard clearing the area. What a beautiful day. The flowers are up, and the trees are so green and the sky is as blue as Sarah's eyes. We give thanks to God all day, every day. Daniel carved out a sign for our fireplace that sums it up, *'But as for me and my house, we will serve the* LORD, Joshua 24:15'."

Thomas closed the journal and looked at his family. "You see, reading from the Bible, has been a great resource for my grandfather's family. God loves us just as much as He did my father's father. Of course, we want to read the Word because we learn more about Him, because Our Lord God is the Word. When we read the Word, we learn about our Jesus and we learn how to live. We learn one of the most important verses in the Bible from Deuteronomy 6: 6-8. 'And these words, which I command you today, shall be in your heart: You shall teach them diligently to your children, and shall talk of them when you sit in your house, and when you walk by the way, and when you lie down, and when you rise up'."

The family joined together as they repeated, "Love thy Lord thy God with all thy heart, thy soul and thy mind, for this is the first and greatest commandment."

# Chapter 9

# Families

"Mom, let me help you. Tommie, get the basket for Mom." Thomas lifted his mother to the top step of the buggy. "You must have packed fifty pounds of food."

"Well, Thomas, I don't get the chance to visit with Delo and Row and their families very often. Want to surprise them!"

Pete and Repete, Thomas' two best wagon horses, were hitched and antsy to get started. With chores and morning activities out of the way, the family started their road trip by eight o'clock Thursday morning.

Once on the main road at Upton, the family traveled directly to Elizabethtown. Although the roads were rough, they were probably in the best shape for the travelers. Since the family would need a full day for their trip, Paul had volunteered to milk the cows so the family would not have to hurry back.

Thomas had the day planned; he would deliver the drawing to Joe Baumgardner who would create the blueprints for the house. Baumgardner, an attorney and a long-time friend, also worked with architecture in Elizabethtown. As the wagon neared the office, Thomas explained that he and Mary would go in, but they would only be a few minutes. Parked under a large oak tree, the buggy should be comfortable until they returned.

The red brick office building on the south end of Elizabethtown was a large, two story house with wide steps which led to a massive front door.

The building was so reminiscent of the house where Mary had lived many years ago that she felt a panic stirring in her chest. As she gazed at the house, bittersweet memories flooded her mind of a secret past when she had been so vulnerable, so hurt.

Drawing strength from Thomas' arm, Mary made her way up the steps. She noted the black iron hand rails had a fancy design and each window had the same fancy ironwork on the black shutters, identical to the house on High Street. Mary gazed at the windows which were long and elegant and held an air of dark mystery.

On the inside, Mary eyed the rooms and furnishings with a quick sweep, perhaps to assure herself that there were no surprises. Stylish drapes hung from ceiling to floor with a large burgundy, oriental wool rug in the center of the room. The furniture, obviously very expensive, was dark and elaborate and created a tone of wealth, a wealth made from the less-fortunate. Mary forced a smile to pull herself from the unwanted flood of memories issued by the house.

Thomas proudly introduced Mary as his new wife, and exchanged pleasantries with Baumgardner as they shook hands. Thomas gave Baumgardner the drawing and a brief description, along with suggestions that Mary had provided. The rest of the day Thomas planned to devote to his family in the city.

"Now, while they are out of sight, we are going to talk." Katherine's tone was firm and both Nellie and Tommie realized that Gran's tone was uncompromising. "First, I will remind both of you that you promised you would be nice to Mary. Did you not promise, Nellie?"

"Yes, but," Nellie was interrupted by Katherine.

"And Tommie, did you not promise?"

"Yes, but I," Tommie tried to continue.

"No, you promised and what I have seen and heard does not sound like someone being nice. Your father chose Mary for his wife and now they are married. You cannot change that. And Tommie, don't roll your eyes. What good is it to study the Edwards' resolutions and your Bible scripture, if you do not live by it?"

"Yes, but Gran, she is trying to take our mother's place," Tommie interjected.

Nellie joined Tommie in the protest, "Yeah, like taking away Mama's dishes and putting her dishes for us to use. Next thing we know she will be throwing out the furniture."

"As far as the dishes go, she has her right to change. Actually, the dishes that belonged to your mother were so heavy, I am glad she changed. Also, she is Mrs. Thomas Cosby and she can change the furniture if she wants. Children, I am telling you, until you make peace with the fact that Mary is your step-mother and the wife of your father, you will spend too much of your time being angry. The Bible says to not give a place to the devil, and that is what you are doing. You are allowing the devil to have a place in your heart." Katherine stopped talking a minute and looked at the children. She could sympathize with them because she understood. In fact, her own suspicions of Mary infected her heart and kept her from loving Mary as she should.

"Focus on having the fruit of the spirit instead. The Bible clearly tells us the fruit of the spirit helps us grow a Christ-like character." Katherine looked at Renie sitting in the front seat, but was listening. "Think about Renie and the influence you have on her."

Katherine continued to talk to the children about the fruit of the spirit. Before long Thomas and Mary were already walking, hand in hand, down the steps of the huge building. "What have I always taught you children about how to treat others?"

Nellie and Tommie answered quickly as they had heard the quote many times.

"Just love them," they answered in unison. Both children apologized and promised they would do better.

"Father, help this family get rid of the hate and anger and just love, in Jesus name I pray. Amen," Katherine concluded.

Even though Nellie and Tommie apologized, Katherine knew that the trouble was far from over. Both children had not been able to accept their father's marriage and sooner or later something was going to happen. Katherine thought about insisting the children stay with her at Delo's, but she figured Thomas would have to face the truth, that his children disliked Mary.

———◆———

Only a block away on Mulberry Street, the family arrived at Katherine's sisters' home. Katherine had not had the opportunity to visit with sisters, Delo and Rowie, for a long time, and she would rather visit than shop.

Katherine had packed a few gifts and food items to give to her sisters' families. As she waved goodbye to her children, Katherine was like a child running excitedly into the large, two-story home to be with her family.

Mary had hoped that Thomas would leave the older children with Katherine. However, she knew him better than to think he would keep the children from the trip today. Still a little paranoid from the visit to the attorney's office in the shady house of secrets, Mary tried to convince herself that she could handle whatever would come her way. By the end of the day, she would have Nellie and Tommie thanking her for being there for them.

"Thomas, we need to purchase new boots for the children before you start on your hardware shopping jaunt. After that, you and Tommie can compare hammers and nails as long as you like."

The large mercantile store was already a busy place with ladies shopping, children whining and the owners busy helping customers. The floor creaked as the family trudged to the back where the shoes were located.

Since Katherine demanded the children make a positive attitude adjustment, both Nellie and Tommie followed Mary's suggestions, to her surprise. All three children, along with Thomas, purchased a new pair of boots. Mary felt she had won a small victory with the children.

Thomas suggested that he and Tommie go to the hardware store while the girls shopped for fabric. Tommie and Nellie exchanged a glance as both had resigned their animosity for Mary. Both knew that they must try to have peace not because of any love for Mary, but because they had promised Katherine and they would at least try.

When Thomas and Tommie reunited with the girls, they found them gushing over their purchases. Mary had made several purchases of calicos, checks, solids, and trims. Nellie had chosen a yellow dotted fabric, and Renie had chosen a blue and white check. Mary also purchased a few of the remnants for quilt fabrics along with some other choice fabrics for dresses. Nellie and Renie chatted about their purchases as they showed Thomas what they had selected, asking advice on which trim looked best. Mary smiled as she thought about how much progress she had made with Nellie. As the family left the store, Mary planned.

On the corner a small bookstore beckoned Mary. "How about we go in here for a minute? Just looking at all the books will be quite an experience."

Thomas and the children followed Mary into the small shop. The windows in front and down the side of the shop provided fresh air and plenty of light which was needed for the small store. The quaint, little store had an expansive display of books. The owner looked like he had been there with his books for years because the books surrounded him where he sat at his desk. The White-haired gentleman knew every book in the store and where each book was shelved as he demonstrated when he greeted his customers giving them directions. Nellie and Renie shuffled through the books on the long table in the middle of the store, while Mary peered at books on the tall bookshelf.

Tommie asked the shopkeeper if he had a book about Daniel Boone.

The old gentlemen looked at Tommie over his spectacles, leaned back in his oak desk chair and stroked his mustache and beard. "I have a book. Now, it is listed as fiction. But, I'll tell you, I know a lot about Daniel Boone, and most of the book is correct. It gives much information about Daniel that is true. Now, who is to say that he went on exactly the same hunting trip, or killed an eight foot bear? I'll get it if you would like to look at it."

Tommie looked at his dad for an okay, and replied to the shopkeeper that he would like to at least look at the book. As Tommie looked at the book, the shopkeeper rattled on with his information about Daniel. "You know, Daniel was called the Prince of Kentucky Pioneers."

Thomas agreed to Tommie's purchase and waited for the girls to make their selections. Renie found a children's book, *The Juvenile Miscellany*, which had illustrations that had already captivated her attention. Nellie chose a book that the shopkeeper had suggested, Susana Rowson's *Charlotte Temple*.

Rummaging through history books, Thomas found the book, *Ramsay's History of American Revolution*. Jokingly, Thomas told Mary, "You will probably have to read to me when I'm in bed if I ever get it read."

Before she could stop herself, Mary replied, "I am glad to see you read something besides the Bible. Well, what I mean is the book is a good selection."

Mary loved books and her favorite hobby was sitting in a rocking chair, an old quilt covering her lap and feet, with a cup of steaming hot coffee while reading a good book. Although, reading days were probably over, she realized. Mary made a selection, a book she had heard about, but not read, *The Spelling Book* by Noah Webster.

Mary explained to Thomas about Mr. Webster who had died just a couple years ago, having done so much for education in America. "Mr. Webster and his wife had eight children. He made many contributions to education by founding the Amherst College in Amherst, Maine. Noah Webster is considered an American hero for all his many accomplishments."

"You are just a wealth of knowledge, Mrs. Cosby," Thomas teased Mary.

"Being a teacher, there are a few heroes of education we know about."

Thomas paid for the books, and the family stepped back onto the street. As the men carried the packages to the buggy the women looked in the windows at the various stores. Nellie loved the shopping experience and could visit all the stores; she could shop all day and never get tired of looking.

However, Renie was hungry and anxious to go eat at the fancy Towne Restaurant. Already tired, Mary was ready to relax and get off her feet. Tommie felt like he could eat a bear if they didn't eat soon. Thomas was just happy his family was behaving.

Tired and hungry, the family was seated at a large round table in the picturesque Hotel Restaurant as they received a menu. "So many choices, I don't know what to order," Nellie said as she looked at the handwritten menu.

The neatly dressed waiter brought water to the table and offered a selection of tea, lemonade or coffee. He suggested that they try the day's special: roast beef on bread with potatoes, gravy, and green beans. An easy banter of conversation followed as the family members made their choices.

Everyone agreed to a special, and while they waited for their food, they talked about their purchases and what fun the day had been. Mary commented on the hat shop on the square, hoping to get a quick visit as she loved hats and owned a hat for each season. Mary excitedly told the girls, "We will have to come to the hat shop before Easter next year to purchase a real hat for you. What about it, girls?"

The dining table was covered with a white damask tablecloth, with a fresh bouquet of flowers in the center. The napkins were monogrammed with the hotel's initial and matched the tablecloth. Hotel silverware rested beautifully upon the crisp napkins. The table looked too beautiful to get stains on, Mary thought. She would remind the children to be extra careful with the gravy. Although, she had to admit that the children had excellent table manners, it was accredited to the fact that Rissa enforced the rules of table etiquette to her family.

Before the meal arrived, Thomas talked with his family. "We have had a good day together. We have bought items for ourselves, which is a good thing. We should remember that when we do something good for ourselves, we need to do something for someone else less fortunate. So, remember today's blessing and think about how you will give thanks to the Lord for our abundance by helping others.

"So, my family, I remind you of the Lord's commands today. Before our food arrives, let's see if we can name all of the Ten Commandments." Thomas smiled at his family. His heart was glad the children had enjoyed the day so much. Still, he wanted them to know there was nothing, not even the goods they purchased, as precious as God's Word and Jesus Christ their Savior.

Starting their long journey home, the family stopped at Delo and Rowie's house. They visited with Katherine's family, enjoying a cup of tea and a cookie. Everyone talked at the same time and enjoyed their visit, promising that they would see each other soon.

Back in the buggy, Nellie and Renie were excited to tell Katherine about everything they saw and did. The day had been wonderful for everyone and Katherine couldn't be happier. She had definitely had a lovely day with Rowie and Delo and all of the children. As she wrapped her arms around Nellie and Renie she thought, there is just nothing like family. Katherine was pleased the girls had the opportunity to be with Mary and enjoy their day. She wondered if the children had been bribed to be good, or if they were naturally getting along better. Either way, she was glad they were nice to Mary.

Katherine poked Thomas sitting on the front seat of the buggy. "Do you think we could stop by Ollie's to check on the baby?"

"You just can't stay away from Baby Oleta, can you?" Thomas kidded Katherine.

"I have to admit I enjoyed my stay with them. I fell in love with that precious family. They are such a good family and that baby and little boy are just the cutest kids!" Katherine went on and on about what they had talked about, how they were so receptive to hearing the Word.

Ollie and Oliver met the buggy and took care of the horses. The children stayed outside and played with Oliver while the adults talked and cooed over Baby Oleta. Everyone agreed she was just the prettiest, most alert baby they had ever seen. Ollie complimented Oliver on how well he had adjusted to a new baby sister.

Lyssa raved about how wonderful Katherine had been with her little family. She told the group how Reverend Morgan had come for a visit. Ollie explained that the Reverend had given them a family Bible and he had prayed with them. They explained with joy, how they felt like the Holy Spirit had come into their hearts and souls, and they were alive in Christ. Lyssa proclaimed that Katherine had opened a door for them by reading the Word to them and by demonstrating God's love.

Thomas said, "We learn in 1 Peter 4:10, 'As each one has received a gift, minister it to one another, as good stewards of the manifold grace of God.' We hope we will always be able to use our gifts to help others."

"Earlier, at the restaurant, Thomas led us in devotion from Deuteronomy. We are instructed to teach the commandments when we rise, when we sit, when we lay down, and when we eat, we are to teach," Mary said, hoping that she had said the passage correctly.

Katherine added that a Christian life was like building a strong house. "A house needs to be built on a good foundation, and that is the same with building character in children. So," Katherine added, "teach those commands as the Lord says, and your children will thank you for it."

Suddenly, Thomas had an idea. "Ollie, would you be interested in a job working for me at the mill? Paul Cox works for me, but he needs some help. Do you think you would be interested?" Thomas had surprised himself with the spontaneity of the question, obviously an inspired thought.

"I sure would, I would love to work for you, Mr. Thomas. Lyssa, is that okay with you? Do you mind if I go to work for Mr. Thomas?" Clearly, Ollie was eager and excited about a new future for his family.

After a brief visit with Ollie's family, the Cosby family was ready to return home. A long day of traveling had taken a toll on everyone. Back home, with chores over, supper on the table, and another day the Lord had blessed the family, the family gave thanks.

# Chapter 10

# The Woodsons

Sunday morning, Ollie packed up his family in the wagon to spend a day at Upton Baptist Church. Ollie and Lyssa were eager to be going to the Lord's house to worship. Today, Lyssa thought, would be a special day.

Pastor Ship brought a message from John 13:34 *A new commandment I give to you, that you love one another; as I have loved you, that you also love one another.*

At the invitation with song of *How Blessed the Righteous Are,* Ollie and Lyssa walked forward and asked to be baptized and join the church. The congregation welcomed them into the church family with hugs and handshakes. Men and women gave them encouragement and assured them they would be there to help them on their Christian walk. The church group assembled outside to have food and fellowship.

Abruptly, the church grounds became a dangerous setting as shots were fired! Men's voices yelling and more shots!

The men warned the women and children to get inside. No church member had guns, so the men hid around the wagons and buildings until they could see what was going on. Straggling from the edge of the woods was a black man and woman. The couple was clearly frightened and afraid of everyone. Thomas ran to the couple and pulled them under a nearby wagon. Within seconds, men with guns came out of the woods.

"Come on out, Woodson. You can't hide from us. We are going to take you in with us," a man yelled as he fired a few warning shots into the air. Oddly, he had no idea where the couple was hiding.

Under the wagon, Thomas whispered to the scared couple. "Stay here and be quiet. I will see what I can do."

Thomas crawled out the other side and held his hands up to the men with guns. "Men, I don't know what you are looking for, but you can't be shooting around here. This is a church service. You don't have the right to come on church property with guns."

"Sorry, sir, but we have every right. We are looking for a runaway slave and his wife. Have you seen them?" the man snarled back at Thomas.

Thomas called some of the deacons from the church to come join him with the officers.

"Well, men they say they are looking for a runaway slave and his wife. Have any of you seen them?" Thomas was holding his breath and saying a prayer that he was the only one who had seen the couple come out of the woods.

"No, we never saw anyone. We heard the shots and started getting the women and children inside," Deacon Cottrell said.

"I did hear something or someone run through the spring over there. I heard it because Bro. Ship's dog started barking at whatever it was," Deacon McKinley confirmed.

That was all it took for the unknown, self-appointed law-men to immediately start running up the spring, yelling and shooting in the air. They had obviously believed the story and were on the chase.

Thomas hurried to the wagon and helped the couple crawl out. "Hurry, let's get you inside before they come back."

The men went inside with Thomas and the family. Thomas explained to everyone what the officer had said about the couple. Thomas explained, "These men will be back; they will come back looking for this couple. Our church has always taken a stand against slavery. If we turn this family over to them, we will be saying slavery is okay. What do you say, people? Are we going to stand together and protect these people?"

Arron Smith, a young man with a family, was the first to speak. "We can't hide them away. What if we get caught? We could be killed for harboring slaves."

Deacon Broadus spoke up. "We hear a message every Sunday about brotherly love and showing good Christian works. Now, when we get to prove what we say, I think we should step up to the Lord's commands, 'Love your brother as you would love yourself'."

A few more of the men spoke up with all the deacons and elders siding with the black couple, except young Arron. Arron felt he was outnumbered and knew he had to side with the church or risk having everyone explain the scripture and pray for him.

"You are right. We have to show the love Jesus commanded us to have for our brother." Arron Smith shook hands with the Woodsons and apologized half-heartedly.

Brother Wesley held his hands up. "Lord unto you we commit this act of love. Show us your will and help us be the hands and feet of Jesus. We pray, Father, you keep the men away from here and totally away from this couple. Keep this man and woman who have come to our church for refuge, safe and free wherever they be. Amen."

"We want you to stay with us. We will bring food in here, so you will be safe," Pastor Ship said giving the couple a hug.

The congregation filed outside to begin the meal and proceed with regular church services—everyone but Ollie's family who stayed and talked with the couple. They introduced themselves and tried to calm the frightened couple. To Ollie's surprise, Lyssa was inviting the family to come to their house and stay for a few days.

"Are you shore bout that Lyssa? I mean you jest had a baby not nearin' a week ago. And I know you been jest feeling fair to middlin' anyways." Ollie stated, his face wistful.

"I feel great, Ollie, and this is my chance to witness and serve my Lord. I want to help others the way I have been helped," Lyssa replied. "Besides, it will give me another person to help with the baby!"

Prayers were answered as the officers did not come back looking for the Woodson family. When everyone had eaten, the church members came back inside to discuss the plans for the family. Lyssa and Ollie explained they would take the Woodsons home with them. Women kindly volunteered their leftovers to help Lyssa, and the men offered to help with seeing them home safely. Thomas reminded Ollie if he needed anything to let him know.

Thomas had a thought. "Woodson, would you want to work for me? Ollie is coming tomorrow to help me at the mill and you men could ride together. We could use another hand," Thomas added.

The man looked confused, but replied, "Yes, sir, I'd like to work. I was trained to build barns and work with the mules and horses where I come from."

Thomas had a feeling the man would work out fine. "You will get paid weekly and we will see what jobs suits and what you enjoy doing the most. Are you a Christian, Mr. Woodson?"

"Me and the wife… we were saved at a revival meeting last year. You said… I would get paid? Is that right?" Woodson asked, dismayed at the offer.

"Honest day's work for an honest day's pay. Of course you get paid. Once you work for me, I will make sure your family is taken care of just like any other family."

On the way home, the Woodson's hid in the back of the wagon, still a little frightened from the earlier chase. Once home, the two families shared a time of fellowship and a meal. The Woodsons, Hobie and Leah, kept thanking Ollie and Lyssa for their generosity. The two couples talked a bit about their fellowship walk with Jesus. Hobie said he was thankful for the men who were hunting them. They forced them to run to the church, right to the people who would help them.

Leah agreed. "You know that is the way it is with the Lord, when we run from our troubles, we can always run right to the Lord and He will give us protection, if we have faith."

Lyssa read from the Bible, the 23$^{rd}$ Psalms. The two families held hands and said a prayer. Little Oliver had gone to sleep early because of the extraordinary day. Baby Oleta, wearing the soft pink gown which Nellie had made, was being rocked by her father. As Lyssa prepared a place in the loft for the couple to sleep, she remembered her pledge to God and thanked Him for giving them the opportunity to spread His love.

Hobie and Leah snuggled in the corn shuck mattress, held hands and said another prayer of thanks to God for helping them find these wonderful people. It was just too good to be true; they had found good friends, good white people willing to risk their lives for them. And what was better, Hobie had a paying job to provide for him, his wife, and in a few months, a baby, a very special baby.

# Chapter 11

# Nellie and Mike

Like old friends, Mary thought as she unpacked her treasures. Mary had gotten up early and put out a pillow she had made, a quilt over the back of a rocking chair, and set the table with her dishes. Her new coffee pot replaced the old one as she made a fresh pot of coffee. Mary ran her hand over the braided rug she had made last winter. This will go nicely in front of the fireplace. Now, with a few of my own things, I will feel more at home and the house will look much more sophisticated, Mary thought.

The men were finishing the chores and Katherine was already hanging out the laundry. Nellie, the first in the kitchen, immediately noticed the changes. Irate, Nellie asked about her mother's braided rug. "And by the way, I like Mama's dishes better than these." Frustrated, Nellie slammed the plate on the table a little too hard and broke the dish.

"Look, Nellie, I'm sorry if I have caused you to become upset. But, this is also my home and I want to use my things in my home. There will be changes, Nellie. Your father and I are married now, and like it or not, we love each other very much. Your father has assured me that I can do what I want with the house so that I will feel welcome. You do want me to feel welcome, don't you, Nellie?"

Thomas and Katherine had stepped on the porch and were discussing the day's plans. "Well, we are going to the Bimbi place after we get enough of the lumber sawed. A lot to do today," Thomas explained.

As the mother and son walked into the kitchen together, they were absorbed in their conversation. "Well, Son, let me know if there is anything I can do to help. I'm working on the laundry and we will make lunch for your workers…what happened? Oh, no, Mary, your dish!" Katherine said as she picked up the piece of the plate.

"Oh, silly me! I was in a hurry and let a plate slip through my fingers," Mary said as she smiled innocently at Thomas and Katherine.

Nellie looked at Mary with a look of dismay. "I'm going to milk the cows. Don't wait on me for breakfast. I am feeling rather sick at my stomach this morning," Nellie said as she left the house.

Fretting all the way to the barn, Nellie spotted Ollie and Hobie headed toward the mill. The men waved to Nellie as she herded the goats in the shed. She realized that her father always recognized good character. So, Nellie thought, why did he marry Mary? How could she have him so fooled? Oh, forget Mary. I'll get the work done and perhaps I can work on Renie's dress this afternoon, Nellie reasoned.

"Nellie, Nellie, are you in here?" Thomas asked as he looked for his daughter. "Hey, Sweetie, are you feeling better?"

"Oh, uh, yeah, better, I'm okay."

"Nellie, we are going to take a supply of lumber and work on John Dales' house, the old Bimbi house in the holler. Do you think you could check on Dolly and the heifer we just bought? Neither are close to calving, but it would be good to check on them since they did not come up this morning. We will be back about lunch time." Thomas gave Nellie a peck on top of her head as he filled his pockets and arms with items that they would need. Soon, the men pulled out with the wagons full of lumber.

After Nellie finished milking Berthie, she carried the milk downhill to the spring house. Intuitively, Nellie gathered the rope, which hung on the wall as she recalled last spring's incident. Using the rope Nellie had managed to pull a calf from a wet-weather pond, an experience she would never forget. Nellie thought about going back to the house for something to drink before the search but she wasn't ready to deal with Mary.

Nellie started calling the cattle and looking for Dollie. As she walked over the fields and looked behind the bushes, she called the cows and looked around and in the pond. They were nowhere to be seen, and the sun was already getting hot. Nellie worried that if there was a problem, the heat would ultimately cause stress on the animal.

Surely, they would not be in the farthest corner of the back field. Nellie walked through the tall grass, glad that Goldie was with her as the memory of the bull snake was too recent to ignore. Looking through the cedar stand, she could not see any sign of the cows. A small cluster of sassafras trees provided shade, so Nellie checked the area, and found no cows. Finally, already hot, tired and out of humor, Nellie saw something that worried her. Dollie was fine, but Bella was down, legs straight out from her body as though she was unable to roll to a side position because of her swollen stomach.

Nellie's own stomach lurched, as she saw the next sight. The heifer was trying to have her first calf and it was coming early. Recalling the day before, and all the activities of the day, Nellie figured maybe no one had even checked on them. Nellie ran the rest of the way, holding on tight to the rope, thankful she had the foresight to bring it. Bella was on her side and the calf's two front feet were outside, but she did not see the calf's nose.

When the heifer saw Nellie approaching, she tried to get up, and finally made it, but she seemed exhausted already. Nellie reminded Bella there were other places she could have chosen to have her calf instead of the open field in the hot sun. Nellie had helped Tommie and her dad pull a calf before, and they had a difficult time, but now she was by herself. The calf needed to come out and the heifer was going to need some help. Nellie talked to the Jersey heifer with her most loving and compassionate cow voice. "Bella, I am going to try to help you, but you are going to have to help me help you."

Nellie made a slip knot in the rope and put the calf's feet through the hole. She gave the rope a tug and it felt secure. Nellie knew she would have to wait until Bella had a good contraction and she would pull as hard as she could. The strength of the next contraction caused the heifer to bawl in pain. Nellie wanted to cry for her because she knew this was a new experience for the heifer and for her also. She pulled with each contraction.

Nellie could barely see the nose of the calf, and it was important to try to get the nose through as soon as possible or the calf would die. Nellie had seen her father as he massaged the cow's birthing canal to stretch and lubricate the area, which she tried. Wiping her hands on her dress she thought, this dress will never come clean.

With the next contraction, Bella fell to the ground and gave in to the birthing process. Both Bella and Nellie were on the ground and with every contraction, Nellie felt there was little progress. The sun was bearing down on them. Bella surely needed water and so did Nellie. Then Bella had a big contraction. Nellie placed her boot on Bella's hip and pushed her weight against the cow while pulling the rope. The calf was still making little progress and at this point it had to be delivered right away. "Please, somebody, help me. Lord, I need help, help, please help, and send somebody!" Nellie screamed.

Nellie kept pulling on the rope with everything she had. Her hands were red and bleeding from the scratching and the burning of the rope, but she couldn't think of that now. It was unbearably hot in the open field and Nellie was wet with sweat. Bella had to be worn out from the delivery and the heat. Nellie had to focus on saving the calf, but it might mean just saving Bella.

"Here, Nellie, let me have that," Nellie heard someone behind her and reaching around with a hoe handle. He was already freeing the rope from her hands. "Girl, you have torn your hands apart. Let's put this hoe handle in the rope and we can pull from each side."

Quickly, Mike was beside her and with the next contraction, they were both pulling with everything they had. Nellie thought, I just can't pull any longer, then all of a sudden the calf started coming out, its head, shoulders, and within a few seconds the hips and back legs. A swoosh of liquids followed after the calf, flowing out all over Nellie, her clothes, and her boots. As she looked at Mike she saw he was in the same predicament, but Mike wasn't worried. In fact he was up, beating on the calf trying to get the calf to breathe.

Nellie got up, shook herself as clean as possible, and asked, "Is it going to live? What do you think, will it make it?"

"Yeah, I think so, but..." As he spoke, Nellie noticed the calf was trying to move its head. Within seconds the calf raised itself and seemed to come alive. "But, as I was saying another minute and we would have lost the calf, and maybe mama."

"Mike, how can I thank you? I could have never delivered the calf by myself. How did you know to come help me?"

Mike was trying to get the heifer up so she could clean the calf. "Well, I was taking the wagon home from the mill and saw you but I didn't know what was going on. Thought I would stop and check on you. Glad I did. Nellie, this was a big job for anyone, let alone a girl!"

"Yeah, she wasn't supposed to calve this soon. I just happened to check on her, or she would probably have died." Nellie tried to say more but the world seemed to be spinning. "I don't feel..." as she started falling Mike managed to swoop her up before she hit the hard ground.

Nellie woke up in a strange bed, with no idea where she was. She heard an older woman talking, felt a cool cloth on her head, and smelled a strong minty smell. She realized it was Mike's grandmother, Mrs. Della Caswell, who was taking care of her. "Now, now, there Nellie, you have had a rough morning. You just lay here and rest. I am going to get you feeling better before we take you home. Mike told me what you kids were able to do. You are exhausted from the heat and the stress of delivering that calf. I took the liberty of taking your dress and boots off. I slipped one of Jena's old slips on you so I could wash out the dress."

"Thank you, but I can go home, if I can just..." Nellie tried to raise herself in the bed, but found she couldn't. Instead, Mrs. Caswell insisted on giving her water in a large spoon. Nellie realized she really didn't have the energy to go anywhere.

"Is she better, Ma?" Mike asked as he peeped in the room. "Is there anything I can do?"

Mrs. Caswell looked at Mike and then at Nellie. "You two kids were lucky to find each other today. Mike, how about riding over to the Cosby's and letting them know where Nellie is? Tell them she is okay, but she probably needs rest for today. We can take her home after supper or in the morning, whenever she is up to it. It's nice to have a girl around, hadn't had anyone but boys in a long time."

———•———

Back at the Cosby place, Mary had confided with Katherine about the china. Mary explained to Katherine that she felt Nellie had just wanted to get away from her for a while. However, the longer Nellie was gone the more concerned Katherine had become. "This is just not like Nellie to stay gone. She would have told us something if she was going somewhere. I'm afraid something is wrong."

"Well, if you want, Renie and I can go look around the mill and the creek. One of us needs to stay here with the food." Mary took Renie and they looked a few places for Nellie.

"Shouldn't we go in the pasture and look for Nellie?" Renie asked Mary.

"No, I don't think Nellie would have gone in the field. It is a hot day and she would have stayed where it is cooler, around the creek. If we don't find her soon, we will go back to the house." Mary thought about the look on Nellie's face when she broke the plate. At the moment she didn't care about

83

the little brat because she had been so mean. After all, she was probably just pouting somewhere and needed to grow up.

The men were coming back from their work at the Bimbi place. Mary and Renie were outside as they ran to meet Thomas in the wagon. Katherine saw that Nellie was still missing as she joined the group. Everyone was asking questions, trying to understand why Nellie was missing.

Just in time, Mike rode down the Cosby hill. Mike tried to calm everyone as he explained the events of the day. "As I was returning from the mill this morning, I saw Nellie in the field. I stopped and the both of us delivered a calf. Cow and calf are fine and Nellie is just tired from the heat and the trials of the morning. My grandmother is seeing to her, giving her water and making sure she rests."

Katherine had several questions, most of them were directed at Thomas. "Why didn't you let us know that you were sending Nellie to look for the heifers? We did not know where she was. We have looked everywhere, Thomas."

"I'm sorry. I didn't think the heifer would be calving and I would have never sent Nellie alone, especially on such an unusually hot day. I feel really bad for her and for you looking for her all morning," Thomas apologized.

Thomas asked Tommie to go to the back field and check on the cow and calf. Make sure they get to the creek for fresh water," Thomas advised Tommie.

As Tommie started to the back field, Renie jumped off her swing to follow him. "Wait, Tommie, I can help you. You might have to deliver another calf, and I can help this time." Tommie laughed at Renie and at the irony of her delivering a calf.

"Tommie will you make a poem about me?"

"Uh…okay, let's see.
Renie Cosby in 1845 is cute little age six.
In 1905 she will be a granma at sixty-six. Renie will see a new century of change, horseless carriages, telegraphs and lights with no flame.
Big machines will fly people through the air, free libraries with thousands of books to share.
People will travel by railroad across the land, from Boston to the Rio Grande.
But first Renie will see a civil war.
Many will die and so much more.

Our nation will be divided and south will fight north.
Slavery will end, reconstruction brought forth. Music and voice will be
sent wireless through the air,
on machines for people to listen to everywhere."

As Renie tugged at Tommie's hand, she looked perturbed with him. "Oh,
Tommie, you're so silly. Will you carry me piggy-back?"

"Yeah, sure! At least I am worth something, huh?"

---

"I will go get Nellie and bring her home so she can rest," Thomas told
the group.

Mike reached out to Thomas and held his shoulder. At sixteen, Mike,
was almost as tall as Thomas but thinner. "Thomas, my Ma doesn't mind to
take care of Nellie. She is resting and Ma is enjoying having her there. She
really needs to rest for the afternoon at least. If it is okay, we can bring her
home later. Looks like you have workers here anyway."

"Tell you what, Mike. I really appreciate you helping Nellie. If your ma
doesn't mind to take care of her, and if it is okay with Nellie, we will see you
later. Again, thanks Mike for all you have done. Don't know what we would
have done without you," Thomas said as he slapped Mike on the back.

Thomas was upset with himself for sending Nellie on such a mission, but
he really didn't think either of the cows was due to calve. Thomas explained
to the men what they would be doing in the afternoon and he left the men
eating lunch at the garden table under the large oak tree.

"Mary, I feel awful I sent Nellie to look for the heifer. I am just thankful
the good Lord sent someone to help rescue her. Thank you for all your
worrying and efforts." Thomas had learned Mary had spent most of the
morning looking for Nellie.

Thomas gave Mary a hug and told her again he was sorry. "I do have a
little good news. John Dales agreed to help us this morning. We took the
lumber to his place and started helping him on the house. He pulled me aside
and told me he would give it a try. So, I feel better to have Pete and John
working together. Still haven't figured out John yet, but maybe that is God's
job, not mine."

Thomas explained they would be hauling lumber to Ollie's place next.
The men were going to work on another room for Ollie's house and another

out-house. With the Woodson family living there, the families needed more room. Mary and Thomas agreed those homes should come before their own wants and needs.

"And…" Thomas said. "We will not be working on a house for Pete and Andrea. Pete and Andrea agreed they would pick up the kids who needed a ride to school each morning. Pete is thrilled he can help Andrea with the education needs of the children in this area. He feels that God is leading him for this mission field."

"So, are you saying…you think you will be able to begin our house before long? Is that what you are saying? Because, I have an idea," Mary said as she winked at Thomas.

Mary continued, "I know we need to get started on the dream house, but, you know how you said someday, when you had the time and some good help,… which you have now, thanks to the good Lord! You said you would build a wing onto the school, a meeting place for the community. Also, there needs to be new outhouses built for the new side, and some improvements to the existing ones."

"I know, I did say that and I have been thinking about the plans for doing something special for the school. Rissa always said the more you could get the parents and public to come to the school, the more they would appreciate the education system and their local school. I have been thinking about making the one large meeting room available with seating around the sides of the building, and several pews like at church. When the ladies want to do quilting they can gather there in the winter. What does that sound like?" Thomas asked.

"Thomas, I think you read my mind. Building something for the school children and the community is the best idea ever. We can wait on building your dream home. Right?" Mary asked. She knew the big house was still a promise Thomas had made to his family, and she knew sooner or later they would need more room. Mary felt maybe Thomas wanted her to have her own home, not one designed by Rissa and built especially for her.

Meanwhile, at the Caswell's, Mike tried to entertain Nellie while Mrs. Caswell was cooking. He teased Nellie about how she looked when the afterbirth had squished out all over her dress and boots. "You looked like you were going to be sick," Mike teased.

"Well, actually I did get sick. But you didn't stop, you were right there with Bella and the calf. I think you probably saved the calf by slapping on it, trying to get some wind into it," Nellie praised Mike.

"I am just happy I came along when I did. You are the one I worried about the most. If you had been out there by yourself when you passed out... well, I am just happy I found you," Mike said as he looked into Nellie's big brown eyes, which were so beautiful that he found it hard to concentrate.

Nellie took Mike's hand in hers and squeezed it. She gazed into his eyes and looked at his handsome face, her heart in her throat, "Yes, thank you for taking such good care of me. I was so shocked when I awoke and I saw your Grandmother. I thank you for saving the cow, the calf and me. You are my hero, Mike!"

Nellie kissed Mike on his hand. As soon as she did, Mrs. Caswell came into the room and told them the meal was ready. Nellie had thought for years she would marry Mike someday and as he helped her out of bed, her heart fluttered. Mike helped Nellie walk to the table, smelling her hair so sweet and soft. Still drunk from the kiss on his hand, Mike pulled out the chair for Nellie and gave her a wink.

Mrs. Caswell said the blessing, praying for the two that they would do the Lord's work together. Silently, she prayed someday these two children would wed. She could think of no one better than Nellie for her Mike. She saw the way Mike looked at Nellie and the way Nellie looked at Mike.

Mrs. Caswell insisted that Nellie eat some of her chicken and dumplings to give her comfort and healing spirits. Mrs. Caswell's fried apple pies with fresh cream proved to be Nellie's favorite. Nellie, Mike, and Mrs. Caswell discussed the church, the blessings of crops, and the health of neighbors. Mike agreed to take Nellie home when the meal was over and her dress was dry enough to wear. Mrs. Caswell enjoyed her visit so much she insisted Nellie promise to come back and see her. Mike hitched Abraham, his best horse, to the buggy to take Nellie home that evening.

Mike and Nellie arrived just as the Cosby family finished supper. Everyone praised Nellie and Mike for their rescue to the cow and calf. Thomas asked Mike to sit while he read the nightly devotion. The appropriate message was about Joshua and his courage. Thomas explained that Nellie had faced a challenge with courage, and God had sent help for Nellie when she needed it most. After the devotion, Mike, Nellie, and the family talked about how God had been there for them when they needed the strength to continue.

"When my grandfather died of a heart attack last year, I thought I couldn't go on. But, I realized that I had to be strong for my grandmother. See, she didn't have anyone but me. My grandfather was Cherokee and he married my grandmother when they were seventeen. Both of their families turned their backs on them. So, I had to be the strength my grandmother needed," Mike said.

About dark, Mike told everyone good night and Nellie followed him to the wagon. "Mike, thank you again for all you did for me today. I honestly do not know what I would have done without you. I was so hot and tired. I hope I can return the favor someday."

Mike looked at Nellie in the glimmer of the moon and realized she was even more beautiful than at church every Sunday. Nellie had stolen his heart when she was eight and he was ten. She was the most beautiful girl he had ever seen. But, he couldn't tell her. He was just a part Cherokee boy with nothing to offer a girl like Nellie. "See you Sunday, Nellie," was all he could say to her.

Nellie reached up and gave Mike a kiss on the cheek.

"Goodnight, my hero!" Nellie said as she turned to go back inside. She watched, waving goodbye as he guided Abraham toward home.

# Chapter 12

# Sharing Stars

Thomas apologized once again to Nellie, Mary, and Katherine for sending Nellie on such a mission. He felt so bad that he had asked Nellie to do something that was his job. What had made it worse was the day had been so hot, too hot for Nellie to struggle with such a difficult task. Delivering the calf under those circumstances would have been a challenge for a couple of men.

Nellie assured him he need not worry. She couldn't help but wonder if her mother had been her guardian angel for the day for she had felt her presence. Nellie liked to think that her mother had guided Mike to her rescue. Regardless, she had spent a wonderful day with Mike and Mrs. Caswell.

With so much on his mind, Thomas could not sleep. No matter how much he was forgiven, Thomas still felt guilty about asking Nellie to do the difficult task. Finally, at three o'clock, Thomas got up and poured himself a cup of cold coffee. Mary was right by her husband's side, trying to give him comfort. The couple went on the porch and finished their coffee. While still dark with the stars shining, Mary grabbed Thomas' hand in one hand and the quilt from the swing in another. "Let's go! I want to show you something."

Mary led Thomas up to the enormous, flat, limestone rock, the proposed site for the new house. Mary spread the quilt and sat down. Patting the quilt, she motioned for Thomas to join her. Before long, the two of them were on their backs looking at the stars. Thomas tried to impress Mary with his knowledge of the universe, but Mary quickly matched his knowledge, pointing to the Big Dipper and the North Star and Orion's belt.

"Where did you learn so much about the stars?" Thomas asked.

"When I was a little girl we would lay on our bridge on Cane Run Creek. My aunt and uncle had a farm, and we built a cabin close to them. We didn't live there; we lived at the store in Cub Run. Occasionally, we would go to the little cabin and spend the night just to get away from the customers. The little cabin was wonderful, some of the best times of my life. Dad taught me about the stars and my mother would make up stories about all the people who live on the planets and stars. She was such a good story teller!"

"Did your mother tell Bible stories?" Thomas asked, realizing he had never talked about the subject with Mary.

"My father told more Bible stories than my mother. You see, he thought the stories had to be told with the correct details, nothing missing. My father believed that his religion was correct, everyone else was wrong, if they did not agree with him. He was a strong force in our home."

Thomas began explaining how his father had taken on the role of the family spiritual leader and the respect that he and his sister had for his Bible lessons. As he talked, Mary reflected on her father and mother and their need to keep their faith secret. Mary's father had taught his family that all the other religions were based on lies. Mary shuddered at the strong will of her father, all she had been forced to live and all she had been forced to lose.

For a few moments the two were silent, looking at the stars, lost in their own thoughts. Mary thought about how her father's pride had resulted in alienation from her and a child that never got to know her grandparents or father. She had heard that her mother had died of a broken heart a year after she was kicked out of their home. The hate for her father consumed Mary's body causing her to tremble.

Thomas reached out for Mary's hand. She was his first. Had he not gone away to Boston for the Baptist convention, he would surely have married Mary. Instead, he left Upton the next day and didn't look back that summer. He had prayed for forgiveness for that day. At least no harm was done. When he and Rissa came home after they were married, he learned that Mary had left to go to school in Louisville. He had never asked Mary about that day. He figured some things were best in the past.

Soon the coolness of the rock was permeating the quilt and their clothing. Chilly, the two cuddled as close as they could get. Then, Thomas pulled the quilt up on both sides to cocoon them together. Romance ignited under the wedding-ring quilt and under the stars. Thomas and Mary would never forget the beautiful moment when the stars winked at their kisses, and the sun rose to a new life beginning within.

# Chapter 13

# Gil and Jeannie

As a summer storm erupted early the next morning, most outside work was halted for the day. Thomas and his workers were taking turn's draw-knifing and sawing lumber in the barn. Due to the rain, business was slow at the mill, so Ollie and Hobie were helping at the saw mill.

Mary felt that she was slowly winning the trust and respect of Tommie and Renie. However, Nellie remained indifferent. Katherine's respect was still another matter. At times, Mary felt that everything was going well between them, but Katherine would suddenly look at her with a look of, disrespect? Hate? No, maybe more like suspicion. Still, she had one more tool to use to her advantage to win Katherine. Still, Mary had no intention of sharing her secret with Katherine and clearing her conscience as long as everything else was going so smoothly.

Katherine had taken the precious patterns out of the family's cedar chest. Usually, Katherine could cut out a dress simply by looking at someone. She called it 'sizing.' However, since Mary and Thomas had spent so much money, she did not want to take a chance on ruining the fabric. Both girls had elaborate suggestions on how to use the materials purchased and were eager to begin.

Each of the females had a job and everyone was getting along well which was a blessing in itself. Mary had the task of cutting the precious materials, while Nellie began stitching the pieces together. Katherine put the hot irons on the stove to press the seams. The work was going splendidly when Goldie began to bark.

Someone was outside in a wagon, in this deluge! For someone to make a trip on such a day like today must be an emergency. Katherine scurried to her room and picked up her rag bag as Mary opened the door to a rain-soaked young man, Gil Spurgeon.

"Mrs. Katherine, can you come quickly? Jeannie is in labor. Her water broke a few minutes ago and I left her there, didn't want to get her out in this storm. Can you please come with me?" begged Gil.

As Katherine was stuffing a few extra rags into her bag, she called Nellie to her side. "Nellie, I want you to stay here. You have been through too much lately. But, be nice, Nellie. Understand?" Katherine said as she let the door swing shut behind her.

The rain was coming down like an avalanche, and even though it was only ten o'clock in the morning, the skies were almost as dark as night and it looked like it could rain all day. Katherine tried to talk to Gil, but the noise of the rain made it too difficult, so she just planned and prayed.

The trip past the small Lucas Grove community had taken almost forty minutes, and Katherine could finally see the house in the distance. Just as she was feeling better about the trip, the back wagon wheel slid into a deep rut and the horse could not pull out. Katherine jumped out, held tight to her bags, and ran down the road to the house. By the time she got in the cabin, she was drenched. Her boots and the bottom of her calico skirt was red clay/ mud soaked. Worse than her physical being, Katherine felt depressed and weird, like something evil was present.

Jeannie greeted Katherine with a forced smile and a "thank you for coming." First, Katherine had to give Jeannie strength and courage to go through this delivery. Katherine tried to cheer Jeannie and talk to her about the baby, whether she wanted a boy or a girl. Despite Katherine's efforts to cheer her, Jeannie began to cry and said she would not be able to have the baby without her mama.

Within minutes, Gil had repaired the wagon wheel, and was at Jeannie's side. "What can I do, Katherine?" Gil asked. "I have plenty of fresh water brought up, but I don't have a fire."

Katherine had taken a quick look at Jeannie and determined it might be awhile before the baby would arrive. "How far away does your Mama live, Jeannie? Do you want Gil to go get her?" Katherine asked.

"Yes, please, please, I can't do this without Mama," Jeannie pleaded.

Gil, soaked and muddy, looked at Jeannie and then Katherine with a worried look. "I will go get her if Jeannie wants," and he was out the door.

Katherine scurried about lighting a fire, getting water on to boil. She fought off the feeling that something was not right. There was an overwhelming feeling of depression, gloom and doom. Oh, silly me, it is just the rain and the storm, Katherine thought. I will pray with Jeannie and ask God to be with us.

As Katherine knelt beside Jeannie's bed, she talked soothingly and told Jeannie that she would say a prayer. Jeannie was quiet through the prayer, but still, Katherine experienced an eerie feeling. Of course, the storm was unrelenting, spreading a bleak ardor about the small cabin.

Katherine suggested Jeannie get up and walk to help her feel better and to hurry the baby along. Jeannie made a couple of laps around the small cabin and then sat in a rocking chair. Katherine talked to Jeannie about her family.

"How long have you lived here, Jeannie?" Katherine asked.

"My family came from Virginia two years ago and settled this area. We lived with my Ma and Pa just up the road, until last fall. Gil and my brother built this cabin." Jeannie grimaced as she had a contraction. She took a few deep breaths before she continued.

"Our grandfather and grandmother came from Germany to Virginia in 1774. They loved Virginia, but they heard of the land Daniel Boone had found and wanted to homestead," Jeannie paused, wiping a tear away. As she stood, she stretched and rubbed her lower back.

"So many problems with living here; we have had crops to fail, and our garden has been destroyed by deer. I just wish my family hadn't left Virginia," Jeannie said as she rubbed her stomach. "Now, this baby is going to be born here with all this hardship, and I just hate it here."

As Katherine listened, she felt she understood the permeating atmosphere in the home. Jeannie was not happy and with a new baby, there would soon be more stress on the young family. "Jeannie, do you have any friends you visit or who come here to see you?"

"Well, no, we have our family and well, they seem to be happy, but me and Gil, well we have had nothing but trouble since we have lived here. Now, this baby is coming into a home which has seen so much strife."

"Now, let's be positive! This baby is going to bless this family and you and Gil will be blessed with more children. Let's walk a little more and then we will examine you again."

Katherine had just finished the exam when Gil and Jeannie's mother rushed into the cabin. Katherine didn't wait, but jumped up, introduced herself, and said, "God is going to bless you with a beautiful baby by the end of the day, for Daddy and Grandma. I'm Katherine Cosby and the baby is not quite ready to come but we can be ready when it does get here."

Jeannie's mother had more of a German accent than Jeannie. "I'm Stella and I help do vhat I can. Jeannie not do vhat I vant her do. Jeannie, you vant shometing to eat? Ja? I made strudel?"

Katherine realized that Stella was the family matriarch, and she would have to step in quickly. "Well, right now, Jeannie should probably not have anything to eat. We need her to drink small amounts so she will not get sick during the delivery. She has a lot of pushing to do. We noticed her pains are coming closer now."

"Ja, vee vill vait for strudel, Jeannie, you need for dee milk. Gil not get strudel."

Gil, apparently not knowing what to do or say, asked Katherine if there was something he could do. There was obviously tension between the two of them, but Gil wasn't going to say anything to get Jeannie upset.

Finding two chipped coffe cups, Katherine poured coffee for the anxious couple as she told them about Upton Baptist Church.

"We have a wonderful church and would love for you and your family to visit. We meet every Sunday at 10:00. We have small group study and worship at 11:00. After worship we have dinner on the grounds, and then the children play. The men and women study the Bible and sing in the afternoons. We usually stay until time for everyone to go home and milk the cows," Katherine laughed.

Stella seemed surprised. "Vhy you eat at church ezery Sunday?"

A bit shocked, Katherine replied, "We observe the commandment, 'Thou shalt remember the Sabbath day and keep it holy.' We believe God wants us to come together at His house and worship, spend time with Him, His church and His people. The Bible teaches us to have communion with one another and to commune with our friends and community. Did you know that the word 'community' comes from the word commune?" Not waiting for an answer Katherine forged forward. "So, we stay and eat and study the Word together. Our time together enables us love and help one another more."

"Humph!" Stella interjected and mumbled a few words in German.

Katherine saw her witnessing was going nowhere and turned her attention back to Jeannie. Jeannie's pains were still not progressing much faster. Somehow, Jeannie needed to relax and let this baby come. She seemed as if she was trying to keep peace between her mother and her husband and not giving into the contractions. Katherine had an idea, at least it could not do any harm.

Katherine always packed a side of bacon, bread, and jelly when she visited a delivering home. Quickly, she sliced a few pieces of the bacon, finished baking the bread, and made plates for Gil and Stella. She asked them to sit, eat, drink their coffee, and start talking about baby names. Perhaps they would start thinking about someone else other than themselves.

While Gil and Stella enjoyed the blackberry jam, Jeannie's pains increased. It wouldn't be long before a precious baby would be blessing their home. Jeannie seemed much more relaxed and put her confidence in Katherine, following her directions.

Baby Spurgeon was born on August 4 or 8-4, at 8:04 that evening, weighing about the same amount, "Your grandson, Stella. He is a beautiful baby, one of the prettiest babies I have ever seen," Katherine said as she handed the baby to grandmother to clean while she worked with Jeannie.

"Oh, little kindchen, you so gutaussehend! Red hair, ja!" Stella said as she cleaned her grandson.

Gil came in the house as he heard the baby crying. "How is Jeannie? How is the baby?" Gil had been banished to the porch when the pains were intense, but no one could keep him away when he heard his baby cry.

Katherine cleaned the bed and explained to Gil what he needed to do. Once again, she explained the process of burying the afterbirth. Gil followed directions just as Katherine had told him.

With the chore finished, Gil was excited about seeing his wife and baby. Stella proudly handed the swaddled baby to Gil. "Here, your beautiful son, Gil. Isn't he prettiest baby boy you ever see?"

Gil held the baby and sat on the bed with Jeannie. "Look, Jeannie, our little boy. He is beautiful. I am so proud of you… and our baby." He gave Jeannie a kiss on her head.

"Have you thought of a name for the baby? With that red hair he could use a good Irish name, like Patrick, Shawn, or maybe Ryan?" Katherine giggled. "Maybe you have a family name for your son?"

Gil held the baby and looked at him with such pride. "Well, we thought of several names, but…well, we thought we would wait to see what he looked like."

"All baby boys named after Opa Stasel. Vhat about Stefan Stasel Spurgeon?" Stella added quite emphatically.

"Could I have my baby?" Jeannie asked. Jeannie cuddled the baby, and Katherine reminded her of the breastfeeding hints.

"Always make sure the baby gets latched on good to the nipple," Katherine explained. "He may take a few times to get the milk, but he will begin sucking, just have patience," Katherine rambled on to keep the tension down. She knew Jeannie could not relax if she was worried about the animosity between her mother and her husband.

Katherine spent the night taking care of Jeannie and the baby. The next morning, Baby Stefan was nursing when Stella insisted she could take care of Jeannie. She said Gil should take Katherine home so she could get some rest. Before Katherine left, she prayed and asked God to bless the home, the family, and the new baby. Gil, Stella, and Jeannie thanked Katherine for all she had done.

"Katherine, I can take you home, and when I get back, I can take you home, Stella," Gil added.

"Nein! I stay here vit Jeannie and little kindchen. I stay, helfen Jeannie. I do vhat I can. I vait on Jeannie vile you go verk!" Stella added stubbornly.

Walking to the wagon, Katherine noticed a hole close to the woods. "What is that hole, Gil?"

Gil walked over to the hole and stood there, shaking his head, visibly astonished. "The hole is where I buried the afterbirth and I placed this heavy rock on top of it."

"Okay, Gil," Katherine said. She was just anxious to leave. There was definitely something weird about the place, and she did not want to stay any longer. As Katherine walked to the wagon, she felt her skin crawl as she had to force herself to walk instead of run.

As Gil and Katherine rode back to the Cosby's, Gil tried to explain Stella's hate for him and everyone in general.

"I rarely meet someone who is hard to love, but I have to admit Stella is a difficult one. We learn in the Bible, Luke 6:28 'Bless those who curse you, pray for those who spitefully use you.' It is difficult, but I have learned praying for someone helps more than revenge."

"Thanks Katherine, for everything, for your attention to Jeannie and all you have done." Gil handed Katherine a coin and added, "This is all we have. Is it okay?" Gil asked. "And, we will try to come to church Sunday, if Jeannie feels up to it. It's time we made more friends like you."

"Gil, you are most welcome to come to church any time, or come and visit with us. We would love the company and Jeannie needs other women for friendships. Now, you go home with your baby and your lovely wife." Katherine waved goodbye and said a prayer for Gil. He would surely need it.

# Chapter 14

# Missions

Katherine was glad to get back home to her family and away from the peculiar, and downright bizarre feeling which had overwhelmed her at the Spurgeon place. The past twenty-four hours had physically and emotionally drained her more than any delivery. Katherine considered the unwelcoming feelings that she had felt at the Spurgeon's and decided she would have to find the cause when she returned to check on the family.

Both girls could hardly wait for Katherine to get settled once she was home. Renie wanted to model her new dress for Katherine while Nellie needed a few tucks in hers. Just in time to do something for my girls, Katherine thought with pride.

"We missed you yesterday. But, the girls and I had a good time. We sewed and laughed and made cookies and ate...," Mary said. "We have some good scraps, maybe to use for a quilt this winter?"

"That would be a good idea. Yesterday, I noticed the young couple had only two quilts. Two quilts, and no baby quilts! We wrapped the baby in a piece of fabric, but it is a shame the baby did not have a baby quilt. How about making a quilt, won't take long and maybe a baby gown? We could take it over to her tomorrow," Katherine suggested.

"Oh, I'd love to. I have some blue check we could use for a gown," Mary replied. "We can spend the afternoon sewing and making plans."

Katherine busied herself with the scraps Mary had set before her as she looked at the notes on the table. "Planning for the new house, I suppose?"

"Well, actually, I have asked Thomas if he could wait on the house awhile, because we have another project that needs attention."

"Another building project? You know, dear, the house is going to take a long time, six months at best, and your house guests are coming in May."

"I realize that, and I do want them to be comfortable, but, there are other things just as important. If worse comes to worse, the company can stay in the small cabin by the creek for a while. Thomas and I have talked about the importance of having additions to the schoolhouse," Mary explained.

Katherine looked at Mary. "Your mission in life is for the children, isn't it? One way or another you are going to make sure those kids have what they need. Before, you gave everything you had to teaching. I am proud you want to continue helping our school."

"Oh, please, thank you, but I just see improvements the children and the neighborhood would appreciate. I want Thomas to build a wing onto the school for a meeting place for special occasions. He said he could build seating around the sides and also have moveable pews so the ladies could use the room for quilting. Or, if the children wanted to present a Christmas program they would have the room for their performance, plus seating for the audience," Mary added excitedly.

After morning chores were completed, Nellie and Renie sat in their swings awhile enjoying the lovely morning. Nellie loved to swing as far as she could, going over the ledge. If she fell from the swing, she would drop about twenty feet; scary but fun. Both girls came in from morning chores and washed their hands and faces. As Nellie listened to the conversation she asked, "Why not use the church for the quilting and performances?"

Katherine knew that she had to explain the circumstances regarding women participation correctly without showing a prejudice toward the church. "The church is good for fellowship and showing love toward our neighbors, but women are not supposed to have much speaking authority, so hopefully, we will be able to use our school for our projects, as the mission project we have discussed.

Since I received that letter from Ms. Polly Webb, I have wanted to get our ladies together to begin our own Ladies Missionary Union. The Doreen Female Society, a mission group at a church in Elizabethtown, has been organized and faithful to missions for over twenty years now."

Nellie asked, "What is a missionary union? Who is Polly Webb?"

Katherine handed Nellie some squares to sew together while she gave Renie a piece of cloth and a threaded needle. "Nellie, Polly Webb is one of the most outstanding young women because even though she can't walk, she has done so much for missions. Polly Webb would be a good example for you because of how she has brought to our attention the role of missions all over the world."[1] Katherine explained. "I will get you the information so you can read it yourself."

"But what did they do, make stuff like we are today?" Nellie asked.

"No, actually, Polly wrote thousands of letters going across Massachusetts and throughout the country. In fact, your grandmother sent me the letter she had sent her. She explained how the group of ladies helps with missions here and in India," Katherine explained.

"I have an idea, as soon as the addition to the school is built, we can have a Ladies' day, and we can organize our own missions group. Just like the stuff we are doing today; everyone can contribute something," Mary added.

"I think it is a great idea. We could even invite someone from the Georgetown or Dorene Organization to come speak to us about what they are doing. We could serve a simple lunch and have activities in the afternoon, like sharing ideas or demonstrations." Katherine was already thrilled about the project.

"This is so exciting!" Mary exclaimed.

Nellie chimed in, "What can I do? I want to do something to help. What about I write letters to the ladies like Polly did?"

Katherine thought it was a great idea and encouraged her to get started soon. "We will send letters to the ladies who go to the churches close to us. Maybe we can encourage them to come and get their church started in missions. The ladies at the White Mills Baptist Church have been doing mission work for a few years. They have a weekly meal which is free for the community. They may want to talk about what they are doing."

"Tommie can make pictures like he did for the house," added Renie.

"Renie, that is a great idea! We will have to give Tommie an idea and some time to get started. We could have several pictures of what missions are doing here at home and in Boston and in India. Good idea, Renie," Mary said.

"Um, today is August 15. It would be nice to have our Ladies' Day before it gets cold, so we won't have to build a fire, but we want to make sure there is enough time for the building to be finished. What do you think about

---

[1] Hunt, Rosalie, We've A Story To Tell, Birmingham: Woman's Missionary Union, 2013

Saturday, Oct. 12? That would give enough time to have the basics of the building finished," Katherine explained.

"Sounds wonderful," Mary added. "The men will be in for lunch soon and we can present our ideas to them. Hopefully, we can get them moving faster on the project. Thomas said John's first day of work would be today, and he will be eating with us. Perhaps the men will help us convince Thomas."

The girls were so excited about their Ladies' Day event they could hardly get lunch out to the men. The day was comparable to their mood, as the sun was shining, the wind was gently blowing; a beautiful day to be eating outside. The large oak table provided a perfect setting for a summer-fresh meal.

Pete said the blessing over the food and everyone began passing the large containers. The girls had agreed to be quiet about the building project until everyone was served. However, their excitement was clearly visible to the men.

"I know something is going on. You women are just too giddy! What's up? Is there a frog in the green beans? Renie, what is everyone giggling about?" Thomas humored Renie.

"We're going to have a girls' day and you can't come but you have to help," Renie blurted out.

"Well, Thomas," Mary said, smoothing the tablecloth. "We have talked about it and we would like to have a Ladies' Day in the new wing of the school as soon as it is built."

"A Ladies Day? A day to get together to make quilts or something?" Thomas asked.

Mary explained the Ladies Day with the focus on missions. Katherine added information about the guests and Nellie explained her part.

Katherine poured more water in the glasses. "Well, we would like to have it on Saturday, Oct. 12, this year. Think you can do it?"

"Let me see if I understand this. You want to invite ladies from other churches to come talk to you about what they are doing with missions. Why not just write letters? For many of them the ride would be over an hour? I can't see anyone wanting to leave home to travel, and what if the weather is bad? What would happen if they have trouble on the roads a long way from home? Do you know anyone who has ever done this Ladies Day idea? How much is it going to cost?" Thomas relentlessly questioned.

Katherine looked a little exasperated with Thomas. "You know those questions are probably the same questions missionaries have asked. Why go there? What if it takes a long time to get there? What happens when I get there and the weather is bad? What if I have trouble a long way from home? Has anyone ever been to that country before? Where does the money come from? If God sends us in the mission field, He will provide."

Pete saw the looks on the faces of the ladies and decided it was time to jump in. "Well, Thomas, the ladies at the Glasgow Baptist Church have a Ladies Day every spring. I think they have a different focus every year, but I am sure they have talked about missions more than once. From what I have heard, it is a time for the ladies to get together and encourage each other."

The ladies thanked Pete and echoed his sentiments. Mary assured Thomas that the cost would be minimal because everyone would be helping with food for the day.

"Well, if you are sure. But, it is no small job. We need to make sure we get the plans soon and no changes after. I hate having to rip out something after we begin," Thomas added, trying to hide the fact that Katherine had made a valid point.

"And do you think you could also have the new outhouses finished by then?" Mary asked. "I think it would be nice to have our new outhouses especially for our ladies."

"Well, I think we probably can have it finished. You ladies will be able to show off a new meeting place and new outhouses." Thomas smiled.

"Well, the point is we are trying to encourage missions, at home, other states and countries. We don't want to show off," Katherine pointed out.

"I don't really see why people go to foreign countries, when they can witness here at home," John said. "There are so many people who need help right here, we could stay busy with witnessing and caring for the poor right around us."

Katherine knew John's argument was a sentiment felt by many folk in the area, so she was prepared.

"Go therefore and make disciples of all the nations, baptizing them in the name of the Father and of the Son and of the Holy Spirit, teaching them to observe all things that I have commanded you; and lo, I am with you always, even to the end of the age'." Katherine paused as she looked at the men for their approval. "Clearly the Lord wants us to spread His Word. This is just a beginning for us."

Tommie had remained quiet as he listened to the discussion. "I certainly agree with you ladies. I have read about missionaries in foreign countries and even though they are challenged with the culture, they are happy to be a witness. You know Mark says in chapter 13, 'And the gospel must first be published among all nations,' and as we spread God's Word it is up to other people to make their decision what to do with it."

"John, we hope your wife, will be able to attend our Ladies Day. We would love to meet her and your little girl. I guess we need to start with a missionary visit close to home," Mary said as she joined Katherine in her plea.

"Well Sallye and Hannah do not get away from the house. Hannah is not right, not like other little girls and Sallye don't want to get her away from the house," John stated.

Mary realized why John and his son came to church and did not bring Sallye. "How old is Hannah?"

"She is almost six, will be Oct. 1, but she is small for her age, and she can't do things other kids do. She won't go to school."

Mary couldn't stand the thought of a little one not having the chance to go to school. "Oh, please, let's try to see if she can go to school. She would like being around other children."

"Yeah, I'm six and I can help take care of her. She can sit by me," Renie pleaded.

John had never felt that Hannah could go to school. She was just too slow; but the women were willing to give her a chance, so maybe he could convince Sallye it would be a good idea. "I will talk to Sallye about it, but I don't know."

Nellie was excited about missions, helping others, and meeting Hannah. "I can't wait to meet Hannah. Yeah, this is what missions is all about, taking care of those around you, here close or in another country."

Katherine realized the work of the family through the mission work was bringing the family closer together than ever. She prayed she could simply forget the dream and the suspicions to accept her new daughter-in-law and love her as she had loved Rissa.

# Chapter 15

# Visits

Thomas Cosby and his men had gotten the supplies and even recruited a few men from church to help. School would be starting in a couple of weeks which motivated the builders to get the work done. Everyone was doing their part to get the building up, and even a coat of fresh paint was going on the original part of the school. Mary was overseeing the work on the new addition of the school. Thomas had built book shelves to Mary's specifications along one of the walls.

Nellie wrote to the pastors of the four local churches and asked them to recruit help with the project. She had also written her Grandmother Wilson for more information on the missions in Massachusetts and information about Polly Webb. Nellie worked with Tommie to develop some art for the walls. They had made a large stretched canvas and used a picture of missionaries feeding children. Another picture depicted a missionary reading from the Bible with several families present. Everything was looking special for the Ladies Day.

Katherine knew she had to get the local ladies excited about the event. She planned to visit as many ladies as she could to get them committed to attending the program. After breakfast, Katherine asked Mary, Nellie and Renie if they would like to go visiting. "We have a long overdue visit, children."

As Katherine pulled the wagon into the Bimbi place, she noticed many improvements to the homestead. The roof had been repaired and a small porch had been added. A new outhouse stood away from the house. The spider lilies were in bloom along with a large hydrangea which framed the little house and made it welcoming. A small black and white dog came welcoming the visitors with his friendly barking. Soon someone cautiously came out the door onto the front porch.

"Hello, how are you?" Katherine began chattering like she had known the lady all her life. Leading the way onto the front porch, Katherine extended a hand. "I am Katherine Cosby, and you are Sallye?"

"Yes, I'm Sallye. Good to meet you," Sallye said, rather timidly.

"Hello, I'm Mary and this is Nellie and Renie," Mary said, trying to put Sallye at ease.

After a minute of chatting about the improvements to the house and the lovely flowers, Sallye seemed to be overcoming her shyness. "John said you might be coming by. He said you wanted Hannah to go to school. But, she can't…she doesn't learn like other kids. She has accidents and messes her clothes. So, I don't think you would want her at school," Sallye said almost as though she hated to say the words.

"She will be okay, I will take care of her," Renie said. "She can sit by me and I will help her. It is my first year at school too, so we can be friends."

"Oh, that is awfully sweet of you, Renie. I just don't know," Sallye was explaining when Hannah peeped her head out of the door.

"Hi, Hannah!" Mary said. "Could she come out and meet the girls?" Mary asked.

"Sure, come on, Hannah. This is Nellie and Renie. They would like for you to go to school with them. What do you think? Would you want to go to school?"

Hannah clung to her mother's skirt and murmured something. She had light blonde hair, with a precious round face. Her lovely, but unusual, blue eyes looked at the group of visitors with innocence.

As she looked up at her mother, she asked, "Soo, ma?"

Sallye picked up the child. "Hannah and I have always been very close. She has to be cared for more than other children. Maybe, if I could be with her, to help her. I don't want others having to take care of her, and she will need extra care. Will you come in? We don't have a lot of room, but you can see what we have done to the place."

As they all gathered around the table, Katherine saw Sallye's talents as well as her gifts of the spirit. Sallye, although still a bit timid, had such a loving, affectionate personality as she entertained the ladies, offering coffee and bread. Mary looked around the cabin and saw so many handmade items: quilts, knitted shawls, and pillows. A stunning landscape painting hung over the fireplace.

"Sallye, the painting over the fireplace is beautiful! Where did you get it?" Mary asked.

Sallye walked to the painting and looked thoughtfully before she spoke, "After Hannah was born, I realized I would be spending a lot of my time alone with her, caring for her needs, keeping her within a safe distance, so I started painting. I've painted several things, but I painted this just a couple weeks ago when we were moving to Hart County. The flowers were so beautiful here, and I had a sense of peace about the place. I just started painting what was on my heart. Of course, the children are my Everett and Hannah. I'm glad you like it. I enjoyed painting it."

Mary was so intrigued with the painting that she had to learn more. "What kind of paint did you use? It looks so thick, but smooth," she added.

"I use egg yolks and mix with them anything I can find for color: poke berries, wild strawberries, sap from horseweed, walnut skins. My oldest, Everett, likes to find bark and flowers I can use to make the pigment for my paint. He is a big help."

"How do you brush it on so fine?" Nellie asked.

"I usually use brushes I make of horse hair." Sallye retrieved some of her brushes from the box under the bed and showed them to Nellie. "I just make them from sticks John whittles for me, and then I put on the horsehair, or whatever I want to make the brush from. The trick is to get the string around the horse hair very tight and then a smooth cut."

The ladies enjoyed their visit with Sallye and Hannah. Eventually, Katherine suggested they move on. She hugged Sallye. "We have enjoyed visiting with you and Hannah. We want to invite you to our first Ladies Day at the school. It will be on Saturday, October 12 and we begin at nine o'clock."

Mary added, "We will serve lunch and have activities during the afternoon. We would love for you to come. You can bring Hannah. I am sure that Hannah and Renie will have a good time while we are listening and learning."

Katherine took Sallye's hand in her own and looked into her eyes, "We want you to come to church Sunday. We will help with Hannah, and we want you to enjoy the fellowship with the other ladies."

Stroking Hannah's hair, Sallye shared with Katherine and Mary that she had never been to church. "Not all of us were raised in Christian homes. My parents never took me to church, and well, I guess I have never learned the value because I have never really wanted to go. John has told me about when he became a Christian. He has told us Bible stories. But, thank you so much for coming. I appreciate your visit and your invitation to the Ladies Day and to church."

Mary had a feeling there was something more, another reason why Sallye had never gone to church and still didn't want to go. Perhaps she was not the only one with secrets.

As they were about to leave, Sallye thought of something, "Oh, wait a minute!" Sallye ran in the house and quickly returned with something in her arms. "Would you please take this quilt? You mentioned a family in need of quilts. I made this one last year, and we don't really need it. If you could give it to someone who does, I would appreciate it."

Katherine took the quilt, thanked Sallye, and gave her another big hug. "See, we are missionaries already, spreading God's love." As they rode away, Katherine realized that their Ladies' Day was much more than just one day, but a lifetime devoted to others and sharing God's love everywhere they would go. She remembered a memory verse from long ago, Psalm 96:3: *Declare His glory among the nations, His wonders among all peoples.*

Katherine remarked as they were riding to their next visit, "We did not ask for a quilt, but God knew we needed a quilt to give to a friend. Thank you, Father for your loving spirit."

The ladies visited Lyssa, Leah, and the children next. While Nellie and Katherine took turns holding Baby Oleta, they discussed the Ladies' Day event. Lyssa and Leah caught onto the excitement from the others and volunteered to help do anything that needed to be done.

"I'm sure we will have jobs for everyone a little later. We are going to try to have breakfast breads, and coffee, since many women will be traveling a good distance. For lunch, we will probably have ham and biscuits with cookies for dessert. Right now, we are open for suggestions for everything," Mary added.

"We will bring raisin bread for breakfast, and we have ham we can share. Is there anything specific you need for us to do?" Lyssa asked. "We can gather flowers for bouquets. Leah has a great hand at flower arranging."

"Sounds wonderful!" Katherine replied. "Right now, we just want to get the women excited about coming to the event. We want everyone to learn what other ladies are doing to promote missions in their area."

Lyssa and Leah offered to go see a few neighbors close to Sonora. Leah offered to write invitations to the Ladies' Day so that they would have a reminder. Lyssa and Leah waved goodbye to the group, and started making their own plans for the event.

Katherine suggested they go see the Spurgeon family next. They had a new baby, and Katherine needed to check on them anyway, she explained. As they pulled the wagon over the rocky road, Katherine had that unnatural feeling again. There was just something about the place that made her skin crawl. She wondered if the others felt the same way. The dead trees which lined the road looked more like scary demons trying to keep people away. The shadows that engulfed the house, made the Spurgeon place an uncanny, spooky, evil-looking place.

Gil was the first one on the porch waving to the ladies. "Jeannie will be glad to see you. Little Stefan seems to be nursing a lot. Maybe you can take a look at him, Katherine."

Mary, Nellie, and Renie seemed reluctant to get out of the wagon until Katherine encouraged them. Finally, one by one they timidly came through the door. Katherine knew they felt the same way she felt, so she assured them that everything was fine.

Jeannie welcomed her guests, but she looked tired. Baby Stefan was crying so Katherine took the baby and started asking questions. "Do you get him to burp after you feed him? Is he getting all he wants to eat before you let him go to sleep?"

While Jeannie and Katherine discussed Baby Stefan, Mary scanned the cabin. There seemed to be a lot of darkness in the cabin—little natural light, casting a morbid look. Gil had hung his spades, grass scythe, and other tools on the wall which made the house look like a barn. The corners were filled with heavy canvas, probably to keep out the cold winds in winter and rodents in summer. There were no extra chairs, and the house did not seem to welcome its guests. Mary couldn't help but compare the house to Ollie and Lyssa's house. One house was so welcoming while the other was quite the opposite.

Jeannie tried to answer Katherine's questions as well as she could, but was confused. "He eats, then goes to sleep in the middle of feeding, then wants to eat again in an hour."

"First," Katherine explained, "you need to make sure every time he gets ready for a nap he is swaddled and can't be moving his hands and feet. They like that feeling of being held. Also, he may be hard to burp and often will get the hiccups. Just part of having a baby, but it will get better."

Mary thought it might be a good time to tell Jeanie about the project since the baby was going to sleep. "Jeannie, we are having a Ladies' Day meeting at the school on Saturday, October 12ᵗʰ, and we want to invite you and the baby."

Katherine joined in the conversation and put an arm around Jeannie's waist. She encouraged Jeannie to attend. "Bring your mother and your sister-in-law. I think they will enjoy it. We are having a program about missions, serving others at home and around the world. Nellie and Renie will be there, and they would love to help with the baby."

"Sure, we would love to help." Nellie remembered the quilt that they had brought with them. "We brought you this quilt for the baby Stefan. Sallye Dales made it and sent it with us to give to whoever we thought might enjoy it."

"Stefan can certainly use it. I don't have anything but this small cloth, so he will have his own quilt now. Thank you so much," Jeannie said looking sad once more. "I wish I had something to give back, but right now I don't have anything. Perhaps, there will be something I can do for the Ladies' Day. Please let me know, maybe Mom and me could make some apple strudel?"

Mary was pleased to get an offer on the food, so she readily accepted. "Please plan on coming and also bring any other women in your family. It will be a day for the women to enjoy being together."

"And, we would love to have you come to church on Sunday." Katherine took her arm from Jeannie's waist and opened the pillowcase she was carrying. "We made this gown and this baby quilt for Stefan yesterday. We hope he will like it."

Jeannie put the baby on the bed. "Thank you so much. I love the gown and certainly can use both of the quilts. Thank you so much. We really do appreciate it."

"You are more than welcome, Sweetie," Katherine said as she patted Jeannie's hand.

"I can't promise anything right now because of the baby, but I would like to go to church. Thanks so much for asking."

As everyone said their goodbyes and headed to the wagon, Katherine stopped and looked at the large rock on the edge of the yard. The rock was about four feet tall and about two feet wide. It looked as though it was stained from something. The woods beyond the rock looked sinister and unwelcoming. Gil came around front to help the ladies get in the buggy.

"Gil, was this house here when you made a homestead?" Katherine asked.

"Oh, no, well, there were rocks like maybe where the foundation of a house might have been. But there wasn't anything here when we settled here, nothing but foundation rocks."

On their way to the next visit, Mary sighed a breath of relief. "Excuse me, but I had the strangest feeling there, it was such a depressing place."

"Me too! I couldn't wait to get out of that house. That place was dark and even with the baby there, it was weird, like something was watching us," Nellie said as she shivered.

"I didn't like it there. Please, Gran, let's not go back there," Renie whimpered. "Can we go home now? I'm tired of mission work."

Relying on instinct, Katherine pulled the reins to stop the horses and got out to inspect the horse breeching. "I was sure this was put on correctly when we left and now it is off." She mended the situation and got back in the wagon. Weird, she thought to herself. Without the breeching, we could have had an accident.

"Just one more visit, and we will go home, Renie. But I do have something in the bag you might like, cornbread and bacon for everyone. We can stop along the creek edge and have a little picnic before we visit Della and Mike," Katherine suggested.

Katherine spread a log-cabin quilt on the creek bank. Mary helped unpack the food; green onions, a sliced tomato, cornbread, and bacon sandwiches. She had managed to tuck away a few rhubarb and strawberry jam biscuits for a tasty dessert.

After the blessing and a picnic lunch, Mary and Katherine enjoyed a beautiful day, resting in the shade and talking about the friends they had visited. Nellie and Renie stepped onto the large rocks along the creek and splashed water on their hands and faces. A day of fun and being together was a treat for all the girls. Nellie admitted to herself she had enjoyed being with Mary. Still, no matter how she tried, something wasn't right.

As soon as they arrived at the Caswell's place, Della hurried out to meet them. She was excited to have company and invited the ladies to sit in her porch swings. Katherine and Mary discussed plans for the Ladies Day with Della.

"Oh, this is such good news," Della said. "I am so glad you girls are doing this. We need to know more about what is going on around us. We need to be able to help others if we can. I don't get away from here much. Seems like there is always something to do, but I will be at the Ladies' Day program. If there is anything I can do, maybe make some fried peach pies?"

"That would be wonderful. Jeannie Spurgeon said that she and her mother would make apple streusel, and we will have ham and biscuits and raisin bread, so that will be great," Mary replied.

Nellie and Renie chased the new puppies in the yard and sat on the grass to play with them. Nellie wondered where Mike was keeping himself.

With the children out of listening distance, Katherine had a few minutes to ask some questions. "Della, we just came from the Spurgeon's, past the Lucas Grove area. Do you know who lived there before them? Gil said there wasn't a house there, just some rocks that looked like there might have been a foundation at one time."

"Oh, Katherine, I can't believe you don't know about the place. Back, oh, I guess more than fifty, sixty, maybe seventy years ago, when the Cherokee was here, there was a massacre. We didn't talk about it much because Daniel, my husband was Cherokee. But from what I heard, the Cherokees killed the family there."

"And you know this because the Cherokee told your husband about it?" Katherine asked.

"Yes, in a roundabout way. The oldest boy had left the house to check his traps. He heard the yelping of the Cherokee and circled back and hid. He got there as the family was being massacred and the house was burning. He hated the Cherokee after that."

"I can certainly understand why," said Mary as she envisioned the scene at the place they had just visited.

"Well, the story doesn't end there. A few days after the massacre the boy, Mack, was caught by the Cherokee and was about to be killed. Daniel's father saved him, let him go and told him where to hide to be safe. He heard the story about seeing his family killed and helped the boy. Anyway, that is the place where Mack's family was killed. Mack dug a hole and buried all the family members together and piled some stones on top. Got to be some bad spirits there," Della said with a fearful look on her face.

Katherine realized why she had felt so spooked at that place. She knew what she had to do. Katherine needed some of the church deacons to help her as soon as possible. The Spurgeon house and grounds needed a blessing and a circle of prayer.

# Chapter 16

# Nellie's Birthday

Corrals were not something Thomas enjoyed building, especially since there were matters that needed his attention more. However, his lovely young daughter was to celebrate her sixteenth birthday and the occasion called for extraordinary measures.

Thomas hammered in the last nail. "Hey, Mike, thanks for helping me get this done today. I couldn't have done it without you." Thomas tested the structure, pushing with his weight against the red cedar boards.

"Have to admit things couldn't have worked out better. Katherine's plan for visiting worked out well with our plans," Mike added as he picked up a couple handfuls of scraps from around his feet.

Mike and Thomas had moved almost all of the lumber from the stack beside the barn. Just as Mike was about to dig up the last piece wedged in the ground, he saw the piece of wood move by itself. Quickly, Mike grabbed a nearby stick, picked up the board and jumped back. Surprised, he stumbled and fell backward to get out of the way.

"What is it, a snake?" Thomas asked laughing at Mike's frightened dance.

"Worse than a snake," Mike replied suddenly breathless. "Was a skunk! That little vermin raised up turned around and I thought I was gonna' be a smelly feller real quick."

Thomas laughed as Mike sniffed his clothes and hands. Mike's quick, frightened measures had been just about the funniest sight and he couldn't tell anyone about it, at least not right away.

Still laughing at Mike, Thomas said, "Yeah, I figure they may want to visit Mrs. Della before they come home, maybe you can get there before they leave. And you could have smelled so good for them!"

The men had worked out a plan to get the corral built onto the barn. Tomorrow would be Nellie's sixteenth birthday and Thomas had a big surprise for her. Nellie had begged Thomas to buy her a few sheep, and although he didn't think it was a very good idea, he had finally given in. The corral was ready and a stall ready for the sheep.

Andy Miller had agreed to bring the sheep over very early the next morning and put them in the new corral. Thomas laughed as he thought of the surprise for all the women when they saw the sheep. He had managed to keep the sheep a secret from Mary. However, Thomas had shared the secret with Katherine because he had asked about Grandmother's spinning wheel.

Della and Mike had been a big help with the surprise. Della had insisted on making pink and blue bows for the sheep. Andy had agreed to bring five lambs, three females and two males. All he would have to do Saturday morning would be to put the bows on the sheep before he had the girls come to the barn. Nellie will be so excited, Thomas thought. Can't believe she is already sixteen! Rissa, you would be very proud of your little girl. She is already a beautiful, intelligent, Christian, young lady.

Thomas straightened his back and rubbed his aching neck. With all the work on the school project and the hurried corral project, he was feeling the stiffness. Thomas decided to go down to the creek and lie in the water, which was the best therapy to ease his soreness. Nellie's birthday on Saturday, church Sunday and school starts on Monday. Quite a lot going on for the next few day. There was still a few things to do to the school addition, but nothing that won't hurt if it didn't get done.

---

Since the mill was closed for the day, Thomas removed all of his clothes, except his underwear and lay in the shallow part of the creek water. The older people believed springs like these had medicinal qualities. They believed that the creek water, which flowed over the rocks, was cleansed of impurities. In addition, because the water picked up the minerals and natural healing spirits, the water was proclaimed as therapy waters. Many people brought containers and filled them with the water because they believed it would heal. Others believed if one would simply sit, walk, or lie in the water for an hour a month, their aches and pains would be cured. Thomas had to agree with that point of view. He could be aching with muscle strain and the cold water would make him feel better and he would not be in pain for a few days.

Looking overhead, Thomas marveled at the beauty of the place. The huge sycamores, maples, oaks, willows, chestnuts, hickories, and elm trees lined the creek bank. The constant bubbling from the springs and the rushing water downstream made it easy to relax.

Thomas thought he had stepped into the Garden of Eden the first time he saw Roundstone. Bro. Daughter, their pastor at the time, had brought a group of boys down to the creek for a picnic and a cool dip in the creek. Thomas thought at the time, I will own this spot someday, for this is the most beautiful place I have ever seen.

Thomas had bought the land and settled when it was cheap. He had never regretted buying the four thousand acres in Hart County. As he lay in the shallow, fifty-seven degree water he thought about his plans for the secret project. He realized he would need to make a trip to Louisville soon and gather more information. Maybe after school was well underway, he could take Mary and have a weekend together in the city. His hope was to take part in the greatest achievement in communication of the century.

Thomas, feeling much better from the cold "therapy," hurried about doing the chores. Tommie was spending the day at the school finishing a few jobs, so he would be back by supper. Thomas didn't want anyone to go out to the barn for fear of ruining the surprise.

The girls were exuberant when they arrived home. Everyone had something to tell about the "best part of the day." Even Renie was excited about her mission work.

After supper, Thomas read from the Bible and talked about how God wants us to get excited about doing for others. "From Second Thessalonians 1:11-12, we read, 'Therefore we also pray always for you that our God would count you worthy of this calling, and fulfill all the good pleasure of His goodness and the work of faith with power, that the name of our Lord Jesus Christ may be glorified in you, and you in Him, according to the grace of our God and the Lord Jesus Christ'."

The Cosby family had a time of praise and worship as they discussed the scripture. Katherine said her greatest hope was to be worthy of the work of Jesus. She added, "I don't want any credit for anything I do on earth, but God receive all the glory and honor."

As Mary listened, she recalled what her own father would have said about this reading in the Bible. Even though she loved Thomas, she could not fully accept his faith or his Jesus. Mary thought, I have called on God and He has not listened to me. He has not helped me when I needed it the most. How do I join in with all my heart if I can't trust God to do what I have prayed for? I cannot turn from my upbringing, no not even for Thomas. And as far as my secrets, well they will be just that. I cannot bear my soul to these people.

"Mary, Mary, are you listening? You must have been deep in thought!" Thomas added as he winked at Mary. "What do you think? Did you feel that you were doing the work of Jesus today as you visited?"

"The work of Jesus, Well, I...I feel that we all felt a higher calling today. My own father always said to do for the One God, Father of Abraham, and follow the Ten Commandments each day. I try, but I never feel that I have done all I can do."

Thomas and Katherine looked at Mary rather curiously. "I think we all feel that we fall short of righteousness. However, Jesus died on a cross to deliver us from the law, for we all sin. We have Jesus living in our hearts to remind us that we can't do it alone," Thomas said quite plainly for all the family to understand. "We simply can't live a righteous life without the grace through Jesus."

Seeing the need to change the topic, Thomas jumped up, clapped his hands and exclaimed, "Since everyone has been out all day, how about we start celebrating Nellie's birthday early? We haven't played games, or sang around the piano in a long time. What would you like to do first, Nellie?" Thomas asked.

Nellie thought for a minute then exclaimed. "Let's play blind-man bluff! And Renie gets to go first!" Nellie teased, excited to see her little sister play the game.

Katherine found the blindfold, a faded waistband of an old apron that had belonged to her mother. She had tucked the saved apron part in the back of her cedar trunk. Katherine tied the blindfold on Renie as the family quickly moved around the room. Renie's job was to try to identify who she found by touching them with one hand. Renie finally found Mary and identified her by the ruffle on her apron. Thomas, Katherine and Mary always made the game fun by not being able to identify who they found, even with the hints from others. Everyone laughed and enjoyed having a good time with each other.

"Let's play Family Fun," Nellie announced. "I'll get the board."

Thomas had bought the board game on his last trip to Lexington. The board game was something new, and the family had learned the rules and played it a few times on special occasions. Nellie put the board on the kitchen table and began to put out the colorful pieces.

"Sounds like a great idea," Katherine said, "but I need to start on a certain cake. You kids can play without me, right now."

"Then let me make the icing, Katherine," Mary added. "I'll make Nellie's favorite cream icing. Is that okay, Nellie?"

"Wonderful, can we eat it tonight?" Nellie teased as she gave out the tokens. "Come, on Renie, get up here." She knew Renie would play for a few minutes and then be on the porch playing with the kittens.

"Nellie, you get to sleep in for your birthday!" Thomas reminded Nellie. "No work for the birthday girl. Tommie and I will have the pleasure of doing all the chores."

As the family played games, they enjoyed being together. Mary talked about school starting while Tommie talked about the sanding he had finished. Nellie talked about the babies, Oleta and Stefan, and Renie talked about Mike's puppies. Katherine talked about the good response to the Ladies' Day Event and Thomas listened to his family, rejoicing in the family's blessings.

Thomas awoke early on Saturday morning. Lots of work to do, and Andy will arrive with the sheep a little after daybreak, Thomas thought. As he went into the kitchen he saw the finished birthday cake on the table. Nellie will be so excited and so will Renie.

Tommie helped Thomas get the cows milked. Tommie finished feeding the horses and goats while Thomas forked manure from Berthie's stall. As they were finishing, they met Andy with the sheep in the wagon. Andy's oldest son Chase and his father-in-law were in the wagon holding onto the sheep.

"Hey, thanks again for bringing the sheep. Nellie will sure be excited," Thomas said to Andy and the others.

"Oh, glad to do it. Nellie seems like she really enjoys the sheep, so hopefully someday she will have a nice herd," Andy replied.

After the chores, Thomas was glad to get back to the house to start the celebration. Days like this one made him miss Rissa so much. Even though he was happily married to Mary, Rissa was still always in his heart. Nellie's birthday reminded him of the love they had shared when Nellie was born.

"Happy Birthday to Nellie, Happy Birthday to Nellie!" Everyone sang to Nellie as they had breakfast. As soon as devotion was finished everyone had a gift for Nellie.

Renie insisted she go first. Renie had made Nellie a braided yellow, red, and blue bracelet. "Thank you Renie, it is lovely. I will wear it the first day of school!"

Tommie presented his gift next. "Oh, Tommie, I love it! Thanks so much!" Nellie exclaimed. "This will hang in my room forever." Tommie had drawn a picture of the cow and calf Nellie had saved, with Mike's help.

"I don't know if you noticed, but you and Mike are in the background, because without both of you, the cow and calf wouldn't have made it," Tommie added. "See, you and Mike are grinnin' like a possum eatin' a persimmon."

Nellie hugged Tommie. "You are the best brother, ever, Tommie! Thank you so much. I love it."

Mary gave Nellie the next gift. It was a box wrapped in pink paper with a red bow. "I hope you like it, Nellie."

Nellie was careful to not destroy the paper or the ribbon. As she opened the box, she found two pair of wool stockings, one beige pair and one gray. "I love them. And I will use them all winter!" As she examined them, she noted a heart on the top of each sock. "I know you knitted the socks, but how did you get this heart on here? That is such a great idea!"

Mary explained, "With wool, you can make a shape just out of working with the wool. I want to teach you how to knit and felt. I bought some yarn and needles for you while we were in Elizabethtown. I didn't wrap them, but here they are. We can get started as soon as you like."

"Oh, I love it! I am so excited about learning how to knit. I have a lot of projects already in mind. I am going to make baby hats, booties, and socks for everybody. Oh, thanks so much, Mary. Thank you so much." Nellie gave Mary a hug. Nellie had to admit that Mary had given her a very thoughtful gift. She was making it difficult to hate her. Still, Mary was not her mother.

Katherine watched Nellie and was proud of the progress she had made. Hugging her granddaughter she said, "I have a gift too, but I think maybe Thomas may want to show you his gift first. Right, Thomas?"

"Okay, then everyone, get your shoes on; we are going for a walk." Thomas was excited and hoped Nellie hadn't changed her mind about the sheep.

As they walked to the barn, everyone was chattering and tried to guess what the gift might be. "What could it be that has to be hidden in the barn?" Nellie asked. About then she spotted the new corral. "What…what is it? Sheep, it's my sheep, I wanted! You said I couldn't have sheep!"

Everyone went through the gate to the inside of the corral and petted the darling sheep. The bows were still on the sheep, marking the girls and the boys. "Oh, how cute, two boys and three girls," Nellie said.

Thomas showed Nellie how they were to be fed and cared for daily. "Sheep are not the smartest animals in the world, so you do have to take care of them. Hopefully, you will enjoy them and they can make money someday. You need to thank Della Caswell; she made the bows for the sheep."

Thomas looked at his beautiful daughter as she petted the sheep. He was so proud of her. "I hope you like the sheep, Nellie. Also, you will need to thank Mike. He helped me build the corral while you ladies were out yesterday."

Katherine told Nellie, "My gift is not going to be as impressive as the sheep, but come on in the barn. My gift is in here."

The family followed Katherine to the barn and watched as she opened the feed stall and removed an old quilt from the back of the stall. Katherine had learned that Thomas was going to give Nellie the sheep, so she had time to get her gift ready and hide it in the barn.

"I hope you like it, Nellie. It was your Grandmother Cosby's spinning wheel."

Nellie didn't know what to say. "This is the best birthday ever! I love it. I can shear the sheep, card it and spin the wool. Mary even gave me the needles to knit, so I have everything I need. Thank you, everybody, I love all my gifts."

Nellie examined the Old Dutch spinning wheel. To think it had been used by her great grandmother! As she ran her hands over the dusty wooden wheel, Nellie saw herself spinning a dream of her own. The spinning wheel would have to stay in the barn for now. Hopefully, when the new house was built she could put it in her own room. Nellie felt that these gifts, the sheep, the knitting needles, and the spinning wheel, were more than just the ordinary birthday presents. These gifts would lead to her future in helping others, giving something from her heart. Also, with these special gifts, she would have an opportunity to give unique gifts to others, gifts from the Hart of Roundstone.

# Chapter 17

# Head to Toe

The cooler temperature of the late night and early morning called for a quilt over the feet. Thomas noticed the air felt fresh and crisp as he headed out to do the chores. The promise of fall weather was already in the air while the trees and the fall flowers sported their glory everywhere. Sunday morning, Sept 2, was a lovely, perfect summer-to-fall day.

At church the wagons and buggies were pulling onto the grounds. Every week or so there would be a new wagon or buggy as new families were joining the worship and fellowship. Hitching posts and fences were around the back and sides of the church where the wagons and horses kept the grass low. Just past the fences and hitching posts was a spring that fed into Big Springs. Late summer meant that the spring was low, and the children enjoyed playing in it after church.

Congregation members were meeting and greeting, and kids were getting kisses and hugs. Lyssa and Leah, along with Baby Oleta, were welcoming visitors. Lyssa had given Leah one of the dresses that Nellie had brought her. Both women, so devoted to their faith, were such blessings to the members of Upton Baptist Church as they arrived. The church had two entrances. Leah was at one side, meeting and greeting and Lyssa was at the other. The two ladies awaited the last family.

"I would guess you are the Spurgeon family with baby Stefan?" Lyssa remembered Katherine telling her about the new family.

"Yes, this is Gil, and my mother, Stella. I asked my family to come, but well, at least I got my mother to come with us," Jeannie said shyly.

Lyssa introduced herself, Leah and Baby Oleta. "Come on in we will introduce you." Lyssa introduced the family to several people before it was time to take a seat. Both new mothers sat close to each other, admiring the other's baby.

Pastor Ship brought a message on *Blessing Those in Need*. The scripture, from Acts 3:6, "Father, help me to be like Peter and freely use the name of Jesus to bless those in need around me," Pastor Ship said as he gave the opening prayer.

After the message, the pastor called for a handshake and welcome to new visitors. At the invitation, a couple came forward and rededicated their lives. Pastor Ship encouraged everyone to take the name of Jesus to bless others around them during the week.

Lyssa asked Jeannie and her family to stay for lunch.

"We would like that, but we really didn't plan to stay. We didn't bring anything and I'm afraid Stefan will be exercising his lungs soon," Jeannie replied.

"Well, then, we hope to see you next Sunday," Lyssa said as she hugged Jeannie and Stella goodbye. Lyssa was a good ambassador for the church and for the Lord as everyone felt her gift of witnessing.

The ladies gathered their carefully packed food and piled it on the large tables. Country ham sandwiches, fried chicken, squirrel dumplings, green beans, tomatoes, onions, beets, boiled potatoes, cornbread, biscuits, sourdough bread, apple pies, peach pies, rhubarb and strawberry pies, cookies, cakes, and jellies loaded the table. No one need go hungry. The ladies made sure the men and children were fed first. The women, though last, could take their time, relax, and talk with friends during their meal.

Baby Oleta was passed around to several admirers and then on to Nellie. Lyssa and Leah were able to fill their plates after making sure everyone else was fed. Both young women realized they did not have this opportunity very often. Being able to take their time to eat and not wait on others was a delight.

Katherine sat in front of Lyssa and Leah at the large picnic table. "I'm so proud of you girls. You two seem like such good friends. I'm glad it has worked out for both of you, your families needed each other."

"Yes, and we have some big dreams together," Lyssa giggled. "Probably that's all it will ever amount to, just dreams, but Leah and I have talked about what we would like to do one day."

"And just what is that, Leah?" Katherine smiled. "Is this something you want to do, or did Lyssa just talk you into it?"

"Oh, I really think it is a good idea, just don't know how we can get started," Leah said.

Lyssa hurried into the explanation. "We would like to have a shop in town, a 'Head to Toe' shop. Leah makes these lovely hats and I think they are wonderful. We can make all kinds, for different weather, for Easter or special occasions."

"And Lyssa likes to sew and make alterations. We would love to open a fabric shop because there is a need for it in Upton," Leah said.

Katherine looked at the two, "So you girls have some big ideas. What about the toe? Where does that come in, Head to Toe?"

"Well," Lyssa said, "I have all the shoe forms Ollie's grandmother had, so we would like to stock some leather for shoe making. And probably we would have ready-made shoes and boots. We think if we had a place in town we could sell our products, plus we would be able to meet people who come our way. We can witness to them and…"

"And, we want to be able to give a Bible to each family who needs one. Every family needs a Bible and many families won't go to church because they think they aren't welcome. But we can give them a Bible, give them a start, and encourage them to come to church," Leah interjected.

"Well, girls, what are you waiting for?" Katherine asked. "Sounds to me like you have a winning plan, we just said lately there needs to be a good fabric shop in Upton, and there is no selection unless you go to Elizabethtown."

"We just don't know how to get started. Guess that's why we have just talked about it. And we need a place to rent or buy, and of course it would have to be cheap. Do you know of a place we could rent, cheap?" Lyssa asked.

"I know a place where you won't even have to pay rent, if you will just fix it up. It needs a lot of work, but it is right on the road, and I think you would have plenty of room. Tell you what, girls, school starts in the morning and I have to be at school for a while, but I can meet you at Upton at about 10:00. I will show you what we own. It may not suit you at all, but you can look at it and see what you think," Katherine suggested.

Leah and Lyssa agreed it was a great idea, and said they would love to meet Katherine tomorrow. As they finished with the cleanup and the Bible study, the girls couldn't keep from thinking about the new store. Lyssa imagined stocking pretty fabrics, laces, and buttons, and meeting other ladies while witnessing to them, giving them a Bible as Rev. Morgan had done with her. What joy!

The two girls couldn't wait to share their news with Ollie and Hobie on their way home. Lyssa explained that Katherine had agreed there needed to be a fabric store in Upton, while Leah explained they had a building, maybe.

"Them's big idies you got, girls, and I want it fir you, but it's gonna take a lot to git a business started. Jest don't want to see you gals git your hopes up and git hurt," Ollie added.

"I have to agree," Hobie replied. "The cost of the merchandise alone would be a thousand dollars, probably. Getting a business started is hard to do in a small town like Upton, but if you girls are willing to work at it, I will sure help."

That evening, after devotion, Katherine told the family about Lyssa and Leah's dream of a store. She explained that she had offered the old building in Upton if they would fix it up. "There's plenty of work to do, I'll admit, but with Ollie and Hobie working together they could fix it up, and the girls could have it rent free, just to keep it from being an eyesore on the Upton road."

"Mom, it is going to take a lot to get the store started. Do they have money to begin? The start-up money would be over a thousand dollars. Oh, I get it, you want me to give them a loan?" Thomas laughed.

"Well, Thomas, the Good Lord has been good to you, and this is your chance to do something really good for someone else. If you could just help them get started, and I am sure Mary knows quite a bit about how to run a business," Katherine stressed.

"You know, I would love to help them get started. My parents ran the store at Cub Run for years until they sold it to the Pence family. I am sure I can help them get started. Plus, I would love to be able to buy supplies at Upton instead of having to go to Elizabethtown or Louisville for fabrics." Mary paused as if she was giving the business deal her consideration. "Oh, Thomas, this is such a good idea for the girls. I hope you will give them a loan, or perhaps I can. I still have the money my parents left me. Let me do this, Thomas. This will be my mission to help them get started."

"Hold on, Mary. I don't mind for you using your money. However, think about it. Upton! How many people are going to go to Upton to shop? It sounds like a wonderful fairy tale, but I just don't see it working. I know Lyssa and Leah are hard workers but it takes more than that." Thomas shook his head and hoped that he had heard the last of the matter as he started to go outside.

Katherine looked at Thomas and covered his hand with hers. "You know Thomas, you are completely right about not appearing to be a good business opportunity. But I do remember a verse in Romans that says 'If God be for us, who can be against us.' Those girls have prayed over this venture and I think God is leading them to this opportunity. And…if you remember the message Pastor Ship brought today…he preached on helping those in need. His passage was from Acts 3:6, 'Father, help me to be like Peter and freely use the name of Jesus to bless those in need around me.' Thomas, these girls want to use their business to witness to others. What a testimony to bless those in need!"

"I agree, Thomas. I know the girls are hard workers and both of them are Christians. With a little help they can not only have a store for the community but be a place to share their faith. I want to help them, if you will give me your blessing," Mary said with a questioning voice.

"You two have it figured out then. You don't even need me. Whatever you do, pray about it and make sure it is the Lord's will," Thomas added dejectedly.

"After school tomorrow, I will go visit them and discuss their business venture. Katherine, please let them know I will help them. I am elated they have the initiative to begin their business venture. I pray God will show me his will," Mary added. For some reason Mary felt that helping the girls with their business would be what God wanted her to do. Perhaps helping others build a business would help her build her faith.

---

School began on Monday morning, September 3, 1845, with a new addition and new outhouses. Children arrived for the first day of school with Pete and Andrea Goodwin and with their families. Mary had brought Nellie, Renie, and Tommie in the buckboard and had picked up Sallye, Everett, and Hannah along the way. Even though some of the children said they would rather stay home, most were happy to be back at school. The school kept filling up with children, and Andrea was glad to have Mary there to help for the first few days.

The desks were double, which meant two students could sit at one desk, so Renie took a desk up front and Hannah sat beside her. Sallye placed a straight-back chair beside the two girls. Mike found Nellie and quickly claimed a seat by her, and the two began to talk about her birthday gift. Tommie sat by Everett, assuring him he would like the new school and teacher.

"The school bell will ring every day at 8:00, and students are expected to be at school with their slates, pencil, and paper and be ready to go to work. All students will have jobs to keep the school clean and safe." Mrs. Mary finished the announcements for students and parents.

As parents began to exit, Katherine decided Mary and Andrea could take care of the school without her as she headed for Upton to meet Lyssa and Leah. The young women were already waiting by the Upton bank when she saw them. She motioned for them to come up the street a half block to where her building was. She couldn't help but notice the expression on their faces when they got out of the buggy.

"I know it looks rough right now, but I think it could be fixed without a lot of problems," Katherine said as she opened the broken front door. "Really, there is a leak in the roof, which is causing some damage. The floor has damage from the leak, but most of it is okay, and you could actually cover the floor damage with a rug after it is fixed. Or, put a new floor down just in this area, which would be your shop area."

The building smelled dank and musty from the obvious leaks. Lyssa handed Baby Oleta to Leah as she tested the floor. Stepping too close to the damaged boards, Lyssa fell through, scratching her ankles and knees on the old jagged boards. "I'm okay, but we are going to have to take this floor out back to the wall here."

Katherine apologized for the accident. Lyssa assured Katherine it was nothing and they continued to look through their dogged determination at the possibilities of the building. Both Lyssa and Leah felt the excitement that bubbled like a teapot.

The girls could make the building work as they were multi-talented and committed women. Katherine led them to the back room.

"This area could be for storage and your office space, to keep your books. There is even a lockbox in the floor."

Katherine showed them how to lift up the latch in the floor. "See, there is a small cellar with a lockbox. That way if you don't go to the bank every day, you won't feel afraid to leave your money here," Katherine explained.

"Well, it will work, I think. I know we will have to do some work, but we just don't have a lot of money to begin with, and there is so much to have to buy to start. I don't know, what do you think, Leah? Do you think we can do it?" Lyssa asked, her excitement a little subdued.

"We can make it look good with a little work, and some new lumber. We should put glass in the windows and fill them with merchandise, put our fabrics on one side and our hats and shoes on another. Maybe paint a sign and hang on the roof overhang to get everyone's attention," Leah added, trying to encourage Lyssa.

"Oh, I forgot to mention…maybe you girls better sit down here on the floor. Um, my lovely daughter-in-law, Mary, told me yesterday she is so proud of you girls, and your dream project. So… she is going to loan you the start-up money!"

The girls squealed and hugged each other until tears began to flow. "Thank you so much Katherine. You have done so much for us that we can never repay you and Mary. We are so thrilled! Now, we can look at this place and realistically think about what we can do," Lyssa said, trying to act calm.

"Mary said she will be at your house after school. Her parents owned and operated a mercantile store at Cub Run for over thirty years. She knows a lot about business and is willing to not only give you a loan, but she is going to help you get started, order supplies, general business stuff. She will meet with you today," Katherine told the ladies.

The exuberance was halted when the door flew open and a man rushed in. "Katherine, I thought that was your wagon. Can you come with me, right now?" Dr. Routt had hurried in with Stella.

"Sure, what's wrong, Doc?" Katherine asked.

"Gil has been hurt and Stella came and got me. Some kind of freak accident in the cornfield. She didn't think it would be good to move him, so I am headed down there. Can you follow me?" Doc asked.

"Sure I can. I'll be right behind you. See you later, girls. Don't forget about Mary after school today."

As Katherine got in her wagon, she blamed herself for Gil being hurt. "I knew the place had some bad spirits and I put off praying and blessing the place. Lord, please, I plead the blood of Jesus on Gil right now. Father, I pray you will help Doctor Routt treat him. The Spurgeon family needs their daddy." As Katherine prayed, she asked forgiveness for not praying for the family and the home sooner. She put her faith in God that He would answer her prayers for Gil as she drove Ol' Dan and her buggy toward the Spurgeon's unwelcoming home place.

# Chapter 18

# The Blessing

Mary explained the process of the business procedure, how to make a list of needs and a list of wants. She mentioned that she would have an account open at Jones Hardware Store for them to get their supplies. Lyssa and Leah had so many questions, but Mary seemed to be addressing them before they had the chance to ask.

"Is Saturday a good day for a trip to Elizabethtown?" Mary asked. "I have an old friend who has a mercantile store and she would be honored to help us. By the end of the day, we should be able to have everything for our beginning order. What do you think?"

Lyssa and Leah kept thanking Mary for her help. "Both of us are good with a hammer and saw, so we can do some of the work ourselves. We will work at the shop each day and try to get some of the work done before Saturday," Lyssa said as she hugged Mary.

Leah added, "Maybe the men can work Saturday while we are shopping, if there are things we can't do. We thank you for your help. Without you, we couldn't begin to open our shop."

"I'm so glad I can help you. If you think of anything, write it down and we will discuss it on Saturday. I want to help you, Lyssa and Leah, in more ways than just being able to help fund your shop, I think both of you have so much potential," Mary added.

"Thomas, come quickly, your mother is not home yet. Lyssa and Leah said Dr. Routt came for her to go with them to Gil Spurgeon's house, something about an accident. Grab a bacon biscuit and let's go. I'm worried about her," Mary said, blaming herself for waiting so long.

Everyone piled into the wagon as Tommie hitched up Sassie.

"Sassie has done a hard day's work already. I'll have to give her an extra scoop of oats when we get back," Thomas said, trying to act like he wasn't really concerned. "She is fine, I am sure. You know Mom; she always wants to help when there's someone sick or needing her."

"I am sure you are right, Thomas, but it would make me feel better if we went over there. Your mom didn't get a good feeling when she was there, nor did I. We learned about the history of the place. Did you know what happened there with the Cherokees?" Mary asked, keeping her voice low. She did not want the children to overhear their conversation.

"Yes, I've heard the story. Expect it is true too. A lot of that went on when this country was being settled. The Indians had a right to the land by a treaty made in Virginia, but the settlers came and run them out. Occasionally, there would be a few young Indians who would get riled up and go after the white people. Just glad we don't have to worry about it now," Thomas added. "Hey, girls, how was school? Tommie said he is going to like school, how about you Renie?"

"It's okay. I have a new friend, Hannah. Her mama sits beside us in case Hannah needs her. I really like school and I like having Mary for my teacher."

"Make sure you call her Ms. Mary at school," Thomas said, glad to get the subject off of his mother. Clearly, he was concerned; she should have been back.

As they rode along, Mary imagined everything that could go wrong. Mary reminded Thomas about the buggy breech that was loose when the four of them were at the Spurgeon home. She kept envisioning the uninviting place and remembering her fear. Surely, Katherine would be there with Gil and Jeannie, probably fixing food for Jeannie when they got there. However, after the story Della had recollected, Mary couldn't help but feel the place was evil.

The wagon rolled unevenly around the large rock in the road. There was no one in sight. The place had a spooky, unwelcoming look as usual, and it didn't help that the fog was rising from the creek. An old black dog saw the wagon but didn't move. He just let out some howls that sounded more like a mournful cry. Katherine's wagon and horse was tied to the hitching post, but she wasn't to be seen.

Thomas and Mary told the children to stay in the buckboard while they went inside. Mary knocked on the door and someone called to come in. Jeannie was holding the baby and sitting beside the bed holding Gil's hand. Katherine was not there.

"Jeannie, where is Katherine?" Mary asked worriedly.

"Oh, she wanted to go outside. She and Dr. Routt worked on Gil's leg for a couple hours, and he left a long time ago. Katherine cooked awhile then said she had to go outside," Jeannie answered.

Thomas and Mary hurried outside and called for Katherine. "Over here, here I am," Katherine answered.

"Mom, what are you doing out here? We have been worried about you," Thomas said, sounding a little upset.

"I'll tell you what I am doing here. Ever since the first time I came out here a week ago, I have had this weird feeling about this place. Then, Della told me the story of what happened here." Katherine stopped and wiped her eyes with her handkerchief. "I stood back here in the woods where Mack would have stood and watched the massacre. That poor family didn't have a chance; they were taken before their time. Mack, a boy, was probably the only one who even missed them after they left."

"Sad," Thomas said, shaking his head.

"Della said Mack had dug a big grave and put them all in it. I wondered if I could find the place and at least put up a marker for them. It's so sad they were killed, forgotten, just left. So I decided I would try to find the place where they were buried, mark the spot and say a prayer over them."

"And did you find a place that looks like it could have been a grave? " Mary asked. "What can we do?"

"First, I'll show you what I found." Katherine led them around a couple of trees to a small clearing with several big rocks scattered on top. "What do you think? Think this could be it?"

"Sure could be. Mom, you have such a dear heart. So, what do we do now?" Thomas asked.

"Well, right now, I just want to say a prayer for them, a prayer for this house and this particular area. Ask God to give a blessing over the house and place because it has seen so much evil. Let's begin by touching the trees, the porch, the house, the spring, the animals, whatever we see, ask God to bless," Katherine said.

As the three of them walked around and prayed, they asked a blessing on the land and the family. When they finished they said a prayer for Gil, Jeannie, and the baby.

"I feel much better, now," Katherine said. "Let's go in and see if we can do anything for Gil tonight. Jeannie may want me to stay the night."

Inside, Katherine told Gil and Jeannie they had prayed for a blessing on the place. She explained, briefly, what had happened there long ago and why she felt the place needed a blessing. Volunteering to spend the night, Katherine hoped she could continue a night of prayer in the little house.

"No, you don't have to stay," Gil said as the three adults asked if there was anything they could do. "I am better now."

Thomas asked, "What happened, anyway?"

"Don't really know what happened. I was in the cornfield with my horse and something spooked her. She reared and when she did my knife fell out of the saddlebag and stabbed me in the leg. My horse reared and threw the bag of corn off that I had picked, and it broke my ankle; I couldn't walk. I drug myself as far as I could but must have passed out, I was so weak. Just a freak accident, I guess. Anyway, I thank you, Katherine. Thanks for coming and helping. But, I'll be okay," Gil said trying to assure her.

"Yes, we appreciate all you have done. You were so good to come help with Gil and then with the baby since I was so upset," Jeannie added.

Getting in the wagons to go home, the family wanted to be gone from the depressing place. Katherine asked if Tommie could drive her wagon for her. The stress from the day had completely exhausted her.

Thomas and Mary drove their wagon with Nellie and Renie in the back. Both girls were tired after their first day of school and were irritating each other.

"You know it seems that when something really good happens, something bad happens, or at least that was what it was today. By the way, Lyssa, Leah and I are going to Elizabethtown on Saturday to order stock for the shop, if that is okay with you, of course. Ollie and Hobie are going to the shop and work on Saturday, to try to get it in somewhat presentable shape. They are so excited, Thomas, and I am so happy for them," Mary said.

"Sounds like you might need your own business, or did you miss teaching school today? Think you might want to go back to teaching?"

"No, I have my own projects I am working on. You are not the only one who has secrets, you-know."

*Debbie Taylor*

"Now, what is your secret, Mary, my dear wife?"

"Well, first of all if I tell you, it won't be a secret. But, maybe you do need to know, because sooner or later you will be able to see for yourself." Mary giggled as she put Thomas' hand on her stomach.

# Chapter 19

# The Discovery

The aroma of coffee cooking on the stove woke Mary early Saturday morning. As she greeted her mother-in-law with a kiss, she prepared to get ready for the long day. Katherine was already frying bacon and baking biscuits. After a few gulps of coffee, Mary ran outside to the porch and emptied what little was in her stomach.

"I thought so," Katherine smiled and said. "You just have that unmistakable glow. You are going to have a baby, aren't you?"

"I guess you are right. I told Thomas last night I thought I was pregnant. I have been getting a little sick each morning, looks like we will have a baby in May. I am excited and scared at the same time, Katherine."

"Oh, honey, you will do fine. You aren't the first to have a baby later in life. You will be a great mother and I am excited about another grandchild. I was planning on going back home to Upton, but if we have a new baby to plan for, along with the new house, perhaps, I better stay here and help you. What do you think, Mary?"

"Katherine, do you really think that we could do without you? Besides, I want to make sure that you are here to deliver this wee one. I suppose you have delivered all of Thomas' babies?" Mary asked.

"Well, all of them but Johnny. I was away at a family reunion and Doc was out of town. But Rissa wasn't due for another month, at least. I had left word with a new mid-wife that just in case, she would know about Rissa."

"And she had the baby while you were gone?" Mary asked almost in disbelief.

"Sure did. By the time Thomas went to fetch the mid-wife and Della Caswell…you know Della is always good to help with births and such. Anyway, he dropped off the midwife, went to get Della, thought he had plenty of time. But by the time he got home, little Johnny had been born. That midwife, left as soon as they got there. Like a thief in the night, she was. Didn't even clean up, course Della did that and was glad to, but I would never leave my mothers like that," Katherine said disgustedly.

"But everything turned out okay with Johnny and Rissa?"

"Well, truthfully, Rissa had problems after that childbirth. You know a lot of first-time mothers have baby blues after delivery. Rissa kept telling us that she heard two babies crying and she wanted to know where the other baby was. Just sad that the midwife didn't take time to care of Rissa, didn't tell her what was happening. Took awhile for Rissa to get through it."

"Oh, my, I better get ready. We have to leave soon!"

After breakfast and devotion, Mary packed up and was ready to go. "Don't you want me to go with you ladies?" Thomas asked.

"I think we can do it, unless you just want to be with us. It will be a day of girl talk, mostly, and a lot of work. I have to admit, the way I feel right now, I'm a little queasy," Mary replied.

"Then, it's done, I am going with you. I would feel better since you will be gone all day, and since we have to protect our little one," Thomas said with pride.

Thomas warned the children to stay out of trouble and to help Katherine. Nellie said Mike was coming to check on the sheep. Tommie promised he was going to clean out the horse stalls. Katherine said she and Renie were going to make a new outfit for her doll, Ella.

Lyssa, Leah and Baby Oleta were ready when the Cosbys arrived. Everyone had packed a snack, and a jug of water. Hopefully, the rain would hold off until tomorrow, but it worried Thomas they would be out for such a long day. Thomas prayed a short prayer for their safety.

Nellie finished her chores. The cows were milked, and the milk was strained and secured in the spring house. Nellie made a special effort to clean the floor, pitching a handful of slivered lye soap, switching with a broom and fresh spring water. Nellie picked up a plate with a chunk of butter and smelled its lovely sweetness. Granma always made a design on the butter. This one had a butterfly. Nellie covered it with a heavy cloth. She checked the late apples stored in the back, taking a perfect apple with her.

As Nellie started up the hill, she scanned the beautiful creek hillside. The enormous walnut and oak trees made an impenetrable covering on the hill. Her favorite trees were the sycamore; the white bark made them so queenly-looking.

Enjoying every crisp bite of her apple, Nellie sat down on the log bench and watched the creek flow around the pebble island where they had played so many times. Squirrels frolicked around the trees and a redheaded woodpecker pounded at a tree nearby. Nellie often sat there above the springhouse, just watching and thinking about how beautiful the creek setting was. She could never bear the thought of leaving this special place. Her father had always told her he was the guardian of God's beautiful land. She understood because the land was blessed with the love of the animals, the fish, the birds, the wildflowers, trees; everything that lived there was happy and blessed.

Nellie walked downhill to the creek and thanked God for all her blessings. The head of the creek was under the three-hundred foot cliff. Huge rocks and ledges formed around the creek, almost like a protection for the many springs that sprang up at the bottom. Often, she had tried to count the springs, but she was never sure how many. She figured there were probably twelve springs that actually surfaced at Roundstone Creek. Of course, every time she visited the creek, she had to drink from the fresh springs. Nellie kneeled beside the shallow water, splashed the cold water on her face and marveled at the freshness.

The creek ran clear most all of the time, except during a really big rain, and then the water might get muddy. She laughed when she thought of Paul's favorite saying, 'That creek, it is just as clare as clare can be!' And it was clear, it was crystal clear! It was Nellie's favorite place in the world, right here with the cliffs, trees, and springs. Nellie thought about all the people who had been there before her. Johnny had been fascinated with the Indians who had lived there, and so was she. Often she visualized families living on the creek, hunting, fishing, cooking, and children playing.

Nellie looked up at the ledge where the boys had found the cache of Cherokee items. Several years ago, Johnny saw something in the crevice and devised a plan to retrieve it. Her brothers had attempted a dangerous adventure to get to the crevice on the cliff. Johnny's tenacity was stopped only by his imagination. Obviously when the items were stashed in the crevice, the huge rock ledge had not been broken off and it was easy to get to it. However, the large rock which had faced the ledge had dropped off and was at the bottom of the ravine. Nellie thought about what Johnny had said to Dad when they found the treasure. "There was something else in there, Dad, please, help us go back. Help me get in there; I have to see what I left," Johnny had said.

"Whatever it is, it is not worth you risking your life. You could fall and get killed trying that stunt. Promise me, Johnny you will not try to get back there again," Thomas had warned.

"Okay, okay, but I tell you there is something I couldn't reach in the crevice," Johnny pleaded with his dad.

———————•———————

"Wow, you are deep in thought! Could have been a bear slip up on you, and you would never have heard it," Tommie teased after poking Nellie in the ribs.

Sitting beside Nellie, the boys continued their conversation about adventures. Tommie pointed to the treacherous ledge. "Now right up there, Mike, is where Johnny got the Cherokee stuff I showed you."

"What, no way, there ain't no way you could get up there."

"Well, Johnny figured out a way. He had a rope harness he wore. We put the rope through a pulley on that tree over there and I was on top of that big rock, see there? So Johnny jumped off the bank and I pulled the rope. I pulled him over to the ledge, like pulling a big catfish out of the river. Then, he was able to swing close enough that he could get the stuff inside, but he couldn't reach all the way in the crevice. So close, if his fingers had been a little longer... Anyway, I thought he was dead when I let him drop to the ravine below. He didn't say nothin' for a while and was pale as a frog's belly. Reckon it knocked him senseless and probably the rope cut off the blood to his legs."

"What did he leave in the crevice? Can we go get it? Bet there is something exciting in there."

"Woo, wait, Daddy told Johnny never to do that again. He said Johnny could have gotten killed trying to recover his treasure," Nellie said as she grasped Tommie's arm.

"Yeah, but he didn't tell me, and I am part Cherokee. I need to find out what is there. Let's get the rope and pulley. Look there, that limb is leaning toward the ledge. Could be with my weight it would lower me right to the crevice," Mike said. Clearly, Mike was not going to be stopped as he was already making his way up the hill.

"Well, as long as you want to try, I am willing to help. That limb wasn't there when Johnny tried to reach the crevice. The tree has grown, of course, and now it would probably be the best way to get to the cave." Tommie was excited as he followed Mike up the hill.

"Hey, guys, be careful. You know Dad wouldn't want you doing this, Tommie! Someday, you are going to learn," Nellie warned.

"Dad wouldn't want us using the harness, but we can climb a tree, just like a couple gray squirrels," Tommie said as he scurried up the hill.

Mike was already skimming up the large sycamore tree and testing the limbs. Tommie was behind him and warning him to take his time and be careful. Nellie was just nervous for the boys. Why can't they just leave it? Certainly they had enough to do without chasing a silly Cherokee feather, or whatever, Nellie thought.

The boys were on different limbs, getting as close to the end as they could. Mike's limb was bending with his weight, and Tommie kept giving him encouragement. Mike scooted close to the end, but the limb wasn't reaching the crevice. Tommie went up another limb above Mike. Mike reached a small branch on the limb Tommie was on and gently pulled it down. Tommie was giving him instructions as he got closer and closer to the crevice. He dared not go any further out on the limb, but it was so close, he could almost touch the crevice now. Tommie reached toward the crevice, but his entire body started trembling from the strain.

Mike said, "Wait, Tommie, I don't want you to get hurt. Let me change places with you. I think with my weight and my arms being longer will work."

The boys changed places on the tree while Nellie watched anxiously. "Oh, please, Lord, keep them safe. They need your safety right now."

Soon Mike reached the crevice. He managed to get his fingers around the rock which framed the prize. "Hey, Tommie, see if you can hold on to my shirt, just to steady me a little," Mike shouted nervously.

As Tommie reached for Mike's shirt, Nellie said another prayer.

"Got ya!" Tommie exclaimed, "Just be careful!"

Mike was able to work his arm around the opening and to the back of the crevice. "Be careful, Mike, there could be a snake in there!" Nellie yelled.

Mike proceeded to reach into the limestone rock opening, apparently not scared of Nellie's snake threat. Within seconds, he pulled his hand out with something like a roll. Both young men scurried down the tree anxious to see their treasure.

Mike unrolled the buckskin cloth and in it was a bag and a piece of paper. "What, I went to all that trouble for a piece of buckskin and a stupid letter!" Mike stated.

"Hey, wait, this could be important. Let's look at it. Yeah and here is a sack of something." Nellie began to read the letter aloud.

> I tracked down and killed a Cherokee brave. These items were on him, but I couldn't stand to carry them with me. I am leaving it here. Someday I may be back to Kentucky, and I will check on it. If someone reads this, well, I guess I didn't make it back.
>
> I am thirteen and I was in the woods checking my traps when the Cherokee attacked my dad. I heard the noise and went to a spot where I could see what was going on. When I got there, it was too late. Four Cherokee had killed my mother, little brother and sister and they piled their pitiful bodies on a rock for everyone to see. They torched the house and hooped and hollered like it was a party. Finally, I shot at the Indians with my slingshot, and they yelped and ran into the woods. I tried to track all of them down, but I only got one of them. I threw my knife at his back as he ran from me, and it felt good.
>
> After I had my little bit of revenge, I went back, dug a hole, and buried my folks. I don't feel bad about what I did, but I wanted someone to know my family is buried behind the house foundation. I piled several rocks on top of the grave. I am leaving Kentucky; don't know if I will be back. Kentucky hasn't been so good to me. May God forgive me for what I did! Mack Jackson

# Chapter 20

# A Baby & Caves

Tommie, Nellie, and Renie were outside with the sheep when they heard the wagon roll in. "How are you going to tell Dad what you found in the crevice?" Nellie asked Tommie. "He isn't going to be happy."

"We could keep it a secret, just for a while," Tommie pleaded.

"Okay, but sooner or later, he is going to find out. Secrets never remain secrets long," Nellie warned. "Let's go. I want to hear what they learned about the orders."

The family was chattering, and everyone full of questions about the day. Mary had packages and gifts to show the family. Mary had convinced Thomas a gift for the children would be nice since they did not get to go with them. She knew she had won Renie's love, but was not sure about Nellie or Katherine. Of course, it would take plenty of time to win Tommie, but she was going to try.

Before Mary had an opportunity to present the gifts, Renie blurted out the news. "Tommie and Nellie went up to that rock and got the thing out of there that Johnny couldn't get out."

Silence "What? Is that true?" Thomas was clearly upset for he had warned Johnny not to go, and Tommie and Nellie knew that.

"I didn't go up the tree. It was Mike and Tommie! And by the way, Renie, it was a secret!" Nellie scolded.

Katherine saw there was going to be a problem, so she diffused the matter as quickly as she could. "Seems I remember a time when I told you, Thomas, not to go to the Widow Lokey's tool shed but you just couldn't help yourself. So, remember that before you start with the lashes," Katherine added shaking her finger in his face.

"I remember, but they could have gotten hurt. After Johnny, I just don't want my kids taking any chances. You have to realize that." Calming himself, Thomas asked, "And just how did you reach the crevice?"

"Well, that tree there by the ledge has grown a lot in six years since Johnny tried to get there. So, Mike and me, well, we just climbed out on a branch till we could reach it. And, Dad, guess what we found!" Tommie exclaimed. "In a buckskin was a letter, and there were arrowheads and stones in a pouch, all rolled up together."

Mike strolled into the cabin where the family was talking about the find. "Hey, everybody! Thought I better come back after I finished my chores. I wanted to explain that it was my idea that we reach the treasure."

"Well, no harm done, Mike. I am glad that everyone is safe. Let's see what you found," Thomas stated as he looked at the children.

Nellie unrolled the buckskin she had stuffed in her pocket. Since she had already read the letter once, she put the emphasis on the gory parts and the sadness where it was needed.

"What a story! That is what Della mentioned when she told me there was a murder and someone was buried there. Her husband was Cherokee, and I am sure he knew some of the story," Katherine said. "Now, I know we have to give the family a proper funeral and a gravestone. Perhaps that will give peace to the place. We will get with Pastor Ship and decide on a good time for a funeral. Thomas, what can we do about a stone for the family?"

"I am sure that the neighbors will want to take up money and buy a stone. We will find out about the cost," Thomas answered.

Tommie spilled the contents of the small pouch that was found in the buckskin. "There might be some value here in this stuff Mack put in the buckskin. Do you think that it might sell for enough to purchase the stone for the family?"

Thomas, Mary, and Katherine looked at the arrowheads and jewels in the pouch. Clearly, the Cherokee had taken some of the stones from other settlers as there were pearls, jade, turquoise and diamonds.

"Good idea! These stones would probably pay for an entire cemetery. However, what about keeping these together for a while, just in case," Thomas mentioned. "I think the community would like to honor the family by helping out with the stone."

Nellie walked outside with Mike as he prepared to leave. The two held hands and walked to the barn where Mike had tied his horse. "You need all those jewels, Nellie. You deserve to have rings on your all your fingers. You are so special," Mike said as he nervously untied his horse.

"Mike Caswell! Jewels are not important! It is how you live your life that is important. You know my dad says if you had a million dollars, you would only want a million more! So, don't figure me as the kind of girl who wants jewels." Nellie looked into Mike's eyes and held her hand flat over his heart. "I just want this, Mike," Nellie whispered so low she didn't know if Mike heard.

Mike hugged Nellie goodbye and gave her a kiss on the cheek. "Since you are sixteen, maybe your father won't mind if I give you a birthday kiss."

Nellie waved goodbye to Mike and ran back in the house, thrilled with the hug and kiss from Mike. Butterflies from head to toe filled Nellie as her mind relived the kiss. Mike was the love of her life and she knew that no matter what her future held for her, Mike would be there with her, together always.

After the family had their meal, Thomas read from the Bible. Thomas talked about his family and how the family would be growing and changing in the next few months. "Soon we will begin work on our new house, which each one of you will have a room. Nellie will be able to do her spinning in her room and Tommie will have a place to do his artwork and store his collection of books. I am sure Renie will soon have a collection also. Mom will get a room on the bottom floor along with us and one other person. Guess who gets to share the downstairs bedrooms?" Thomas grinned as he asked the children.

"Well when Mama's parents come, you said they had to sleep upstairs. Who else is coming? More company?" Nellie asked.

"Oh, Thomas, just tell them. We, or I am going to have a baby," Mary said.

"A baby?" Renie said and she looked at Nellie. Renie's face was downfallen. Her bottom lip started to quiver as she realized she would no longer be the baby of the family.

"Sounds okay to me. I just don't get excited about babies. They cry a lot, don't they?" Tommie asked.

Nellie knew she had to think fast. "Oh, Renie, you get to be the big sister now. The baby will probably love you more than anybody."

Renie wiped away a tear and agreed that she would be the baby's favorite of all the family.

Mary asked Renie to come sit in her lap as she talked to her about how much help she was going to need. Renie was being asked to grow up which she hadn't had to do before today. Mary had not anticipated such a reaction from Renie.

Suddenly, Mary remembered the gifts. "Thomas would you care to give the children the gifts we purchased for them?"

Thomas, for the first time, was glad they had bought the gifts. He hadn't realized the impact another baby would have on the family.

"Renie, why not come sit in your father's lap, and we will let Mary hand out the gifts? She was the one who carefully picked them out for you."

The children were touched by Mary's thoughtfulness and showed their appreciation by their thanks. Katherine was happy to see the children accepting Mary and the baby. If she could rid her own mind of the suspicion of Mary. Why the dream and why the feeling that there was something about Mary that was a dark secret?

Later when Katherine and Mary were not around, Thomas whispered. "Tommie, I am proud of you, even though I wouldn't have wanted you to do what you did. You and Mike solved a mystery we would never have been able to solve if you had not retrieved that letter. But, don't do it again, not without me!" Thomas tried to act mad, but he was actually pleased with the boys.

Sunday morning church services gave Katherine and Thomas the opportunity to approach Pastor Ship about the Jackson family. "We were wondering if we might hold a funeral service for the family?" Katherine asked.

"Also, we would like to have a stone erected for the family. Since four of the family members are lying there in the grave dug by a thirteen-year old, it would be nice to have a stone," Thomas added.

"What about I mention it this morning at church? I am sure we could take up a special offering for them. I can't think of anything better for us to do than to erect a stone for the family," Pastor Ship replied.

The church members felt honored to give an offering for the stone. Thomas offered to get the stone up as soon as possible. After that, the pastor would hold a belated funeral for the family. Mary suggested she and Tommie draw a design for the stone. The stone should be attractive, especially since it would be so close to the Spurgeon house.

# Chapter 21

# Cave Hunt

Thin slices of apples filled the dishpan as Katherine sat in her favorite rocker on the front porch slicing the last of the tart red apples. Her family had certainly changed and there would be more changes. Katherine considered the morning's devotion. First Thessalonians 4:1-3, Paul wrote... *we urge and exhort in the Lord Jesus that you should abound more and more, just as you received from us how you ought to walk and to please God.* As Katherine thought about the passage she realized that once a person is sanctified by Christ, she is constantly being molded or changed into what Jesus wants her to be. "Father, I pray I will be continually connected to you and my life will show it to others. Give me a heart like yours, Father," Katherine prayed.

Nellie opened the front door and stepped over Goldie who was chasing rabbits in her sleep. "What are you going to do with the apples, Gran?" Nellie asked as she noticed that she had scared Katherine. "Oh, sorry I didn't mean to scare you."

"Oh, that's okay, Nellie. Are you feeling better?" Katherine asked.

Nellie had awoken with a headache and sore throat and didn't feel like going to school, which was unusual for Nellie. Nellie sat beside her grandmother on the swing. "Don't know if I feel better, just tired of being in bed."

"I was just thinking about our morning devotion. I pray as we work on the Ladies Day that we will have a heart like Jesus." Katherine handed Nellie one of the apple slices. "I am going to dry them. What do you think? Are they sour enough for a good apple pie?"

Nellie made a silly face as she chewed the apple. "So, does an apple have to be sour to make a good pie?"

"Like people, apples can be used many ways. Some apples are good the way they are. Some apples, like people need a lot of help from sweetness."

Nellie interrupted. "So, you think Mary is a sour apple and we have to help her to make her sweet and good? Something is just not right with that apple! Have you noticed that she never prays to, or talks about Jesus Christ? She prays only to The Lord, Our Father."

"Yes, I have noticed, but maybe we are just not familiar with her upbringing. She has said that her father had a very domineering way," Katherine said hoping to change the subject.

"You know the Ladies' Day event is less than a month away. I think we have volunteers for jobs for the day, the food and flowers and the clean-up. I like the theme that you suggested, 'A Heart like Jesus' because Christians want to be more like Jesus."

Nellie picked up another apple slice. "Yes, and Mary bought some red wool yarn and is making hearts for the ladies to wear. I think everyone will enjoy our guest speakers and the special singer."

Katherine picked up the last of the apples in her dishpan and began cutting off bad spots. "It was so nice of Linda Johnson to donate her old piano to the school. Thomas said that he would get it moved for us before the big day." Feeling of Nellie's forehead, Katherine sighed.

"You still feel a little warm. Nellie, we just need to pray for the success of the meeting. Our goal should be to get the message out to the women about the spreading of God's Word all over the world. There are so many countries and people who do not know the Lord and do not have Bibles to read."

Nellie kissed her grandmother on the cheek, "Yeah, Lyssa and Leah have a really good idea, to give each family a Bible as they witness to them. But, I think I will go back to bed."

Nellie was quickly growing up and Katherine could see how much she was like her father and her mother. Katherine prayed for her grandchildren to find Christian spouses when that time came. She had always prayed that whatever her grandchildren did in their lives, with their spouses, or alone, they would always follow the instructions of the Lord.

As Katherine finished the last basket of apples, she realized they still had the crib Renie used as a baby. She would ask Mary if she wanted to use it. If not she would give it to Lyssa for the shop. That would be one way to help them as they worked.

Katherine had a couple of buckets filled with the thinly sliced apples. She covered a new tin with a thin layer of muslin, placed the evenly spread slices, then brought the material back over and covered them. Covering the apples insured that the gnats, flies and other insects would be deterred.

"Goodness! You finished all the apples before I could help." Mary stepped upon the porch and picked up a slice of apple for Thomas and herself. "Um, so good."

"Nothing like a good apple!" Thomas said as he munched on the slice.

"Isn't the dance next Saturday night? A luscious apple pie would be good to take! Your apple pies are the best. Your crust is always so flaky it shatters." Mary smiled at Katherine as if trying to win her favor.

"That's a good idea, but, of course Edna Mae always takes an apple pie. What about a tom turkey? I was wondering if we might take turkey with sage dressing."

"Oh, that's a good idea. I'll take a large bowl of corn salad. We still have a lot of peppers and onions, and it will be something different," Mary said as she lifted a brow. "I just hope the dance doesn't get out of hand. I thought last year that we might have some trouble."

Thomas gave Mary a hug as he stepped off the porch. "We will make sure if there is any drinking they do it outside of the dance. I will put your apples on the chicken house roof as soon as you get them ready. Hopefully, we still have a few hot days to get them dried."

"Thank you, Son. I will leave them on the table and you can get them any time. Thought me and Mary might go check on Lyssa and Leah. What do you think?" Katherine looked hopefully at Mary.

"We can go right now, if you want, and be back by the time the children get home. And we could take a few apples for an apple pie," Mary added.

"Oh, would you want to let them have the old crib in the barn? I know they could use it in their shop for Baby Oleta, but didn't know if you might want to use it," Katherine asked.

"That's a wonderful idea. Sure they can have it. Not that it wouldn't be good enough, but I am sure Thomas will want to make this little one a crib. We can load it and be on our way."

At Roundstone School another school day was over as Andrea waved goodbye to the last student.

"So much to do, every day is a challenge," Andrea said to herself. Thankfully, her thoughtful husband had agreed to come back to school and pick her up after he had taken the children home. Pete enjoyed taking care of the children and she needed the time to get a display on the wall and grade some papers.

Andrea said a prayer for each of her students. She walked around the classroom and prayed a blessing on each chair and desk. As she was finished her prayer, she heard horses approaching.

Opening the door of the schoolhouse, Andrea saw two men on horses, "Ma'am, I'm Sheriff Konner and this here's my deputy. We're lookin' for a man on the run. We know, for sure, he killed an ol' woman in town and injured her husband. Mr. Wiseman, the injured man, was able to identify the man, so we know he's our killer. We want to search around the place and make sure he is not here," the sheriff said as he slid off his horse.

As soon as they left, Andrea felt unsafe. "Now, this is silly. I know the Lord is with me and will protect me. I will be fine," she told herself. "Until Pete comes, I will continue with my work."

---

At the Cosby place, Thomas was draw-knifing a log when the sheriff and his deputy rode up. Sheriff Konner told Thomas what had happened. Tommie and Mike had just gotten home from school and were listening to the news from the sheriff.

"We figure he came this way. Someone saw him running on foot at the top of Roundstone hill. You haven't seen him, have you?"

"No we haven't. We will check the cabins, barns, and buildings. Do you think he has a gun on him?" Thomas asked.

"Don't know, after shooting and killing Mrs. Wiseman, he shot Mr. Wiseman, Hank. But old Hank was able to go get help. The low-down murdering thief took their money and hightailed it this way. We did find a gun on the road, but it was empty. Figured he ran out of bullets," Sheriff Konner said. "We will help look, don't want you running up on him by yourself. He could have another gun."

While the men started the look for the fugitive, Mike and Tommie began their own investigation. "Tommie, let's look at that map of Johnny's. I bet the killer is hiding in one of the caves," Mike said.

As the boys were in the loft looking over the map, Nellie overheard their conversation. "We can start here at this wildcat cave and then go over to the mushroom cave. He could be hiding out there," Tommie said.

Mike thought a minute as he looked at the map. "No, he won't be in the wildcat cave; it's too small, and he couldn't get in and out without a lot of trouble. He would be in one of the caves that is easier, like the mushroom cave or this limestone cave right here," Mike said as he pointed to the map. "What do you say we go over and just look to see if he is hiding out there?"

As the boys came down from the loft, Nellie begged, "Guys, don't try to be heroes. You need to stay here where it is safe. You could get yourselves killed."

"Hey, we aren't going to try to get him, we are just going to sneak around and see if he is there, then we will get the sheriff to come get him," Mike said.

"Boys, be safe," Nellie told them as they left. Nellie prepared a snack for Renie and herself and said a prayer for the boys' safety. Seemed like she was doing a lot of that lately. "Renie, let's work on our knitting right now since we can't do the chores."

Both girls had learned from Mary how to knit and purl which was all they needed for their hat project. They were making a ribbed edge to their red wool hats. Both girls needed to concentrate: knit one, purl one, knit one, purl one.

"Where do you think the killer is, Nellie? Do you think he might come in our house?" Renie asked.

Nellie put down her knitting and gave Renie a hug. "Hey, sweetie, I am here, and I will protect you. Nothing is going to happen to you. Our Dad is close by, and I am sure he will be back in to check on us soon. Gran and Mary have gone to town, but they should be back soon too. Don't worry," Nellie said as she gave Renie a kiss on her auburn curls.

"Now, I forgot where I was," Renie said. "Do I knit next or purl?"

"Let me see, okay, your last stitch looks like a purl, see this little bump, that is why it is called a purl, so the next one is a knit."

"You are so smart, Nellie. I love you. You're the best big sister ever!" Renie smiled at Nellie. "Are you like Mama, Nellie?"

Nellie thought for a moment and replied, "Renie, I wish I could be like Mama. She was the best mother anyone could ever have. Mama was beautiful,

145

and you look a lot like her, more than any of us. She was so smart, she could do anything. Mama played the piano, and the banjo. She made baskets from oak trees, and could cook anything. She decorated the house with flowers and all the things she made, like quilts and the art pieces. Our mother was also a dedicated Christian. She made sure she prayed before she did anything. She was the best, Renie, and I am so sorry you didn't have long with her. But she is an angel now, in Heaven looking down on you, protecting us now."

Thomas rushed in, "Nellie, do you know where Tommie is? I have looked everywhere."

"Well, Mike was with him. They thought they might go look in the Wildcat cave or the Limestone cave for the killer," Nellie said. "I didn't want to leave the house to get you. I was scared."

"That's okay; Nellie, you and Renie stay here. I am going to tell the sheriff where the boys are. They may be onto him. We hadn't thought about hiding out in a cave. Did they take the map?"

"I think they did, but I heard them say the mushroom cave is close to the Stahls' place and the Limestone cave is close to Steve Caldwell's place," Nellie said, anxious for both boys.

"I'll be back, girls. Stay right here. I don't want to have to worry about you, too!"

# Chapter 22

# The Witness

---

"Look!" Mike said pointing at the rock which had recently been skinned of its moss. "Here's tracks where he's come this way. Must be headed for the limestone cave."

"Which way here?" Tommie whispered as he looked at the map. "If he knows where the cave is, he will turn...supposed to be a big rock here... where..."

Both boys stopped to look at the map. "Right here, it is. So we go straight after we turn at the rock, right?" Mike asked, trying to keep his voice from shaking.

"Yeah, looks like it. Maybe we can pick up a track soon." Tommie looked around for tracks. "This looks like maybe he jumped over this fallen tree." As soon as Tommie saw where the outlaw had jumped over the tree, he motioned, "This way!"

The boys were being as quiet as possible, still, a little scared but running on adrenalin. "It's not much farther, just down this hill," Mike said as he pointed the direction. The boys slowed down as they started sliding on the leaves and branches which littered the hillside.

"Why don't we split up? I'll go on that side, and you go around the hickory over there," Tommie whispered.

The boys were on both sides of the cave as they took their places, each hidden behind large trees. Tommie sneaked a peek at the cave entrance well hidden by trees and rock in front of it. Although they didn't see anyone, they could hear a sound like beating on the ground with something. Mike was anxious to try to get a look inside the cave. He crawled along the side of the ledge where he couldn't be seen. Feeling courageous, Mike rose up and peeked over the edge. He saw the murderer beating on the ground. What is he doing? Mike thought.

Mike motioned for Tommie to get help while he made sure the killer didn't escape. But then, what was he going to do when the killer tried to get away? Hit him with the map? Mike ducked his head and tried to calm down. His heart was beating so loud he was afraid the killer would hear it. Something came down over his head binding him. He could not move.

"What do we have here? Looks like a kid, an Injun kid even. Guess I could get rid of you without anyone even worrying about you." The man holding him down was stepping on his head and Mike could not free himself.

"Come on up here, boy. I can use you!" He said as he yanked Mike up by the shirt collar.

The sheriff didn't say this guy was really big! Mike thought, trying to fight back. "Let me go," Mike whimpered. "I won't tell anyone you're here. Just let me go."

"No, can't do that, we got to stick together now, son. See, I figure they won't find me for a while and when they do, I have you to bargain with. I have to thank you for finding me, I guess. Meanwhile, don't even try to get away, or I will shoot you in the back. You probably already heard that I don't care to shoot people, make no matter, young or old, and I'll shoot you if I have to," the killer said huskily.

Mike sat in the corner of the cave, as he hoped and prayed the Sheriff would rescue him. He figured since he wasn't tied up, he could run away when he had a chance.

"And, oh, if you are thinkin' about runnin' I'm going to tie you up right here so you will be my hostage for a while. A few years ago, me and a friend explored some of the caves around here, so we had ropes. Lucky, for you, we left the ropes, so I can tie you up instead of me killin' you right now."

The killer pulled ropes first around Mike's wrists, and then he pulled and yanked on them again. Mike was reminded how the ropes had cut into Nellie's wrists. Now, he really knew how much it must have hurt. Next, he pulled a rope over Mike's ankles and did the same, yanking and pulling at the rope. The killer seemed to want Mike to know he didn't care to hurt him or even kill him.

"My name is Mike, what's yours?" Mike asked. Maybe, he could get to know him, at least before the man killed him.

"Bob," he answered as he watched the opening of the cave.

"Well, Bob, wish we weren't meeting like this, but maybe God brought us together for a reason." Then, Mike started singing hymns. "Shout glory to God, all the earth!" Mike kept singing and singing louder with each verse.

"Stop singing!" Bob yelled.

"I am reminded of Paul when he was imprisoned. He thanked God for his blessings and he sang. This song is a song from the 66th Psalm. "Come and listen, all you who fear God, let me tell you what he has done for me." Mike was astonished at his own courage and the words that were coming to him. Although he was scared, he still had a peace that was a comforter.

"I don't want to hear it," Bob grumbled.

"Okay, I will change songs, 'Hear, O Lord, my righteous plea; listen to my cry...'" Mike continued to sing while Bob peered out the opening.

"You know Bob, when you have Jesus in your heart, you have faith. Do you know my Jesus, Bob? He is always with me, and he has told me in his Word he loves me. John 3:16 says 'For God so loved the world that He gave His only begotten Son, that whoever believes in Him should not perish but have everlasting life'.

"You, see Bob, God loves everyone, even the worst sinner in the world. If you believe Jesus Christ is God's son, and that he was born, crucified, and raised from the grave, He will save you. Bob, do you feel like you need a Savior? Do you want me to pray for you?" Mike asked Bob.

"I don't want to talk to you about God. I had a good friend who talked to me about God, and then God took him away. So, if God is so good, why did he take my friend?"

"We all have people who are taken away from us. My mother died when I was only three. But, I have the assurance I will see her when I get to heaven because she was a Christian." Mike couldn't tell if he was making headway or not, but he kept talking.

"No matter what we have done, God will forgive us of our sins if we pray for forgiveness." Mike watched Bob for a sign.

"I will never be forgiven because I have sinned worse than anybody. God knows what I have done. I shot and killed one person and maybe two because I hated them for what they did. I know God is not going to just forgive me."

For the first time, Mike was not afraid of Bob. He was seeing a different side of Bob and he felt a compassion and love for the man. Mike paused, said a silent prayer.

"Bob, I love you, and God loves you. I am not worried about what you may do to me; I just want to be your friend. I want to say a prayer for you. You can join me if you like, or just listen," Mike explained.

"Dear Heavenly Father, we praise you for the wonderful Lord and Savior you are. We know your Word promises whoever comes and asks forgiveness will be saved. Father, today we come to you asking forgiveness of Bob's sins. He believes in Jesus Christ, that he is the Savior, and he was crucified for our sins, but was raised from the dead. He believes you can forgive him."

Mike opened his eyes and saw the big man beside him, but more importantly, all the ropes were loosened. Mike was filled with the spirit as he asked, "Do you want to pray with me now, Bob?"

Bob knelt beside Mike and repeated the sinner's prayer. A miraculous thing happened, something Mike would never forget. The big man was on his knees beside Mike, sobbing, asking God's forgiveness. Mike prayed, Bob prayed, and Mike thanked God for His love.

When the two opened their eyes, there were others surrounding them. The sheriff, his deputy, Thomas, and Tommie were there.

The sheriff brought out his gun and said, "Bob, you are under arrest for the murders of Mr. and Mrs. Wiseman. I am going to take you in."

Bob willingly followed the sheriff's instructions, and as he lifted his head he said, "Thank you, Jesus for saving my soul. I know I did wrong, Sheriff, I will go along with no trouble."

Sheriff Konner took Bob while Tommie pulled the ropes off Mike. "You wanted more rope, but this is a heck of a way to get it, Mike!" Tommie became serious, "I heard you witnessing to that guy. You did a great job. I don't think I would have been so brave."

"Well, I always heard when the time comes, the Holy Spirit will lead you to what you need to say, and it happened, Tommie. I felt the words coming out of my mouth and I felt a love for that man, Bob, one of God's children. I praise God for what He did here today, and I will never forget it," Mike said.

"I don't think anyone will forget it, Mike. We better get you home. Your grandmother will be worried about you." Tommie slapped him on the back and gave him a hug. "You have been an encouragement to me, Mike."

Thomas checked in at the house. Katherine and Mary were home with the girls. "Do we have an extra Bible, Mom? I want to go to the jail and give the prisoner a Bible and talk with him a few minutes. We witnessed an amazing thing awhile ago. I will let Tommie tell you about it; right now I am going to catch up with the sheriff."

Sheriff Konner was putting the prisoner in jail when Thomas walked in. "Could I have a moment with the prisoner, Sheriff?" Thomas asked.

"Sure, Thomas, but you know, just because he got right with the Lord, doesn't mean he isn't accountable for what he did. Murder is murder."

"I know, Sheriff, I just want to talk to him a few minutes," Thomas replied.

"I'll give you ten minutes, then you have to leave," the sheriff said.

"Thank you, Sheriff," Thomas said as he went in the cell and took a seat. "Bob, I'm Thomas Cosby. I am sorry to hear of the trouble that happened. However, I heard what you did today, asking for salvation, and I am proud to have you as a brother in Christ." Thomas extended his hand and they shook hands. "I wanted to bring you this Bible to read. It belonged to my son. I am sure it will be a help to you."

"That is good of you, and I appreciate it. I know I won't have long to live here on this earth, know I face a hanging. What I did was wrong, and I have to pay for it. But because of all that, I met my Savior and now I am a new person in Christ. Thank you, Thomas."

The two men embraced and Thomas left the jail. He had witnessed the power of God in church, at home and many places, but there was something about that cave where the Holy Spirit was so strong, he would never forget. He would never forget how Mike had witnessed to a complete stranger, a killer at that! Mike had proven he was a disciple of Christ.

# Chapter 23

# Family Lessons

"The mayor said the dance would go on as scheduled for Saturday night. He said Mr. and Mrs. Wiseman would not have wanted it cancelled. They had always prepared and went to the dance together," Thomas said as he relayed the information to the family Tuesday evening.

"You know, Mrs. Wiseman would have enjoyed having a fabric shop in Upton. She sure did love to sew." Thomas suddenly looked at Mary. "How is the shop coming along?"

"When we were there yesterday, we helped paint and clean until we heard the news. The men repaired the roof, and the girls pulled up the planks in the old floor and replaced them. They are pretty handy with tools! Leah built a couple of the pine shelves herself. Lyssa has pulled nails out of the walls where they have been for years. They will be getting the merchandise in another week or so. It is beginning to really look nice, don't you think Katherine?...Katherine?"

"Oh, sorry, I had my mind on something else. Yes, dear, yes it is beginning to look like a shop." Sitting up straight in her chair, her arms folded, she appeared as though she was going to make an announcement. "When I went to the Spurgeon home, when Gil was hurt, Dr. Routt told me he was going to retire, leaving as soon as he could to tie up all his business matters. Moving to Chicago with his daughter. He isn't doing well, having a lot of trouble with his knees, his back and just old age, I guess." Katherine waved her hand as if there was nothing else to do about the matter.

"Oh, no. Well, we hate to see him leave. Say, we could use Saturday night as a going away party for the Doc," Mary said, trying to make the best of the situation.

"Good idea," replied Thomas, "but I don't know what we will do without a doctor. Mom does a lot, but even you can't take his place, Mom."

"Well, I won't. Doc Routt said he has a doctor coming from Lexington. Says he just wants to come to a small place, a good Christian community, so he can semi-retire. He doesn't have a family, just the doc, so he plans on getting here within a month." Katherine gazed at her biscuit as if she was trying to decide whether to take a bite.

"That's great! It's hard to get a doctor in a small place like Upton, so we are blessed to have someone." Mary helped herself to another piece of bacon and tomato. "Getting back to Head to Toe; they are working hard. Lyssa ordered a stand for the window. She wants to make an outfit from her fabrics, and display them each month with a different seasonal look. She has some good ideas."

"So does Leah. You know she told me how she learned how to make hats. When she was a slave in Virginia, her master made her make hats for their mercantile shop in the city. She knows how to make wool hats, straw hats, women's fancy hats, and just about anything. Both girls know how to make shoes and boots, plus they are going to sell ready-made shoes. They have some great plans," Katherine bragged.

"Yeah, and I love the name, 'Head to Toe' because they will have it all. Wonder if they will have underwear and slips?" Nellie asked.

"They are planning a section of underwear, socks, slips, handkerchiefs. You know, Nellie, you and Renie might make some of those knitted hats to sell in their shop. I am sure they would appreciate getting the extra merchandise to fill the store," Mary suggested.

Nellie smiled at Renie. "What do you think? Do you think we can remember what stitches we are on, Renie? I think it is a really good idea, but it takes me so long, and I want to use some of them for Christmas gifts, if I get them made," Nellie said apologetically.

Mary reached for Nellie's hand and patted it. "I understand, completely. I just can't wait to see the fabrics they have ordered. They were trying to choose which fabrics to buy for children's wear, and finally I told them to buy all of their choices. I think both of the girls have really good taste."

Katherine and Mary began clearing the dishes off the table so Thomas could read from the Bible and give the devotion.

"Leah is expecting her baby in late December, may be a Christmas baby," Mary added. "I am so glad we took the crib to the girls. Both of them will be able to put their babies in it while they are working."

"You know, it is wonderful how they became such good friends. It is like God led them right to the church, and Lyssa and Ollie adopted them as family," Thomas said as he turned the pages of the family Bible.

Katherine wiped the tablecloth clean of crumbs. "You know, some people live a lifetime without a really good friend. For Lyssa and Leah, the color issue has never been a problem. Just shows you that all folk, no matter what color they are, are more alike than different. In fact, God made people with hearts for love, and they can choose to have a heart like His, or be indifferent to Jesus and others."

"Ollie and Hobie are good friends, too." Tommie joined in the conversation. "They are always looking out for one another. They work together side by side and get along like brothers. They learn from each other."

"That is the way it should be for all of us, Tommie. We get impatient with others and lose respect. In fact, if everyone would remember the gifts of the spirit, and make them the attributes of their lives, we would be better individuals, a better community and country. Think about it, patience, kindness, joy, long-suffering, wouldn't we all get along better?" Thomas asked.

On Thursday morning, the family left early to leave the prepared food at the church. They would spend the morning at the Wiseman's home where the bodies were laid out, then go to the church for services. The burial would be at the Big Springs Cemetery. Finally, everyone would gather back at church for lunch.

The children had a lot of questions about the Wisemans while at the wake. Nellie admitted she would never go in that house again without thinking about where the coffins had been.

The community turned out for the wake as the Wisemans were always beloved friends and neighbors. People talked about the terrible tragedy and how the murdering varmint should be hung by his toes, or other body parts. Everyone had their own take on the awful death of the Wisemans, but no one had room for a prayer for Bob. No one offered to say a prayer for a killer.

At the funeral, Pastor Ship preached about following the right path, doing what the Lord wants His children to do and not what they want to do. Pastor Ship mentioned Bob had received salvation and wanted to be baptized. Pastor Ship told the group about Bob who had been faithfully reading the Bible.

"Really a sad funeral, wasn't it?" Mary commented.

"Well, funerals do tend to be sad," Katherine replied. "Sad because they only had one daughter, Cindy, and she had run off with that Bob! Bob had been an orphan and lived from one relative to another until he ran away and took care of himself. That was probably why he knew where the cave was; he had been familiar with the community. Now, we don't even know where Cindy is. Bob said he would tell everyone when it was the right time. You know, he might even have killed her."

"That's right, he could have. Who knows?" Mary said, nodding an affirmation.

"Don't you think Pastor Ship did a good job with the sermon?" Thomas asked, needing to change the subject. "I thought his choice of scripture was unique; don't think I have ever heard that scripture as a funeral message. Proverbs 16:25, 'There is a way that seems right to a man, but its end is the way of death'."

I wonder if Bob thought he was right, and the Wisemans thought they were right. He made a good point," Thomas continued. "The phrase is repeated several times in the book of Judges, I think it is chapter 21 that says 'everyone did what was right in his own eyes'. What we should be doing is what God says is right."

"The good outcome is that Bob was saved through the experience. And to think he was led to Christ by a sixteen-year-old boy," Katherine said.

After the meal, the group, traveled to the Spurgeon place. Thomas and his crew had already placed the stone. Nellie and Renie had picked a nice bouquet of wildflowers, tied with yellow satin bows, for both funerals. As they were traveling, the family speculated on the slain children.

"Just think," Nellie said, holding on to the bouquets, "one of those children could have grown up to be a preacher or a missionary, or maybe a doctor for a community like ours."

Katherine concluded, "Of course it is always a tragedy when a family perishes, like this one, well…Mack did survive, but the worst part is no one was there to grieve with Mack, to help him through the tragedy. No one there to offer hope, the hope that we have in Jesus Christ, and that one day we will see our loved ones again, the ones that have gone on before us."

"Dad, do you think it would be okay for me to take notes at the funeral? I would like to send an article about the funeral to the *Louisville Journal*."

Thomas looked confused. "Sure, I don't think anyone would mind. What made you think of that, Tommie?"

"I don't know, just in case someone, somewhere, knew Mack Jackson or some of his family. Think I will sketch a picture of the gravestone and send it along with the article."

"Sounds good to me, Tommie, but I doubt they will publish it. A little place in Hart County would not get much attention as a big town like Bowling Green or Lexington, but go ahead, give it a shot."

Before the funeral began, Pastor Ship asked Nellie to read the letter from Mack Jackson. The letter explained the death of Mack's family. Nellie had practiced reading the letter, making sure to be loud enough for everyone to hear, while putting the dramatic touches where needed. Visible shock from the mourners, gasp, and pity waved through the crowd. Although Thomas was a little skeptical about reading the letter detailing Mack's revenge, he agreed it was best everyone heard the details of what had happened so long ago.

# Chapter 24

# Dance Preparation

Saturday brought a full day of cooking and preparing for the annual fall barn dance. Thomas had shot a tom turkey at daybreak and the big bird had been in the outside oven sending tantalizing smells around the open outdoors. Katherine had made cornbread dressing with her fresh sage, an apple pie, and a big bowl of creamed potatoes with chopped green onions.

Mary had finished preparing a large bowl of green beans and a bowl of fresh corn salad. She also prepared a pecan pie from a new recipe she had gotten from her friend on Saturday. She finally cut herself a small piece to make sure the pie was as good as it had been warranted by her friend.

"Ummm, I could eat the whole thing. It's delicious," Mary said while no one was listening. "Guess I am already enjoying foods more, for both of us, Wee One."

"Something smells!" Mary mumbled aloud as she remembered the turkey was on the outside pit. Running outside, Mary saw the black turkey was smoking. Grabbing the turkey from the fire, she flung it on the cedar bar. What a mistake, a silly mistake, Mary thought as she dipped her hand in the bucket of cold water. The turkey was probably ruined so why had she picked it up? As she cooled her hand, she thought about her mistakes, how she had plunged into other activities and been badly burned. The scar on her hand would eventually heal, but the scars she had on her heart would never heal because of the shame and guilt she could not admit to her family.

"Oh, dear, what have you done?" Katherine ran to Mary and examined her hand. "I am so sorry, I should have watched Tom more carefully. But, you shouldn't have been messing with my Tom!" Katherine laughed. "Now, you have hurt yourself. That is probably going to leave a scar."

"It's okay, Katherine. I'll put some salve on it. It is my fault. I do stupid things without thinking, and then I suffer from it... anyway, we need to get things prepared for tonight."

Nellie waltzed out to show Katherine and Mary. "What do you think? Would it look better with my hair up or down, like this or like this? Or should I do half up like this, or what? Gran, do you think you could fix my hair?"

"Sure, sweetie, but we would like to talk to you just a minute, and then I'll try to fix your hair. You know, you are sixteen now and becoming a lovely young lady. Sit down a minute; we want to talk to you. There are going to be boys, including Mike, in your very near future who are going to see how pretty you are," Katherine wagged her finger at Nellie.

Mary jumped in, "But, Nellie, remember, don't give your kisses away. You are far too young and even if you were older, your kisses need to be saved for your wedding night."

"That's right, Nellie. Girls let boys kiss them, then one thing leads to another, and sometimes the girl doesn't want it to go any further, but the boy does, and the next thing is the girl is with child. Often the boy decides to get out of the picture." Katherine shook her head, obviously remembering far too many babies born without fathers around.

"Yes, I have seen it happen over and over, Nellie. So, we are saying we love you, and you are certainly beautiful, but you should save your kisses for your husband on the night of your marriage. Okay, promise?" Mary asked as she looked at Nellie with a penetrating look.

"Okay, okay, I promise! All this because I asked to have my hair fixed?" Nellie smirked.

As the food was being packed Mary gushed, "Katherine! You are not ready! Go, go, and get ready now!"

Katherine clucked around the baskets of food for a minute then ran to her room. A few minutes later, she glided out of her room. The family looked in awe. Katherine had pulled her graying hair atop of her head in a loose bun with curls around her neck and ears. She had on a beautiful violet silk dress that accented her tiny waist. The violet color was a perfect accent for her skin and hair.

"Granma, you are beautiful!" Tommie exclaimed.

Thomas whistled and both Nellie and Renie gave Katherine a hug.

"You look beautiful, Gran. You never dress up like this, even for Sunday. I am so proud of you." Nellie raised a brow and gave a cheery whistle.

As Mary came out of her room, she noticed Katherine, "You look incredible, Katherine. Is that the dress you said you wore when you married Thomas' dad? It looks great on you!"

"Yes, it is. You know when Nellie said she was going to dress up a little, it gave me an incentive to dress up also. This dress has been in the cedar chest all these years and not doing anyone any good. So, I thought I would wear it. The necklace was a gift from Parson the year before he died."

"Well, you look great. For a sixty....three? You are in great shape and the size you were at eighteen. You look, beautiful, Katherine," Mary stated as she checked Katherine's hair.

Katherine didn't offer to help with the food. Instead, she marched to the buckboard and had a seat before the others took their places. Katherine scooted over to let Renie sit beside her, while she scolded herself for being so vain.

All the wagons, buckboards and buggies were headed in the same direction, to Erik Goodlin's barn. He had the biggest barn in the neighborhood and the large barn served well for the yearly fall dance. Food was being carried in and stacked on tables on one side of the barn. Everyone greeted with hugs and handshakes as they looked forward to an evening of merriment.

On the other side of the barn was a small band of three gentlemen, a banjo player, fiddle, and a harmonica player. Eager to get started they commenced their routine of tuning their instruments.

People were already beginning to get onto the dance floor. Mr. Goodlin had three platforms made of wood which were 10 x 10 foot sections. They were pushed to the middle of the barn. Often people would dance on the floor of the barn, but to make a good heel-clicking sound, one needed to be on the platform.

"Attention, attention, everyone!" Mr. Goodlin was shifting his weight from one foot to another as he tried to get the attention of everyone. "The food is ready, I suggest everyone eat and then during dessert time, I will have some announcements to make. So, fill up and get ready to dance the night away!"

Sallye and John made their way to Pete and Andrea to share a couple of bales of hay. Both girls had brought a quilt to cover the hay to prevent hay itch. The two couples had become very good friends since school had started. The arrangement was good for both Sallye and Andrea. Sallye wanted to be close to help with Hannah and Andrea appreciated the extra pair of hands. Andrea had immediately recognized Sallye's talents for working with children, as well as Sallye's artistic talents.

Thomas had thanked God many days for Pete and John who had worked so well together on the building projects. Both of the men had learned from each other and from Thomas. The two men felt they could build about anything, including the new house, which was a big topic of conversation for the night. More important than the building of the house was the building of their spiritual minds as they felt a closeness to Thomas and to the Lord through sharing the Word as they worked.

Most of the folk from church were at the barn dance. A few churchgoers had their doubts about dancing, but most of them didn't have anything against it, as long as the church covenant did not object. The church considered the local dances a good way to reach those who didn't come to church, to share food and fellowship.

Arron Smith and his family had just arrived at the dance. When Hobie and Leah arrived at the church a few weeks ago, Arron had been the only member to voice an objection. Although he had apologized, he still harbored negative feelings. Arron entered the barn with an air of pessimism and was upset about the killer of the Wisemans. He made no pretense of telling everyone how he felt. Interrupting a group of men at the door of the barn, Arron began shouting insults aimed at the law for not taking care of the killer.

"I think we ought to go down there and get him out of jail and hang him. You know he did it, killed those old people. They didn't have a chance. He should have been hung instead of going to jail. That is just what is wrong with people today, letting a killer like that sit in jail while those nice people are dead."

Thomas tried to calm him down by telling him Bob Wright was going to have his day in court soon. Yet, Arron did not want to listen to what the others were telling him.

"You know, it is our fault. When we let people come in our community, and we lie to protect them, we are asking for trouble. That is where we made our mistake letting those slaves settle here. Killers and runaway slaves! No wonder!" Arron was truly wound up, and Thomas suspected he may have been drinking.

Grabbing Arron from behind, Thomas pulled Arron away from the others as he knew one person could ruin the dance. Trying to calm the young man, Thomas suggested, "Why don't you take your lovely wife and go get something to eat. Tonight is supposed to be a fun night. Worry about the other stuff later."

Thomas signaled for Mary to come talk with Anjolee, Arron's wife. Anjolee had just joined her husband as she noticed he was becoming loud and argumentative. Hopefully, getting them to talk about other things would calm him, get them in the party spirit. As the four of them began to talk, Anjolee stopped in mid-sentence.

"Where is Adam? I thought you were watching him," Anjolee said nervously as she started looking around.

"I thought he was with you. He was right behind you as you were coming in," Arron replied, looking around the last place they had been.

"I was putting the food on the table and while I was talking and putting the food in place, he went to be with you. I thought you were watching him." Anjolee was becoming more upset, while everyone was learning about the missing three-year old.

The barn party soon turned into a search party. People started looking for the child behind the hay, on top of the hayloft, everywhere, but the child was not in the barn. A few of the men went outside and looked around the outside of the barn. Although everyone agreed little Adam couldn't have gotten very far that quick.

———————————

Ollie, Hobie, Lyssa, and Leah had gotten a late start to the party, and were in the buckboard several hundred yards away from the Goodlin barn. Ollie sat in front, Everett between Ollie and Hobie. Lyssa sat behind Ollie with Baby Oleta, and Leah sat behind Hobie. The group anticipated a night of fun and dancing while Leah scoured the countryside for fall flowers.

"Oh, I would love to have some of those cattails over there in the pond. Perhaps we can ask Mr. Goodlin for some for a flower arrangement," Leah said as she eyed the tall cattails waving in the pond.

"Well, as long as they aren't near a pond. They will eventually take over a pond. They are beautiful..." Hobie stopped as he eyed the pond. "Leah, do you see something in the cattails? Stop, Ollie. Something is caught in the cattails."

"Yeah, there is something in there, but I can't tell what it is," Leah exclaimed as she jumped out of the wagon before Ollie had come to a complete stop. Both Leah and Hobie were looking and running to the pond. As they neared the pond, they saw a child in the pond clutching the cattails.

Quickly Hobie kicked off his boots and waded out in the water. He tried to reach the child, but kept slipping deeper in the pond mud. The child was becoming upset as he tried to get away from Hobie, an unfamiliar face. The child was in the deep part of the pond, going under while Hobie took sinking steps toward the child. Finally, Hobie was close enough to reach out and get the child, when he too, slipped in the water, almost over his head.

Hobie tried to pull his feet out of the deep mud in the pond. As Hobie talked to the child, he tried to get the child to trust him and to take his hand.

Leah waded into the pond on the side with the cattails, seeing that Hobie was getting deeper into the water. She reached for the child with one arm but could not reach him. Mashing down some of the cattails, she told the child to grab hold of the pretty flowers. The child reached for the strong stems on the cattails. At least, they would hold him up for a while.

Desperate to help, Ollie ran to the wagon for a rope. Finding a small piece of rope, he flung it to Hobie and began pulling him out. Holding the arm of the child, Hobie pulled the child from the cattail and held onto the rope. Leah had made her way to Hobie and the child as she tried to help both her husband and the frightened little boy.

After what seemed like eternity, Leah pulled both of them to the safer water. Leah held the child who was screaming with fear. Hobie pulled himself out of the pond and lay in the grass for a minute to catch his breath.

Men were searching the fields all around the barn. Ollie yelled at the men and told them they had found a child. Arron Smith and his father ran to Ollie's wagon and met the couple with the child. Leah held the child clinging to her.

"Flower, daddy." Little Adam clutched the broken cattail during the escapade and giggled at Leah.

Ollie explained that Hobie and Leah had just barely seen him as they were going by. The couple had jumped in the pond to save the child. Arron and his father thanked the couple for saving little Adam.

"He would surely have died if it had not been for you," Arron said, through his tears. "I am so sorry that I made my objections to you. Please forgive me, and may God forgive me."

After hearing Adam had been found, Anjolee ran up the road to Adam. She repeated her husband's feelings, thanking the couple over and over between her sobs. The two finally took their son back to the barn and wrapped him in the quilt they had brought for the hay. Inside, the Smith family made an announcement to everyone about what had happened. Arron apologized for being so negative toward Hobie and Leah. Both Arron and Anjolee praised God for the miracle they had seen. Without the Woodsons, the barn party would have turned into a wake.

All of Nellie's friends had arrived and were already dancing. Where is Mike, Nellie thought when she felt someone's hands around her waist. About to slap the intruder, Nellie spun around to see Mike.

Mike looked at Nellie, enjoying how beautiful she was. "You are beautiful, Nellie, and I can't wait to dance with you."

Nellie felt a tingling sensation and a thrill deep in her soul. "Wish I hadn't made that promise!" she whispered.

# Chapter 25

# Barn Dance

"Could I have your attention, please? Attention, up here, please! Our Mayor, Mr. Bymel, has a few words before we start the dancing and fun. Please direct your attention to our Mayor. Mr. Mick Bymel."

"Thank you, Erik. We want to give a hand to Erik Goodlin for allowing us to use his barn for the Upton Fall Dance. He does this every year, so please put your hands together and let him know that we appreciate it!" Mayor Bymel said as he clapped vigorously.

The audience erupted in a round of applause while Erik bowed, smiled sheepishly, and nodded.

"We are certainly thankful little Adam Smith was found and now safe with his mom and dad. In case you hadn't heard, the Woodsons found him in the pond up by the locust thicket. We are blessed that they found him when they did." Mayor Bymel shuffled through his notes.

"Katherine Cosby wanted me to announce that there will be a Ladies' Day at the school building, the new addition, on Saturday, October 12th, beginning at 9:00. The ladies are having a full day of activities with guest speakers and special music. They will serve a light breakfast and a lunch. The emphasis is on local, national, and world missions. You women need to keep that in mind and go; men are not invited!" Everyone laughed and looked toward Katherine.

"Now, while we are on the subject, and yes, folks I am trying to make this fast, I know that most of you are itching to dance and would rather me shut up, but just a couple more things I want to address."

Mayor Bymel took on a different tone as he began talking. "I went to see Bob Wright at jail. He is the one who killed the Wisemans. Bob told me the reason he went off and shot Mr. and Mrs. Wiseman. Now, I am not trying to defend him in any way; what he did was wrong and he should be punished for it. However, I wanted you to know that, even though sometimes we see things only one way, there is another side to the story." The mayor stopped, cleared his throat and looked at the crowd.

"You see, Bob married the Wiseman's daughter, Cindy. The Wisemans did not want Cindy to marry Bob because they said he was no-good and Cindy would not be happy with him. You may remember, Bob was an orphan and lived here and there, taking care of himself during his teenage years. The Wisemans had their reasons to dislike him, but Cindy and Bob were in love. They left this area and got married. They were living and doing okay in Nashville until Cindy got sick. She wrote home to her parents to please send money. Cindy was going to the doctor and needed money for the doctor and medicine. Her parents wrote back and said they would not send any money, she had to come home. Cindy wrote again and explained the situation, and Bob said that she was too weak to travel, her health was deteriorating rapidly. They wrote again they would be glad to help her when, and only when, she came home.

"Unfortunately, Cindy died a few weeks ago and Bob just couldn't take it any longer. He made a trip to see the Wisemans and when he got there, they saw him through the window. Scared of him, they got all the money they had and told him to leave. The Wisemans just thought the money was all he wanted. They kept telling him to take the money and leave. Mr. Wiseman had gotten his gun out and put it on the table as he was arguing with Bob. Bob stuffed the money in his pocket, and then he told them about Cindy. He figured he would use the money to buy Cindy a proper gravestone.

"Bob said he told them about Cindy's sickness and her death. They screamed at him and told him he was lying, they knew he was just trying to get their money. They kept screaming at him telling him that Cindy wasn't dead. Mr. Wiseman became so mad that he got his gun and threatened to shoot Bob. He told Bob it was his fault that his daughter was sick and that he should die like a dog. Bob reached for the gun to take it away from him but the gun went off and shot Mrs. Wiseman. Another wrestling over the gun caused Mr. Wiseman to be shot. He yelled at the Wisemans and told

165

them that it was their fault. He said he just couldn't take it any longer. He just couldn't understand how they could be so stubborn, just because they didn't like him. He knows he did wrong, and he will hang for what he did, but he felt like that was all he could handle. Now, he is in jail waiting for his trial.

"Okay enough of that. We have one more item to bring up and we will begin the festivities. Our beloved doctor, Dr. Routt, has said he is retiring and going to Chicago to live with his daughter. As a matter of fact, Linda Johnson is also going to Chicago. She is leaving Upton because her son married Dr. Routt's daughter. They may be making an announcement on that later. However, our good doctor would not leave us without medical attention. Tonight we have the honor of having Dr. Larimore here. Dr. Larimore, would you come up here and address the folks?"

As Dr. Larimore stepped up on the platform, everyone was trying to get a good look at the new Doc. He was dressed in a gray suit with a white shirt and gray stripped tie. He had striking silver hair about the color of the suit. He was a tall gentleman with glasses and a beautiful smile. His charisma seemed to charm everyone without him saying a word.

"Thank you, Mayor," the Doctor said. "I am from Lexington, and I am wanting to be semi-retired. I want to get away from the rush of the city and retire in a small community. I didn't know for sure if this was the place until today. After I got here and looked around, I realized this is truly the place I want to be. So, after I close all my business dealings, sell my home in Lexington, I will be here for good. Looks like, Upton, you have stolen my heart!" As he finished, he looked right at Katherine. Their eyes met for the first time as they looked at each other and felt an instant bond.

"Thank you, Doc, and we are mighty glad you chose Upton to semi-retire. You will have a great helper with Katherine. Now, let's start the music! Everybody have fun!"

As soon as the music started, couples began to flood onto the dance floor. Doctor Larimore made a bee-line to Katherine. "I assume that you are the invincible Katherine whom everyone admires so much! May I have this dance?"

Katherine, who was never at a loss for words, suddenly was shy and had a bug in her throat. "Yes, excuse me, yes, I am Katherine. Doctor Larimore, it is so good to meet you. And yes, I will dance with you."

The two of them danced as many dances that night as the young people. They seemed to have unlimited energy. The Doctor would talk to others for a few minutes and then would have Katherine again in his arms dancing the night away. "Katherine, you are really light on your feet. What are you about thirty-six?" Doctor Larimore asked.

To everyone's surprise, Deacon Avery asked Carolyn to dance. Mary noticed they danced several dances together. Yet, Mary did not see that sparkle in Carolyn's eyes. There was almost a fear instead of enjoyment. Mary wondered what Carolyn's secret was.

Mary and Thomas danced and excitedly told others the good news, that they were expecting a baby in May. Thomas was so happy and so proud of Mary. He had thought he would never be happy again after Rissa died. God had His plan in our lives, thought Thomas.

However, it was Mike and Nellie who were the main attraction. Everyone said how great they looked together. Everyone told Thomas that Nellie was developing into be a beautiful young lady, and he had better watch out for Mike. Thomas knew he didn't have anything to worry about with Mike, for Mike was one of the few good guys.

As Thomas danced with his wife, he said, "Yeah, we may have a wedding there," nodding at Mike and Nellie, "in a few years, I hope, but it does looks serious."

"I agree, Thomas, but I can't think of a better young man."

As Mike and Nellie swirled around the dance floor, Nellie looked into Mike's eyes. She saw so much there. Mike was sweet, curious, intelligent and so cute, she thought. She remembered Gran's words, "Nellie, when you start looking for someone to marry, or even date, you look for a good Christian man. The Bible says we need to be equally yoked."

As Mike held Nellie in his arms he felt like the luckiest guy in the world. Nellie was perfect in every way. He ached to make her his, but he had to have God's permission for Nellie. Mike had told the Lord he would be His disciple, so he had to keep his promise in mind which was so hard to do when he was so close to this beautiful young lady.

# Chapter 26

# The Drunk

Thomas tiptoed around the bedroom, trying to avoid the squeaky floorboards. The children needed their sleep as they had worn themselves out at the party.

Sauntering into the kitchen Thomas discovered Katherine at the table, already with a cup of coffee and the Bible. "Good morning, Mom. Why are you up so early?"

"Couldn't sleep. Just too much excitement for the night. What did you think about Dr. Larimore? Thomas, what did you really think?" Katherine asked, keeping her voice low.

"Seemed like a good man to me, and he was really smitten with you. Of course, I don't know why not, my mother is beautiful, inside and out," Thomas said as he kissed her silken hair.

"I am going to get a head start on the chores. Let the children sleep; they need the rest or they will be cranky for the day," Thomas said as he pulled the buckets from the wall pegs.

As Katherine worked on breakfast, she also prepared extra ham and biscuits for the church service. With the extra biscuit dough, she would make some fried apple pies. Pastor Ship would make sure to grab a couple of his favorite pies to take home before they disappeared.

Hearing pans rattling in the kitchen, Mary was soon up helping Katherine. "I'll shuck that corn and cut it off to make a big bowl of creamed corn to take. We still have so much corn, even though you planted extra for the deer and the groundhogs!"

The family enjoyed Sunday morning breakfast of ham and eggs with some of Granma's special apple butter on a buttered biscuit. "Mmmm, I think I could eat five or six biscuits, Katherine, they taste especially delicious this morning," Mary said inhaling the smell of the butter-topped brown biscuit.

When everyone was dressed and ready, the family joined Thomas on the porch. The children sat on the floor of the porch, swinging their legs off the side. Katherine and Mary sat in the large rocking chairs. Cat Callie was in Renie's lap, purring, making biscuits, while Goldie was at Tommie's side wanting her ears rubbed. The sun was sending the warm rays through the trees while the family awaited the warmth of the light of the Word.

Thomas lovingly turned well-worn pages in his Bible and began the devotion. "Psalm 118:24: 'This is the day which the LORD hath made; we will rejoice and be glad in it'." Thomas said as he looked at his family. "We really should rejoice every Sunday we are alive and be ready to worship our Lord and Savior. Whether it is a good day for us, or if someone along our way causes us to have a bad day, it is still the Lord's Day and we should rejoice. For even a bad day is worthwhile. Good events or bad events, either way, it is a day the Lord has made. So, family, let us be glad we are going to the house of the Lord to worship, to praise our Lord, and give Him the honor and the glory He deserves. Now, if we are ready, let's pack up and go."

The family loaded the buckboard with the day's church meal. The children chattered in the back, while Katherine was in front talking with Thomas and Mary.

In the little time that Dr. Larimore and Katherine had not been on the dance floor last evening, Katherine had talked with many of Dr. Routt's patients about their aches and pains and their sorrow of losing their doctor.

"A lot of people do not trust a new doctor, you know. They have depended on Dr. Routt for years and it is hard to change," Katherine continued.

"Yes, but we have to be able to change as we face new challenges when they come our way. And by the way, he doesn't look like much of a challenge, Katherine," Mary said as she giggled.

The three adults continued talking about the dance, some new faces and the troublemakers. Of course, everyone praised Hobie and Leah for their help with little Adam. Tommie and Nellie were comparing notes about all the young people at the dance, and a couple they did not know.

Storm clouds rolled in and created a darkness in the west. The wind picked up and the imminent threat of rain caused Thomas to think about putting the cover on the buckboard as he scanned the skies. "Think I will wait a few minutes to put the cover the buckboard and see if this storm is going to hold off a while. Always heard that a storm that comes up so quickly is a warning that trouble lies ahead."

Renie had the back of the buckboard to herself and she made good use of it by singing to herself. She enjoyed the ride and like her mother, was fascinated with all the flowers, the yellow daisies, the ironweed, the purple asters, the blue cornflower; all were so stunning in early fall. Gazing at the sides of the road for unusual flowers, Renie saw something by an old apple tree.

"What is that?" Renie yelled to the others as she pointed ahead.

About that time, the wind started blowing and the rain began to plummet. Hastily, Thomas stopped the wagon, and he and Tommie worked against the wind to pull up the cover. Renie kept trying to get the attention of the adults as they scurried about trying to cover on the wagon but no one was paying attention to her.

Soon Renie saw that the bag of rags appeared to be a person. "Hey, everybody, there is someone over there under the tree. He looks like he is dead."

At first, Tommie and Nellie thought she was teasing but quickly they began to yell for Thomas to stop. The adults finally saw what was causing the commotion. Someone was under the apple tree and he looked dead.

Quickly, Thomas stopped the wagon, jumped off and peered through the rain. Katherine and Mary had taken notice and were already out of the wagon. Thomas told Tommie to get under the cover and stay with the girls.

When the three approached the old man, they were disgusted at the sight.

"He must have wallowed in manure, or he has really soiled himself." Thomas held up an empty moonshine bottle and showed Mary and Katherine. "I reckon this is his problem. The old scoundrel has tried to drink away his problems."

"We need to take him home and clean him up, then feed him. He must feel awful. Can you carry him, Thomas?" Katherine asked.

Thomas looked confused, "We are on our way to church. You want to take him home and take care of him while we miss church?"

"Well," Mary confessed, "what is most important to God, for us to go to church or for us to help this old man. Don't you think we need to help him?"

"Since you put it that way, I guess you are right." Thomas bent over the man and started talking to him, telling him he would take him home with them, get him out of the rain.

"Leave me be!" the old man mumbled just loud enough to hear.

Katherine bent over the old man and began talking to him, "We can't leave you out here in this rain. You need to go home with us, let us get you cleaned up and get you something to eat."

"I said, no!" The old man was louder and acted like he could hit someone, waving his left arm.

Thomas said, "Okay, he doesn't want us to take him with us, so let's just leave."

The three of them started to walk away, but Mary stopped them. "It is raining, he is drunk or sick, and needs our help, and we just can't leave him. He needs to eat and get some clean clothes on. He smells awful, and look, his clothes are filthy rags."

Thomas went back to the old man, bent down and started talking to him. He put his hand on the man's shoulder and was very gentle as he told him he wanted to help him.

At that point, the old man took a swing at Thomas, and said in a slurred speech, "I said I don't want you helpin' me! Go on now, you hear? Get outta here and leave me be."

Thomas told the women to go to the wagon, "That man does not want to be helped! Let's go. If we hurry, we can make it to church." The three of them started walking, reluctantly, to the wagon.

The three children were peeping from the cover of the wagon. "Aren't you going to get the old man?" Nellie asked.

"Yeah, you just can't leave him there. He might die," Renie said.

"Well, he probably won't die, but he does need some clean warm clothes and a meal, don't you think, Dad? You aren't going to leave him there are you?" Tommie asked.

"Yeah, we can't leave him. Tell him Gran, we need to take care of him. Dad, can't you take him to our house and fix him up?" Nellie pleaded.

Feeling guilty, Thomas stopped and turned to retrace his steps. "Well, I will try again. But, if he won't go this time, I am quitting," Thomas warned. Mumbling to himself, "I knew that storm was warning me of something, I should have kept driving."

Mary, Katherine and Thomas walked back to the man and told him they were not leaving without him. The old man didn't protest as much this time, and even if he had, it would not have done any good. Thomas picked up the old man and threw him over his shoulder. At the wagon, Thomas gently lowered him in the back.

As Thomas took the reins, he complained about the smell, and said his clothes would never come clean. He said if it was left up to him they would have left the old man there with his bottle. Katherine and Mary tried to help Thomas understand, but he just wasn't happy, having to go back home to clean up an old man who didn't want any help from him and his family.

Katherine, Mary and the children went inside while Thomas stayed with the visitor. Katherine heaved a pot of water on the stove for the bath. Thomas put the metal wash tub on the front porch along with a towel and some soap. Soon, the ladies had the tub full enough and Thomas was taking care of the old man on the porch. The women and children stayed inside reading from Isaiah while Thomas helped the old man get in the tub.

Katherine found some of Thomas' old clothes and handed them to Thomas as he retrieved his shaving cup and razor from the cupboard. The old man told Thomas he wasn't going to shave, but Thomas insisted he shave because he would be presenting himself at the family table.

Katherine and Mary were setting the table with the food they had originally loaded into the wagon for church. As soon as the old man was finished and dressed, the family would share their food with him. Thomas asked if there was anything he could get for him. The old man looked up at Thomas with almost a look of disbelief.

Thomas invited the old man into the kitchen and helped him settle in a chair at the table. He introduced his family and waited for the old man to introduce himself, but instead, he just looked down and occasionally grunted. Although more than a little put-out with the stranger, Thomas blessed the food and began passing country ham biscuits, green beans, corn, and tomatoes. The old man, who said at first he wasn't hungry, began to eat. He cleaned his plate and asked for seconds, then finished with a fried apple pie.

The rain had stopped and fortunately, it looked like the day wasn't a complete waste. "Well, Sir, we are going back to church. If you want to go with us, jump in the back of the wagon and we will take you with us. I am afraid there isn't anything for you to do here today, but you can join us in fellowship at church." Thomas tried to be as pleasant as he could.

The old man told Thomas he would not go to his church, but he would take a ride. He made sure he was sitting on the back of the wagon on their trip back. Thomas figured he wanted a chance to jump off whenever he wanted to, and Thomas really didn't care. After all, he wouldn't even tell them his name, or say thank you for their trouble.

Nellie kept looking back at the old man on their way to church. She noticed the man's shoulders were shaking, and he would wipe at his eyes. "I bet the old man is crying. He feels bad about what he did," Nellie told Tommie.

Katherine and Mary bragged on Thomas as they explained that they were proud of him. Thomas had the hardest part of helping the old man. The worst part was the old man didn't say he was grateful, nevertheless, he surely was.

"Plus," Katherine said, "You were a wonderful example for the children. You did a good deed, when you didn't have to."

"And remember what you said this morning, if someone along our way causes us to have a bad day, it is still the Lord's Day and we should rejoice." Mary reminded Thomas. 'This is the day which the LORD hath made: we will rejoice and be glad in it'."

# Chapter 27

# Sunday's Explanation

The two big, red horses responded to Thomas' pull on the reins, tramping into the last spot along the hitching fence at church. Even before the wagon had come to a standstill, Tommie jumped from the wagon and tied the horses to the posts.

Trying to escape the same questions, Thomas made his way to Dr. Routt. He had noticed that the old man had taken refuge with the doctor as soon as they had stopped.

By the time Thomas made his way to Dr. Routt, the old man had left, and Thomas didn't see him anywhere.

"Doc, good to see you. Doing well?" Thomas asked.

"I'm fine, Thomas. So glad to see your family last night. Good-looking family, Thomas," Dr. Routt said as he shook hands with Thomas.

"Doctor, I noticed you were talking to an old man a minute ago. Do you know his name?"

Dr. Routt looked a little stunned, "Of course I do, Thomas. That's Louis White. He is a good friend of Dr. Larimore. In fact, he traveled here with Dr. Larimore."

Thomas could not keep his surprise contained. "No, not that old man. Couldn't be."

Dr. Routt looked hurt. "Well, Thomas I know I am getting old but I think I know someone's name. He has been a good friend for many years. Our families visited when we all had families."

"Well, is he an alcoholic? Is there something wrong with him?" Thomas asked, more than a little confused. "See Doctor, we were on our way to church this morning when Renie saw someone lying under a tree, so we stopped. We talked to the man and he was drunk, completely out of it. I told him we would take him home and clean him up because he was dirty and smelled like a cow pile, but he told me to leave him. I actually was going to leave him, but the kids and Mary and Katherine, too, they wouldn't let me. So, I carried him to our wagon and took him home. We made him a hot bath, gave him soap, a towel, even a razor. I gave him some clothes to put on. We fed him and brought him up here. He wouldn't tell us who he was, his name, where he was from, nothing."

Doctor Routt scratched his head. "I don't know why he would do that. Louis has worked hard all his life, never has been an alcoholic, as far as I know. He has a dental practice in Lexington and is getting ready to retire also. He is a good man, and I can't believe this would happen. Well, I mean, he is not a Christian. In fact, he doesn't believe in God. But, he is a good man. I just don't understand, Thomas."

"Is Doctor Larimore here?" Thomas asked.

"Yes, he is, or he was here. Saw him talking with Pete and Andrea Goodwin. He's interested in the education system here. He was talking to both of them about school attendance."

"Okay, I'll find him." Thomas was certainly confused. Was all of this a joke, to make them look silly in front of Dr. Larimore? What was his motive? Maybe, he really is an alcoholic, but didn't want anyone to know. Now, where was Dr. Larimore?

"Hi there, Thomas! How are you today?" Dr. Larimore said as he shook hands with Thomas. "Just saw your mom, she didn't have time to talk. She's a lady on a mission."

"Well, Doc, I am on a mission, right now," Thomas said, becoming a little nervous. "I am a little confused. Your friend Louis was drunk, lying under a tree in the rain. We took him home, I helped him take a bath, gave him clean clothes, and we fed him. We brought him back here. Still, he would not tell us his name or anything about himself. Doc, what is going on?" Thomas had become rather loud when Mary found him.

"What, Thomas? Dr. Larimore knows that old man? The drunk?" Mary asked, looking from Thomas to Dr. Larimore.

Dr. Larimore had a complete look of surprise. He didn't know what to say until finally he replied, "I, I don't know. Are you sure that it was Louis? I am really confused, too."

"Excuse me, Doc, I know the man, I saw him naked. He was talking to Dr. Routt who identified him as Louis White." Thomas took a deep breath and continued.

"Well, we have interrupted fellowship services because of this ordeal, because of a man trying to make us think he was a drunk, or maybe he was, I don't know. You know, I think I will take my family and go home. Good day, Dr. Larimore."

Mary and Thomas rounded up the family and started home. Mary tried to explain to everyone what had happened; between Thomas interjecting his displeasure.

"I think he was trying to make fools out of us, make us look like country hicks," Thomas said disgustedly.

"I don't know, I think maybe he is a secret alcoholic and wandered around drunk," Mary said trying to offer a solution to the problem.

Nellie spoke up. "I felt sorry for him because on the way back to church, he was sitting with his back to us. His shoulders shook and he wiped his eyes and put his head in his hands. He was crying for bothering us or being in a bad shape in the first place."

Katherine shook her head. "I can't believe any of those ideas. This whole thing has been just too weird. And the worse thing is we didn't get to go to worship service, and we totally disrupted fellowship service. When we get home, let's don't even mention it. Forget it!" Katherine said emphatically.

———◆———

Enjoying a peaceful afternoon Thomas and Mary read until they heard a buggy. "Now who in the world would that be?" Thomas asked as he shaded his eyes to see who the uninvited Sunday evening guests were.

The driver was Dr. Larimore. As they rolled in the front yard, Thomas could see the scowl on Dr. Larimore's face. Beside him sat the old man, Louis White. Both of the men left the wagon and walked onto the porch where Thomas and the children met them.

"Could we go inside, Thomas? I would like to straighten out this matter, if I possibly can," Dr. Larimore sighed.

"Sure. Children, maybe you better stay out here and play ball, let the adults talk awhile," Thomas advised.

"Would anyone like something to drink?" Katherine asked.

"No, Mom, let's just sit here until we get a good explanation from these two guys," Thomas said as he eyed the two men with disfavor.

"First, please let me say I am sorry this happened today. I am truly sorry," Dr. Larimore stated as he shook his head and looked at his hands on the kitchen table.

"Last night, when I got back to Dr. Routt's house where I was staying, I was raving about Upton, about Katherine, about all the nice people, about the church, a church that is open all day on Sunday to observe the Sabbath. I was truly inspired with the people here. I said that I have the feeling God is here among all these good people. I guess you could say I felt the Holy Spirit moving in this community. I went on and on to Louis last night. He said no place was that good, and he figured more than half of the people were hypocrites. I told him I truly felt these people were good, honest God-fearing people. These people take care of their neighbors, they live by God's commandments, and they love each other." Dr. Larimore shook his head and sighed.

"I should have known Louis was going to do something to prove his point, but I would have never guessed what he did. Do you want to explain now, Louis?" Dr. Larimore asked.

"Okay, maybe I got a little jealous. Keith heard about this town from Dr. Routt, and he said he was leaving Lexington, just like that. He thought he would go to a small town that believed in God and worshipped every day, not just Sunday, but they were, I think he said 'Christ-like' people. Then last night when he came back from the party, he talked for hours about how nice everyone was. He went on and on. He mentioned Katherine's Ladies' Day project to promote missions everywhere. He mentioned the different families and what they had done, like the family that took in the slave family. Of course, the little boy who would have drowned without the slave family who risked their lives to save him. And the young couple who are giving so much of their time to the school when they don't have any kids. Most of all, he made the Cosby family sound like saints. In fact, it sounded like everyone here wants to be a do-gooder. Finally, I thought, I will just show him. I will show him, given the opportunity to do something for a stranger, someone who they don't know, who is a stinking mess, someone who drinks, who they object to, I will show Keith they are just like everybody else. They will turn and look the other way," Louis said as he looked down at the table.

Thomas couldn't hold back any longer. "Yeah, but how did you know we would see you? You were taking a chance. What if Renie hadn't seen you? You could really have been able to say we passed you by if Renie had not seen you."

"Chances are one of the six of you would have seen me. I heard all about the family last night so I knew all about you and when you would be leaving for church. The wind and the rain was not what I was bargaining for though. Anyway, instead of leaving me the way I told you, you insisted on taking me home with you. You not only gave me a bath, let me shave and gave me a new set of clothes; you took me into your home, a complete stranger, because I would never tell you my name. And, you fed me."

Mary spoke up, "But Nellie, said she saw you crying on the way back to church. You were shaking and wiping your eyes."

"No, Mary, I was laughing, because I had pulled the trick off so well. I was able to completely fool you into thinking I was a stinking, old drunk. But after I got through laughing, I realized Keith was right. You are good people and would do anything for another person. So, Thomas, Mary, Katherine, I am sorry for what I did. I tested your faith and your real compassion for people. If you had gone on and left me there, I could have proved to Keith that this was not the place for him. However, your family has shown more compassion and love than I have seen in a long time. Now, if you will accept my apology, we can shake hands and try to forget this ever happened. Okay?" Louis asked.

Thomas put out his hand and shook hands with Louis and Dr. Larimore. "May I share a Word with you from the Bible, Louis?"

"No, Thomas, not now. I have always lived a life of not believing in God. I have to admit I do believe in Him more now than ever before. But, right now I am too much of a sinner for God to have me. I am not ready for the next step. I'm ready to go if you are Keith," Louis answered, apparently anxious to leave the tenderness and compassion of the Cosby family.

"Well, I hope this clears everything up for you. I am sorry, too, that it happened. But, I am very proud of you, all of you. You showed your love for a complete stranger." Before Dr. Larimore and Louis headed back to town Dr. Larimore told the family, "I think the theme of your Ladies' Day is very evident; you clearly have a heart like Jesus."

# Chapter 28

# Good Foundations

Using both hands Mary smoothed the large white sheet of blueprints spread on the kitchen table. Thomas pointed to a particular section of the plans. "Right here."

"Are we ready to go, Boss?" John shuffled in the kitchen and waited for Thomas.

"Yeah, we probably are. Mary had a question about the front portico. From the looks of it, the house may need to sit a little further back on the hill," Thomas added, still looking at the blueprints.

The house design had taken on a southern revival style. The *Savannah Gazette* had displayed a picture of a southern mansion of the particular style in an issue that summer. Mary had seen the newspaper on their visit to the bookstore in Elizabethtown. Nevertheless, the most important aspect of the house was that it would be comfortable for their family.

John studied the blueprints and pointed to a section. "We can sure go back a little more, but we need to make sure you have your mind settled before we start on the foundation. Got rock ready to place today. Make sure you know where you want it, then no turning back," John warned.

Thomas and Mary agreed it would be a good idea to back up the house closer to the trees. The problem was they didn't want it to be so far away from the existing road. The cobblestone road was laid during the early 1800s, and they wanted to be able to use it as a drive to the house. However, backing the house up more meant they would have to create another cobblestone drive.

"Will any part of this house building be easy, Thomas?" Mary asked, wiping her brow of perspiration from the morning work.

"The worst part is trying to get the house finished by May when your guests are coming." Thomas winked at Mary. "I'll see you later."

John and Pete were moving the foundation rocks when Thomas joined them.

"Hey, John, how about you lift and I'll grunt?" Pete teased.

"How about we both lift and we both grunt?" John answered.

"Guys, we just want to make sure there is bedrock there. If not we will have to dig down. This is one of the hardest parts of building, getting the foundation level and strong. Just like our lives, when we build our lives on a strong foundation, Christ, we know we will stand through all the storms of life. Men, I want this house to be able to withstand the storms, the wind, and rain."

"You're right," Pete said as he surveyed the sight again. "I have a pick if we need it to start breaking rock. Hey, John, can you help me move this foundation stone? We will carry it backward, what...about five feet?"

"Yeah, that looks right according to these measurements. We will move it and measure again anyway," John answered, although he was not eager to move the blocks more than was necessary.

Soon the men realized they would have to dig down to bedrock to set the foundation rock. As they were digging John started hitting flint.

"Well, look at this, a bunch of arrowheads in this hole here. This is what the Indians called a hominy hole, isn't it? They had filled it up with their arrowheads and left them here."

The men picked them up by the handful and put them aside where they would not be harmed. As they scraped the limestone rock, they found another larger hole. The men kept digging, afraid that the hole was all the way through, but it made a big, gentle dip, as big as a large dishpan.

"Hey, Thomas come look at this. This looks like a bowl or a dishpan in the rock," Pete said as he scraped back the dirt and sod.

"Yeah, that is a beautiful sink, isn't it? We want to make sure the limestone sink is stable, not on top of another rock," Thomas said.

Thomas was concerned about the evidence of the Indians having been there many years ago. He didn't want to build on top of or close to an Indian burial ground. However, in the area there were so many flat rocks, he figured there couldn't be a burial ground close. Looking at the numerous arrowheads made him wonder, much like Johnny would have wondered about the Indians who had lived there many years ago. Surely the Indians had also stood overlooking the creek, watching the deer, the ducks, and the squirrels. Without a doubt, they loved it as much as he and his family did.

"You know, men, I can really feel sorry for the Cherokee when they had to leave this area. First, they were tricked because they were told the Virginia territory did not include what we know now as Kentucky. Yet later, they were told Kentucky was included in their original treaty. They sold out beautiful lands in Kentucky for practically nothing."

"Yeah, course I really can't feel sorry for them after the many pioneer that they killed and scalped," John said.

"Don't you mean, 'scalped first and killed?' Pete asked. "Yeah, I heard my Granpap talk about…hey, do we want to go back any more, right here? Maybe we need to stop and measure, no need to dig out any more than we have to."

Thomas looked at the angle and decided to measure. "Yes, I think we stop digging here, and let's start stacking foundation rock on this side. What were you saying a while ago about your Granpap, Pete?"

Pete and Thomas picked up and moved the rock together. "Granpap said his granddaddy was with Daniel Boone when they came through the Cumberland Gap. He said that Daniel declared Kentucky was the Garden of Eden. Most or all of the paths had been made by buffalo and Indians, so other areas were untouched. Granpap told how they had to hatchet their way through, to make most of the roads as they went. They were afraid to go to sleep because of losing their hair. Sometimes the Indians would get into where the horses were tied up and they rode off on them, never saw them again."

"Yeah, I don't think I would have had that much determination to live in Kentucky. I would have told them that they could have it and I would keep my hair," John said as he moved another big rock.

"But, it is the white man, settling everywhere, putting up fences and building homes and killing out the wildlife, like the buffalo. We are the ones, not the Indians, who are making the country look so different than a hundred years ago," Pete said, scooting another rock into place.

"Let's see if this is level and we will measure where the rocks go on the other side before we carry them over there," Thomas said. "Hopefully, we will learn a lesson how we mistreated the Indian in the past, and we will not make that mistake again."

"Well, don't you think we already have?" John said, "I mean what we did to the colored folk. I know you do not go along with slavery, or Pete or myself, but most of the people south of here do have slaves and think nothing of it. So, it seems like we keep repeating our insensitivity toward others."

"I agree. So much of the time, human nature is so that we take advantage of others. Thomas, what do you think is the greatest single lesson or command we can learn from the Bible?" Pete asked.

"In Matthew 22:37-38 Jesus said, 'You shall love the LORD your God with all your heart, with all your soul, and with all your mind. This is the first and great commandment, and the second is like it: Love your neighbor as yourself'. That's the greatest," Thomas replied as he looked toward the heavens.

"Guess there would be no need to have laws or a sheriff if we even observed the second commandment, to love your neighbor as yourself," Pete said.

"No war, no fights, no stealing, no jealousy, no adultery, all if we could love our neighbor as ourselves." John moved another block. "But that is hard to do. I don't think I can love everybody. Some people I don't even like, Thomas. I am ashamed, but I don't want to love everyone."

"Then pray and ask God to give you a spirit of love for everyone. Start by smiling at everyone you see, then when you see a person who is hard to love, ask God to help you love that person more. Soon, you will find yourself loving more and smiling more and being able to love all of God's people more. First John 4:20 says, 'If someone says, I love God, and hates his brother, he is a liar; for he who does not love his brother whom he has seen, how can he love God whom he has not seen?' So, pray to love people more and the more you try, the easier it becomes."

"Thomas, I want to know how you can remember all those scriptures." John asked. "I can try to remember a verse, but then it leaves me."

"Well, it does take a lot of study, and I read the Bible every day. If I want to witness to someone then I need to know the scripture. When you say scripture, it has power in it, because the scripture is the Word and the Word is the Lord. The Holy Spirit will use that scripture to help witness to the lost," Thomas explained.

"Thomas it is a special treat to work for you because I get to hear about the Bible every day. I always go home and tell Andrea something you said. Often we look it up in our Bible and read and try to remember it. Do you want to move these rocks over here now, Thomas?" Pete asked as he pointed to the pile of rocks.

Thomas said, "Let's measure, then we will see. My advice to both of you is to start every day with the scripture and end every day with the scripture. When you do that, God fills everything in between."

# Chapter 29

# Renie

"It's time," Renie whispered softly as she touched Katherine's hand.

Katherine had been asleep, but seemed to wake a few seconds before Renie had come to her. The rest of the family continued their slumber with no idea of the adventure ahead for Katherine and Renie.

Without another word the two dressed. Katherine scribbled a note and left it where Thomas would find it. No need for words for both of them knew their mission. Twice before, Renie and Katherine had been guided by the Holy Spirit to minister to the needs of someone nearing the gates of heaven.

Both Katherine and Renie seemed to be able to read each other's minds on such occasions. Instead of getting a horse for their trip, the two walked to the saw mill and hauled the boat from the timbers it rested on. Like good soldiers aware of their mission, they moved with swiftness and dedication. Katherine prayed for strength to get the little boat in the water and for a successful trip to Mrs. Audie Bearden's place. Going by the creek would be much faster than taking a buggy as the good roads were not easily accessible from the Bearden's place.

Pushing off from the little island in the creek was the easy part as they started their journey downstream. Thankfully, the moon was almost full and it brought a blessing as the two paddled around the rocks and sand islands. Both the young girl and the older woman knew what they were to do, and words were needless, but prayers were indispensable.

Katherine prayed unceasingly and whispered scripture from Mark 12:31, "And the second, like it, is this: You shall love your neighbor as yourself. There is no other commandment greater than these."

Renie, sitting in front of Katherine, felt the prayers and scriptures and whispered them with her Grandmother, her mentor.

Watching the moon reflect on the rippling waters, Katherine prayed not only for Mrs. Bearden but for Renie and herself. Katherine whispered, "But straightway Jesus spake unto them, saying, 'be of good cheer; it is I; be not afraid'."

In the Gosser's farm bottom, the creek widened and became too shallow for the boat. Katherine and Renie got out of the small boat and picked it up to carry it through the stretch of shallow water. About one hundred feet downstream, the creek narrowed again and deepened enough to put the boat back in the water. Paddling and guiding the boat Katherine prayed once more. "Father I pray for Mrs. Audie that she will be comfortable and we will be able to minister to her needs."

Only a few minutes had passed since the couple had put the boat in the creek. Katherine knew it wasn't much further. She remembered a footbridge which marked the Bearden farm. Tugging the boat up the bank, Katherine tied it to a tall river birch.

Trudging up the hill to the Bearden place was the roughest part of the trip, as the path had long since overgrown. Briar vines stuck to their clothes and honeysuckle vines tripped them. Relying on her memory of where the house was located, Katherine and Renie plodded up the hill, not complaining, or even talking as they journeyed.

A dog announced the arrival of the couple. A small, brown dog barked a couple of times and ran to offer his greetings. He seemed glad they were there to help. The dog's barking aroused someone inside.

The door opened to a sliver of candle light.

"Hello, Luke," Katherine called as she saw Mrs. Bearden's son open the door just wide enough to see out. "We came to see your mother."

Thirty-five year old Luke opened the door a little wider to see Katherine and Renie who were now on the porch. "Ma…sick," Luke said, pointing inside at his mother.

Luke was the only child of Mr. and Mrs. Bearden and was never able to leave the care and attention of his parents. Oddly enough, Luke had some of the same features as Hannah, like they were related. He had the same odd shaped eyes, the small stature, a sweet smile and a loving personality. Luke had been limited to what he could learn and do, but his parents had taken care of him the best they knew, and they had loved him so very much.

Mr. Bearden had passed away ten years ago from heart ailments, and Mrs. Bearden had taken care of Luke and herself as best she could. Neighbors and the local church helped occasionally.

Mrs. Audie appeared asleep when Katherine and Renie approached her bed. Katherine spoke gently to the little lady as she lightly stroked her forehead, "Mrs. Audie, we are here to help you. Renie is here with me, and we will help you with anything you want us to do."

Mrs. Audie opened her eyes and tried to focus on Katherine. "Water," was all she could whisper.

Finding a spoon and a cup of water, Katherine lifted Mrs. Audie's head enough for her to have a small spoon of water.

"Mrs. Audie, I want to give you a dishpan bath and freshen your bed, if you feel like it," Katherine said as she didn't really know how long Mrs. Audie had. Although she hated to disturb the woman, she knew that the bed was too soiled for her to die in the mess. At least, Katherine and Renie could help with cleaning the bed.

Mrs. Audie nodded and gave an approving smile. Katherine got bathwater ready in the dishpan she found in the kitchen.

Renie knew her job without being told as she started talking with Luke. Emptying the contents of her visiting bag, Renie engaged Luke in her play. She had put her slate and a chalk in the bag along with her new book and a couple of carvings her father had made for her. Picking up the carvings, Luke said something that Renie didn't understand.

Meanwhile, Katherine searched through the chest to find a clean gown, undergarments and sheets. She was watchful with Mrs. Audie as she gave her a quick bath, just enough to make her feel a little better. Getting rid of the soiled sheet, she sang a hymn and talked with Mrs. Audie as she proceeded to try to make the bed a little more comfortable for her fragile patient. Mrs. Audie was seventy-five years old and had been in good health until the past year. Her health had deteriorated and for the last couple of weeks she had become bedridden.

After Katherine had finished with the bath and the bedding, she whispered to Mrs. Audie that she should rest awhile. Mrs. Audie closed her eyes and slept for a couple of hours. Katherine was sitting beside her, holding her hand. Renie had joined them and was rubbing her forehead and her hair while holding her other hand. The two simply wanted Mrs. Audie to know that someone was there for her.

Abruptly, Mrs. Audie's eyes opened and she reached for Katherine's hand. "Luke, Luke..." she whispered worriedly.

"We are going to take care of Luke. I will take Luke home with me, and he will always have a home. Don't you worry about that, Mrs. Audie, you rest now," Katherine said assuredly.

Mrs. Audie seemed to let go of her worries as she resigned herself with a look of sweet solace on her face.

"Gran, do you see them?" Renie whispered as she gazed all about the small cabin. "Do you hear them? They are making such a beautiful sound, their wings, I suppose. Gran, they are beautiful. Don't you see them? There are a dozen at least, and they are magnificent."

Katherine looked at her grandchild who was so enamored with the sight of the angels she looked like an angel herself. "No, child, I don't see them, but I feel their presence. When we get older we lose the ability to see through the eyes of innocence. But, I can see and hear them through you."

"Then I never want to grow up. They are beautiful, Gran, and they have come to take Mrs. Audie to heaven to be with Jesus. I remember when they came for Mama, the first time I saw and heard them. They are so beautiful I wish I could go with them."

"We are not ready for you to go with them, Renie. You are such a blessing to me and to this family. How can we do without our little angel here on earth?"

Luke sensed his mother was getting worse as he knelt beside her and put his cheek on hers. "Ove 'ou, Ma," and the tears began to roll down his face.

Giving mother and child time together, Katherine pulled a Bible from her bag. She knew that Mrs. Audie was a Christian, for her life was a testimony to others. Although Katherine did not feel the need to witness, she felt the need to read a few comforting verses.

"Luke, would you care if I read a few verses to your mother?" Katherine asked.

Luke shook his head and wiped his face of his tears; as though he was resolved to what he knew was coming.

Katherine read a few verses from Psalm 139 and prayed as the four of them held hands. "Father, help us make this time comfortable for Mrs. Audie as she prepares to meet her husband and Jesus."

Recognizing the signs, Katherine knew Mrs. Audie probably wouldn't last long now. She had the clammy skin, deep-set eyes and a pallor color.

"Father, what do I do about Luke? Should I spare him seeing his mother die, or should I let him be with her as she slips away?" Katherine whispered her prayer, hoping that Jesus would help her know what to do.

As though Luke knew what Katherine had asked, he held onto his mother's hand and gently kissed her.

"Goodbye, Ma," Luke said as he wiped his tears once again.

Mrs. Audie took two deep breaths and was gone, on her way to heaven.

———◆———

At the Cosby cabin, Thomas read Katherine's note. He hitched the horses to the buggy and started on the journey. The sun was just beginning to come up when Thomas arrived at the Bearden cabin. He peeped in at Katherine and told her he would get the boat and be right back.

Katherine and Renie had done all they knew to prepare Luke to go with them. Although he did not want to leave, he gathered a few things to take with him. Renie helped Luke put some clothes in a pillowcase along with his mother's Bible.

Katherine explained they would have a funeral for his mother, and they would bury her. Luke took Katherine's hand and led her to the back yard. There in the back yard was a small gravestone, Luke's father's gravestone. Luke had already faced the death of a loved one, his father and now his mother.

"You would like your mother buried here, beside your father. Is that right, Luke?" Katherine asked.

Luke nodded a 'yes' in reply as he headed to the wagon.

On the way home Luke sat up front with Thomas. "I remember when you were born, Luke. I was seven years old, and I saw you with your mama and dad. They were so proud of you. You were a cute little baby boy," Thomas said trying to bring a little cheer to the situation.

Luke acted as though he understood. "Funeral?" Luke asked Thomas.

"Yes, the funeral will be tomorrow or the next day. We can go see your pastor and ask about the time and place," Thomas explained.

Behind Thomas and Luke sat Katherine and Renie, settled in for the ride home. Renie put her head in Katherine's lap and soon fell asleep. As she slept, she dreamed of Mrs. Audie and Luke. Mrs. Audie was showing her something in her dream, but Renie could not understand what it was. Trying to listen closely to Mrs. Audie, Renie found herself struggling until she woke herself.

"Gran, I had a dream. Mrs. Audie was trying to tell me something, but I wasn't able to understand."

Katherine ran her hand through Renie's hair, "Dear, don't worry, it will come."

The weary group arrived at home while Thomas and Luke took care of the horses. Meanwhile, Katherine and Renie hurried to the house to warm a few leftovers from breakfast. Mary had made breakfast and left to spend a day at school with Tommie and Nellie. When the men had finished with the morning chores, the two came in, eager for bacon and eggs.

The first thing Luke noticed was the piano. He pointed to the piano and seemed to be asking permission to touch it. To the surprise of the family, Luke began to play the instrument, mostly chords and runs, but it sounded heavenly. Mrs. Audie had played for her church and had an old organ which was probably how Luke had learned.

Luke played for a few minutes, then promptly stopped and went to the table. The family clapped and praised Luke for his music. Luke thanked everyone and was ready for breakfast.

"Thomas, since Renie is tired, why not let her stay home from school today and get some rest?" Katherine asked, knowing that Renie was exhausted and wouldn't be functional at school.

"I think that is a great idea. She can rest and when she wakes she can help me clean the manure out of the barn stalls. What do you think, Renie?" Thomas teased.

Katherine suggested they take a nap together. Perhaps Renie would understand her dream and feel secure if they were together. Katherine had always heard from the old folk that the deceased person's spirit remained on earth for three days, until it left, never to come back. If there was a message Audie wanted to give Renie she would need to learn of it before the end of the three days.

Snuggling next to her grandmother, Renie felt secure. They talked a few moments about the events of the night and before long Renie and Katherine were sound asleep.

Thomas checked on the two and pulled a light quilt up around them. Their "gift" was such a blessing to others but brought such demands on the two of them, emotionally and physically. The last incident had been so different from the others, one that rendered everyone, even Katherine and Renie, helpless.

The heartbreak of the beloved Taylor family had reached the hearts and lives of the people, not only the Upton and Roundstone area, but in the three counties, Hart, Hardin and LaRue.

The tragedy had happened over a year ago, and still Thomas felt such pain for the family. Oddly enough the devotion he had given that morning was from the book of Job. Job had told his wife that we should not only accept the good from God but also the trouble. He remembered telling his family that when times are good, we should be happy; but when times are bad, we have to consider that God has made the one as well as the other. Therefore, no one can discover anything about their future.

Renie had slept for two days at the beginning of the tragedy. No one could fathom that the two incidents were connected. Thomas had traveled to ask Dr. Routt to come pay a home visit on Renie as he feared Renie would not wake. Unfortunately, the doctor was with the Taylor family.

The terrible accident had happened that morning as Mrs. Taylor and her daughter, Brianna, were in the buggy on their way to see a family member. A rattlesnake coiled in the road caused the horses to become frightened and they reared. The buggy turned over and Brianna was thrown out onto a large rock. She was killed instantly.

The doctor was with the family that morning but paid a home visit that evening to the Cosby home. Dr. Routt examined Renie and concluded that he could not find anything wrong with her, except a low grade temperature. He had to admit he was bewildered with Renie's sleep. He advised the family to keep a watch on her and she would probably be fine in a day or two.

Renie slept through the day and night, murmuring something in her sleep. On the second day of her sleep, another tragedy, the same family, more heartbreak to endure.

Mr. and Mrs. Taylor had left their house that very evening to go to town to purchase a coffin for Brianna. Friends were at the house sitting with Brianna's body as she was laid out in the living room. Their son, Brice, was in the wagon while they were in the buggy behind. As they were driving they watched a horrible scene unfold before their eyes.

A large buck deer, possibly influenced by rutting season, had decided to charge across the path, right in front of Brice's wagon. When the buck charged into the horses, they reared, which caused the tongue of the wagon to twist, throwing Brice over a cliff and down a hill.

As the fear-stricken parents ran to Brice's side, he was already dying. He looked at his mother as he whispered his last words, "Goin' to see Brianna. Love you, Mom, Dad. I see angels coming to take me to Jesus."

The Taylor family had lost two children, their only two children in less than twenty-four hours. Their pain had been difficult as they asked God, "Why?" The entire community grieved with them for everyone knew their children were Christians and were ready to go to heaven but everyone had to ask why. Why would a loving God let this happen to one of his own?

Pastor Ship told the parents that it was certainly okay to be angry, as a part of grieving. "Sometimes bad things happen to good people, but as Christians, we have to be able to accept the good with the bad. The Taylor family had Brianna and Brice for fourteen and seventeen years, loving them and learning from them, and they were taken to be with their Heavenly Father."

The funeral for the siblings was held the next day at the church. The morning had been rather bleak, with rain showers, coming and going. At the cemetery a large crowd gathered to show love to the family. The pastor said a few words from Genesis regarding God's covenant to man and the rainbow. He talked about the new covenant, being the blood of Jesus to cover our sins. As he was delivering the words of his last message to the family, a double rainbow formed in sky.

"Oh, look," as people began to gaze at the sky and point to the double rainbow. It was obvious that God wanted to remind every one of His children that He is a loving God and He is keeping His covenants with them.

"Well," Pastor Ship concluded, "this sign from God is obviously a message from Him that He is keeping His covenant with us. Praise God for His gifts of these two children. Now, God will have two beautiful angels making heaven even sweeter for us as we wait to join them."

The crowd worshipped and prayed as they had never done before. The funerals had not been 'hell, fire and condemnation' for sinners, but a sweet invitation to become a Christian and let your light shine as the two Taylor children had done. Because of the service, Mike, who had been Brice's best friend, had responded to the invitation and accepted Jesus Christ. Because of the death of two good friends, Mike had become a disciple of Christ.

After the incident, Thomas realized that Katherine knew all along that Renie was sleeping to avoid the critical time with Brianna and Brice. Somehow, the child knew the tragedy would happen and she could not help.

Thomas joined Luke happily rocking in the rocker on the front porch. Thomas sat in the other rocker and rocked with Luke as they watched the creek flow easily along. Luke pointed to the squirrels as they ran up the trees, and the birds flying overhead. Thomas relaxed with Luke, for time is all we really have.

# Chapter 30

# School Day

Bible reading was always the first part of the day at Roundstone School. The students were quiet as they observed this special devotional time. Most of the children were churched, but a few never heard the Bible except while they were at school. Andrea Goodwin recognized the awesome responsibility this job meant. Mrs. Andrea read from Hebrews 12:11: "Now no chastening (disciplining) seems to be joyful for the present, but painful; nevertheless, afterward it yields the peaceable fruit of righteousness to those who have been trained by it." Placing the Bible on her desk, Mrs. Andrea continued.

"Remember, students we talked about the word discipline the first of the school year. Someone give me a sentence using discipline," Mrs. Andrea asked as she walked around the classroom watching the faces of her students.

Geri's hand went up. "I have to use discipline when I don't want to do the dishes, but I know when I do, the kitchen will look better and I will please mama by doing my job."

"Good, Geri," Mrs. Andrea said in an encouraging voice.

Mike raised his hand. "I had to use discipline to get up this morning because I wanted to sleep more."

"I think we all have to use discipline when we try to get up in the morning. Mike, good sentence. Now, Nellie, what do you think this verse means?" Mrs. Andrea asked.

Nellie placed her index finger on her lip as she thought for a minute. "I think sometimes studying can be a discipline and sometimes I don't want to do it, but I will have peace when I have learned how to read, write, and do my arithmetic problems."

"I think that is a very good practical use of the verse. You have looked at the verse from a fundamental use. Anyone else have a comment on today's scripture?" Mrs. Andrea asked.

"Sometimes I have to make myself listen when my Dad does the devotional. Sometimes my mind wants to wander. I guess you would say I have to discipline my mind to listen. Like Sunday morning, Dad read a lesson from Psalms 118, I think. It says, something like; 'Today is the Lord's Day, and we will rejoice and be happy in it.' Dad talked about how we are blessed with a new day every day, and we should always be happy and accept any challenges that come our way. He put that verse to use when he picked up an old man on the road and took care of him," Tommie explained.

Mrs. Andrea took a minute to expound on what Tommie had said, to break the message down a little more so that everyone could understand the lesson Tommie had learned. All the children quoted the scripture with Mrs. Andrea three times, as they did every morning.

Mrs. Andrea had written the day's lesson on the blackboard: Today is Monday, September 23, 1845. The sun is shining, and we are going outside this afternoon. We will have a lesson on nature.

Children used their slates to write the morning lesson. Afterward the students went through lessons in the *Kentucky Primer*, the *Kentucky Speller*, and Harrison's *English Grammar*. Mrs. Andrea worked with the advanced arithmetic students while Mrs. Sallye worked with the beginner's arithmetic.

Sallye enjoyed giving assistance at school. She admired Andrea, and wished she knew better how to help her. A student who needed help with reading or writing would often ask Sallye for help. If the student needed more detailed instruction, Sallye would summon Mrs. Andrea.

Sallye envied the students in the classroom, as they had the chance to learn about the Bible. She had run away from home when she was barely fifteen. Sallye had not come from a Christian home like many of the people at Roundstone. Seems like everyone here is a Christian, everyone but me, Sallye thought. She believed in God, but knew God could never forgive her for her sins.

As Sallye checked on Hannah she thought, I'm sure God made Hannah the way she is as a punishment to me for my sins. But, I love her so much I wouldn't change her for my sake at all. I love her just the way she is. Watching

Hannah quietly doing her printing, Sallye's heart was filled with love. "So precious, my little Hannah," Sallye whispered.

During lunch, Sallye and Andrea shared time together. "Sallye, you are a natural with the children. I really appreciate your help. And Hannah is doing so well. She is a precious little girl."

"Thank you, Andrea. I just don't want to be in your way, or do something wrong, so always tell me if I make a mistake."

After lunch, Mrs. Andrea took a seat in the middle of her students. "Many of you were at the dance on Saturday night. I enjoyed seeing you all dressed up and dancing. All of you looked so nice, and I realized for some of you, you will be making decisions which will affect the rest of your life. So, I would like to talk to you about some of the options you have. Someone tell me what you would like to do when you get out of school."

Ruthie Avery was first to answer. "Get married and have a baby."

Expecting that answer, Mrs. Andrea needed to address that issue. "Good answer, Ruthie, and I know that is important for many young girls. However, I do want you to know there is more out there for you than getting married and having children. Kentucky now has several schools which are very good. Young women can go and be trained for many vocations. Now, there is a woman in Kentucky who is going to graduate and become a doctor soon. I want you to think of other things you could do with your life besides getting married and having children. Anyone?" Mrs. Andrea was hoping to get good class participation.

"I want to go work in missions, if it is the Lord's will, of course, but I think I would love helping other people. Maybe being a midwife would be good since I have helped Gran deliver babies," Nellie answered enthusiastically.

Geri shyly answered, "I would like to be a teacher like you, Mrs. Andrea."

"Great answers, girls. You know you can do anything you set your mind to do. There are schools which are eager to help you with your goals," Andrea encouraged the girls.

"Boys, what about you? Do any of you think about your future? Do you have goals for your life?" Mrs. Andrea asked looking at some of the boys.

Tommie was the first to answer. "I would like to be an architect. I like to make drawings of houses and put them to scale. I did a drawing of our new house."

"I know, Tommie, I was there the day you showed it. You did a good job, and you will make a great architect!" Mrs. Andrea encouraged him. "Mike, you are going to graduate soon. What do you want to do?"

"Well, I don't know exactly, but I think I would like to mine for a while, get some money before I get married and settle down. Then, I would like to be a farmer, raise cattle, sheep, goats, chickens and have a lot of kids. I just want to get rich in the gold and silver mines before starting a family."

"Getting rich is not necessary, though, Mike. Rich does not equal happy. Many people are heading to North Carolina to the gold mines to get rich. However, the experience of seeing the country on an adventure would be nice for any young man. All I can say is follow your dream, but keep God's will in mind for your life," Mrs. Andrea advised.

Mrs. Andrea took the students on a walk around the edge of the woods. She asked them to observe all living things: plants, trees, and insects, everything that they saw. Many of the students knew the particular names of the trees, and they could explain if the tree was good for burning in the fireplace, or for building, or for bearing fruit. Mrs. Andrea encouraged the students to look at the trees as beauty and asked the students to name their favorite tree.

Students had good class discussion talking about the various types of trees, explaining their favorite and why. Mrs. Andrea and Mrs. Sallye remarked that they had learned from their students about the trees. Mrs. Andrea explained the homework assignment. "If you could be a tree, what kind would you be and why," she explained.

The lesson had been engaging for all the students. Mrs. Andrea had pleased everyone when she said they would go out each afternoon and observe nature. The last thirty minutes of the day was spent writing and/or drawing about their nature expedition. Mrs. Andrea challenged the students to enter a writing contest about nature. The contest was a nation-wide contest and there was a cash award.

Mrs. Andrea pulled Tommie aside. "Tommie, I would love for you to enter the contest. I told the other students to write on nature. However, the topic can be anything that you wish. You have such writing potential, that I feel that you might have a good chance to win. Give it some thought and hand it in a week from today."

As the students were going back in the building, Nellie pulled Mike aside. "Mike, why do you think you have to be rich to get married? Working together and building a home is what I look forward to. Really, Mike, I don't want you to leave and go off somewhere mining."

"Nellie, I will not marry anyone before I have something to offer. I don't have anything of my own and I want to be able to offer my bride a home, with nice things. My good-for-nothing father married my mother and did not give her anything but a hard time. I will not do that to you, well, I mean, to anyone I marry."

Nellie took Mike's hand, looked directly into his eyes and said very firmly, "I will marry you, Mike Caswell, just you wait and see. We will have a good life together despite your wanting to run away and dig for gold. We are going to live right here at Roundstone and be happy the rest of our lives. That is unless the Lord wants us to go on a mission field somewhere. I have known I was going to marry you for a long time, and you are not going to change my mind. Understand?"

Mike smiled and nodded to Nellie. However, he knew there was something God wanted him to do, he just didn't understand right now. As much as he loved Nellie, he knew he had a calling, not so much the mines which he had mentioned, but for something which God had not entirely revealed.

# Chapter 31

# The Attic

In her pocket apron Katherine held the envelope that Renie had found at the Bearden cabin. While at the Bearden place, Luke, Thomas, and Tommie had taken turns digging the grave. Neighbor ladies had helped Mary take care of the house by cleaning and arranging the furniture for the wake. Katherine had fixed Audie's hair and dressed her. Other friends and church family had paid respects that afternoon, bringing food and memories to share. Members of the church had offered to buy a coffin and purchase a gravestone. Word was spread throughout the community that the funeral would be the next morning.

Renie had been anxious to get to the Bearden cabin that morning.

The day before, when the two had been napping, Renie had awakened. "I know what it is, Gran. There is a letter that we need to get at Mrs. Audie's. An important letter."

As soon as the Cosby family arrived at the Bearden home, Renie burst into the house and quickly looked around for what she needed. Finding the loose hearth stone on the floor of the fireplace, Renie pulled and tugged on it. Urging Renie to let them try, Katherine and Mary pulled at the stone and finally managed to budge the stone from its place. Pulling it away from the hearth, they found the letter. Katherine immediately read the letter.

September 25, 1836

Dear Audie,

We heard that Clyde passed away a few months ago. We would like to come see you and Luke. We know that Clyde would not have let us visit, but since he has passed away, we would like to come. How is Luke doing? We have worried about you trying to stay there without any help. We want you and Luke to come live with us. We have a big cabin here and there is plenty of room for you and Luke.

You remember Aunt Lizzie. Well, she fell and broke her leg and is not doing good. Her husband, son, and daughter-in-law are taking care of her. They live in Tennessee and we don't hear much from them. You know the Jackson family was never close to this side of the family.

Anyway, we would love for you and Luke to come and live with us. It is just Austin and me and we would be a big help to each other. I know that Austin and Clyde had their problems, but we don't have to worry about that. Please let us know if we can come see you, or if you want to come to our house. I want to be close to my sister and my nephew now that I am getting older.

Love you,
Your sister, Marie Stanel

Early that morning, Katherine had mailed a letter to Marie, Audie's sister, telling her of Audie's death. She used the address on the envelope and hoped it was still the correct one. She knew there was no way for Marie to get there for the funeral, but at least she would know.

The church family, neighbors and friends arrived for the funeral on Saturday morning. The preacher said a few words, and the body was lowered into the grave. Friends were concerned and asked what would happen to Luke. Katherine explained she had told Audie she would take care of Luke, or at least make sure he was with someone who would take good care of him.

Each morning, Luke left with Thomas to take care of the chores. Luke had taken an immediate kinship with Thomas and the two were becoming great buddies. He had also made friends with Nellie as they learned to play a lively duet together on the piano.

I wonder what kind of house Dr. Larimore lives in, Katherine thought. Although he had told her to call him Keith, she just didn't feel comfortable with that informality yet. He had told her that as soon as he finished all his business dealings, selling the house, packing and closing his practice in Lexington, he would be there to see her again.

Katherine felt she had met someone very special on Saturday night, but wasn't ready to put her trust in him. When the doctor had stood on the platform and addressed the people, his eyes had met hers, and she was ashamed, but sparks flew. She even felt flushed when he held his gaze on her. He probably won't even come back, and if he does he will not think about me, at my age. Why would he?

Katherine gathered a few fried pies along with some country ham sandwiches to take on her trip. She left a note for Mary. Katherine took the smaller buggy and the first horse that Thomas wasn't using. The day was beautiful, with a slight chill in the air; the leaves had begun the first phase of turning into their majestic fall colors. Of course in Kentucky, it could take an entire beautiful month for change. Fall was Katherine's favorite season even though she dreaded winter coming more and more every year. There was just something about the fall, pumpkin pie, cold molasses, a harvest of late vegetables, the glorious colors of leaves which made fall so beautiful. Also, one could sit back on the porch with a hot cup of coffee and rock without worrying about being too hot or too cold, or the garden work.

Mrs. Velma Thomas' house was Katherine's first stop. She chatted with the feeble, ninety-year old lady while doing a few chores for her. Promising a quick return, Katherine left the food and hugged Mrs. Thomas goodbye.

Katherine stopped at another couple of houses on her way to town and told the ladies about the Ladies' Day event. Promises of food and attendance looked encouraging for Katherine.

The next stop for Katherine was at Head to Toe to pay a visit with Lyssa and Leah. More improvements were being made by the girls, and the rough building was becoming more like a business place.

"Hello, hello, anybody here?" Katherine called as she walked into the shop.

Both girls were in the back trying to sand a rough table the men had built for them. The table was tall, built to cut fabric on, which was good, but it was extremely rough.

"Girls, what about covering the table with some strong, sturdy fabric? You might be sanding this time next month if you try to get it perfectly smooth."

"Yeah, we thought of that, but the fabric is so expensive we hated to have to use that much to cover the table and then we could cut it as we cut material. What are you up to today? We thought you would be in Lexington by now," Lyssa teased and winked at Katherine.

"I had much rather be here with you girls," Katherine replied giving both girls hugs.

"I don't know why," Leah said. "That Doc is a good looking fellow, and he had the eye for you, Ms. Katherine. Didn't he, Lyssa?"

"Sure did. You are a very lucky woman, Katherine," Lyssa teased.

"I am a blessed woman, girls. The Lord has blessed me with a rich life, good health, a good family and friends, and a good church. I love my friends and neighbors. Anyway, I wanted to ask you when you thought you would have your opening day?"

"Leah and I have looked at the calendar, and we don't want to open until after Ladies' Day. We will open on Monday, Oct. 14. We expect it might be slow that week, until Saturday, but we will have time to do more work, if we need to," Lyssa said.

Leah added, "We have plans to help all we can for the Ladies' Day. It's very important. We would like to give everybody this little reminder about our store opening. Here's what I printed."

"Amazing! Leah, did you make this yourself?"

"Yes, Mrs. Katherine. Now, I just have to make about fifty more," Leah said.

The card was a small piece of paper with a picture of a needle and a thread and it appeared the thread had stitched the words, 'Head to Toe' and below that was a heart. She had printed the address below. The card looked professionally done.

"Leah, you did an excellent job! Where did you learn to print so well, so evenly?" Katherine asked.

"Well, my master in Tennessee had me do her writing for her, and it had to be done perfectly. I was allowed to go to school and learn a few things at the plantation's school for the slaves. Hobie got to go too because his master wanted him to be able to measure and do carpentry work, so he learned to read, and he is good at arithmetic," Leah said. "We would have stayed with them, but the older couple died. Before they died, they gave us a certificate of freedom. When the son came, he was mean, and he whipped us, and he shot at Hobie. He said that he was going to sell one of us, and we would not be together. First chance we got, we ran. We would rather have died than have been split up."

Katherine saw Leah wipe a tear from her cheek. "Leah, you are such a sweet girl, I can't see how anyone could be mean to you. Just like God remembered his covenant with Abraham, Isaac and Jacob, He heard the groaning of the Israelite people, and He brought them out into the Promised Land. So, God brought you out and delivered you to Lyssa and Ollie. Now, both of your families are together and being blessed." Katherine spoke emphatically.

"Well, I came here to work. Is there anything I can do?" Katherine asked.

Lyssa looked around the room. "Well, the baby is asleep right now, so you don't have to rock. We bought some of this oil cloth to cut up and put on the shelves. We want it to come over the edge like this. All of the shelves need this. Also, we need more painting to be done, but you can't do it in your good dress."

"Well, let me help on the shelves. I can cut and place this while we talk," Katherine insisted.

Leah remembered the attic and asked, "We haven't been in the attic. Is there anything up there, besides bird and wasp nests?"

"I don't remember. My husband bought this store when it was for sale thirty years ago and we just never did do anything with it. Let's go up and see," Katherine said.

Thankfully, they still had the ladder they had borrowed from Mr. Risen down the street. They put the ladder under the attic and Katherine scampered up like a squirrel. She pulled at a latch and the top fell open. Sticking her head over the top she peered in each direction. Small windows on both ends of the storefront let in a little natural light.

"Hold on, girls, you may not need to come up here. Well, let me see if there is anything to look at, if not, you can save your energy." Katherine pulled herself up to the floor of the attic. Giving her eyes time to adjust she looked around. There was a leather pouch, like a saddle bag, close to where she stepped up. She picked it up and felt something inside. Hope that isn't a mouse nest in there, she thought.

"Girls I am going to pitch something down. Watch out," She said as she dropped it. Looking over the floor of the attic, Katherine picked up a few objects she couldn't identify and slipped them into her pocket.

Behind the chimney, almost as if intended to be hidden from view was a small trunk. Katherine bent to see if she could open it without taking it downstairs but the trunk was locked.

Hmmm, now what am I going to do? Probably too heavy to try to get downstairs, Katherine thought as she grabbed the handle on a side and tried to move it. Giving up, she descended the ladder downstairs.

"Uggh! You have dirt all over you!" Lyssa said. "We looked in the pouch, looks like a diary of someone on a journey, tells about the weather each day, what they did, how much Indian relics they saw, that kind of notes. Guess it would be pretty interesting."

"Was there anything else?" Leah asked.

"Yea, there was a small trunk, but it must be filled with lead because I could not budge it. It is locked, so the lock would have to be sawed off. And, you girls are not going to be able to get it down by yourselves. I pulled and pulled and didn't get it to move an inch. Why don't you have your men to come by tonight and check it out?"

"Okay, we have a lot to do here anyway," Lyssa said. "Hey, Katherine, I have a dishpan here, and water in the jug. Pour yourself a pan of water and clean up a bit."

"Listen to that: she doesn't want me to get her shop dirty, Leah. What do you think of that?" Katherine teased.

Katherine helped the girls for a while before she realized she needed to be getting home to chores. There were still some green tomatoes and peppers which would make some green tomato relish. Thomas had bought another crock and she might as well make good use of it.

As she rode home, she could not keep from thinking about Dr. Larimore. How silly of me, I can't keep my mind off him. Truth was, she had thought about Dr. Larimore much of the time since Sunday. Perhaps she was just a silly old lady, but there seemed to be something there, and she couldn't wait to see him again.

———◦◦———

School was out about the time Lyssa and Leah went by school so they picked up Oliver and went home to fix supper. When the men came home, everyone shared a meal of beans, onions, bacon and cornbread. The women shared part of their day and the men, laughingly, exaggerated about how tired they were. Ollie and Hobie enjoyed the job of working with wood but they were really tired at the end of a day.

"Then you probably don't feel like going back to the shop, I guess?" Lyssa asked.

"Aw shucks, I'm feelin' mighty worn out." Ollie said stretching his legs out and his arms over his head.

"What about you, Hobie? You too tired to go to the shop?" asked Leah.

"Yeah, I'm pretty tired, would just like to put my feet up out on the porch and rest awhile before we start doing the chores," Hobie admitted.

"Well, Leah, guess we could get some big, strong men to help us get that big, heavy trunk out of the attic, couldn't we?" Lyssa asked Leah.

"Say, what? Get what out of the attic? What attic? What are you talking about?" Ollie asked so quickly Lyssa didn't get a chance to answer.

"Well, I thought you weren't interested. You are tired, dear, don't worry, we will ask someone else to help us tomorrow. That old trunk at the store is probably filled with rocks anyway, it is so heavy."

Ollie and Hobie jumped up, and they were hooking the horse up to the wagon before the girls could get Baby Oleta ready to leave.

"Landsakes women! Y'all better be hurrin' it up. We ain't got all day!" Ollie yelled back at them.

Little Oliver asked why they were in such a hurry. The girls explained to Ollie and Hobie they didn't have to be in a hurry; the box had been in there for several years, and it wasn't easily going anywhere.

On the trip to the shop the men were speculating what could possibly be in the box that would make it so heavy. When the treasure hunters arrived, Ollie quickly climbed the ladder with Hobie and Leah close behind. Lyssa, Baby Oleta, and Oliver stayed downstairs.

All three tried to pull the trunk to lower it downstairs, but the trunk was not moving. "Look, the trunk has been nailed to this beam across here. It's not going to budge unless we open it and pull out the nails." Hobie said turning the lock over.

"Well, we have wasted our time, because this trunk is locked," Leah said as she kicked the side of the trunk.

"Mighty lucky for us, I jest happened to pick up this here awl. Let's see here." Ollie bragged as he twisted the awl in the lock. Grunting, Ollie pulled down on the awl and the lock popped off.

"Wow!"

# Chapter 32

# The Trunk

Ollie carefully lifted a couple pieces from the trunk. "Well, I be a possum in a hen house. Ain't them jest the purddiest rocks you ever saw?"

"What is it? What's in the trunk?" Lyssa asked anxiously from downstairs.

"Well, it's a box of rocks, I guess," Leah answered as she held a rock up to the light.

"Here, I will hand this to you," Ollie said as he stretched to hand one of the smaller pieces to Lyssa.

"The box is full of these, most are bigger."

"Let's take out these bigger ones so we can try to get the nails out. See here, there are two nails holding the trunk to this attic beam," Hobie said as they were removing the contents. "How about you stand on the ladder, Leah, and hand them down to Lyssa."

Lyssa put baby Oleta in the crib and the group passed the stones down to Lyssa and Oliver. The stones, arrowheads, and bones were put on the large table the men had made for the fabric. The excited group examined the rocks carefully, holding them to the window for close examination. Most of the stones were purple, white, and blue, but there were a few coral stones and lots of quartz.

"These are beautiful! There are so many different colors, sizes and depths of intensity," Leah said, mesmerized by their beauty.

"Where do you think they came from?" Hobie asked. "Looks like it is a collection of oddities, too. Look, this here looks like bones instead of rocks."

"Sure does. These here are surely bones. And this here, look, it looks like an imprint of a foot, and this one is a leaf," Ollie said. "Somebody did a lot of digging, and some of this here came from caves, like this, looks like cave rock."

"These are beautiful. Do you think we can display them in our shop?" Lyssa asked. "I think a lot of people would like to see them."

"I don't know, they are... actually property of the Cosby family because it is their building," Ollie said. "They may want them, and we'll have to ask. Don't know, may be worth something."

"Yeah, we need to get them to come and look at the collection," Hobie said. "They may have an idea of where they came from."

"Could Oliver have one to carry in his pocket?" Lyssa asked.

"Sure, don't look like it would do any harm. I'm sure Ms. Katherine wouldn't mind," Ollie added.

A bit disappointed that the trunk didn't contain gold, or coins, the families started home, satisfied they had solved the mystery.

Leah asked, "Would you care if Oliver and me went on down to the Cosby's and told them what we found? Lyssa you want to go?"

"I really need to get Baby Oleta ready for bed. But, please go and tell Katherine the news."

Oliver played with his stone and chatted with Leah on their way to the Cosby's. "Mrs. Andrea told us to bring something for show and tell. I didn't know what to take, because Mama said I couldn't take my baby sister. Now, I have something to tell about, but I don't know what it is," Oliver said, turning the stone over.

———— ·•· ————

"Guess where I got this! Guess! Aw, you won't know. It's a...it's a...what is it Leah?"

As Leah and Oliver told Katherine the story about the discovery, Oliver held, rolled, and examined his stone. "Could I keep it, Ms. Katherine?"

"Sure you can. I don't even know how it got there. The others are doing chores but we will get them to come to the house for a few minutes. Oliver, would you want to go to the barn and tell them to come up here, as soon as they can?"

Oliver was off to the barn while Leah talked with Katherine. Mary joined them on the porch as Thomas, Nellie, and Tommie came from the barn.

"Hey, Leah, what's up?" Thomas asked. "This must be important for you to come out here at this hour."

"I sure hope we haven't done anything wrong, but the trunk in the attic... well we pried it open and we were able to get the contents out. Oliver, show them what was in the trunk," Leah said.

Once again, Oliver dug in his pocket and brought out the sparkling purple amethyst.

"That is feldspar," Mary said. "I don't think it is really worth a lot, but it is beautiful, isn't it."

"Ollie said he thought the other larger rock was cave rock, a magnificent stone too. Some of it is sparkly and heavy," Leah added. "I'm just sorry now that we pried the lock open, but we were anxious to find out what was inside, and we didn't have a key."

Suddenly, Tommie became interested in the conversation, "You say key? I wonder if the key that was in Johnny's box, the one he gave me, could be... do you think it might be the key to the trunk, Dad?"

Tommie ran inside and climbed up to his room in the loft. Scratching through the bag of arrowheads and rocks he found the key. Tommie jumped down the last half of the ladder anxious to get outside. "Dad, do you think this key would fit a trunk? Maybe that is Johnny's trunk of treasures. He told me he had more stuff somewhere, but I never knew where it was."

"Well, it could be. Johnny was always on adventures, going everywhere digging, going places he shouldn't and sometimes getting in trouble," Thomas said.

"We can find out when we go look at the rocks. Hey, there was a journal in the pouch. I bet it holds the secret," Katherine said.

"Yeah," Leah added. "We really didn't look at it very good, but it listed directions, dates and maps."

"Sounds like Johnny," Thomas said. "There isn't anything he wouldn't do to get special rocks. He had a fascination with caves, stones, Indian things. I warned him over and over to stay out of trouble. So, he might have thought if we saw the collection of stuff he had, he would get in trouble. Could very well have been his. We will have to check it out as soon as possible."

"Thank you so much, Leah, for coming out here and letting us know about this. We appreciate it. You know, I completely forgot about the trunk and the pouch. I had other things on my mind," Katherine admitted.

Leah and Oliver waved goodbye as they rode back home to their family. Oliver was happy he did not have to give up his stone. "I have a good show and tell for tomorrow. I can't wait to tell them about Johnny hiding his treasures."

The Cosby family finished their chores that evening and sat on the porch to enjoy the cool evening. Thomas and Katherine could not keep from talking about the trunk, and all the places Johnny had been to create such a collection.

"What worries me is that he was going to dangerous places. He could have been killed there in an accident, and we would have never known where his body was. At least, with him drowning, we found his body." Thomas spoke with a shaky voice as he kept his head down.

"I never understood, if Johnny was a swimmer, how come him to drown?" Mary questioned.

"It had rained all night and when the creek is up, there is a whirlpool which forms in the deep section across from the mill. I figure Johnny got caught in it, could not swim out and was sucked under," Thomas said, sadly.

"That's so sad," Mary said. "There is no telling what he could have done with his life. He could have been another Daniel Boone, from the way he explored. I am so sorry he died so young, with so much potential."

"But, now we have another clue which Johnny left us. With the journal, we can read about where he went and what he did. It is like Johnny is sending us a message," Katherine said.

"Well, let's not get too excited: it may or may not be Johnny's stash. We will know more when we get to see it. I say we pick the kids up after school tomorrow and go to the shop. We can see it together. I know Tommie wants to be there, and he has the clue to the trunk. Without the key, we wouldn't be able to fit the pieces together," Thomas said.

Tommie couldn't sleep. He had always missed his brother, but now he missed him more. Perhaps he would be able to read his journal and figure where Johnny was going all those times when he would be on his adventures. Tommie remembered how upset his dad would become when Johnny disappeared while they were working. After Johnny had finished a chore, he was nowhere to be found. Dad would get so aggravated with Johnny and tell him every time to stay close by, to help with the chores and not go wandering off. One time, Tommie remembered, a neighbor had told Dad about seeing Johnny miles away coming out of a small cave with his pockets full of rocks. Tommie remembered how Dad had warned him he could get hurt, bitten by a snake, or something, but Johnny's thrill of the search was so powerful he could not be pinned down.

At breakfast the next morning the family continued to chatter about where Johnny had been and what he had found. After the devotion, the children were off to school, and everyone began their chores, trying to get through the day, focused on one thing, to get to the shop. Thomas, Pete, and John talked with Ollie and Hobie about the treasure find, and reluctantly went to work.

Katherine and Mary managed to stay busy by working on the green tomato relish and pickled eggs. Apparently, the hens were producing more eggs since the weather had cooled down a bit. The smaller crock would hold several dozens of pickled eggs which would be good during a long, cold winter.

Katherine chopped green tomatoes, onions, red peppers and a bit of yellow squash until her shoulders were hurting. "I will do the rest of these tomorrow. Not as young as I used to be, and my body tells me lately," Katherine said as she rolled her shoulders.

"I can do the rest after lunch. We have so much in the cellar, now, it is almost full and we don't have the rest of the beets pickled. We may try to dig another cellar next year, plus one under the new house, Thomas told me. I think we are going to need it especially with Rissa's parents coming for a while."

"For a while? I bet you they are coming to stay, dear. They know Thomas will be a good son-in-law and take care of them in their old age. But, another cellar would be great. You can never have too much room to store vegetables. And don't forget, there needs to be plenty of room for the potatoes, and we still have all the pears to gather in. What are we complaining for, God has provided us with all this abundance of fruits and vegetables and we need to thank Him instead of complaining where to put it and how to save it. We probably need to take a bushel basket of vegetables to Ollie's bunch. They would love fresh vegetables."

"Yeah, I noticed their garden is pretty skimpy. What with the baby being born this summer, they haven't had a lot of time to work in a garden. With Leah and Hobie to help, they will have a huge garden next year, I expect. You know, I am excited about Leah's baby. I have some pretty yellow yarn that I am going to make a hat, mittens and booties," Mary said.

"And I have some green and yellow material that would make a baby gown. After lunch, we could just sit outside on the porch and sew and you can knit and we will talk about the babies. I have got to get a few things prepared for my next grandchild also!" Katherine said as she winked at Mary.

The two women enjoyed their afternoon together, working on baby clothes. Suddenly, Mary changed the subject, "Well, when do you think Dr. Larimore will be back? Did he say a particular time to expect him?"

"Not really, just as soon as he could get everything finished." Katherine paused and made eye contact with Mary. "Mary, I would like to tell you something. Even though you might not respect me after I say it, but, well, how do I say it?" Katherine paused.

"You have feelings for Dr. Larimore, don't you? It's okay. It is normal for you to have feelings," Mary said trying to assure her.

Katherine shook her head. "You don't understand. Mary, oh, I am ashamed to say it, but when I danced with Dr. Larimore, or Keith, he asked me to call him Keith. Anyway, when I danced with him, I felt things, feelings, I had never felt before. Maybe I did long ago, maybe I had those feelings for Thomas' father, but I don't remember."

Mary took Katherine's hand. "It is okay, Katherine. You are a normal human being, with normal feelings. And you are in great shape, you are sixty-three and look like forty-three. You are a beautiful lady."

"Mary, I can't wait to see him again. You know, we told Nellie she couldn't kiss, we made her promise, made her promise, Mary! That she would not give her kisses away. But, you know it is exactly what I want to do, kisses and more," Katherine said ashamedly.

"Katherine, I understand. It is not a sin to have wants and desires. You know just because the commandment says 'Thou shalt not commit adultery.' Does not mean someone your age, widowed, and can't have feelings for the opposite sex. God wants us to enjoy each other…" Mary said as she laughed and gently tapped Katherine on the hand.

"Thanks, Mary, for listening. I just thought at this particular time in my life, I was over with love. And now, things are changing. I have to admit, I want to be with him in every way. I have fallen in love, Mary, a silly old woman who is in love," Katherine said as she wiped her apron clean.

———— ·• ————

Anticipation caused the day to be incredibly long even with everyone trying to keep busy. Finally, Thomas hitched the horses to the buggy and the family started the trip that would, hopefully, solve the mystery.

The large fabric-cutting table displayed the stones and cave rock beautifully. "Oh, what a collection!" Katherine gasped as Tommie ran past and up to the attic.

Tommie was anxious to see if the key was actually to the trunk. With the key gripped tightly in his hand, he scrambled to the attic to check it out. Seconds later Tommie yelled to the family, "The key fits the lock!"

The pouch was among the collection. Katherine picked it up, shaking her head, "I should have recognized this pouch yesterday. I gave Johnny this pouch when he was about six years old. He had collected some rock at our place and I gave him this to hold his rock. The pouch was Parson's and I thought Johnny might be able to use it. He certainly did. And, you know, Thomas, looks like this journal tells where he went and what he did, and when he did it. There is another person mentioned in the journal as just David. Sounds like he had a friend who helped him, or maybe was with him sometime. Wouldn't it be nice to know who he was?" Katherine asked.

"I remember giving him this journal when he was ten. He had scraps of paper he would use to write on. One year when Rissa and I were shopping for Christmas gifts we found the journal. She suggested we buy him it for Johnny. I am so glad we did, and I am glad he used it," Thomas said.

"You will be proud of what else he used it for, Thomas," Lyssa said. "Johnny said he witnessed to his friend, saying he had planted a seed. Johnny wrote prayers and blessed the areas he visited. He prayed he would not take or do anything to the land that was not right with God."

Holding Johnny's journal gave Thomas a sense of pride and curiosity. As the others were saying goodbye, Thomas flipped through a few passages. There seemed to be many scriptures, maps and a lot about David. Turning the pages to the last entry Thomas read:

> I can't wait to tell David! And everybody else! David promised his grandmother that he wouldn't open it till his 18th birthday but I thought why not? Not in a million years would anybody have dreamed this could happen! I knew we were connected somehow! The one guilty of the crime has passed away long ago, so we look forward! Such great news! I'll get David and let him tell the family!

Unfortunately, my son, this secret died with you, Thomas thought. Oh well, it was probably nothing really important. Johnny always got excited over little things. Yet, I will always wonder.

# Chapter 33

# The Invitation

The envelope lay on the table directly under Katherine's hand. Mary needed to sneak a look at the return address. The letter, under Katherine's watch, was a long-awaited letter from Dr. Larimore. Katherine had obviously read and reread the letter, paying little attention to anyone else in the room.

Mary memorized the address and wrote it on her stationery. She would write an invitation to the doctor for their party on Oct 5. Although Katherine had not revealed the contents of the letter, Mary could tell the letter contained words of love and promise from Dr. Larimore.

Quickly, Mary wrote an invitation to Dr. Larimore and addressed the envelope. She would need to get it in the mail...that night for it to go out in the morning's early mail, so he would have time to get it. Now, for a reason to go to town! With her being pregnant, Thomas would not let her go by herself. She had to think of a reason to get him to take her.

As soon as Thomas finished his work, Mary asked if he could take her to town. She took him aside and told him of her sneaky idea. He didn't agree at first, but she soon convinced him it was very important. In the kitchen, Mary explained to Katherine that she and Thomas wanted to go see Bro. Ship about a church matter. "We won't be gone long, Katherine, do you mind to watch the children?"

Katherine assured the couple they would be fine and to tell Bro. Ship and Marlie she said *hi*. Her efforts to encourage them to wait until Sunday, didn't work as Mary said she also wanted to see if the shipment had arrived at the shop.

In town, Mary went to the post office first to place the letter in the mail. Postmaster Billy had a letter for them. The envelope Katherine had addressed to Marie Stanel had something scribbled on the front. *Marie and her husband are both deceased.* Oh, how sad, they never got together and shared sister time that they probably both wanted, Mary thought.

———————◆———————

Baby Oleta was demanding attention from Lyssa as Thomas and Mary arrived. "Why, come in and visit for a spell," Leah exclaimed as she saw the Cosby couple. Pulling out a chair for Mary, Leah winked. "You need to rest those feet when you can."

"Oh, Mary, you just have to see the stuff we got in today. We got in a shipment yesterday and one today," Lyssa said excitedly.

"Look at this material. Feel it! Is it not just wonderful?" Leah asked. "This fabric feels as smooth as a baby's bottom."

"And it is beautiful," Mary said. "Are you going to have time to make an outfit for it and get it displayed by opening day?"

"I don't know, I hope so. Problem is, I don't know which fabric to use to make an outfit. All of them are so pretty. And, Leah and I want to make a new dress for ourselves for the Ladies' Day. I haven't had a new dress and neither has Leah, so we are ready to pick out something for ourselves. We are going to pay the shop...just wanted you to know we are paying customers," Lyssa added.

"Oh, I know dear. It is your shop and I trust you. I have faith in this shop. I think it is going to be a really good business. I can help you pick out the color that matches your hair and eyes, whenever you get it unpacked," Mary said to assure the girls.

Mary could have stayed and looked at the fabric all evening, but she knew Thomas wanted to get back, so they said their goodbyes. On the way home, Mary and Thomas talked about the party invitations, and the guest list.

"I feel like I am a mother of all of your workers, Thomas. They seem to look to us as parent figures. I love those kids, all of them, Pete and Andrea, Ollie and Lyssa, Hobie and Leah, John and Sallye, and they all seem like our family. I just hope Geri's mother, Carolyn and Deacon Avery will enjoy being with each other," Mary said.

"Yeah, I feel the same way about those kids. I feel like they are my family. And, I think it should be like that, to love the people around us, take pleasure in being with them, working, worshipping, or playing together. And, it is so important we try our best to lead them as God would have us," Thomas added.

Mary put her arm through Thomas' arm. "You are constantly leading them, giving them scripture, helping them understand."

"Well, I try to give them the scripture and the interpretation and then try to show where it applies in their life. I have to admit, I wasn't sure about John for a while. But now I feel the Lord led him and his family to Roundstone and to us."

Thomas thought for a minute about those closest to him as he said, "You know, I have heard it said the longest trip there is, is the trip from the head to the heart. We can know the scripture, but if we don't live it, apply it daily to our lives, then it is not doing us any good. We should always strive to have a heart like His." Thomas stopped talking long enough to kiss Mary and he continued.

"I have noticed our 'children' all have different gifts. It's important all of them are helping each other and making the whole body stronger. Ephesians 4 states, 'And He Himself gave some to be apostles, some prophets, some evangelists, and some pastors and teachers, for the equipping of the saints for the work of ministry, for the edifying of the body of Christ'. God gives gifts for a reason," Thomas added.

Thomas thought for a moment and continued. "And you know the gifts do not necessarily mean we have to be a preacher or a teacher, we can show peace, kindness, goodness, love, which comes from the Holy Spirit, to all. These are the gifts I see from all of our children, these younger people. Mary, I pray for discernment all the time, that the Lord will give me the spirit of discernment, to know the Lord's will, and not my will," Thomas said humbly.

Once home, Thomas hurried to help with the remaining chores while Katherine and Mary put supper on the table.

———•———

"Sorry to have to leave you, just had to get a chore finished," Mary said sheepishly. "You should see the fabric and supplies that the girls have received. They are so excited, and I am excited for them. I may have to be their first customer. They are excited and both of them want to make a new dress for the Ladies' Day. They will be good advertisements for their shop, won't they?" Mary asked.

"Yes, they will. I want to buy some material for Renie and some baby material soon, too. Just have to make a baby dress for little Oleta. She is just the cutest thing!"

"Oh, I almost forgot!" Mary said as she dug into her pocket. "I received this at the post office. Looks like Marie died before her sister Audie. So sad, to think all those years were wasted and they didn't get to say goodbye to each other." Mary shivered at her own statement as she knew all too well the pain of wasted years, time being away from loved ones.

Katherine sighed as she held the envelope which contained the letter she had written to Marie, Audie's sister. "Just another case of someone dying and the family not knowing about their loved one. So sad. I was glad we could have been there for Mrs. Audie. It would have been terrible for her to have died with just Luke there. Could have been days before anyone knew about it."

The family finished their meal and Thomas read from I Corinthians 12:18, 'But now hath God set the members every one of them in the body, as it hath pleased him.' Thomas discussed how all parts of the body are needed, and even though some parts are not as important, we would not want to have to live without them. He asked the children what part of the body they would be willing to give up.

"I would probably give up my little toe," Renie said. "But I wouldn't want to."

"Neither would Jesus. He doesn't want to give up any of us. He wants us all to be a part of the body of Christ. We should make a dedicated decision to be a part of the body of Christ," Thomas added.

How could I ever hope to be a part of a dedicated body of Christ? Mary thought. That requires too much faith from me right now. Mary recalled how her father had chastised others for their belief in Christ. Yet a verse from Mark kept coming to her mind, 'Lord, I believe, help though mine unbelief.'

# Chapter 34

# Cosby Party

Guests invited, plans made, the Cosby's fall party was underway. Nellie and Renie had been to the garden early to gather the late vegetables; sweet peppers, tomatoes, onions, potatoes, corn, green beans and beets. The air felt like frost any night, so the vegetables threatened by low temperatures were gathered. Colorful vegetables were piled in baskets and the remaining stored in the cellar. A few baskets, which had been filled with the garden delights, were ready to send home with guests.

During the last few days, Thomas had read most of Johnny's journal entries for devotion. Thomas wanted a few minutes to discuss some of Johnny's journal with the company on Saturday night. He wanted the guests to share an insight of what Johnny's heart was really like. The journal had revealed much of Johnny's character that even the family had not known.

Unfortunately, Mary had another secret to deal with. What was she going to do and say when and if Dr. Larimore did show up? Would Katherine be upset with her because she had sent him an invitation without her knowing about it?

"Katherine, why don't you go clean up and put on a fresh dress so you will look nice for your guests. You might want to redo your hair; too, it's falling down a little."

Katherine frowned, but didn't argue, as she left to tidy up a bit.

Mary thought to herself, it was a blessing to have company, especially company you love. She thought about her guests who had become so much like their family. Pete and Andrea made such a cute couple. They were so much in love with each other and they prayed together about making choices in their lives. John and Sallye, with their sweet children, were such a nice family. John took part in the church and he always brought Everett, but Sallye still stayed at home with Hannah. She wished she could do something to help Sallye feel more comfortable with Hannah at church.

The entire community had grown to love the Woodsons and the Bookers. Both families had taken care of each other so well. Hobie and Leah had come into Ollie's home right after the birth of Baby Oleta, so Leah had been a big help to Lyssa. Now, Leah's baby was due around Christmas, and they would be there for each other, helping at work and at home. What an example of brotherly love the families had demonstrated to others.

When everyone had arrived, except Dr. Larimore, the company settled down to listen to the devotion given by Thomas.

Thomas opened his Bible to I Corinthians 13:4-8. "I will be reading what we like to call the love chapter. 'Love is patient, love is kind. It does not envy, it does not boast, it is not proud. It does not dishonor others, it is not self-seeking, it is not easily angered, it keeps no record of wrongs. Love does not delight in evil but rejoices with the truth. It always protects, always trusts, always hopes, always perseveres'.

"I wanted to read these verses because they aptly apply to us tonight. Mary and I discussed you, our honored guests, and we agreed we love you like family. We want you to know if you need us, we are here for you. Our family has come to love you, because God first loved us. What a miracle is the gift of love. Have you ever had someone say for the first time, 'I love you?' Do you remember how that made you feel? I am sure you felt special. Well, you are special because God loves you. He loves you so much he gave his only begotten son that whosoever believeth on Him would not perish, but have everlasting life. God loves you and wants you to accept his love. When you recognize you are a sinner, and you want Jesus to come into your heart and save you, you are ready for God's eternal love. You will learn to have the love we talked about here in Corinthians. When you have this kind of love in your heart, it will show in everything you say and do. I don't know if we have anyone here who is not saved, but this was the message I felt the Lord wanted me to say tonight," Thomas said as his voice was swelling with emotion. Unaware to Thomas, one person had truly taken the message to heart.

The guests talked about when and where they first accepted their Lord and Savior into their hearts. Pete told about his experience in a small country church. John told about being saved in the field while working and then his falling away from church a few years ago.

Several guests told about that special someone who had been an inspiration. Ollie and Hobie talked about how much Thomas had inspired them with his faith. Others talked about verses of the Bible that helped them witness. Everyone agreed there were often seeds planted. Years later the person would follow the road of salvation because of that seed planted long ago.

Thomas opened Johnny's journal and shared a few of Johnny's insights. He read to the group how Johnny had witnessed to a friend and the friend turned away from him, but he prayed he had planted a seed with David that would someday be cultivated. "Johnny wrote a verse from 1 Samuel 18:3, *Then Jonathan and David made a covenant because he loved him as his own soul.*"

Katherine spoke what the others were thinking. "I wish we knew this David because our Johnny must have loved him dearly."

Tommie and Nellie led while the group sang gospel songs that engaged everyone in the musical part of the evening. Trusting that it was better to end in a high note, Nellie concluded the performance with a prayer and a blessing for the meal.

Mary and Katherine asked for help to take the food outside. Luke scrambled to be the first to help get the food on the table. John said the blessing and soon everyone was around the table and bowls were being passed. Ooohs and ahhhs were shared around the table as the food was passed. Compliments went to the cooks for an amazing meal.

"What better sounds than friends enjoying food?" Thomas mumbled to himself as he flashed a grin at his family. People loving each other, worshipping and spending time together, was just the best! It just doesn't get much better than this. "Thank you, Lord, for giving us this day," Thomas whispered.

With all the noise of the multiple conversations, no one seemed to notice a buggy was heading down the road—no one but Mary for she had kept a vigilant gaze on the road all night. Carefully, she made her way from the table to the road.

"Hello, Mary!" Dr. Larimore called out. "How are you doing? I was so glad to get your invitation." He took Mary's hand and shook it and then gave her a little hug.

"I want to apologize for the invitation being so late, well, not giving you much time. But, I didn't know your address until I saw it on the envelope you sent Katherine," Mary said. "Please come on over. We have plenty of food and you can get a plate."

Behind Katherine, Dr. Larimore made a sign for everyone to be quiet. He bent over and kissed Katherine on the cheek. She was so startled she almost choked.

"What are you doing here?" Katherine asked. "You weren't supposed to be back here for several days." Katherine was praying her nervous, school-girl lovesickness didn't show to those good people. "Well, fix a plate and join us. We all can scoot down and give you room."

Soon the desserts were being sampled and the vegetable bowls were being carried in the kitchen. Katherine jumped up to help.

"No, Katherine you are not helping, there are plenty of us to help without you. You get dessert for you and Dr. Larimore. We will take care of everything."

Dr. Larimore finished his food and told Katherine he didn't have room for dessert and wondered if they could go for a walk before the sun started going down. Dr. Larimore said he had heard so much about the place he wanted to see some of the Roundstone wonders before dark.

Katherine first took the Doctor to the back of the house where Rissa and Johnny were buried. She was proud of the stone Thomas had designed for his Rissa. Katherine explained how he had called Rissa the Hart of Roundstone. Doctor Larimore admired the beautiful heart-shaped stone as he commented on the workmanship.

Hand in hand the couple walked to the third spring and to the blue hole. They walked across the spring overflow and down the path to the creek. When they reached the head of the creek, Katherine explained the process of the mill. The couple sat on a fallen tree and watched as the squirrels ran back and forth on the trees.

Dr. Larimore reached for Katherine's hand. "I see why you said this place is so beautiful, it certainly is. So, this water runs down to the river, right?"

"Yes, it makes a lot of curves and turns, then spills out in the river. We think this is a little piece of heaven. We bring the Bible down here and read when we have time. Gives new meaning to the living water," Katherine said.

"Katherine, I have thought about you ever since I left. I know we have not known each other very long, but I haven't felt like this since I graduated from medical school and met Molly. But Molly has been gone for a long time. I have spent too many years alone, without a companion. I have looked for someone, but no one was the right one. Not until now."

The doctor kneeled on the sand on one knee and said, "Katherine Cosby, will you marry me?" Then he handed her a small box.

She opened the box first and looked at the amazing diamond ring, "Yes, yes, I will marry you!" Katherine laughed and threw her arms around Dr. Larimore. The couple sat on the makeshift bench, held hands and shared hugs and kisses until they felt guilty about staying away so long.

Katherine wished that moment would last forever.

# Chapter 35

# Story Time

Dr. Larimore and Katherine, more like love-struck teenagers than seniors, walked gingerly back up the hill. "Shall we tell them the good news?" Dr. Larimore winked and squeezed Katherine's hand.

"We were getting worried about you," Thomas said. "We've laid a fire and are going to tell some stories. Any story you would like to tell?"

"Sounds great! Maybe we can have a contest of who tells the best story. Could I offer a prize for the best story, Thomas?" Dr. Larimore asked as he dug in his pocket. "I have a reason for asking, to be last. And, I have a coin here for the best story. How's that?"

The first story was from the host of the party, Thomas. "Now, my story is one my grandfather told me, and he claimed it was true.

One time long ago when my grandfather was a young man, he was invited to go fox hunting. There were a lot of foxes in Kentucky back then. Anyway, he met a group down about Cub Run and they said, if we get separated for any reason, go to Appleby General Store in Cub Run. So, they all started out on their horses.

They had hunted for a while, and then Pa's dog, Spot, he wanted to go off in another direction. So, Pa followed the dog into a thicket. Before long, there was a cloud that came up and the rain started. Pa tried to get his dog to change directions but he wouldn't do it. He just kept on going the same way, away from the fox hunters. Then, through the pouring rain, Pa spotted a light way up ahead. He thought, well, I might as well see what that is. He rode up to the barn. There was a woman there trying to get her horses and cattle out of the corral and into the barn. She was all by herself so he rode up and asked if he could help. She thanked him, and soon they had the livestock in the barn and the door closed. Since it was still pouring rain, he asked if he could sleep in her barn, as he was soaked and didn't want to ride back to Cub Run.

The lady suggested he come in and get a cup of hot coffee, and he could dry out by the fire. He was much obliged to do so because he was really wet. When he got in the house he sat by the warm fire and quickly dried out. The little cabin was bright even though it only had one candle on the table. The lady explained that her husband had gone up north for a cattle buying trip and she expected him back any day. Pa sat at the table with a cup of coffee and rested.

The lady had a little girl, Lilly who was about five years old. She crawled up in his lap and started talking to him asking him about his family. She had ribbons in her hair. She took out one of the ribbons and told him to give it to his little girl. Putting the ribbon in his pocket, Pa said that he would give it to his little girl, for he knew she would like it. After he finished his coffee, he told the lady that he would go to the barn and sleep. He assured her that he would leave as soon as it was daylight, and that he wouldn't bother them when he left.

Before daylight, Pa saddled up and rode out because he wanted to meet the others as soon as possible at the store. When he got to the store everyone asked him where he had been. Pa told them what I just told you. Well, them fellers they got as white as ghosts. No way, they said. That's not possible. They argued with him. Finally, they told him, that he couldn't have been there. See, that lady, her little girl, the house and the barn burned down fifty years ago. Every so often somebody will come by and tell that story. But you, sir, had to have dreamed it.

Pa, being a good man and not one to argue said, well you are probably right, and he packed up his gear and got on his mare and left. About a mile or so down the road he thought he would have a chew of tobacco. When he put his hand in his pocket and got out his tobacco he felt something else, a red ribbon." Thomas finished with a pretend ribbon in his grasp and a scary look on his face.

"Awww, well, I don't know if we will tell our story. Yours is too good," Pete said.

"No, no, I am sure you have a good story, and I want to hear a story from all of you," Thomas said.

John and Sallye told their story next. Their story was funny and everyone laughed at the storytellers. Both of them helped tell the story and occasionally argued good naturedly about the events.

Della said that she would go next. She told a story about a young Cherokee couple and their love and tragic ending. Putting so much emotion in the story, Della had the women wiping the tears away.

Pete and Andrea told their story about an Irishman and his journey to find a pot of gold. The Irishman ran into a Frenchman, a Spaniard, a Russian, an Englishman and an American. Each one told him where the pot of gold was taken. It was a funny story and Pete and Andrea used the Irish accent which made it even better. They did a great job and everyone cheered.

When all the storytellers were finished, Dr. Larimore had his turn.

"Well once upon a time, there was a young doctor, he graduated from school and met a lady and made her his wife, Molly. They had a good life together, but never had any children. They were a happy couple and had many friends. Molly became sick when she was only thirty-six. She lived only one year after, and she died. Being a doctor and not being able to help his wife made the doctor feel guilty plus depressed. The doctor grieved for years and he said he would never love anyone again. He visited her grave every day and worked hard. The doctor worked for thirty years after that and finally one day, he realized Molly was gone and he was alive. He started looking for someone to love, someone to share his life with, a loving companion. He looked everywhere but he did not find her. One day, after forty-five years of practicing medicine the doctor was ready to retire. Then one weekend he went to a little town and as he was talking to the people there, he realized this was just what he was looking for, a Christian community that believed and proved they loved their neighbor. Then he saw her, he saw the woman he wanted to share the rest of his life with. She was radiant, the most beautiful woman he had ever seen. The minute their eyes met, he knew they were meant for each other. He didn't see her again for a while, but he thought about her all the time. He made up his mind, life is too short to put off happiness. He would ask her to marry him. And you know what she said?" Doctor Larimore looked at Katherine.

Katherine laughed and said, "She said, 'yes,' and she held up her hand with the diamond ring on it."

The group stood applauded, shook hands, had hugs and kisses for each other. "What a wonderful story!"

"Great story, Doc!"

"You won, Doc!"

"That was the best story ever!"

"So, I guess that means I can keep this nice coin?" Dr. Larimore laughed.

"Yes, yes! You told the best story, one we will never forget!" Thomas added.

Patches' kittens had been cuddled and rocked and adored by all the children. Each child had a kitten to take home. When people started standing to get ready to leave, a jealous Goldie saw her opportunity to chase the kittens. A couple barks and the kittens scratched and scattered away from their captive hands. Renie immediately screamed for Mike and Tommie to come to her rescue and retrieve the kittens from their hiding places. The guests were picking up kittens, trying to calm them down without being clawed by the ferocious little beasts.

Mike asked Nellie to hold the lantern because he thought two kittens went under the blackberry bushes by the barn. Crawling on his stomach, Mike saw the kittens hiding as deep in the bushes as they could get. He managed to pull one out, but the other kitty ran deeper into the bushes.

The blackberry bushes had plenty of thorns and Mike was constantly getting his shirt hung on the vines as he slithered along the ground. Nellie was telling him he didn't have to get the kitten but Renie was crying because that particular kitten just happened to be her favorite. Mike managed to grab the kitten as Renie started calling for it.

Just as he started to crawl out he saw something that caught the light from the lantern and made a reflection on the barn. "Nellie, see if you can lower the lantern close to the barn, about where my head is."

Maybe there was another kitten, Nellie thought. She leaned into the vines that stuck and pulled at her clothes, as she lowered the lantern through a break in the foliage.

Mike started crawling out of the blackberry maze holding onto something, but it wasn't a kitty. Standing, Mike opened his hand and showed Nellie the prize, the reward of his efforts.

"What is it?" Nellie asked, taking the shiny thing from Mike's hand. "It looks like a chain and magnifying glasses, and, what do you think this is?"

Mike looked at the gold wad of metal in Nellie's hand. "I can't tell, but you can figure it out. Ma is wanting to go home and I have to go while I have a way."

Mike took Nellie's empty hand and kissed it. "Goodnight, Nellie, I enjoyed the night. Well, I better go, Ma is waiting."

Saying goodbye to the others, Nellie slipped the gold metal thing in her pocket. She and Tommie helped the guests with the horses and baskets of vegetables. Thomas and Mary hugged each family member goodbye and encouraged them to come back soon.

"Take care of my girl, Thomas. I am going back to Dr. Routt's house. I will be at church in the morning. Since I am engaged, I will have to settle down and act my age," Dr. Larimore declared as he got into his buggy.

When Thomas and Mary got back into the house they found Katherine looking at the calendar and making notes. She was so preoccupied with admiring her ring, writing on the paper and looking at the calendar she didn't realize her son and daughter-in-law were beside her.

"Oh, okay, now, it looks like the wedding will be a Christmas wedding. I think Friday evening, Dec. 20 at 6:00 sounds good. Now, Thomas, you will give me away and Mary and Annie will stand up with me. I am going to buy some silk the girls ordered for their shop for my wedding dress. The wedding will be at the church and we will live at my house after the wedding. Some of the guests can stay at my house and if you don't mind, maybe some can stay at your house?" Katherine asked.

"Oh, my, slow down, Mom. You are going a little fast. We are so happy for you. I think you are going to be very happy and you certainly deserve it. Love you, now you go to bed and we will put everything up. Go!"

As Mary and Thomas put away the food they talked about the evening. "It was a great evening and the engagement announcement just topped it off! The stories were wonderful. I thought I wouldn't quit laughing at the story John and Sallye told. What fun!" Mary said.

"And Della's story, quite a love story, kind of sad."

"Pete and Andrea did a good job on the Irishman. Didn't they do a good job with the accent?" Mary asked. "But your story, you said it was a true story, you know it's not! Shame on you! And, by the way you are going to have to make up a new story. You have told that story a few times, so next time, new story!"

"Yeah, but that story has been passed down from my grandfather and we have told it for years, and I tell it so well," Thomas whined.

"Good reason to give it a break, okay." Mary snuggled up to Thomas. "Thank you for a wonderful evening. I really enjoyed your devotion. It was the best topic considering the doctor proposed. I still can't believe it! Who would have thought?"

"Dad," Nellie called to her father from her room. "I wanted to ask something. Did you like our show?"

"Sure we did, Honey. You kids were the highlight of the night. The singing was great and your accompaniment was wonderful! I'm sorry. Did you think we didn't enjoy it?" Thomas asked.

"Well, I don't know. I guess I'm just sad. Gran will be leaving us, and I will miss her. Renie will too."

Renie was already asleep next to Nellie. Thomas and Nellie looked at each other, as they realized their lives would be different. Katherine had always been dependable for them, always there and always an encouragement to them. Everything would sure be different when she was gone, and Nellie was the first to realize how much different.

"We will make it, Nellie; we will do fine without Mom," Thomas said. "We have been lucky to have her with us up to now."

"But now, Nellie, we need to let her have the wonderful life she deserves to have. She can have the rest of her life to enjoy being with someone she loves," Mary said.

"Now that Granma is getting married I won't be able to help her deliver babies. I always learn something when I go with her," Nellie said sadly.

Mary knew she could not possibly fill Katherine's shoes, but as she spoke, she realized how much she needed Nellie. "Nellie, I know you will miss Katherine, and so will I. But, you will be needed so much now for this baby. You will definitely be a part of shaping his or her life just as your grandmother has for you. So, in a way, you are kind of taking Katherine's place for a while. Do you think you can do that?" Mary asked.

"I suppose. But, I will miss Gran." As her dad and Mary left the room, Nellie ached with sadness. Her grandmother had become her mother, her best friend and her mentor. I will miss Gran too much. Maybe she will let me live with her and I can go to school from her house. I can go with her and Dr. Larimore on their visits. Maybe I'll just get married to Mike and we will have our own home. Mike, oh…

Thomas and Mary were still putting up vegetables and dishes when Nellie remembered the thing that Mike had found. Nellie jumped out of bed and dug in her dress pocket.

"Dad, Mike saw this as he was looking for a kitten. What do you think it is?"

Thomas looked in her hand and shook his head. "Looks like a big glob of gold to me. What do you think, Mary?"

225

Mary put down the dishes she was cleaning and wiped her hands. As she looked in Nellie's hand, she exclaimed, "Oh, goodness! That's my necklace that I lost! Guess I lost it the day we were picking blackberries. The vines were pulling at our clothes and aprons so bad I went to the barn and got a hoe, so I probably lost it then. Oh, I am so glad Mike found this! I thought it was gone forever."

# Chapter 36

# Church

The piano keys felt cold as Nellie made a few soft practice runs preparing for the first hymn. Bowing her head, Nellie said a prayer for God to touch her hands with His guidance, especially since it would be her first Sunday as church pianist.

Sneaking a look at Mike, Nellie hid a wave. Mike winked at Nellie sending her heart fluttering and her head spinning. That promise! How she wished she hadn't made a promise to not give her kisses away!

The congregation had been stunned as Della Caswell came in with Mr. Lucas Avery, Deacon Avery's father. Lucas had surprised her when he went to pick her up in his buggy that morning. Last night, they had sat together during the meal, the entertainment and storytelling. Lucas had shared with Thomas before he left last night that he was glad he had been there. Lucas told how the devotion on love, then the story from Dr. Larimore really got him thinking. He wanted to enjoy love again; to experience having someone to share good times and bad.

Dr. Larimore and Katherine walked in together, as people whispered about the couple. Nellie watched the older couple sit together and actually had a twinge of jealousy. After all, Granma Katherine had been filling the role of mother for the last two years. Truth was, Nellie had never seen her grandmother prettier or happier.

The music was uplifting and the Holy Spirit was definitely among the congregation as the message was delivered. Pastor Ship brought a soul-searching message entitled *A Heart for the Lord.*

"Please turn to Jeremiah 24:7 'Then I will give them a heart to know Me, that I am the LORD; and they shall be My people, and I will be their God, for they shall return to Me with their whole heart.'

"Tell me, congregation, have you stopped listening to the still, small voice of the Savior? If you are a Christian, will you, today, draw closer to the Lord? For those who are lost, will you allow Him to come into your heart? Ask Him to become your personal savior and invite the Holy Spirit to come and live inside you.

"People, I ask you to pray for forgiveness of sins, and be blessed through the Holy Spirit," Pastor Ship declared.

Upon the invitation, John Dales went up to have prayer. Sallye was so moved from the devotion the night before that she wanted pray at the altar. When John went forward, she followed behind him. Sallye fell at the altar and began to pray. There was so much in her past and she felt God could never forgive her, but she was so burdened, she cried out to Him for forgiveness of sins.

As a young girl, her father had forced her to have sexual relations with him, natural and unnatural ways. Sallye's mother would not, or could not do anything to protect her, so Sallye endured years of abuse. As soon as she could run away, she did and she never looked back. She had never gotten in touch with her parents. Sallye had harbored so much hatred in her heart for her father and her mother that she could not begin to forgive them. However, before she could love the way Jesus loved her, she would have to ask forgiveness of her sin of hate.

Sallye prayed a sinner's prayer and rejoiced in the fact that Jesus loved her. Tears flowed and women and men surrounded her giving her their blessing. Sallye professed her faith and told the church she wanted to be baptized and join the church. She wanted to read and study the Bible and learn more about Jesus Christ, her Savior.

Gracious ladies gave Sallye hugs and men came by to shake her hand and give her encouragement. Sallye had never known any people as nice and filled with such love as these people. She felt like she had found a home with them and she wanted to get to know all of them better.

John had asked God to help him lead his family closer to Him, and now his prayers were answered. He shook hands with everyone and there was plenty of shouting, clapping and singing. The service was spiritual food for everyone and no one was ready to leave. Finally, the church was dismissed and the meal was blessed.

Gil, Jeannie and baby Stephan were at church along with Jeannie's mother, her brother and sister-in-law. The families had brought some food for fellowship and were excited about the Bible study after the meal. Saving Dr. Larimore a seat close to the Spurgeons, Katherine asked how the baby was doing and if Gil was healing okay. Katherine hoped they would say something about the stone that was put up for the Jackson family.

"Keith, I don't think I have told you about what we learned about Gil and Jeannie's property, have I?" Katherine asked.

"No, I don't think I have heard that story. What about it?" Dr. Larimore asked.

"Do you mind if I tell him?" Katherine asked Gil and Jeannie.

"No, go ahead. At least it is a good story," Gil said, good humoredly.

Katherine started, "About seventy years ago, a young boy, about thirteen years old, had left his house, I think to check his traps," Katherine proceeded to tell the story about the Mack Jackson family.

"Wow, that is sure a pitiful story, and it is a true story?" Dr. Larimore asked.

"Yes, and the boy tracked down one of the Indians and killed him. Then he returned and dug a hole large enough to bury his family. Although he piled rocks all over the grave, there was no sign that someone was buried there."

Gil continued the story, "So the church took up an offering and put up a stone for the family. Says, *The Family of Mack Jackson*."

"And how do you know this is true?" Dr. Larimore asked.

"We found a letter Mack had left confessing to killing the Indian and telling about what the Cherokee had done to his family," Katherine said. "I will tell you how we came about the letter some other time."

"So now we have a grave marker beside our yard," Jeannie added. "I guess it is something we will always be able to talk about, telling a story of the Jackson family."

"Do you mind that the gravesite is there beside your house, Jeannie?" Katherine asked.

"Well, there isn't anything I can do about it. I doubt they wanted to be massacred and put in a grave together either, but that is what happened. And, you know, I think their spirits can rest now since the story has been told, and people know what happened there, and what happened to the family," Jeannie said. "We are much happier too, maybe because of Stefan or who knows?"

Talk continued about that year's crops, and plans for the next year. Jeannie was thrilled about how they were going to build onto their cabin. The small family had big plans. Jeannie's family joined in the conversation, but often used German when they were talking between themselves.

"Putting on the armor of God." Pastor Ship announced the study for the afternoon as the congregation quietened to listen. "Let's get into study groups because I would like to assign scriptures for discussion."

After a lively discussion with questions and answers from deacons and pastor, the group was dismissed with a circle prayer.

The newly engaged couple caught Pastor Ship to ask him about a date for the wedding. Friday, December 20 was confirmed. "What an honor, Katherine! I have always been inspired by Katherine, and she has mentored me and my family since I have been at the church. I am so happy for both of you." Pastor Ship hugged Katherine and shook hands with Dr. Larimore. "You have a good one, there, Doc. Not a better woman anywhere."

# Chapter 37

# Guilty of Love

Riding home on Sunday evening after church included an array of lively subjects for the family to discuss. "Isn't it just wonderful news? Della and Lucas, and maybe a wedding soon. You know, Thomas, I think last night had a lot to do with that. What a great couple they are!" Mary squeezed her husband's arm and smiled proudly.

"And what about Sallye! She gave her life to the Lord and she was so happy!" Thomas interjected.

"I think Thomas had something to do with that. Reading from the Bible and talking about salvation to the group last night had an effect on Sallye. I noticed her as Thomas was talking and she seemed to be taking in every word. Thomas, I think God led you to invite John to work for you and everything fell into place, according to God's will. Isn't it exciting when we reach out on faith to someone? I thank God for Sallye and John and for their sweet family," Katherine gushed.

"And did you notice Leah's stomach? It has really popped lately. She will be such a good mother. With her and Lyssa working together they will be such good help to each other." Mary rubbed her own stomach and straightened her posture. She was beginning to feel the baby move which was a blessing.

"You know, I will never forget the look on Hobie's face when Arron took the baby bed to Leah. I think Arron and Anjolee really wanted to show them how much they loved them as their Christian family," Thomas said as he looked up and whispered a 'Thank you, Jesus."

Katherine held her ring out and looked at it as she talked. "They definitely had a change of heart, and to think they gave their baby bed to Hobie and Leah for their baby. What a gift of love."

Everyone agreed both Babies, Oleta and Stefan were growing, and would soon be sitting up alone. Thomas even noted that Deacon Avery was sporting a new hat.

"Oh, yes, good news! Andrea asked me if I could teach for her tomorrow. She wants to take the day off to be with her family visiting from Cave City. I hope it is okay. I told her I would love to help. I am so excited," Mary exclaimed.

"It will be wonderful for you and for the children—a nice treat. Make sure you don't push yourself too much, you don't need to wear yourself out, dear," Katherine said.

"Oh, I won't. I did sit up last night and worked on my necklace. Did you hear, Katherine? Mike found my necklace in the blackberry bush by the barn. I suppose I lost it there the day Rissa and I were picking blackberries. We got in the vines and they tore our clothes; vines were springing out everywhere. That is when I went and got the hoe to push them out of the way. Anyway, I will get to wear it to school tomorrow," Mary explained.

Monday morning Mary was up early and excited about her day. After devotion, she slipped on her dress for school, then carefully put on her necklace. Hurrying the children along, Thomas went to get the horse and buggy. Katherine stopped Mary long enough to look at her necklace.

"I have never seen a necklace like that before. Where did you get it?" Katherine asked.

"My grandmother bought it for me when I got my first teaching job. A tinker came through the community selling his wares and she bought it. She wanted me to have something special. See, there is a pair of glasses here, a 6" ruler and a pair of scissors, here. Then it all folds back like this. I thought I had lost it forever. It has always been the most useful item because I always have it around my neck at school. I think I will try to find someone who makes these and give one to Andrea. I feel like she is my upstart anyway," Mary said laughingly as she picked up the rest of her supplies and hurried the children along.

Once everyone was out of the door, Katherine grabbed the table to keep from falling. Surely, she did not see what she thought she saw. When Mary opened the necklace and showed the scissors, a vision flashed before her eyes, the shiny blade she had seen in her dreams! Practically once a month ever since Rissa had died, Katherine had the same dream! Rissa with a tree and a rope, then something gleaming and very sharp.

Katherine poured herself a cup of coffee and sat at the table. She had a strange feeling about Mary for a long time, as Mary seemed guilty of something, as though she was hiding something from her. Mary had the opportunity to use the blade of the scissors and cut the rope when she left the kitchen to go to the outhouse. But how would she have known the rope would break and cause the tree to fall on Rissa? Yet, saying she had to leave right at the time the tree was to fall was too much of a chance.

According to Katherine's dream, she felt the rope had been cut, causing the rope to snap. The old adage that a chain is as strong as its weakest link is absolutely true with a rope.

However, Katherine had to admit she had always been just a little jealous about how Mary flirted with Thomas before Rissa died. Even Rissa had mentioned it jokingly to Thomas. Also, everyone knew Mary had not wasted any time after Rissa died to smother Thomas with her female wiles.

What was she to do? If she confronted Mary with her suspicions, their relationship would probably be ruined. With the baby due in a few months, Katherine knew she did not want to take any chances.

However, if there was a chance she was guilty, she should pay for what she did. How could she have fooled everyone into thinking she was Rissa's friend when she had planned her death? Perhaps she was letting her imagination run away with her. What would she advise someone if they had a problem like this one? For sure, she would tell her to pray and ask Jesus to direct her. She would ask her friends to pray with her and ask for an answer, for guidance.

Katherine prayed for wisdom to know how to handle the situation. Thomas would be home soon. Should she tell him what she feared? Maybe she would go to see Della or to Lyssa and Leah and ask them to have prayer with her. What if they asked, should she tell them?

Perhaps a cup of coffee and time would help. She sensed that so many times Mary had wanted to tell her something, but changed her mind. Clearly something had been bothering her. Had Mary wanted to admit her guilt?

Katherine felt she should not talk to Thomas. He had work planned for the day, and who could say her theory was believable? No, she couldn't mention it to her son. Ordinarily, she would not mention a problem to her pastor, but she felt led to go talk to Pastor Ship. Getting away for a couple hours would be best. There were plenty of biscuits and bacon left over from breakfast and Thomas could help himself. She could talk to Pastor Ship and a few friends before she had to come back home.

Katherine spent a day of visits before she felt she had the courage to return home to face Mary. She felt God had told her to confront Mary with the facts and get everything in the open.

As soon as Thomas brought Mary and the children home, Katherine sent them on an errand. Thomas realized the two women wanted to talk.

Katherine made some tea and asked Mary to sit awhile. "Mary, do you have something you need to share with me? I have learned some information I am going to ask you about, but I would rather hear you tell me first."

Mary became upset, her eyes filled with tears and her hands began to shake. "You are right, I should have shared with you and Thomas long ago, but I just couldn't do it, because I know I was wrong."

Mary took sips of tea in order to receive the strength to deliver her confession. Katherine felt compassion for Mary; she couldn't help it. Mary was still her daughter-in-law no matter what. She put her hand on Mary's arm and encouraged her to take her time.

"Four years ago I came here to start a new life. My last job was at a large school in a poor section of Louisville. I taught with some good friends and we started comparing notes. We found at least one girl or boy in each grade level at school were being physically or sexually abused. I am not talking about touching. I am talking about perverted acts by a family member or friend of the family. The children would show signs of abuse, or we would suspect through other ways. We tried to get something done, but no one would do anything about it. Because, when it comes down to it, a child will lie to protect family members because of fear.

"Finally, we couldn't stand it any longer. We made a pact together. We would get the child away from the home, and not let the parents know. We provided a home for thirteen boys and girls. I quit teaching to stay with the children during the day and teach. The others kept their jobs and watched out for more abuse. When we would get the children, they had had nothing to eat, were beaten black and blue and were so abused sexually that they peed on themselves. We all chipped in to be able to have a home for the children.

"We were doing great, taking care of those children, giving them an education, a good warm bed, with good food and proper medical attention. Then one day someone found out where the children were going and made a big deal. My friends were very good. They tried to make it work legally, but we couldn't. Of course, I was the one who was really targeted, and the story was retold according to the abusive parents who wanted the children home to work or for sexual favors." Mary remembered the insults that had been hurled at her when the children's parents learned of her religious teaching, one of the complaints brought against her.

"Anyway, my friends gave me a month of their salaries and told me to run, to find a place where I would not be despised and hunted by the law. What we wanted to do for the children blew up in our faces. But the thing is… I would do it again if I knew there was a child being abused." Mary thought about telling the rest of the story, how she had taught the children that the New Testament of the Bible was a lie and that Jesus was a lie, as her father had taught her. However, she knew that she could not include that information if she ever wanted to be a part of the Cosby family.

"So, that's my dirty little secret. The money they gave me is saved in a stocking. I know I should have told Thomas about being wanted by the law, and about the money. I feel really selfish about keeping it a secret, but, well, that's it." Mary wiped her tears and asked Katherine for forgiveness.

Katherine was confused, and she did not know what to say. After seeing Mary go through the pain of telling her about the abused children, she couldn't bring herself to ask her about the necklace, not right then.

"Well, do you forgive me?" Mary asked.

"Um, of course, of course, dear." Katherine didn't really know how to reply.

Mary wiped a tear and asked, "How did you learn about it? Well, it doesn't matter. I confess we probably took the wrong steps. But after seeing those children mistreated I couldn't stand it any longer."

Katherine felt sorry for Mary, but somehow she had to get the truth out; she had to ask the questions and find out what happened. "Mary that was not at all what I wanted to talk to you about. I hate to ask these questions but I have to have some answers. I have prayed about this all day, and we, well, we need to talk about it.

"The day Rissa was killed was a terrible day for all of us. One of the worse things about it is we don't really know what happened. The rope was strong, but yet it snapped into. Mary, did you cut that rope with the blade on your necklace, causing the tree to fall on Rissa?"

Mary looked like she had seen a ghost. Suddenly, Mary felt like the blood was about to drain out of her body. Her mouth instantly became dry and tingly, and she could not catch her breath. Clearly, she was so shocked she couldn't talk. Trying to blink back tears, Mary tried to remain calm, but her heart was beating so fast she wanted to scream.

"No, I did not touch the rope. I don't know how you think I could have cut the rope to kill Rissa and not Paul or Thomas. Katherine, I certainly did not cut the rope! Rissa was a friend, a good friend, and I would never have done anything to hurt her or anyone, for that matter."

Katherine put her arm around Mary and asked forgiveness for allowing herself to think she could have been guilty. She explained the dream with Rissa, something shiny, all the evidence, and both women agreed Katherine had a valid concern. Mary asked Katherine if she really felt that Rissa had been murdered, or if it was an accident.

Katherine explained how she had the dream repeatedly, as though it was a warning something was wrong. "Mary, would you care if we talked all this over with Thomas? I think we need to get everything out in the open and I am sure he will feel like I do, that you are completely innocent of everything. Do you feel like going through this one more time?"

"Yes, please, let's get this over. I will call Tommie and have him go get Thomas," Mary said sadly.

Thomas looked puzzled when he rushed in the cabin. "Is everything alright? Are you feeling okay, Mary?"

"I am feeling well, but…I have something to explain to you. Something that is well overdue. Please sit down and let me tell you my dark secret."

Mary proceeded to tell Thomas about the children in Louisville, how she had ran from the law, about the money, and how sorry she was that she had kept the information from him. At one time she considered telling the rest of the ugly truth, but she couldn't.

"Don't worry about that, Mary. What is in the past, stays there." Thomas slid his chair back to get up when Katherine stretched her arm out to stop him.

"There is more, Thomas, about another matter," Katherine said dryly.

"Thomas, I suppose my imagination got out of hand. However, I have been blessed with a gift of dreams and visions. Anyway, a month after Rissa died I started having dreams of Rissa, a rope, a tree and something shiny. I did not know what the shiny thing was. This morning when I saw the blade of the scissors on Mary's necklace, I started drawing some conclusions. I know I am an old woman, but this is the way I saw it." Katherine steadied herself as she started through the explanation.

"Mary excused herself that day to go to the outhouse. She could have cut the rope in the barn then. You admitted the rope looked like it had been cut on one side, not just worn. Mary had the necklace on which would have helped her cut the rope. She just happened to be in the barn looking for a hoe when the tree fell over on Rissa.

It was enough for me to think maybe Mary could have done it."

Thomas interrupted, "How could Mary have known how the tree would fall? She wouldn't know what would happen if the rope was cut. Mom, I understand your dreams and visions, but I don't think Mary is responsible, not at all."

"I know what you are saying, Thomas. I am sorry, and I am so sorry, Mary. Yet, why have I kept having the dreams? When I saw the necklace, the blade flickered just like in my dream. Do you understand, at least where I am coming from on this?" Katherine was pleading for forgiveness.

"I'm sorry, Mary." Thomas picked up Mary's hands and held them in his hands. "Please forgive us, Mary. What do you say, Mom?"

Hurriedly, Katherine jumped up to comfort Mary with a hug. Denying the apologetic act, Mary escaped Katherine's touch and stood at the door of her room. "Wait a few days, then apologize, if you really mean it. I know there is still some suspicion in your heart. Please don't apologize until you really do mean it." Mary closed the door behind her.

# Chapter 38

# Raising the Roof

---

Mike and Nellie walked through the field covered in beautiful yellow, red and orange daisies. As they spread the wedding-ring quilt on the grass, Nellie pinned the quilt edge with the picnic basket. Stretched out on the quilt, the two talked about getting married someday and having children. As they looked up at the blue skies, Nellie nestled under Jack's arm. "I love you, Nellie," Jack whispered.

Nellie and Jack gazed at each other their hearts filled with love. Then Mike held Nellie in his arms, kissed her, and she kissed him back, warm loving kisses.

Nellie let out a scream and sprang up in the bed. It had been a dream. Her promise to not let Mike kiss her had worried her more than she thought. The dream had been so real. As she tried to go back to sleep she thought about how much Mike meant to her and wondered if she meant the same to him. Was he really serious he wouldn't get married until he had made a fortune in mining? For the first time, Nellie really wondered if it was God's will for them to be together.

Nellie's youth had been so different from Mike's. A couple of years ago, Katherine had told Nellie about Mike's mother. She had been the only child of Della and Daniel. After her death, Mike's father brought three-year-old Mike to Della and Daniel to raise. He said he just couldn't keep Mike; he was too distraught and needed time to heal.

Della had confided in Katherine, that although Mike had been only three years old, he said he remembered the night his mother had died. His father had come home drunk and his parents had argued. His father had beat his mother and started whipping Mike with a belt when his mother intervened for him. Mike's father then beat his mother until she couldn't get up. Finally, she crawled in bed with Mike and slept, and although she was a bruised and a bloody mess, she told Mike she was okay. The next morning his mother got up to fix breakfast and she fell dead. Of course, it wasn't quite the story Mike's father had told when he dropped Mike off with his grandparents.

Della and Daniel had been wonderful grandparents, seeing to Mike's education, taking him to church, making sure he had what he needed, but it still wasn't the same. The grandparents had to work hard to build Mike's confidence and get over his grief. Mike had always missed his mother but he had never missed his father. In fact, Mike had blamed his father for his mother's death.

Mike will be at the house tomorrow, helping with the building, Nellie thought. I will go back to sleep, and talk to Mike tomorrow, since we are taking the day from school to help. *Yawn.* I will tell Mike that if he wants to chase gold mines, I will go to Boston to school and live with my grandmother and perhaps that will...

---

Thomas pulled his tired body out of bed. Work that week had been grueling, trying to keep ahead of the work orders for the men and the weather. He really hadn't told anyone, but Thomas felt God was leading him to get the house built. Although the family would definitely use the house for the in-laws and his growing family, the Lord had told Thomas this house would be important someday. Thomas had to admit he wrestled with the thought of 'house pride.' The Lord had provided him with plans and His blueprints, so possibly he would live to see the real reason for the house.

The morning's Bible reading was from Psalm 127:1, A Song of Ascents of Solomon. 'Unless the LORD builds the house, they labor in vain who build it; unless the LORD guards the city, the watchman stays awake in vain.'

Thomas asked everyone to be in prayer for the house. It would be a difficult day to raise the sides of the house. Mary and Katherine pleaded with Thomas to be extra careful. The possibility of someone getting hurt worried Mary. Tommie had begged to stay home from school to help. Finally,

239

Thomas agreed. He could use a "watchman," someone to watch to make sure the workers were always safe.

The wagons came rolling in about eight o'clock. Ollie and Hobie brought Lyssa, the baby and Leah. In another wagon were Pastor Ship, Deacon Avery, Erik Goodlin and Mayor Bymel. In the last wagon were three more men from church.

Thomas opened the workday with a prayer that the Lord would bless their work and watch over them. The ropes were in place, in case of an accident. The men had been given instruction on what to do. Finally, they were ready to raise the first side. Nellie watched as the men gave everything they had to lift the heavy frame. With the first frame up, Pete and John were up on the top nailing the side to the top rafters. While they were completing the task, other men were gathering around the next side.

Katherine and Mary watched for a few minutes as the second wall was going up. It looked like Pete and John had the hardest job for they were very high off the ground hammering and pulling at the sides, trying to make sure everything was level.

"The whole thing makes me nervous," Mary said. "Thomas said they would go slow and make sure that safety was the main issue today. They seem to be moving along."

By dinner time the frames for the sides of the house were up and Pete and John were ready to bring up the other rafters. Thomas suggested everyone take a break, eat dinner and rest awhile. The morning had been quite stressful. Thomas needed to relax awhile, and he was sure everyone else did.

The women carried the food to the large tables outside and Pete blessed the food. The meal was filled with joking and good humor. Some of the men had their reservations about the water closets, and all had questions.

Thomas explained how the water was brought from the creek with a pulley system which had been installed years ago. Their water barrels were always full because of the system, which would help with the pressure in the water closets.

"Now, all the women will want us to install water closets in our houses!" Mayor Bymel laughed and said. "Probably plenty of other new things that will make our simple homes look obsolete."

After lunch the rafters were raised and the roofing process was started. Ollie and Hobie joined Pete and John on the top of the house. The men hoisted the heavy frames while the men on the top of the house used the ropes to pull them up. Thomas was scrambling between the two places to help secure the frames.

With the first rafter frame in place, the next one came easier until they were all up. Thomas told the men they could go home. Most of the people had to leave to go to school for the children, including Pete, so work was stopped, but the house had the side frames and rafters.

Before the group left, Pastor Ship asked everyone to bless the house. All the women and men held hands and made a circle while Pastor Ship said a special blessing on the house. Thomas and Mary thanked everyone and most of the crowd dispersed.

With the workers and onlookers gone, Nellie and Renie went inside the new house. Mary and Katherine joined them, pointing out the various rooms. "This house is so big. We will have way too much room," Mary said.

"No, I think before you know it, the house will be full. You remember, your family is increasing," Katherine said as she patted Mary's stomach.

"How about we get our chores done for the night and rest? I am really tired. Guess the stress of the building really got me today," Mary said.

"What about you just lie down, Mary? You have done too much today. Go rest. We can manage without you," Katherine told her.

Mary didn't argue. Probably just the stress of the day, but she didn't feel well. Mary pulled the quilt back and snuggled in the bed. That morning Katherine and Thomas had apologized to her again. Somehow, she did not believe them. She felt the heartbreak from Katherine's accusation of Monday. She had not been able to sleep for worrying about the accusation and about always living in their suspicion. Mary had worried so much about the accusation that she had become sick from worry and lack of sleep. No matter how much she had been hurt, she couldn't say anything. She had also kept a secret—one she was truly guilt of. Mary cried again until she had a headache. She was tired and upset with her husband and her mother-in-law. Yet, the two of them did not realize how they had hurt her so deeply.

Thomas took a moment to look at the house, to plan the next few days. That time of year brought uncertainty of weather, so he would push forward. Looking around at the beginnings of the house, he thought about the future. Thomas had a vision of the house being full of children and family, but he also had a vision of the house being used to help others.

Tap, tap, tap. "Nellie, Nellie, I have to see you. Wake up!"

"Mike, what in the world?" Nellie crawled over Renie to look out the window. "Hold on, I will be right there." Nellie slid her shoes on and still half-asleep, tip-toed to the porch. There was Mike, on the steps. "What are you doing? No, be quiet! We don't want to wake my dad!" Nellie whispered as she hurried off the porch pulling Mike through the yard down the path behind the house. Watching the front of the house, Nellie shook Mike's arm, "What are you doing? Why are you here this time of night? Don't you know my father has a gun?"

"Nellie, Nellie, stop, please let me answer your questions. I have not had any rest since you said what you did earlier today."

"What, Mike? There is nothing I could say to get you here at this hour."

"When you said that you would go to Boston to go to school, remember… when we were working on the house. I heard what you were telling Mary and Katherine. Of course, you meant for me to overhear, didn't you?"

"Well, Mike, I just want you to know that I am not going to pine away waiting for you to come back from your mining adventures. I am not going to wait for you. In fact, I am not going to wait at all. If that is your dream, then I have my own." Nellie folded her arms in defiance when she realized she was in her gown.

"Nellie," Mike cupped Nellie's elbows, "I want you to realize that my good-for-nothing father married my mother and had nothing. He was never worth a nickel and made her life miserable. I want you to have everything you deserve. I won't marry you until I have something to offer you. Do you understand, Nellie?"

"Oh, Mike, yes, I know, but that stuff is not important to me." Nellie put her arms around Mike's neck. "Mike, I love you!"

Without thinking, the two embraced and kissed. The world seemed to stand still for Nellie.

Finally, Mike broke the spell. "Do you promise you will wait, at least a while for me?"

Another kiss followed with Nellie's promise. "Yes, Mike I promise…I promise, oh no, Mike! I promised I would not give my kisses away and I…"

Just then the couple heard the front door bang shut. "Oh, no, Mike, go. Get out of here!"

Luckily, Mike had ridden his horse to the fence which was not far for him to run through the woods to ride home. Nellie, though had a dilemma, what was she to do? What would her dad say if he caught her outside, even by herself, he would have questions.

Frozen, Nellie stood where she was until she could figure out what her dad was doing, where he was going. He didn't seem to have a purpose, he definitely wasn't coming to fetch her. She would just walk up to him, tell him she couldn't sleep. Umm… no not a good idea; He might see her in the white gown, think it was a ghost and have a heart attack. Hide, she had to hide! There behind the large sycamore, she could hide from her father.

Something had awoken Thomas and he couldn't go back to sleep. With the building tomorrow and the heartbreak of the ordeal with Mary, he felt he just needed to talk to someone. It had been a long time since he had come to talk with Rissa. But something had told him to go outside and talk with her. As Thomas knelt beside Rissa's grave he began to confide with her as he always had.

"Rissa, I need you more all the time. I love Mary, but something has been revealed that I have to talk to you about. I know that you don't know what happened that awful day. See, Mom thinks you were murdered. She has had visions of the tree, the rope and something shiny. Well, see the rope was cut. Someone had to have cut the rope, just enough for it to tear into when the tree pulled against it. So, when Mom saw the necklace that Mary wore, she assumed it was Mary who had cut the rope… that she meant for you to be murdered. And, the fact is that Mom has always had these visions and, you remember, Rissa, most of the time she has been right! Well, I can't believe that Mary would, on purpose, have done that. But, it sure looks like someone did. Oh, Rissa, what am I supposed to do? Help me, please, understand this!"

Nellie put her hand over her mouth to keep from blurting out to her dad. No wonder she had felt like there was something going on with Mary. So, Gran and Dad have reason to suspect Mary of murder. Her mother's murder!

# Chapter 39

# Ladies' Day

Excited about their first Ladies' Day, Lyssa and Leah arrived early at the school with food and flowers. "We are putting the food on the long table, Lyssa. If you and Leah will be in charge of the breakfast, I would appreciate it. Thomas built a fire in the school room, so we could have coffee. You can get it started any time; I have the pot and coffee here." Katherine rushed about making sure everything was ready for guests.

Nellie greeted each guest, gave them a program and directed them to the breakfast table. Being included in the activities for the day was exciting as Nellie had dreamed of being a missionary for the past few years. Gran had trusted her with presenting information about Polly Webb and she prayed she would make her proud. Nellie had kept quiet about the information she had learned from her eavesdropping. That week had been busy with all the preparations and Nellie wanted to focus on God's will.

The addition, still smelling of new wood, created an atmosphere of harmony along with a spiritual blessing. Tommie's stretched canvas paintings of the missionaries in foreign countries were absolutely masteries of art. Tommie had also used a long piece of stretch canvas to write the theme of the day, *A Heart Like Jesus*.

Flowers on the front table were combined with fruit and vegetables, peaches, apples, grapes, squash and pumpkins piled around them. The breakfast table was covered with Katherine's embroidered tablecloth and loaded with breakfast breads, butter, and sliced fruits. The theme seemed to be flowers, food, fruit and female fellowship.

Katherine had placed her heirloom quilts on the pews which gave the room a homey atmosphere. Beautiful quilts created a ready source of conversation between the ladies. Almost every lady had made a log cabin quilt, or a nine patch, or a maple leaf.

The ladies kept arriving until about nine o'clock. The group from Dorene Ladies' Missionary Society was at the church early, and had enjoyed breakfast and fellowship with the other ladies. Nellie's prelude signaled quiet as the ladies took their seats. Katherine welcomed everyone and gave the devotion and prayer. She introduced the speaker from the Dorene group as Elizabeth "Beth" Moss.

Beth, an incredible speaker with a vivacious energy, was younger than the others in her group, probably in her late twenties. Beth was dressed in a more fashionable dress and her poise and beauty made it easy for everyone to keep their interest. As she began to talk the excitement was contagious. Beth warmed the audience by making them comfortable, telling a few jokes about herself. She told a story so inspiring and yet so funny that Nellie knew she would never forget it.

Beth smiled mischievously as she started her tale of one of her speaking engagements. "Recently, I had to take my two darling little boys with me to a church where I had been asked to speak. While I was speaking, the boys acted terrible. The boys talked, cried, squirmed, and finally I said, 'I am like Stephen today. He had to suffer in Christ. I am suffering here because of my boys. But my point is because I have a message to share, my love for Christ, I hope to inspire you that instead of breaking I will be like Stephen and I will suffer because of Christ and the cross. Life is not always easy when we take up the cross. And somedays your cross may be two little boys'." Beth said as she giggled.

"You know, afterward people came to the altar to give their lives to Christ. My point is… we have to show others we believe so strongly in our Lord and Savior that we will carry the cross through not only good times, but through the times we feel we could quit, or go home, or even pick up the boys and go home!"

Beth expounded on her travels with her husband, and the boys. They had taught Bible study groups in various places. She described their visits and stays in homes, sometimes not in the best accommodations, but they always made it. The Lord always provided them with food to eat and a place to stay. Beth had a beautiful testimony of how her family was serving the Lord.

Katherine was about to introduce the next speaker when she had an idea. "Many of you already know each other, but there has to be something that you don't know. So, why don't we introduce ourselves, give your name and your favorite Bible scripture, with a brief explanation of why."

The ladies started with the introductions and before long the meeting turned into fellowship meeting and greeting. Nellie had trouble picking out her favorite, but when it was her turn she felt she had the perfect verse. "My verse is Proverbs 31:30, 'Charm is deceitful and beauty is passing, but a woman who fears the LORD, she shall be praised.' I chose this verse because it reminds me of Beth. Beth works to give God the glory and honor, and I would truly like to be a disciple like Beth."

The next speaker was Linda Wells. Linda told a story about a Virginia girl who married as a seventeen year old to Rev. Shuck who was a 23 year-old missionary. [2]Henrietta Shuck was one of the first ladies who inspired the many women around her to get interested and do something about missions. Henrietta was everything to everybody, a hostess, a mother, a wife. Unfortunately, the many roles took their effect on her body.

Linda's expression softened, "Ladies, we know how much time it takes as a wife and mother, but she was able to do that and more. Henrietta made time to write letters informing people of the needs and accomplishments of missionary work. In 1842 the Shucks moved to China, Hong Kong. Henrietta helped develop the first Chinese church. However, after her fifth child, Henrietta died, but the impact of her ministry has continued. She has left a legacy which continues today to inspire women and to promote missions worldwide."

The ladies stood and applauded. Katherine announced the verse, "Galatians 2:20, 'I have been crucified with Christ; it is no longer I who live, but Christ lives in me; and the life which I now live in the flesh I live by faith in the Son of God, who loved me and gave Himself for me.' Henrietta Shuck has been a good example of dying for Christ."

After two wonderful missionaries had shared their messages, Nellie was next on the program. A wave of panic attacked her body and Nellie quickly said a prayer. With her voice quavering, Nellie stiffened her spine and began.

"We begin with a quote from Polly Webb,[3] 'Dear sisters, let us arise,' was the call in 1812 to women. When Polly was eighteen, she heard a missionary's sermon that would affect the rest of her life. She devoted her life to missions,

---

[2] Hunt, Rosalie, *We've A Story To Tell*, Birmingham: Woman's Missionary Union, 2013

organizing meetings in her home, sending letters to other women to help spread the word. What makes Polly Webb even more interesting is the fact she was paralyzed from the waist down at age five. However, her handicap never affected her desire to serve the Lord and spread the Word through missions all over the world.

Thanks to Polly many missionary groups are being developed." Nellie closed with, "No matter what we do, big or small, if we do it for the Lord, that seed will be established."

Nellie ended with a presentation of "An apple has four seeds". She cut the apple open and showed everyone the four seeds. "How many trees could possibly start from these four seeds? Everyone answered four. Then, if these four seeds made four apple trees, how many apples would we get in a few years, one, ten, a hundred, who knows, but we know it started from one apple. Let's take our stand with one apple and plant those seeds."

The sound of applause was an affirming message to Nellie that she had succeeded in her quest to inspire the ladies about missions. Nellie pressed her lips and eyes closed and thanked God for helping her get through the presentation.

The food table was prepared with fried chicken, country ham biscuits, cookies, cakes, pies, vegetables and fruits. The ladies took their plates and filled them with all kinds of goodies. The women joked that it seemed eating well was a Baptist tradition, at church and community functions.

Lunch was a treat for the ladies and for the mothers who had brought their babies and children. Nellie, Renie and Geri helped with the children, taking them outside and letting them ride in the small wagons which were usually used to carry water. The school room next door was useful as the mothers were able to take babies to feed and change. The new addition, the school room and the new restrooms helped make the day more comfortable and fitting for the ladies. Katherine, Mary and Nellie were proud to have been able to host the meeting, to represent the missionaries and most of all, their Lord and Savior

After lunch, the ladies sang again, another song from the book of Psalms.

Katherine announced the next speaker, Becky Graham who spoke on Busy Hand, Busy Missions. She explained how ladies in many churches were working on needs for the community or elsewhere. Becky had brought samples of some crafts her ladies had made.

"The ladies from our church group get together every Thursday afternoon to make clothes for the needy babies and children. We have learned that certain projects work better at particular times for us, but you may find projects are different for your group." As Becky talked she placed her large basket on the table and donned her apron which had pockets full of surprises.

"We have spring and fall bake sales on the sidewalk around the bank. From the proceeds of the bake sales, we send hard-earned money to our foreign missions. One Sunday each year, we have a bean and cornbread meal and we give any change collected to the local hunger fund. A friend of mine runs the fund and is always appreciative of help from churches and organizations." Looking through the basket, Becky found a newspaper article about her friend and the local hunger fund. The article was passed around for everyone to see. She continued to explain that the fund had helped many people.

"One year our group helped Beth and her family. Beth mentioned her work with us earlier, I think. We made knitted hats and booties for babies and sent them to Beth to use as she needed. The knitting was one of my favorite projects and I have patterns for them if anyone wants them." Becky dug through her apron pockets and found several examples of the knitted projects which brought ogling from every lady.

Becky's last project was the crowd favorite. As soon as she pulled the project from her basket the ladies were declaring that they would make at least one. "I make the rag dolls for our precious little girls. I use a variety of colors for the hair and the girls enjoy choosing a hair color that matches theirs. Some dolls have curly hair and some have straight, but they are all fun. For the boys, my husband created a barn which has doors and holds barnyard animals. Before Christmas, we recruit our husbands to make wooden toys for the children, such as these." Becky picked up some small wooden animals from her basket and passed them around for the ladies to examine. The animals were not finely carved, but one could tell what they were. Suggestions came from the audience as well as the speaker on making more projects.

"You know, many times the older men can't work outside, but they really want to help with missions. So they enjoy whittling, and remember it doesn't have to be perfect. Patterns for the rag doll and the farm animals are available for those who would accept the challenge. Remember Ladies, do not try to do it all. Something is better than nothing. He has a job for each of us." Becky used a rag doll to tell the audience goodbye.

When she was finished, once again the ladies clapped and told her how much they had enjoyed her presentation. Katherine stood before the crowd and agreed with everyone that the day had been great and she hated to close, but she knew her guests had a long way to go.

Lyssa spoke before Katherine had time to dismiss. "Katherine, I think all of us have truly enjoyed this day. I think we ought to have this day as an annual event to get together and share and also see our guests again. We have learned so much from you we want to make sure we see you again."

When the ladies were finally dismissed, Katherine and Mary walked with the ladies to their buggy. "Let's keep in touch," Mary said. "We are excited about what we have learned and we will let you know how our church accepts the challenge of missions."

"Well you know, at least you have planted the seed. There will be plenty of opportunities now to help spread the gospel," Beth said.

The other ladies thanked Katherine, Mary and Nellie for getting the Ladies' Day together. Some ladies said they never even knew such things were being done and they were so glad they had come to hear the speakers. Some of the local women suggested they try to get a Thursday work group together since they now had the wing to the school. Without a doubt the ladies were enthused about missions.

The congregation of women and children said goodbye and waved as they traveled up the hill, leaving Roundstone. What a wonderful day we have enjoyed together. Mary thought, as she sat on the steps of the building for a rest. "I'm tired. This has been a long day, a good day, but a long day."

"Did you get a count of how many women were here, not counting children and babies?" Katherine asked.

"I did. I counted twenty-seven women. I think it was a great crowd, especially for our first Ladies' Day," Mary replied.

Katherine, Mary, Nellie and tired Renie agreed. It had been a great day. Katherine told Mary to go home and get some rest. Katherine volunteered Renie and Nellie to help take care of the dishes. Mary, very tired, took her advice and left with her horse and buggy.

As Katherine, Nellie and Renie packed all the plates, glasses and silverware from breakfast and lunch, Nellie figured she would be washing a lot of dishes this evening.

Katherine read her mind. "You know one of the jobs of being a servant of the Lord is not always being the star of the show and giving the best presentation, like your apple illustration. Sometimes it is doing those lowly jobs like washing dishes. That is often where we learn how to be humble and be a servant of the Lord."

Nellie agreed and as they rode home, she thought about what it would be like to be a missionary in a foreign country. There would be many challenging jobs away from home. Although it looked and sounded like it would be a great way to live a life, there would be a lot of times when it was the dishwashing of the day, and not so much the delightful apple illustrations. Something Nellie would have to think about!

# Chapter 40

# The Good and the Evil

Andrea used her teacher's calendar to pencil in the date for the Fall Harvest Program. "Sallye, let's plan for Friday, November 8 at six o'clock in the evening. Don't you think that will give the children enough time to memorize their parts?"

Sallye gazed over Andrea's shoulder at the calendar. "I think that sounds good. Andrea, I want to thank you again for giving me this opportunity to help you and to be with Hannah. I have so enjoyed my time with you in the classroom."

"Sallye, you have been such a help to me and to the students. I don't know what I would have done without you. Hopefully, we can get some volunteers to bring cookies for the evening. How about we eat our lunch before the students come back?"

Andrea and Sallye were enjoying lunch, sharing their apple desserts, when Sallye spotted someone unusual outside.

"Someone is out there talking to Mike," Sallye said as she walked to the window to get a better look. "He is by himself, on a horse."

Andrea walked to the door and cautiously went outside. She didn't like for anyone to come after school had started, especially someone she didn't know. Although Andrea felt a little timid in the situation, she knew she had to have courage.

"Okay, students, lunch break is over; time to get back into the building."

The students were disappointed to have to come back in, but reluctantly followed orders. However, Mike, was still talking to the man. The shady-looking character looked at Andrea and said something to Mike. Getting off his horse, he swaggered up to the door beside Mike.

"I'm Mike's ol' man and I want to take him fishin, then I'll take him home."

"I really can't go," Mike said. "I have a test this afternoon, so I have to stay."

"Yes, you do, Mike, I am glad you remembered, but even if you did not have a test, I couldn't let you go with the man, even if he is your father. Sir, this is a school day, and I have never met you," Andrea said. "Mike, do you know him as your father?"

"No, I really don't. I don't remember what my father looked like. He left me with my grandparents almost thirteen years ago," Mike said, not looking at the man scowling at him.

"Okay, so I will wait until after school. I will take you home and then we will get your clothes. You are coming to live with me," the man said, showing his exasperation. "It's time you spent some time with your ol' man."

Andrea guided Mike through the door and told the man he would have to wait until after school to talk to Mike. Andrea and Sallye had heard the story of how the father had dumped Mike at the grandparent's door and left. Now, he wanted Mike back in his life? Why?

Andrea had heard that the father lived up north. As she pictured the crowded cities with the factories, she wondered, who would want to live there with the stench in the streets, the lack of places to live and the forced child labor. That's it! He wants to take Mike north so he will be forced to work and he will get the pay from Mike's labor. A young boy the size of Mike would be a profitable worker, one who would be able to work long, hard hours. What could she do to prevent the father's diabolical plan?

As soon as school was over, Mike's father met him at the door. Seeing the gloat in his eyes, Andrea watched the father order Mike to hurry up. The irritating man rode the horse while Mike walked. Perhaps they would change places after a while, but she really doubted it. Andrea had seen his kind many times, a selfish, uncaring man who had no right to be called a father.

Sallye offered to ride out to see Thomas. He would know what to do.

As soon as Sallye and Hannah found Thomas and told him about what had happened, Thomas headed for Della's house. By the time he got there, Mike was gone.

"Oh, Thomas, Salin, Mike's father, took him. He took my Mike," Della said between sobs. "He demanded that Mike get his clothes and what he would need. And he said he had to have a horse for Mike."

"Della, I will try my best to track them and catch up with them. Do you have any idea where they were headed?"

"No, no, I don't have any idea. Mike didn't want to go but he didn't want me to worry, so he told me he would be okay. I know that Salin wanted to get away as soon as possible before the neighbors stopped him."

"I will see what I can do, Della. Say a prayer for Mike. God will watch over and protect him."

Thomas tried to track the horses, but they had obviously taken to the backwoods. Riding horses through the creek a ways would make tracking futile. He decided to go to the sheriff and ask him to track the boy and his father.

"Thomas, I would love to help. But, see, the problem is that Mike went along peacefully. You know the boy's father has the right to take him, even if the grandparents did raise him." Sheriff Konner leaned a shoulder against the building as he studied his boots. "Sorry, Thomas. I can notify the authorities in Hardin and Jefferson counties," the Hart County sheriff explained.

"Anything, you can do to help, we would appreciate, Sheriff."

"Well, the boy might try to get away on his own, but that could get him killed. You know, someone like that wouldn't care to kill again. Better say a prayer for him, Thomas. It's not a good situation."

The two men shook hands and Thomas rode home to give the family the news. As soon as they heard the unfortunate news, the women decided to ride out to see Della.

Both women said a prayer for Mike and for Della. Nellie insisted on tagging along as she remembered all the negative things Mike had said about his father. Mike's father had certainly not been a father to Mike and Mike resented his selfish ways.

Della met the group at the door and welcomed them. "Thank you for coming, but there is not anything you can do."

"Della, we heard about Mike and we wanted to come say a prayer with you for Mike." Katherine said as she hugged Della.

Della kept talking about how no good that Salin was. Her lower lip wobbled as she gasped a sob. "I've always known that Salin killed my daughter, Abby. But me and Daniel never could prove it, of course."

Katherine busied herself in Della's kitchen, fixing a pot of coffee. The apple fritters she had made that morning would help to take the edge off the pain.

Della continued to talk, worry crinkling her brow. "Just the mean way he had brought Mike, told him he had already buried Abby, and expected us to pay for her burial. Of course, we paid him what he wanted and we were glad to get our grandson. Mike, oh, Mike." Della paused as she looked at Nellie. For the first time she realized that Nellie was probably also hurting.

"Nellie, I'm sorry. I didn't think about you and Mike."

Nellie, swallowing back her fear, tried to reassure Della. "We are praying for Mike, and I know that God will keep him safe."

"I thought we were shed of that good-for-nothing scum. Just what is he up to? Why does he want Mike? Mike don't have no money, just a few dollars I gave him when he left." Della stopped to take a bite of her apple fritter. "Salin mentioned that they had a lot of ridin' to do, to pack plenty of clothes. Oh, that's right, he did say they were headed north, and that Mike would need his jacket."

Mary cleaned up the crumbs from the fritters and picked up the knitting that Della was working on. As she examined the work she realized Della was knitting a pair of socks, probably for Mike. As she put the work down, she shivered at the thought that he might not be back to wear them.

"Salin said that Mike had to have a horse because he didn't want him to hold him up. They needed to move on. Other than that, I don't have an idea where they could be going." Della dropped her head, too upset to say any more.

Katherine moved to Della and put her arm around her. "I will stay with you tonight. I don't want you to be alone. We will keep praying for Mike, which is the best we can do for him."

Before Nellie went to bed that night she knelt in prayer, "Father, please watch over Mike and take care of him. I am willing to give up Mike if it be your will. Please, just bring him home to us."

---

Mike was glad his wise grandmother had stuffed his pockets full of food. His father rode ahead and took a swig from a bottle occasionally. He looked back at Mike occasionally, but didn't seem to care if Mike was comfortable. Finally, they stopped for the night. Mike asked if they could build a small fire, since it was cool at night. Salin said he didn't care. He showed Mike his bottle and told him the bottle was his warmth for the night.

Mike picked up a few sticks and branches to start a fire. Luckily he had brought matches with him along with a canteen of water. The bacon biscuits and the beef tack his grandmother had put in his quilt roll was definitely a blessing. The quilt was large enough for him to make a small pillow and use the rest for his bed. As he snuggled in for the night Mike prayed. "Lord, give me strength and help me through this, and, Lord, I know I am not supposed to bargain with you, but, Lord, if you will get me out of this, I will dedicate my life to you. Amen."

The next morning the two were up at daybreak. Salin had not told him where they were headed, so he had to be patient. Mike asked him how much longer they would be riding, but Salin had no time for answers.

"We'll stop at the mercantile store and get something to eat, if you move along. We need to be making better time, we got things to do up north." Salin coughed and spit before getting on his horse, never looking at Mike to see if he was ready.

Soon they came to a small trading shop, and Salin went in. He told Mike to stay put. Mike slid off his horse and watered the horses while he rested. Salin wasn't seeing his horse got anything to eat or drink, so it was up to Mike to take care of both horses. He crossed the street to the livery stable and got a couple of scoops of oats, which he paid for. As he was bringing the buckets back for the horses, he saw his father paying for his purchases. When Salin came out, he dropped a hard biscuit in Mike's lap.

"Let's go," Salin grumbled at Mike as he stumbled toward his horse. It was evident that Salin was already drinking so early in the morning.

"The horses aren't finished with their oats. Can't we wait just a few minutes?" Mike knew he didn't want to get his father riled up at him, but he had always been taught to respect animals and feed them before you feed yourself.

Salin grumbled, finally sat on the step and ate his bacon sandwich. Mike clearly saw the pattern. Without a doubt, it was all about what Salin wanted.

Mike had to design a plan. He had heard his Grandmother cry so many nights when they thought Mike was asleep. She and her grandfather had cried together about Mike's mother and their suspicions that Salin had killed her.

One night after they had gone to visit their daughter's grave, he heard them talk about what they had learned that day. Friends of their daughter told them how she had often had bruises and they knew Salin had beaten her when he went home drunk.

Mike had to handle the situation very carefully. He knew if he made any mistake and he would be found out, he would never get what he needed. Mike thought about Joshua and how brave he must have been, as he recalled his memory verse, 'Have not I commanded thee? Be strong and of a good courage; be not afraid, neither be thou dismayed: for the LORD thy God is with thee withersoever thou goest.'

Mike repeated the verse over and over. How glad he was that Pastor Ship had encouraged the congregation to repeat the scriptures, as he would always say, "There is power in the Word of the Lord."

# Chapter 41

## An Arrest

As Pastor Ship stepped on Della Caswell's porch, he heard Della's sad greeting. "Come on in Pastor, but I'm no good company today."

Pastor Ship sat at the table with Della as he drank his coffee. "Della, we have to trust in the Lord that Mike will be alright. You know, he is quite an ingenious young man, and I have faith in him."

"I know God will watch over him, but, it is just, well, Salin killed my daughter. And I have to admit that I have wondered many times where God was when Salin was beating her. And if Salin could kill someone as sweet as my daughter, well, he could just as easily kill Mike. I don't think I could handle that; I really don't." Della wiped her brow and stood up. "Well, Pastor, I hate to run off, but I have work to do, now that Mike isn't here, I am trying to keep up with his chores."

---

Once on the trail, Mike knew his father would begin drinking soon. While Salin had gone to relieve himself, Mike emptied part of his dad's whiskey so he would run out a little sooner. Planning to get Salin to go to a store or bar for liquor would give Mike time to go to the sheriff's office.

After riding a couple of hours or more, Salin was ready for a drink. Emptying the last of his bottle, Salin's nostrils flared, as he looked at Mike with distrust. Thankfully, they were close to a little town where they could stop and rest.

"We'll stop here. I can go in and have a drink while you take care of the horses, Boy."

Salin gave Mike orders not knowing that he was doing exactly what Mike wanted.

Mike took care of the horses first, tying them to the post at the water trough. Once Salin was inside, he went to the sheriff's office to ask for help. Mike told the sheriff the story, and what he planned to do. The sheriff said he would be there and all Mike had to do was to get him talking.

Salin was at a table talking to some other men, eating and drinking. Mike went in and sat close to Salin, but at another table.

"Boy, I'm not ready yet, you go on out and wait for me." Salin waved his hand toward the door as if he was shooing Mike out.

"Well, if you don't mind, I would like to just sit here and have a nice glass of water. I'll even buy you a bottle of whiskey since I would like to rest awhile longer," Mike said as he stretched his long arms and legs out, giving the impression his back needed a rest.

"Now, that's my boy! Didn't know you had money, Boy. Hey, we'll talk about that later." As Salin drank, the others began to leave. Mike was hoping they would stay, but even drunks couldn't stand to be around a mean, ornery character like Salin.

Not wearing his badge, the sheriff came strolling in as if he was a regular customer. Sitting behind Salin, he could listen and give Mike support if he needed it.

Mike prayed that he would have the courage he needed to accomplish the task. "Hey, Dad, I'm really glad you came and got me. I was tired of living with my grandmother. You know, men can live together with men better than having a woman with them, right, Dad?" Mike asked.

"Yeah, women! Just have to give 'em a little of this once in a while." Salin raised his fist, and he acted like he was hitting someone.

Mike sucked in his breath and prayed his fear wouldn't creep into his face. "Yeah, my grandma carries on all the time about you and my mother. I say if she whined the way my grandmother whines about everything, she needed a good beating." Mike could hardly say the words because it wasn't true.

Suddenly Salin gave Mike a look as if he didn't believe him.

Mike had to do a better job of acting and give it everything or he would lose it all. "I saw my grandfather beat my grandmother and she would still whine. Stupid, silly women, what they need is a good beatin, don't you agree Dad?"

Salin looked at Mike this time with more respect. He poured himself another drink and downed it. "Well, sometimes you just have to show them who is boss."

Nerves were getting the best of Mike and he had to think fast. "Yeah, that constant whine, whine about fixing supper, whine about milking and doing the work. I tell you it would make me so mad, and my grandfather, well he would take it till he couldn't take it anymore and then wham!" Mike hit his fist against his palm as hard as he could.

Salin took another drink and leaned where he could get a good view of Mike. "Yeah, I agree. Your mother was a whiner. You know I would warn her to shut her trap up, and I would have to shut it up for her, smacked that mouth closed a few times. She wouldn't listen to me and if I came home after having a drink she would whine and cry and pray for me. The praying for me was just too much, and I beat her every time she started that 'Jesus, help him!' stuff. She just wouldn't give it up, no she kept on whinin' and praying for me to stop drinking. The last time, I hit her so hard, her head bounced off the floor like a ball. Yeah, that shut her up. She didn't fuss at me anymore, I sure saw to that!" Salin laughed and stretched out with his hands behind his head as though he had done a great deed.

At that point the sheriff stood up. "Sir, will you please, stand up!" Quickly, the sheriff had a pair of handcuffs on Salin. "You are under arrest for the murder of your wife, Abby Steele, thirteen years ago. You are coming with me."

Mike followed the sheriff and Salin to the jail. "I'll be back out, Mike, you stay here," the sheriff said, while Salin was shouting at Mike.

Mike waited for the sheriff. "Son, what you did was brave, took a lot of courage to do that. You can go back home. I will send one of my deputies with you. Since I was there and heard the confession, you will not have to appear in court, but it might be helpful. We will see what the judge says. Thanks for putting this guy behind bars. Your mother's killer is finally going to pay for what he did," the sheriff stated adamantly.

Mike thought about his Dad in jail, maybe getting the death sentence for what he did, mostly because what Mike did to put him there. Mike felt bad because he had no compassion for his father. During the years he had seen how his grandparents had suffered over the death of his mother. His mother, how sweet and faithful to the Lord she was and now justice was hers. Salin wouldn't hurt anyone else again.

# Chapter 42

# Bob

In jail at Hart County, Bob was waiting for the circuit judge to make his rounds. Bob realized he was going to hang for what he did. He had read the Bible every day and memorized verses which gave him comfort. People from the church and others brought Bob food and had prayer with him. The people had been nice to him considering what he had done. Bob wished he could erase that awful day, but it had happened, and he had to take his punishment. People could not get away with murder. The sheriff had warned him, it would be a quick trial.

On Monday morning, the prisoner was brought in the courtroom. Bob looked around at the courtroom; there sat the people who had brought him food and encouragement the last few weeks. They looked at him with a sigh, realizing there was no escaping a guilty verdict.

The trial was over quickly. Sentencing would be in the afternoon. During the day, he had several visitors, people bringing him sandwiches, fried chicken, pies, candy; so much food, he couldn't eat it all. Each one of them said prayers for Bob in hopes they would give him encouragement and strength for the next day.

The judge announced the prisoner stand as he read the sentence. "The prisoner, Bob Wright, has been found guilty and will hang until death on Friday of this week. Son, I suggest you take the next few days to get your affairs in order."

As Bob was escorted back to jail, the local people gave him a pat on the shoulder. They knew the sentencing was inevitable, but it was still a shock when they heard it. Bob asked the sheriff if he could say something to Thomas.

Bob shook Thomas' hand as the two entered the cell together. "Thomas, there is money hidden in the cave I went to. Please see that the money is used to buy a gravestone for Cindy. She is buried at the Nashville Memorial Cemetery. That is my only wish, for you to take care of my Cindy."

Bob was ready to turn away and he remembered something else to say to Thomas. "Will you be with me on the day of the hanging? I would like for you to be there and say a prayer before… well before it happens."

Thomas assured him that he would be there. Although Thomas knew justice had to be served and Bob deserved his punishment, he knew it would be the hardest thing he would ever have to do, to watch the young man die.

That evening he told Katherine and Mary what Bob had asked. Of course, he had assured Bob that he would do what he asked. "Tommie, we will go over to the cave tomorrow. Bob said that he hid some money there for Cindy's grave. Hopefully, it will still be there."

In other news, Thomas shared with the family, the sheriff had mailed a letter to the Hart County Sheriff. He had told him about how Salin was arrested for the murder of Della's daughter. "What about paying a visit to Della?" Thomas asked. "I think she would like to know about Mike as soon as possible."

The family loaded up and made the trip to Della's place. Mr. Avery was with Della, helping with the chores. Thankfully, he had spent a lot of time with her since Mike's absence.

"Now, he will pay for murder of my Abby, and I will get my Mike back home," Della said, as she heard the good news. Although no one actually knew how the arrest had happened, they figured that Mike had used his ingenuity to get Salin arrested.

The next afternoon, Thomas and Tommie went to the cave to find the money. Mike had told Tommie that he had heard the prisoner stomping on the floor of the cave. As the men looked around in the cave they saw an area that looked like it had been disturbed recently. Sure enough, the money was all there.

"Just think," Thomas said, "this could have been prevented if the Wisemans would have just sent the money for Cindy's medical needs. Sometimes, we think we know best, but we need to trust in the Lord and he will give us our direction."

The weather had taken a dip in temperatures over the past week and it was time for hog killing. The help would be there on Thursday morning and the process would begin. Although the children wanted to stay home to help, they were not allowed.

Katherine showed Mary how the hams were prepared for curing, some were salt cured and some brown sugar cured. The pork bellies were prepared much the same way, using a lot of pepper.

When the children came home from school, they hurried to the large, iron cracklin' pot. Ollie was stirring the huge black pot sitting on a pile of wood beside the woodshed. The smell of smoke and the aroma of frying pork fat caused the children to remember the good times of the past when the family embraced the experience. Ollie had already taken up a basket full of cracklin's which the children were eager to taste.

"Ummm, fresh cracklin's! They're the best!" Renie said as she filled her hands and pockets.

Ollie cautioned the children to stay away from the fire and to be careful. He explained tomorrow would be another full day and if they wanted to help they could bring up more firewood. Katherine and Mary would be making lye soap with the fat rendered from the cracklin's.

Nellie raced into the house and asked if she could stay home to help make the lye soap. Katherine promptly told her 'no' and asked if she could help clean the kitchen. The day had been very tiring for her and Mary.

"Gran, how do you make lye soap?" Nellie asked.

Katherine was busy cleaning the tables with hot water, but stopped long enough to explain. "We use the fat we rendered today and we put wood ash and lye water; that's the water leached through wood ashes. Why, you aren't going to be making any by yourself are you?" Katherine asked.

"Who knows when we will need a lot of soap to clean up a big mess? Odd, we use a lie to clean up filth," Nellie said as she looked at Mary. The overheard conversation between Nellie's father and her mother's resting place had weighed heavily on her mind lately.

"L-y-e and l-i-e are spelled differently, Nellie, but I get your point," Mary replied without a smile.

"What's that smell? What's cooking?" Nellie asked.

"Oh, come look," Mary said as she lifted the top on the large cooker. "Hogshead. Doesn't it look delicious? It has vinegar, salt, pepper, onions, and it is falling off the bone, just about ready to eat."

Nellie covered her mouth with her hand and walked away quickly. "I know someone who needs the brains in the hog's head." Nellie added quietly.

The children changed clothes to begin chores. Renie grabbed the egg basket and was on her way to the chicken house. Nellie fell in behind her with the buckets. Both girls wanted to complete their chores to get back to the house and eat a few more cracklin's.

Bessie was at the barn, ready for her evening milking. Nellie put some feed in the trough and let Bessie in the stall. Sitting on the milking stool, Nellie rested her head on Bessie's warm belly. The cow was soft and warm. Bessie had a wonderful cow smell which brought back memories of when she first started milking. Bessie must have known Nellie was having a moment as she looked back at Nellie with those big brown eyes.

Watching the frothy bubbles forming in the bucket, Nellie dreamed about Mike. She had always thought that she and Mike would be married someday and maybe become missionaries. However, since Mike had been through the experience with his father, he seemed different. Mike had seemed so reserved when they talked at school that Nellie was sure something had changed. Of course, Mike's obsession with his plan to get rich with gold mining worried Nellie. Still, that wasn't it. There was a change in Mike and she couldn't help but be upset that he was not the same. Perhaps she could get him to talk more freely if they were alone, and that is what she would have to do.

The family enjoyed the fresh hog meat with homemade sauerkraut, cornbread and white beans. Katherine reminded the family she had a little over a month to stay with them and she would be getting married and living in Upton with her new husband. She took every opportunity to tell Thomas and the children they would have to work harder the next few months to help Mary. Because Mary's due date was the first part of May Nellie and Renie would be out of school and would make great helpers.

"Now, Mary, please go put your feet up. You need to go rest. This has been a difficult day for you. I can tell you have really pushed yourself." Katherine gave Mary a side-hug and waved her off to her room.

Mary didn't argue with Katherine as she was more than tired. Throwing herself on her bed, Mary let all the frustration, hurt and anguish surface. Tears gushed and she sobbed so hard she shook the bed. Even though Thomas and Katherine had apologized again, the apology was not genuine. Not being able to sleep, and being pregnant were not good combinations.

# Chapter 43

# The Trip

Thomas could not sleep the night before the execution. He was up early reading his Bible and praying. It would be one of the hardest days he would ever have to face. "How, Father, how will I get through this day? Please be with me for I have not the strength to do this by myself."

"Thomas, is there anything I can do for you? I know this situation has you worried." Mary said as she made a pot of coffee.

"No, no, go back to bed. It is too early for you to be up and this is just something I have to work out for myself. Besides, you look tired." Actually, Thomas had thought for a week or so that Mary looked bad. Perhaps she was just trying to do too much, he thought to himself.

"No, I want to stay up with you. I want to be with you and at least you know I am here, like you will be there for Bob today." Mary stood behind Thomas and wrapped her hands around his head, kissing him on top of his black, unruly hair.

"I appreciate that, Mary. I just feel so bad for Bob. Somehow, I feel like I could have done something about this whole thing. There is just something about Bob Wright that I can't figure out. It is like I know him, but I don't."

"Well, dear, I don't see how you could have done anything about what Bob did. You weren't there, and you didn't know Bob. Please stop feeling guilty for something you didn't do." Mary sat beside her husband and held his hand.

"Mary, when Mike witnessed to Bob, I saw something very familiar. I didn't understand the familiarity with Bob when I went to the jail and took the Bible, or the many times I talked with Bob over the past several weeks. Yet, there is something so familiar about Bob. You know, perhaps I saw him somewhere long ago. Just wish I knew."

During breakfast, Thomas explained he would go to the hanging, take the body to the Upton cemetery and he would say a few words at the gravesite. "If you ladies want to come about 1:00, we will plan on having the funeral then. I am sure it will take that long to get the body…"Thomas couldn't continue.

Mary touched Thomas on the arm. "We will be there. If there is anything we can do, please tell us. We want to help you get through this."

Thomas hitched up the wagon to his best horse, Old Dan. With the unfortunate load the wagon would be carrying, and having to go through the muddy cemetery at Upton, Old Dan would have a work out.

Thomas was allowed to go into the cell with Bob when he got there. The hanging was to be at 9:00 and it was only 7:30. Thomas took his Bible in the cell and prayed with Bob. They read scripture together and talked easily. Although Thomas' heart was breaking for Bob, Bob was actually courageous. Again, he admitted he had done wrong, but with Cindy gone, he really had nothing else to live for.

"Thomas, my father died when I was seven, then my mama died when I was ten. My aunt tried to take care of me, but she had her own children and I was always a burden to her family. My grandmother was the only one who really tried to take care of me. Then, you know what, she died! After that, I just started on my own, wandering around. I would do small jobs for people here and there. Just work enough to get a meal and then sleep in a barn. There were times that I wished I could just die because I would be so cold and so hungry. But, God wouldn't let me die."

Swallowing the lump in his throat, Thomas sighed. "I wish I could have been there for you, Bob. Surely, I could have helped."

Bob explained when he was about sixteen, he met a friend. "Don't you know, he died! So, a couple years after that I met Cindy. She was the best thing ever happened to me. I fell in love with Cindy and she fell in love with me. Her parents didn't like me from the beginning. I didn't have anything, so I don't really blame them. But I decided I would work hard every day to give Cindy everything she deserved. We left and went to Nashville where I heard I could get a job. We were doing fine for the first couple years, and then Cindy got sick. I would have taken her back home and left her if I had of known she was going to die. I loved her so much. So, you see, everybody I loved has died and left me, so it is time I join Cindy. I had a good friend tell me about Christ years ago, and then, when the boy witnessed to me that day in the cave, everything came together. Thank you for listening, Thomas, thank you for being here."

Thomas shook his head, trying to keep the tears back. "I am going to take care of everything afterwards. Next week I will go to Nashville to get the stone for Cindy. Is there anything you want on the stone in particular?"

Interrupting the conversation, the jailer came to the cell. "Son, the judge wants to see you."

"What, why?" Bob asked, very confused.

"Don't know, son, just come along with me."

"Would it be alright for me to come with Bob?" Thomas asked.

"Uh, I guess. He can tell you to leave if he wants." The jailer seemed to be concealing a secret.

"Sit, Bob, sit down, please. I see Thomas is with you today. Morning, Thomas! How is Katherine and the family?" Judge Winston certainly seemed to be in a cordial mood for an execution day.

"Good, good, what is this about, Judge Winston?" Thomas was confused but saw a ray of hope for Bob.

"Well, seems I have overlooked some important information in this case. First, Bob, we found this letter, torn up, in the garbage" Judge held some pieces of paper together for him to see. "What can you tell me about this? Where did it come from?"

A very nervous Bob dropped his head and cleared his throat. "Well, see I never meant for anyone to see that letter. I don't want Thomas or anyone feeling sorry for me."

"That is not the point, Son. Answer the question. Where did this come from?"

"Well, me and Johnny were best friends as teenagers and we had the same birthday. So my grandmother gave me that letter and said I couldn't open it until I was 18. She passed away right after she gave me the letter. So Johnny said that he would put it in his bible and we would open it together on our birthdays. Except he died and I forgot about it."

The judge looked even more confused. "Then how did you manage to get it now?"

"Well, Thomas, here, see…he brought me Johnny's bible and one day I turned to the scripture that Johnny had talked about so much, 1 Samuel 18. There was the letter, but somebody had opened it and I figured they didn't want me to know about it. I'm not anyone to be proud of that's for sure. Anyway, I read it and I don't want anyone to know what it said. I don't want to bring shame on the family." Bob said with his head low.

"Son, I have never done this before. But I have given this a lot of thought. I have reviewed my decision in you case. First, you acted in self-defense as far as I can see. The gun was not yours. It belonged to Hank Wiseman. Correct? I even saw the letters that you and Cindy had written to her parents for help."

The judge took a minute to look over his notes as he looked from Bob to Thomas. "Bob, this is a little difficult for me. Are you saying that you do not want Thomas to know what this letter says?"

"Uh, er…yes."

"Well, this is a very different case. However, I am going to change my sentencing from hanging to one year in jail. That is if you, Thomas, can take complete charge of Bob here when he gets out. I expect to never see him in my court again. Are you willing to take him under your supervision after he completes his jail sentence?"

Thomas could not believe what he was hearing and without even considering, he blurted out, "Yes, yes, of course!"

"Okay, Bob, this is your requirement. I expect you to complete your sentencing with no issues in jail. Good behavior, understand?"

"Yes..yes sir!" Bob answered as if in disbelief.

"And when Thomas comes to pick you up on the day you get out of jail, you must, you must, understand? You must tell him about the letter. Alright?" The Judge shook his head as if not understanding the young man.

"Sure, I will do that."

"Okay, until then, you will go back to jail and stay. Thomas, I heard that you have a trip planned for Cindy's gravestone in Tennessee."

"You know, your mom was my sweetheart and she broke up with me when I went off to school. Broke my heart. I've always had a weakness for Katherine. I guess that's why when I saw that letter I had to do something. Well, I better shut up." Judge Winston quickly left the office.

In shock, the two sat looking at each other until the jailer came in.

"Thomas, thank you for Johnny's bible. It saved my life. Because you brought me God's Word to read I have been pardoned from a death sentence."

As Thomas explained the previous episode to the ladies they rejoiced in the unbelievable news. Still, Thomas wondered what the letter was about. Could they stand not knowing what the letter said until next year? "Mom, what in the world did you do for Judge Winston to make such an impression on him. I think you are the reason that the judge changed his mind."

"Oh, Thomas, we courted back then and I was foolish to break up with him. But when he came back I did something for him he said he would never forget." Katherine smiled shyly.

"Okay…and what was that?" Thomas asked as he looked at his mother a little differently.

"Well, for now, let's just say that God gets all the glory for miracles. Judge Winston now believes in a God that can perform miracles!"

The three of them had met at the cemetery as planned. Katherine was the first to suggest that they get along with their business and talk more later.

A letter from Nashville was at the post office for Katherine. Katherine had sent the letters to Hobie and Leah's parents a few weeks ago, inviting them to come for a visit. The letter was from Leah's mother Pearl. She tore open the letter and read it quickly.

> Dear Mrs. Cosby,
>
> I received your letter and I would love to come visit my daughter and her husband. I do not have a way to get there, though. Please tell Leah I love her and I miss her.
>
> God bless.
>
> Pearl

Mary and Katherine went to Riders to make a few grocery purchases. We could make two trips in one, she planned. I will send a letter to Ms. Pearl as soon as possible so she can prepare to come back with us.

Quickly, Katherine wrote to Leah's mother and made a trip back to the post office to get it in the mail. She wanted Pearl to have as much time as possible to think about the trip and plan. Every woman wants their mother around when they get ready to have a baby, and she was sure Leah's mother wanted to be with her daughter's family.

Thomas worked outside for a long time, putting more framing on the house. When the children came home from school, he started the chores. The day had been a long, stressful day and he would quit finally and be with his family.

After a meal and devotion, Katherine excitedly told Thomas about the trip to Nashville "And I figure while we are in Nashville, we can pick up Leah's mother. She can come back with us so she will be here for the baby."

"Mom, yes, I agreed to take care of the gravestone, but it is a long way down there and back. Do you think you can ride that far without being completely worn out? Because, you can't, it would wear out anyone. Mary can't go either, it would be way too much for her. I will take Tommie with me but I doubt Leah's mother would want to ride back with us," Thomas said.

"But Thomas, I have to go. I have to be there to pick her up. I have already written her and told her that we are coming. So, see, I have to go with you. I will be fine," Katherine begged.

Mary said she would love for Katherine to pick up a book for Nellie and Thomas. The books would make great Christmas gifts, she suggested. Katherine said she would pick up something for Renie also.

On Saturday night, the family discussed and planned the next week. Everyone knew their jobs and if they needed any help, they could ask Paul at the mill to help. Mary assured them they would not need him and everything would be fine. Nellie said Mike also had offered to help, if they needed him. Pete, John, Ollie and Hobie would not be there until Thomas returned. Hopefully, they would be back for the Fall Harvest Program at school.

On Monday morning Thomas and Katherine drove the buggy to Upton and left it at Katherine's house. Dr. Larimore walked with them to the stagecoach depot. Dr. Larimore insisted on saying a prayer for them before they got into the stage coach, then he shook hands with Thomas and gave Katherine a hug and a kiss.

"Be safe," Dr. Larimore told the two.

"We will be fine, Keith," Katherine said as she pulled up into the stage coach.

They had barely gotten on the road when the gentleman opposite them started talking to Thomas. "Scott is my name, sir and you?"

Thomas introduced Katherine and himself. A conversation flowed between the travelers, as they learned a little about their traveling companion.

"So, Thomas, what do you think about our new President Polk?" Scott asked. "He made a name for himself with the Mexican War. Did your area have many men to fight in the war?"

"Yes, sir, we had a couple men killed and one man who had never returned to his family. Our part of the country is against slavery, and therefore the biggest majority of the men had mixed feelings about helping Texas since Texas was for slavery, you see."

"Oh, you know there are rumors of war because of so much rumble about slavery? Have you heard of Cassius M. Clay?" Scott didn't wait for an answer but proceeded to explain. "He was an officer under General Taylor in the Mexican War and he has written and published this paper, *True American*, which is an anti-slavery paper. He lives in Lexington and right now he is confined to his bed, very sick. Hopefully, he will get better and he will continue his petition against slavery. I will give you this paper; you will find it interesting," Scott said as he rolled the paper up and handed it to Thomas.

The first stop was several miles down the road and Katherine was very happy to stop, stretch her legs and use the outhouse. The station had a large corral, several rooms for overnight stays and a small restaurant. They were told they could order a cup of coffee and pie, but nothing which would take any longer. Katherine and Thomas took the opportunity to have something to eat and drink to prepare them for the long trip ahead.

Scott was the first back on the stage coach and he began talking as soon as they were loaded. He obviously knew a lot about politics because it was his favorite subject. He talked about Governor Letcher and what he was doing in Frankfort. He was responsible for getting the railroads under contract in Kentucky. "Just think," Scott said, "we may have a railroad going between Louisville to Nashville in the next few years. It will really speed travel. A lot more people will be traveling then. You know travel is education. The more I travel the more I learn," Scott continued.

# Chapter 44

# Rebecca

Another stop for the horses and a bit of refreshment for the passengers was right on time. Thomas and the Professor were ready for lunch while Katherine had rather take a walk and have some quiet time. The stage coach manager warned the group that the stop would be about one hour, no delays. They would be picking up another passenger.

While the men went to the large, comfortable dining room, Katherine walked around and looked at the mercantile display next door. The store which obviously catered to the lay-over folk had a mouth-watering selection of candies. Katherine purchased a little of each of the varieties as she told herself it was to take home to the kids, but she had to sample them.

While Katherine strolled through the depot she noticed what appeared to be a mother and father with their daughter. Immediately, Katherine saw the parents were upset with the young girl as they made no body contact, no hugs, not even smiles. Instead, they wagged a finger at the girl and shook their heads as though she was a contemptible person. Katherine wondered if the girl was even their daughter, for they didn't seem affectionate toward her. The parents acted as though the young girl was repulsive, as they kept their distance and barked commands at her. Katherine noticed the luggage and realized that the luggage belonged to the young girl. Possibly, she was the one who might be riding with them.

The stage coach manager was giving a hefty call for everyone to board. Sure enough the girl started toward the coach. Katherine noticed the man and woman who were with the girl. They did not give her a hug, but more of a stern, goodbye, as they left her there with her heavy bag. Katherine offered to help her with the bag but she refused the help. Through eye contact and motions, Katherine conveyed to Thomas that he could sit together with the Professor and she would sit with the young lady.

After the anxious passengers were settled in the coach, Katherine introduced herself to the young lady. She replied, not looking at Katherine, appearing not to want to have anything to do with anyone. The new passenger, Rebecca, stared out the window to hide her tear stained face. Katherine was at a loss to try to comfort her for Rebecca obviously did not want any help. Katherine decided she would put her hand on top of Rebecca's and tell her whenever she wanted to talk, she was there for her.

A good way down the road Katherine removed her hand. "Rebecca, may I ask, where are you going?"

"I am going to Nashville to my aunt's place," Rebecca said softly looking from her hands to the window outside.

"Oh, and will you be going to school there?"

Rebecca just shook her head no and continued to stare out the window.

Then Katherine noticed the little bump on her stomach. Katherine tried to figure out what to say. "We are also going to Nashville and we are bringing back a friend's mother. She is going to be there when her daughter gives birth to her first child. I am going to be a grandmother, my eighth grandchild. A baby is a very exciting event." Conversation came easily for Katherine and she could talk all day about her grandchildren but she wanted to give Rebecca a chance to add to the conversation if she wanted to.

Rebecca was silent, wiping the tears from her eyes with a handkerchief, keeping her head turned to the window.

Katherine didn't know what to say, but figured she would share more until Rebecca told her to be quiet. "I am a midwife and I deliver babies in our area. This year has been a real crop of babies, one set of twins and several others. A baby is one of God's most special gifts," Katherine chatted on.

"Well, some people think it is special, others think it is horrible!" Rebecca shrugged as she wiped her tears from her face.

"Are you a Christian, sweetie?" Katherine asked. "Because we believe that every baby is a gift from God."

"I am a Christian." She paused and said with a huff, "My father is a Baptist minister. I suppose you have guessed that I am pregnant." Rebecca motioned to her stomach.

"I assumed that," Katherine said. "Was that your parents at the stagecoach depot?"

"Well, yes, and they are very unhappy with me," Rebecca answered. "Actually, I was adopted when I was a few weeks old. My real mother had me and wasn't married, so she gave me up for adoption. The only thing she left me with was this gold locket." Rebecca showed Katherine the small gold locket around her neck.

Katherine noticed there was an "E" on the locket. What does the E stand for? Was that your mother's initial?"

"No, my mother named me Emily, but my parents did not choose to keep the name. This is all I have of my mother's. My parents have reminded me constantly that I was going to turn out just like my real mother. Now I have, so, they want to get rid of me and my baby. They are sending me away to my Aunt Beckie's house and then I am supposed to give the baby up for adoption." Rebecca seemed anxious to tell Katherine about everything now.

"Oh... do you want to give your baby up?"

"No, I don't and I told them. I love the father of my baby but they won't let us get married."

"I will pray for you right now that God will take care of you and your baby. He will lead you and guide you, if you are willing to listen," Katherine said as she began her prayer.

When Katherine finished her prayer, the two of them sat for a while without talking. She did not know what to tell Rebecca. This situation had to be one of the most difficult situations for a young woman. Everyone makes mistakes. Just this mistake was one that couldn't be corrected. Yet, something positive could be done. She wondered about the young man who obviously had a big part of the problem. Wouldn't he stand up to the parents and tell them he wanted to marry Rebecca?

Katherine thought about Nellie and Renie. The talk they had with Nellie about her kisses had been very direct, leaving no room for Nellie to misunderstand the message. Yet, everyone knows about the heat of the moment and what the heart wants, the heart wants. No one knew better than she, because of the love she and Keith shared.

At the evening lay-over, everyone gathered around the large table for supper. The meal was fried chicken, biscuits and gravy with strawberry preserves which Katherine and Rebecca enjoyed after the long afternoon ride. Both ladies were tired and dusty from the long ride and went to the room they shared. Katherine asked the depot host for a dishpan so they could take a quick bath before retiring for the night. Rebecca thanked Katherine for being with her and taking care of her.

"Would you care if I read from the Bible?" Katherine asked Rebecca.

"I would like that, please," Rebecca replied. Rebecca had already built a bond with this nice lady who was not judging her, but trying to help her, a stranger.

"Reading from Psalm 127 vs. 1-3 'Behold, children are a heritage from the Lord, the fruit of the womb a reward. Like arrows in the hand of a warrior are the children of one's youth. Blessed is the man who fills his quiver with them! He shall not be put to shame when he speaks with his enemies in the gate'." Katherine stopped reading and looked at Rebecca.

"Rebecca, do you want to marry the father of your baby?" Katherine asked as she closed her Bible and looked at the young lady sitting across from her.

"Yes, yes, I would like to, but my parents are strictly against it. They would never permit it."

"Rebecca, how old are you?"

Rebecca looked at Katherine, "I'm eighteen. I know I am old enough but I do not want to go against my parents and their wishes." Rebecca ran her hand over her baby bulge and kept her eyes from Katherine.

Not wanting to sound disrespectful to Rebecca's parents, Katherine still had to say what was on her mind. "I may sound like an old wooden spoon beating against a bowl. But, Rebecca, if you want to marry the man you love, you have to stand up for yourself and your baby. You have to do what your heart tells you. You may not be ready for marriage, as your parents must feel. Your young man may not be perfect, but if he is the father of your child, then the two of you need to make a home for your baby. If you give the baby away, then you will never know what becomes of it. Don't you want to be a part of the baby's life?"

Rebecca began to cry, putting her hands over her face. Katherine moved to the cot where Rebecca was sitting and she put her arm around her.

Rebecca took her hands away from her face and wiped her red-rimmed eyes. "I guess I'm afraid they will be right. I won't be a good mother and he won't marry me anyway."

"Does he know where you are going?" asked Katherine. "Did you tell him you are expecting his baby?"

"No, he doesn't know. I haven't seen him for three, maybe four months. He has been working out west and would be home any day, so they wanted to get rid of me before he came home."

Katherine thought a minute and looked around the room. She asked, "Rebecca, why don't we write and tell him where you are and about the baby. He can meet you in Nashville, and the two of you can decide what to do."

Rebecca agreed and wrote a letter to the father of her child. She and Katherine left it at the depot to be mailed.

"Katherine, I thank you so much for helping me. Writing this letter is the best thing I have done and whether he shows up or not, I have done my best."

Katherine said a prayer that the young man would do the honorable thing and show up at Nashville.

The rest of the trip was more enjoyable for Katherine and Rebecca as they watched the Kentucky landscape trail off into Tennessee. After their scheduled rests that day, the stagecoach finally arrived at the Nashville depot at 8:00 that evening. Katherine asked Rebecca if she would want to spend the night there since it would be too late to arrive at her aunt's house that evening. She agreed and Katherine and Rebecca shared a room again. Katherine used every opportunity to give Rebecca some confidence and encouragement.

"Rebecca, I suppose you are named after Rebecca in the Bible?"

"No, not really. I was named after my adopted great grandmother, Rebecca Boone."

"Really? You are Daniel Boone's granddaughter?"

"Yes, I am. But I prefer to say that I am Rebecca Boone's granddaughter. You see, Rebecca had ten children plus took care of other children and other families while being the homemaker, the trader for supplies, the hunter and fisher, she did everything while Daniel was out running around in the wilderness. Everyone knew about Daniel Boone, but everyone forgot about Rebecca. One time Daniel hadn't been home in months and it was a cold, snowy winter. Rebecca was in a tree trying to shoot a deer for food for their family. After she shot the deer she had to skin it and butcher it so her family would have some food. That's only one example of the many times she had to do everything while her man was off somewhere playing in the wilderness with the Indians. She kept a journal and wrote about her many adventures of taking care of a family while her husband was off on another adventure. I truly enjoyed reading the journal. It has inspired me."

"And you think you can't raise a baby? Adopted or not, you have it in your bones! You can do anything if you are a granddaughter of Rebecca Boone! You have no excuse. You have a great example to follow. Wow! Granddaughter of Rebecca Boone! I can't believe it," Katherine said as she teased Rebecca.

"Adopted, but thank you, Katherine. I guess you are right. I do need to keep that in mind. If my grandmother could do what she did, surely I can take care of one child." This time it was Rebecca who gave Katherine a hug. "Thank you so much, Katherine, you have been such an inspiration to me."

"If you are ever up toward Upton, please look us up. Katherine Cosby. Oh, well, I told you that I am getting married on December 20." Katherine had not wanted to talk about her engagement to a handsome doctor, considering Rebecca's unhappiness. However, she did want her to know a little more about him. "He is a wonderful gentleman, Dr. Keith Larimore and he and I are so much in love. We are going to spend the rest of our lives loving each other and being available to help others through our medical practice."

"That sounds wonderful!" Rebecca hugged Katherine and they said goodnight. The next day would be a busy time for both ladies.

Early morning Thomas and Katherine started their assignments. Thomas wanted to get their mission accomplished as soon as possible. The address of the monument company and the information of the cemetery was safe in Thomas' hand as he summoned a coach.

Waiting for the coach, Thomas talked with Katherine. "Mom, I don't know if I like the idea of you out on the city streets unaccompanied. I really wish you would stay at the hotel until I can get back to take you shopping."

"I will be fine, Son. You take care of your business and I will get everything finished so we won't be delayed."

The coach was picking up Thomas as he called out to her. "Just remember, we have to leave in the morning for the stage coach at seven."

Thomas was anxious to get home. First, the children would be having their Fall Harvest Program after school on Friday. Mary had assured him she would be there, in case he couldn't make it. However, he wanted to be there for his children. Also, Mary had been on his mind ever since he left. She had either not felt well, or something was going on with her. Surely she wasn't still upset over Katherine's suspicion. Both of them had told her they didn't believe she was responsible for Rissa's death and she had forgiven them for their suspicions. Could it be with this being her first pregnancy, she was not adjusting well to the pregnancy. Thomas admitted to himself that he felt a strange urgency.

Katherine had a list of things she wanted to do. First she wanted to visit Leah's mother and make plans. Gripping the envelope with the address, Katherine took a buggy to Ms. Pearl's place. Knocking on the door, a bit of fear gripped her. She knocked again and she heard someone come to the door. "Yes, ma'am."

"Ms. Pearl, I am Katherine Cosby, a friend of your daughter," Katherine said as she extended her hand.

Ms. Pearl shook hands with her and invited her to come in. The two ladies chatted about the weather and the city. Katherine asked if she still planned on going with her back to Kentucky. Ms. Pearl motioned to her bags packed just inside the bedroom door. She said she would be ready whenever they were ready to leave. She had made arrangements with her son to take over her café.

"We will need to pick you up at six in the morning, to make sure that we have plenty of time to catch the stage coach."

"Oh, I assure, you, Ms. Katherine, I will be ready. I can't wait to see Leah and Hobie. I just can't thank you enough for helping me get to my children."

Katherine took the buggy to a few shopping places and bought Christmas gifts for the family. A bookstore on the corner of Main Street caught her attention. The bookstore was the largest she had ever visited and she quickly became absorbed in the merchandise. Finally, she decided on a book for Tommie, *Guy Mannering and The Astrologer*, a novel by Sir Walter Scott. She purchased *Sense and Sensibility* by Jane Austen for Nellie. Katherine shopped for a gift for Dr. Larimore and found something she felt was very special.

Ms. Pearl was true to her word, she was ready and waiting when the buggy came to pick her up at six o'clock the next morning. Katherine thought as Ms. Pearl was thanking them again, she would really like to be her friend. Ms. Pearl had that mellow, southern drawl with nuances of musical notes. What a lovely lady, Katherine thought.

# Chapter 45

# The Note

The ride back home had been exhausting, but Ms. Pearl kept Thomas and Katherine charmed with her stories about her children, the café, and much more about her colorful life. The trip being one of the few times that Katherine didn't do most of the talking. She and Thomas thoroughly enjoyed Ms. Pearl's anecdotes and tales of life as owner of a cafe.

Thomas felt badly. they had missed the children's program at school, but it couldn't be helped. With the delay on one of the lay-overs, the travelers had no control on the time spent away.

Glad to get back to Roundstone, the three stopped at Ollie's. Leah and Ms. Pearl rejoiced at seeing each other. What a glorious, emotional reunion! The group held hands and prayed a prayer of thanksgiving before Katherine and Thomas left.

It was late when mother and son carried their bags into the house. Both agreed they were happy to be home and too tired for bed, so they sat at the table awhile to relax. As they enjoyed a cup of the morning's, cold coffee and a piece of leftover cornbread, Katherine noticed an envelope on the table addressed to both of them.

"Thomas, look! What in the world?" Katherine started tearing apart the envelope when Dr. Larimore stumbled into the kitchen, scratching his head and wiping his eyes.

"Hey, you two, how was the trip?" Dr. Larimore asked, unaware of the note on the table.

Katherine was opening the envelope and taking more interest in the envelope than Keith, as both Katherine and Thomas were beginning to worry about this envelope. Why was Dr. Larimore here?

"What are you doing here?" Thomas asked.

Dr. Larimore scratched his head again and said, "I'm not really sure, but Mary asked me to come spend the evening and the night with the children. Said you would be here tonight or in the morning. I agreed and that is all I know."

Katherine read the letter aloud.

Dear Katherine and Thomas,

I am sorry to have to leave but I have thought it over and I cannot have any suspicion between us. I realize there are too many unanswered questions. I do not want to live in a household which has the least bit of suspicion of me. I can say over and over I did not have anything to do with Rissa's death, but you will never trust me fully.

I am truly sorry this has happened. I have no intention of returning, so don't try to find me. We will be fine. Tell the children I love them.

Love,
Mary

Thomas jumped up, ready to go look for Mary. Dr. Larimore and Katherine grabbed an arm. "Thomas, you have no idea where to go to look," Dr. Larimore said.

"And it is late. You couldn't find her tonight. Also, her note said that she did not want to be found," Katherine added.

Thomas stayed up all night, torn between guilt and grief, so worried he couldn't pray. Katherine was by his side all night saying prayers for her family and asking forgiveness for Mary's hurt.

The next morning, Thomas left instructions for the work with Katherine. He had to leave, to do something toward looking for Mary. First, he would tell Paul what was going on and ask him if he knew where Mary had gone yesterday.

Paul was already milling when Thomas walked down to the mill. He finished the load of corn and gave his boss his attention. Thomas told the story of what had happened to Mary. With shame and guilt, he told Paul about the necklace, how Katherine suspected her of murdering Rissa.

Thomas was so distraught he left the mill, walked through the woods and threw himself on the ground. He couldn't stop crying, so he prayed for wisdom; he asked the Lord to help him get his wife back. He lay on the cold, wet ground and cried and prayed until he thought he could shed no more tears.

Finally, Thomas pulled himself together and went back to the mill. There were no customers, so Thomas and Paul were alone. "Paul, will you pray with me? I don't know why but the Lord wanted me to come to you and pray before I left to look for Mary. Would you pray with me?"

Paul nodded and bowed his head. Thomas put his hand on Paul's shoulder and prayed with all his wisdom and all his strength and was filled with the Holy Spirit. Thomas felt like his cup was running over; he had an unspeakable joy and peace. As he finished his prayer, God led him to tell Paul that he was forgiven.

Paul broke down and between his sobs he explained his part in the mystery of Rissa's death.

"Rissa was the only woman who ever treated me nice, ever treated me like a man. She would bring me milk and cookies and she took time to make me feel special." Paul was having a difficult time telling Thomas, but he continued.

"I am sorry, so sorry, but I fell in love with her. She was the most beautiful woman I ever saw. I know she didn't mean it, but she was so nice to me, I took it that she liked me, I know she liked me. She liked being around me and talking to me. Nobody else has ever done that. Rissa was not only beautiful but she was a nice person." Paul stopped a minute, choking up before he could finish.

"The day we were cutting wood, I saw my opportunity." Paul pulled a knife from his pocket. "I always carry this here knife, so I knew I could cut the rope which would cause the tree to fall on you and I would have my Rissa. I have cut a lot of trees and I know how to make them fall, but the tree did not fall the way I figured it would. Instead, the tree killed the only thing I ever loved, my Rissa."

# Chapter 46

# A Revelation

A chilling wind was blowing when Thomas prepared to get the sheriff. Going back to the house, Thomas dug through his cedar chest for his warm winter coat.

"Mom, I have to go to town. Don't know when I will be back. Explain later." Thomas made a quick exit of the house before Katherine could stop him.

Paul had promised he would stay there and turn himself in. He just wanted some time to be alone. Thomas hated to turn Paul in to the authorities because Paul had always been special. Paul was a good worker and never complained about his work, which made him a treasure to Thomas. Nevertheless, Paul had committed a crime and he would have to let the sheriff know what had happened.

When Thomas and the sheriff arrived at the mill, Paul was gone.

"Well, Thomas, I am not surprised that he is gone. Most criminals when caught will run instead of waiting to be taken to jail."

"But Paul is not really a criminal. I thought Paul would stay here and wait for us. Think I will see if he took the cash in the money drawer." Thomas went inside and opened the cash drawer. There was no money, only a note, obviously from Paul.

> Thomas, I saw you with Mary.
> Paul

Thomas looked at the note and quickly put it in his pocket. He suffered a pain he had never known, a pain from guilt combined with grief. Even though he loved Mary, there had been a small amount of suspicion; the suspicion had caused Mary to leave his family. Suddenly, he realized what a tragic mistake he had made. Thomas wanted to look for Mary and bring her home, even though Mary had told him he could not find her and not look for her.

Thomas prayed for the Lord to help him with his grief and guilt. He also prayed for wisdom to know how to find Mary. Early the next morning, when sleep had finally come, the Lord spoke to Thomas. "Thomas, have faith and patience. You will find Mary when it is time."

Certainly, Thomas had no idea what the message meant. Yet, he was given a calmness and patience that Mary would be fine. Meanwhile, Thomas would attend to his work, building the house for Mary and his new baby.

---

Ollie and Hobie began work on building the kitchen, more determined than ever to do a good job for Thomas.

The two men had discussed and planned the raising of the walls. Both men agreed they could get the walls up by themselves since the building was much smaller than other walls they had put up. The two men had already put up two of the sides and they started up with the third side, the south side, when Ollie's foot slipped and he lost his balance. Hobie could not control his side as it slipped and Ollie lost control of the wall. Before they knew it, the wall was crushing down on them. The crash brought Thomas and the others running. They found Ollie and Hobie under the heavy structure. The men raised the wall while Ollie and Hobie crawled out. They assured Thomas and Pete that they were okay. They would call when they needed help. Meanwhile the structure was repaired to raise for the second time.

Both men had cuts, scrapes and bruises. The odd part was that both men had cuts on their arms in the same area. Hobie looked at Ollie's cut, and shook his head, "This is a sign, brother. This is a sign this house will see the black man's blood and the White man's blood spilled together," Hobie said rather thoughtfully.

"Hobie, don't mean to be onery, but jest why do you think that there's a sign?" Ollie asked.

"All the older folk taught us to look for signs, blood spilled while working together. This blood means that more blood will be shed."

"Now, good brother, I shore do hope you're wrong about that, cuz it kinda spooks me."

Hobie looked deep in thought as he was trying to remember the spoken words of his elder. "I remember hearing the elders say that 'Two working on a beam, blood colors to redeem, blood spilled leaving a mark, and future will be dark'."

"Ollie what was our devotion this morning? Wasn't it from Hosea?" Hobie asked.

"Yes, it was about the North and the South kingdoms being divided. Do you think that was a sign?" Ollie asked, truly concerned with Hobie's revelation.

"Oh, I am not sure. Let's get back to work. Pete, we have this side repaired and are ready to lift it, want to help?"

The men put the last two sides up and took a few minutes to rest with a dipper of cold water. Pete told Hobie he had heard him talking about a sign. "I haven't told anyone but before me and Andrea left Haywill, I had a vision. It was of a large white house and there were many people and a lot of pain and suffering. Do you know what my vision might mean?"

Hobie shook his head, "No, sir, I don't know. Do you think it could be this house?"

"Oh, I don't know. I haven't mentioned it to anyone else because I thought they would think I'm crazy," Pete said as he jumped up to get back to work.

After work on the house was completed for the day, Thomas and Katherine took the children on a walk to the creek. The day was unseasonably warm and the creek was beautiful. As the family sat on the stones around the creek, Thomas and Katherine tried to explain why Mary had left. They asked the children to forgive them for even suspecting Mary could do such a thing.

"We are so sorry. Mary has left and it is all our fault," Thomas said as he threw a pebble in the creek.

"No, Dad. That is not the only reason she left." Nellie took a deep breath for she knew she would be in trouble, but she had to tell the truth now.

"Nellie, I don't think you understand how she was hurt, and don't think that you did anything. This was our fault, actually my fault," Katherine said as she hugged Nellie.

Nellie stood up to give her some courage. "No see, last Thursday Mike came over after school. He wanted to tell me about his time with his dad. He promised the Lord that if he got out of the situation with his dad that he would give his life as a disciple. He was crying because he said he loves me but he had to follow God's will for his life."

"But Nellie, I don't think…" Katherine tried to help her granddaughter as she was obviously hurting.

"Just let me finish, Gran! See Mike held me and we kissed. Yes, Gran, we kissed. And about that time Mary came around the corner of the barn and saw us. Of course she reminded me that I had promised not to give my kisses away. Well, that was all it took. I told her that I knew that Gran had suspected that she killed my mother and…"

"Nellie, how did you know that?" Thomas asked in disbelief.

"One thing at a time, let's just say I overheard a conversation. Can I wait some other time to tell you about it?" Nellie asked sheepishly. "So, you see, it was me, it was my fault she left. That happened on Thursday and she left Friday night."

Stunned from the admission from Nellie, the family returned home, finished the chores and Thomas read from Genesis 29, the love story of Jacob and Rachael. He talked about how a man will do just about anything for the woman he loves. Thomas explained how much he loved the children's mother, Rissa, but his love for Mary was real and he wanted his family back together again.

The children went to bed and Katherine and Thomas stayed up to talk awhile. Katherine wanted to talk to Thomas, apologize again. "Thomas, I really don't see how you keep from hating me. All of this was my fault. My dreams have just bothered me for so long I thought when I saw the blade, there was a good chance Mary had murdered Rissa. I am so sorry. Will you forgive me, Thomas?"

Thomas got up and walked over to the bucket and used the dipper to get a drink of spring water. He rubbed his head, stretched his back, and sat down beside his mother. "Mom, there is something I haven't told you. You see, I had my suspicions also." Thomas stopped; obviously it was hard for him to reveal his reason for suspicions. He tapped on the table with his fingers. "Mom, there is something Mary and I both feel guilty about but we would never have told anyone. The only reason I am telling you now is because I don't blame you for feeling the way you do." Thomas stopped again, walked across the floor before having a seat again.

"Before Rissa died, you know, after Johnny died, Mary became friendly. You remember Rissa teasing me about Mary?" Thomas had to stop because he was becoming so nervous.

Clearing his throat, Thomas continued. "Do you remember the day you took Rissa and the kids to Elizabethtown for a visit with family? Well, I remember telling Rissa just a day or two before that, I would not go. Mary heard me and she knew I would be at home working." Thomas stopped talking, walked across the floor again, trying to bring himself to finish.

"Rissa had been gone only a little while before Mary came in her buggy. I saw her at the house and, thinking there might be something wrong, I went to the house. When I got here, at the house, Mary was putting food on the table. She said she had come to cheer me up. I told her I didn't need to be cheered and I needed to go back to work. Mary made me sit down and she started to massage my back and before long she had my shirt off. She took my shoes off and massaged my feet, all the time telling me how she knew how depressed I had been over Johnny's death. She repeated that she just wanted to cheer me up, make me feel better."

Thomas stopped again, went to the water bucket and dipped another drink of water. He continued, "The thing is I guess I was depressed, or at least I felt all alone. After Johnny's death, Rissa and I grew apart, we stopped being together. I missed her so bad, but she just couldn't get over Johnny's death. Her grief overpowered our love."

Katherine reached out to Thomas and patted his hand. "I can understand how Rissa would withdraw, but you knew you had to help her, to help her work through the death of your son."

Thomas continued, "I know you are right. I should have worked harder to help Rissa. Instead, I threw myself in my work and kept too busy to think about Johnny."

"So, what happened that day with Mary?"

"Well, Mary told me she knew I was feeling too anxious and depressed. She said she wanted to cheer me up and she knew how. Before I knew it, well, I tried to say no, I really did. Finally, she told me she loved me and she wanted to make me happy just for one day. Just for one time, we could be together. I was so weak, and I should have walked away, but I couldn't."

Katherine dropped her head, fought back the tears. "So, was that all of it, just that one day? Tell me Thomas, it didn't happen again, did it?"

"No, it was the only time," Thomas answered.

285

"Thomas, I am your mother, and I can still tell when you lie. It didn't stop there did it?" Katherine asked, but really hoped she was wrong.

Thomas got up again, walked around a minute and sat back down. "I couldn't stop with Mary. It's no excuse, I know, but Rissa and I were not together, or I would have never done it. It continued with Mary until about a month before Rissa was killed, she got better. We renewed our love and we were so happy again.

"I couldn't go on seeing Mary, so I told her that Rissa was better and I had to end our adulterous affair."

Katherine sat up straight, stretched her arms on the table and looked at Thomas. "She didn't take the rejection well, did she? So that is why you think she may have killed Rissa."

"As a matter of fact, Mary was upset, said I had taken advantage of her for the second time. And that I should have never married Rissa in the first place."

Katherine couldn't control her shock but did not understand. "The second time? She had no right to say you shouldn't marry Rissa. Was she crazy?"

""No, Mom. Remember the day before I left for my trip to Boston? Mary was my first."

Katherine pretended to cover her ears. "I don't think I want to hear this. Oh, well, come clean while you are at it."

"She said she would get me one way or another." Thomas put his head on the table unable to look at Katherine any longer. "I have prayed and asked forgiveness so many times. I know God has forgiven me but I will never forget my sins."

"Oh, Thomas," Katherine said, clearly upset with her son. "Now, I know why you read the wedding vows from Hosea. It took me awhile to realize where it came from and then I feared why. I can't judge you, Thomas. Only you have to answer to the Lord. I have always thought that adultery was a terrible sin. Thomas, sin carries penalties. I am going to forget you ever told me this. I want it to never be mentioned again."

Katherine got up. "One more question, did Rissa know?"

"No, I don't think so, but I knew."

Nellie couldn't sleep. She knew all too well that Mary's leaving was her fault and now that they knew the real killer, it was up to her to get Mary back home. Making plans she fell asleep, and finally let go of the guilt of the ordeal.

Quietly Nellie left the house before daylight. She would get Ol' Dan hooked to the buggy and first pick up Mike and the two of them would go after Mary. She was fairly sure she knew where Mary was hiding out.

Nellie woke Mike and Della as the sun was just beginning to come up. Quickly, she explained the situation and told Mike that he just had to go with her. Mike wanted to keep most of the information from his grandmother, so he moved quickly, putting on his boots and jacket.

"What if she is not there, Nellie? Come all this way, and you know your dad is going to be upset with you. I can't believe you told him. Ugggh, bet he is mad at me."

"Oh, quit your whining. I told him what it was, a kiss, that's all. Now, which way is the Fletcher cabin? Do I turn right or left?"

The kids arrived at the Fletcher cabin as an old man headed to the barn to milk. He stopped, waved and motioned for them to go inside. Obviously, he knew why they were there.

"Nellie, Mike!" Mary was obviously surprised to see the young people. "What are you doing here, and how did you know to come here?"

Nellie and Mike took the first seat they could find and Nellie started rambling as fast as she could. Her goal was to get back before her father became really upset and sent for the sheriff. "Mary, first of all, we know who the real killer is. We will explain that later on our way home. Please get your things as soon as you can so I can get you back home where you belong. I am so sorry that I have been mean to you. Please forgive me."

"Uh, I…uh, well yes, I forgive you, but how did you know to come here? I thought no one would ever find me here." Mary looked at her Aunt Tula who was pouring coffee for everyone.

Nellie giggled. "I guess this is your Aunt Tula, right? You probably don't remember but you talked so fondly about your aunt and uncle one time at school and I never forgot their names because they were so unusual. Tula sounded so much like tulips that I drew a field of tulips around their cabin, just as you described and put a mailbox out front with 'Fletcher' on it. So, you see, I really was listening!"

On the way home Nellie explained how her father had learned about Rissa's killer. Mary seemed stunned from all the news, but grateful for the graciousness of Nellie and Mike.

Renie was the first to hear the buggy roll down the hill. Everyone ran outside, and before the wagon could be stopped, Katherine, Thomas, and the children ran around the wagon, calling out to Mary. Katherine was the one to help Mary down from the buggy and she gave her a hug and a sincere apology. Thomas hugged Mary and welcomed her back home. When Renie had her turn to hug Mary, she told everyone they had to be especially good to Mary because she was going to have two babies in a few months.

Thomas shook his head and told the family, "Guess we are going to have to start listening to her more. Renie knew we would have Mary back, she never doubted it."

Katherine insisted the family sit at the table and enjoy breakfast together. Mary was anxious to talk with her family and give an explanation for the last few days. "I would like to explain a few things to my family. First, I didn't feel the apologies were sincere and now that the real killer is found, it is not an issue."

Mary continued. "When I left here, I was feeling sorry for myself. I went to my aunt and uncle's home and realized that others have needs which are real. I was so blessed while I was there. I cooked and cleaned and helped them. In fact I gave them my horse and buggy. They couldn't go anywhere, so now they can. It felt good to help Aunt Tula and Uncle Minor."

Sipping the hot coffee, Mary sat her china cup back in the saucer. Taking a deep breath, as if to summon the strength and gumption to complete the challenge, Mary continued. "The beautiful gift that came about because of all of this hurt and pain from humiliation is that I now know Jesus Christ, my Lord and Savior."

"What do you mean, didn't you know Him before?" Katherine couldn't help but interrupt and ask.

"No, Katherine, I knew of Him, but I didn't know Him. There is a big difference. First, let me explain. My father, excuse me, I know we are not supposed to speak ill of the dead, but forgive me when I tell you that my father was not a Christian. He would not let the name of Jesus be discussed around him. He believed in the Bible, the Old Testament only."

"Then who did he think Jesus was?" Katherine could not hold back her curiosity.

"Well, I think he considered him a prophet. My father thought that his faith was the only way to believe. He believed that anyone who did not go to his church was going to hell. Anyway, once I was finally able to pray to Jesus for redemption of my sins, Jesus heard and he came into my heart. The

experience is something I will rejoice and share with others as long as I live."
Mary stopped to take another sip of her coffee.

"We are so proud of you, Mary. If I had only known, I would have
helped in some way. I just figured you were a Christian when you came here."
Thomas picked up Mary's hand and held it between his.

"Only because I wanted everyone to think that I was a Christian. You
know, I feel kind of like the invalid beside the pool. You know...the one in
Jesus' miracles. Well, he had been sitting by that pool for thirty-eight years,
which happens to be my age. All that time, he sat beside the healing pool,
when he could have been healed long ago, if he had been ready. You see, I feel
like that was me, just sitting around not ready to be a Christian, just watching
life go by. Now, I know Him. I really know Him."

Katherine moved from where she was sitting and gave Mary a big hug.
"I am so happy for you, child! You have a wonderful testimony and your face
shows that you know Him."

"But that is not all. I feel that God has laid something on my heart
that I want you, my family, to know. When I was eighteen I was living in
Bardstown with my aunt. One evening on my way home from school, I was
beaten and raped. I dropped out of school, went home because I was so upset
and humiliated. Unfortunately, my father would have nothing to do with me.
He sent me away and told me that I had to get rid of the baby." Mary's voice
quavered as tears glistened in her eyes.

Stunned, the family waited, not knowing what to say. Finally, Mary
began again.

"I did not know the man who raped me, but that didn't keep me from
wanting to keep my baby. However, my parents told me that they would never
let me come back home if I didn't get rid of the baby. I was barely nineteen
when she was born and I didn't know what to do. The world is not kind to a
mama with a baby and no father. Finally, in desperation, for food for both of
us, I left her at an orphanage. The only thing I left with her was the clothing
and blankets she had and a small locket."

Mary took a deep breath and sighed. "Guess you weren't expecting this
kind of mess. The thing is, I want you to know what has happened. I'm
sorry, Thomas. I feel like the Lord saved me for a purpose. I want to find my
daughter, if possible."

"I understand, and I will help you all I can." Thomas kissed Mary's head
as the family tried to put everything in perspective.

"Mary, you said you gave your daughter a locket? Did it have something on it?" Katherine asked, disbelieving that it could possibly be Rebecca's.

"Oh, yes, I remember. I spent my last five dollars on a gold locket with an 'E' on it, because her name was Emily."

Katherine tried to maintain a neutral expression. "Mary, I know that I have caused you so much pain. If I find your daughter for you, do you think you could forgive and forget the hurt I have put you through?"

Mary shrank back from the table, unable to speak as she gave a nod to Katherine.

# Chapter 47

# A Baby

Mary wanted to know everything about Rebecca, her eye color, hair color, any birthmarks, and any distinguishing characteristics that she could form a picture of her daughter.

"Mary, just don't get your hopes up. You know, I could be wrong."

"But, Katherine, how could you be wrong? The age is right, and her hair color, eyes and physical characteristics are so much like mine, how could it not be my Emily?"

"I'll admit it seems like there could be no mistake. After all, she has the locket. How many eighteen-year old girls would have the locket, especially with the 'E' on it? I just don't want you to be disappointed if this girl is not Emily." Katherine squeezed Mary's hand and thanked God for answered prayers.

The two women talked all day about the chance encounter that Katherine had with Rebecca and how it had obviously been God's will that the two had met. Even though Katherine regretted having to tell Mary that Rebecca was pregnant and her parents were sending her away, Mary was glad she knew.

"I just can't wait to see her, to meet her and help her, if I can. Are you sure you don't remember where she was going to her aunt's house?"

"No, Dear, the only thing she said was that she lived somewhere in Nashville. For right now, let's just pray that we hear something from her. I did invite her to the wedding. Who knows, maybe we will hear something.

You know, I felt like I really bonded with her." Katherine said as she finished the last stitch on the baby quilt.

———— • ————

The children came home from school, chilled from the freezing rain. Thomas advised the children they would need to get their chores finished as soon as possible because he feared the weather would just get worse. Wood was stacked on the porch to keep it dry in expectance of a winter storm.

Everyone had come in for the night and was glad to be in the warm house. Just as they were to sit down for the evening meal, they heard a wagon coming down the road. Soon someone was jumping onto the porch. Thomas was at the door before the guest had a chance to knock.

"Come in! Terrible night!" Thomas was going to continue but Bill interrupted.

"I know it is bad outside, and going to be worse, but Betty is starting to have her baby," Bill Moore said. "She asked for Katherine to come right away."

"What about I go to Upton and get the Doc? I can be over there in… an hour or a little more." Thomas feared for Katherine to be out in the weather.

Mr. Moore looked at Thomas and then at Katherine. "Betty said that no man has ever delivered any of her six babies and he wouldn't now. She wanted Katherine to deliver this one just as she had before."

Katherine went to her room and gathered her things together. Renie followed her grandmother and took her hand. Katherine looked at the child's face, ashen and painful. "Renie, let me take care of it this time. I know you want to be there, but it is too bad for you to be out. Please stay here with Mary and help her."

Katherine ran back to the kitchen with her things and Nellie was right behind her pulling on her warmest clothing and packing a few of her things, in case she had to stay a couple days.

Thomas did not want Nellie to go, but he was afraid to tell her she couldn't for he knew she would be a big help for Katherine, and with the weather getting bad, they might need all the help they could get. "Mom, I will go with you and Nellie," Thomas said.

"No, you won't. Your place is here with Mary and the children. Give Renie extra attention tonight. I will take care of Nellie, if you don't mind for her going with me," Katherine said rather worriedly as she filled a pillowcase with items she would need, plus the new baby quilt she and Mary had just finished.

Bill Moore, Nellie and Katherine were soon in the covered wagon. The trip would be less than thirty minutes on a normal day, but with the rain, and the road conditions, it would probably take almost an hour. When the group finally reached the Moore home, the three were freezing. Clothes and hats were soaked. It would take a few minutes before Katherine could even get warm enough to do the examination. She and Nellie washed their hands in lukewarm water while they were waiting.

Katherine talked with Betty, asking her about the frequency of her contractions. Judging from Betty's face, she didn't seem totally conscious, hopefully she was not close to delivery. Finally, Katherine had warmed her hands enough she could begin her examination. Nellie was beside her, asking questions and trying to learn all she could. As Katherine finished the exam, she explained it could be a couple hours, not really sure because Betty was not the typical laboring mother.

The children were in the loft playing and were out of the way. Yet Katherine was concerned the children may have not had anything to eat. She explained to Nellie if the children could eat and perhaps get full they might go to sleep early; so they would not be in the way during the delivery. Katherine asked Nellie to get the pork out of the bag and fix the children something to eat. Quickly, Nellie had food on the table and called for the children to come down.

The children were like stair steps, four boys and two girls, and Katherine had delivered all of them. Katherine had to hug each one of the children, pulling them close to her and kissing them on their heads. She reminded the children to wash their hands, to eat and then go to the outhouse before they went back upstairs. Love the little darlings as she did, she still wanted to get them upstairs out of her way as soon as possible.

Katherine had not been able to get this family to come to church, so she rarely got to see them. Nellie had kept her informed about the three children at school. They missed a lot of school and when they were there they didn't have clean clothes and she suspected they didn't have food in their lunch bucket. Nellie had often shared her lunch with the oldest girl.

"You know, Nellie. I wish someday the school would teach girls and boys how to raise a family, how to take care of their children. I know Betty and Bill do their best, but they just don't know how." Katherine quoted the verse from I Thessalonians 5:14-15, "Now we exhort you, brethren, warn those who are unruly, comfort the fainthearted, uphold the weak, be patient with all. See that no one renders evil for evil to anyone, but always pursue what is good both for yourselves and for all.' Christian families and church families tend to comfort each other, to help each other not only to build faith, but to help in practical ways when needed." Katherine sighed and shook her head, just so much mission work to do at home.

Katherine examined Betty. "Betty, you are too thin. You haven't been eating much have you?"

Betty sighed and seemed too tired to talk. "Too many little mouths to feed, they need it more than I do."

"But you need strength for you and this baby," Katherine said as she looked at Nellie worriedly. "When was your last contraction? Do you remember?"

"No, I don't remember. I'm just so tired. I don't think I can do this. I don't have the strength," Betty mumbled.

"Well, we are here to help you. Nellie has fed the children and sent them to the loft to bed, so we will concentrate on you." Katherine tried to sound cheerful.

Katherine was more than a bit concerned there could be a problem. Despite Betty's wishes a man doctor not be around, she would feel much better with the Doc there. As Bill was bringing in an armload of wood, Katherine cornered him and told him she would feel better if he would go get the doctor. She tried to not alarm him, but he did need to know the urgency of the trip. Bill agreed and got the mule out of the barn and hooked him up again for his trip to Upton.

Nellie had three pots full of water heating on the small stove. Picking up the poker she poked at the coals. As she threw another stick of wood on the fire, she glanced at Katherine's face, full of concern.

The women did what they could to get Betty comfortable, putting a quilt behind her head and back to help her sit up a little. The mattress was very sparse, made of a corn shucks, but they had been flattened and of little use to soften the bed.

At Betty's last delivery, Katherine had explained to Betty and Bill that Betty needed to make the baby her last, or at least wait three or four years before trying to have another one. They had agreed they would not have a baby for a while due to Betty's health. She had been barely fourteen when she had her first baby and had not given her body time to recover before she had the next baby. Betty had never been very big, but she clearly had lost more weight from the last time Katherine had seen her. Instead of gaining weight with this baby, Betty had lost weight which was not good. Katherine was worried.

Betty seemed to be going in and out of consciousness. Katherine tried to time her contractions, but they were not coming regularly. What seemed like hours to Katherine was actually less than an hour for Bill to return with the doctor. Katherine hugged Keith as he came in and then she pulled him aside. She told him her fears and Bill saw the worried look on both of their faces.

"She is going to be alright, ain't she? We need her. Please, help her, I don't know what we would do without her," Bill pleaded as tears rolled down his face.

Katherine put her arm around Bill and tried to calm him, but she knew it didn't look good. Keith began talking to Betty, very calmly assuring her he was to help deliver her baby and Katherine was with him also. Betty was unresponsive, and Dr. Larimore became more worried. Quickly he started his examination, grabbed Betty's wrist to get a pulse, and then opened her eyelids. Katherine joined him. "What do you think? Is there anything we can do?"

"She is fading away, Katherine. Why don't you see if you can talk to her, maybe say a prayer for her?" Doc said.

Remembering Renie's warning, Katherine knelt at the bed and held Betty's hand. "Betty, I don't know if you can hear me, but I want to say a prayer for you, okay? Our Heavenly Father, we pray for Betty and her baby. Give us your comfort and help Betty as she goes through this trial. Father I pray you will fill her with your love and your spirit at this time of need. In Jesus name, I pray, Amen."

Katherine held Betty's hand and stroked her hair and forehead when she became acutely aware of the presence of angels in the room. She couldn't see or hear them, but she felt their presence. Dr. Larimore was monitoring Betty and watching Katherine at the same time. Having been around death many times, he had also felt the presence of angels.

"Katherine, we can save the baby if we act quickly. Get Bill to go outside for a while. He doesn't need to be around right now."

Katherine went to the fireplace where Bill was poking at the fire. "Bill, we would like for you to step outside for a minute, if you don't mind. We will let you know something in just a few minutes."

Bill reluctantly followed orders, without asking about Betty. Katherine thought he probably knew Betty was slipping away, but he didn't want to say it aloud.

Doctor Larimore had already rolled his sleeves up and had his scalpel ready. Katherine knew but asked anyway, "She is gone, isn't she?"

"Yes, and if we don't hurry the baby will also die. Just help me as I get started here, we need to get the baby out as quickly as possible." Dr. Larimore's voice was shaky.

A few seconds later, Dr. Larimore was pulling the baby out. She was a small baby, and it was hard for the Doc to keep the slippery little girl in his large hands. Katherine was standing by with cloth to clean the baby as soon as he had her. Baby Girl Moore let out a scream to Katherine's relief. Bill heard the cry and came running back in the house.

"Is Betty okay...please tell me she made it," Bill said. He looked at the blood-soaked sheet which covered Betty's body, completely over her head. He knew his wife was gone.

Katherine talked to Bill as Nellie cleaned the baby. As she tried to comfort Bill, Katherine felt awkward as she witnessed the grief of the man, now a widower with seven children. She didn't know what to do next, so she offered to let him hold his baby. He looked up at Katherine with the saddest eyes she had ever seen, and said he couldn't.

Bill sat in a straight-back chair and began to sob. Katherine sat with him and told him they had done everything they could, but Betty just wasn't strong enough. She told him she knew someone who could nurse the baby and they could take the baby to her, if that was okay. Bill agreed.

"Bill, how about I take the children to my house for the night? You can come with us. We will come back in the morning and help take care of Betty's body, but the children do not need to stay here tonight. They can spend the night at our house," Katherine said.

Bill shook his head in agreement. "I, I gotta stay here with Betty. But I sure do thank you for taking the kids for the night. They don't need to stay here tonight."

Nellie told the children to bring their warmest clothes; they were going to spend the night at Katherine's house. The children thought it would be fun to spend the night at Katherine's, so they readily put on their extra layer of clothing. Doctor Larimore had driven his buggy, and they all piled in the buggy together.

Katherine explained to Dr. Larimore they should stop at Lyssa's house. Hopefully, Lyssa would be able to nurse the baby at least for a day or two until other arrangements could be made. They would take the children to Thomas' house where they could provide for the children a night or two. Bill would need time without worrying about the children, just time to grieve. Dr. Larimore agreed.

It was late when they arrived at Lyssa and Ollie's house. Katherine knocked at the door and announced herself through the door. When Ollie opened the door he was quite surprised to see Katherine holding a baby. Katherine explained what had happened and how the baby now needed milk; could Lyssa feed her?

"Of course, I will take care of the baby." Lyssa immediately reached for the baby and lovingly cradled her. "I will let her nurse now and later I will get something warm and cuddly on her. Does she have a name yet?" Lyssa asked.

"No, Bill is too distraught right now to name her and we are taking the other six children to our house for the next couple days. They certainly don't need to be at the cabin. We will go back tomorrow morning to help Bill take care of the body," Katherine said.

# Chapter 48

# The Children

It was about midnight when Dr. Larimore drove the group to the Cosby home with the children fast asleep. Katherine, Nellie and Dr. Larimore carried the smaller children into the warm house. The other three were able to walk, although they seemed scared and unsure of where they were going. Katherine and Nellie kept assuring the children they would be warm and comfortable inside the house.

Mary and Thomas were already saying a prayer for the Moore family when the buggy rolled in. They sensed what had happened because of Renie's demeanor. Thomas went outside to take care of the horses while Mary helped get the children warm by the fire. Katherine and Nellie started making quilt beds on the floor for the children.

Mary asked the children if they would like a piece of cake with a cold glass of milk. Little eyes looked at the pieces of cake like it was a Christmas! Disregarding the spoons, the children dug into the cake with their fingers. Cake littered the table and the floor as well as the children. Mary began cleaning little faces, hands and hair as she got the children ready for bed.

The children were so tired they were asleep almost as soon as they lay down. The adults looked at the children and mentioned how cute they were, just little angels. Katherine explained how Lyssa had the baby, which was a real blessing. Lyssa, always a help to others, didn't have to think twice. She took the baby girl and immediately started to care for her.

Dr. Larimore started to leave when Thomas encouraged him to stay the night. "We don't have a lot of accommodations, but if we are going early in the morning to Bill's house to get the body and take care of the burial and funeral arrangements, you don't need to have to go all the way back home," Thomas said. "I have already taken care of the horse, giving her some oats, water and bedding for the night."

Katherine and Mary agreed. What a truly sad time, one that they felt the need to be together to support to each other. Dr. Larimore agreed he would sit in one of the chairs and sleep. Katherine insisted he take her bed and she and the girls would sleep together. With everyone tired and worn out, no one argued.

On Saturday morning, Thomas arose early to get the chores started. He woke Tommie, and they were able to get out without waking the children, although Tommie had plenty of questions. Katherine hadn't been able to sleep, so she got up and started breakfast. The children started waking, and they wanted to know when they were going back home to their mommy and daddy. Katherine told them they would probably go home later, first they had some things to do, like have breakfast. She had made a big meal, and the children were surprised to get to eat all they wanted.

After the family had breakfast, Thomas gave the devotion by telling a Bible story. He told the story of Little David and the Giant. The children listened and asked questions. Thomas explained sometimes we have something happen that is so big, we think we can't go on. We get sad and cry and want to give up. But, like David, with the Lord's help, we can make it.

Nellie, Renie and Mary knew they had a big job to keep the children happy, for a few hours. As soon as Tommie was finished with his chores, he came back to help with the children. Renie brought two kittens inside for the little ones to play with. Nellie and Mary held children and rocked.

Later that morning, Katherine, Dr. Larimore and Thomas headed toward Bill Moore's place. Thomas took his wagon and Katherine rode with Dr. Larimore in his buggy. Thomas realized his wagon had been used far too much lately to carry a coffin.

Thomas had left a few minutes before Katherine and Dr. Larimore, so he arrived at Bill's place a little earlier. He went to the house, knocked, entered but Bill was nowhere. Calling for Bill, Thomas walked around the house, thinking maybe Bill had gone to get some wood as there was no fire. Thomas walked to the side of the house, and looked toward the woods, when he saw Bill. He was hanging from a tree. Bill Moore had hanged himself.

Thomas met Katherine and Dr. Larimore as they drove up in their buggy. Katherine shuddered and wept as Thomas explained Bill's whereabouts. Katherine blamed herself as she said she should have stayed with him because she knew he was depressed.

"Katherine, you were needed with the baby and the children. Even you can't be everywhere and God understands." Dr. Larimore took Katherine's hands and held them together, kissing her hair.

The weather had cleared, and they were able to take the bodies in Thomas' wagon. Thomas took care of cutting Bill down while Katherine and Doctor Larimore prepared Betty's body to be moved.

Preparations for burial took all morning. Dr. Larimore and Katherine went to the mercantile store and purchased two coffins while Thomas went to see the pastor about the funeral. He visited a couple of the families from church that knew the Moore's. Once the graves were dug at the Big Springs Cemetery, the bodies in the coffins, the funeral planned, it was time.

Katherine and Mary dug through clothes which Nellie, Renie and Tommie had outgrown. The Moore children had worn clothing, basically rags, with stains and holes. Luckily, they were able to find something for all of the children. At least they could dress warmly enough to be at the graveside for a brief funeral. The three adults tried to explain to the children what had happened, although they did not have the words which could explain the tragedy, for the children and the Upton community. The funeral was quick to avoid any confusion for the children, and the family returned home with the orphans.

At church on Sunday morning, the six Moore children walked in with Katherine, Thomas and Mary as though they belonged to them. Nellie, Renie and Tommie had made the children feel at home. The congregation of the church discussed the sad happenings of Friday and Saturday. Pastor Ship explained to the congregation that the children would need a permanent home as there were no grandparents or relatives to their knowledge.

Pastor Ship was closing his message when three people entered the church. An old man, probably in his nineties, was assisted by a younger man, in his fifties. A lovely, gracious lady followed the two men. All three met Pastor Ship in the aisle with a handshake. The younger man asked, "Are you Pastor Ship? I sent you a letter."

"Yes, I am, and I am so glad to have you visit our church. You may talk with the congregation. I haven't told them anything," Pastor Ship said as he motioned for the three to go toward the pulpit.

The three strangers made their way to the pulpit. The younger man addressed the congregation. "Good morning, Congregation. We are here at the request of my father. A few weeks ago, we saw an article in the newspaper about a funeral and gravestone for the Mack Jackson family. We read about your generosity and we were so encouraged by a group of Christian people having such concern about others. We decided we wanted to come and meet you folks and tell you how much it meant to us to see that article in the newspaper. My name is Jason and this is my father, Mack Jackson."

Gasps, murmurs and whispers were heard in the congregation as the group realized this old man was the Mack Jackson they had heard about. The Mack Jackson who had killed an Indian and buried his family in a mass grave, then left the community.

Mack Jackson came to the podium with the help of his cane and his son. "I want to thank this church and this community for everything you have done for my family. Somewhere I think they know what you did for them. I want to thank the young men who found my note and the one who wrote the article. Will Mike Caswell and Tommie Cosby please stand?" The old man watched as the boys stood.

"I want to thank you and shake your hand before I leave." Mack Jackson pointed a shaky finger at the boys. "Without you finding that note, I would have never known about the gravestone. I had forgotten where this place was, had no idea how to find it. Had it not been for the article in the newspaper, I would not have been able to come back to my home place. For years I have wanted to return, but I didn't know how to get here.

Also, I had hate in my heart for the Cherokee for killing my family. God probably wouldn't let me know about this place because I had such hate in my heart. I think He protected this community from the kind of hate I had. When I saw the article in the paper, the church had taken an offering and put up the gravestone, I broke down and cried. I finally forgave the Cherokee and I asked God for forgiveness. At ninety-two years of age, I let go of hate and I allowed Jesus to come into my heart. I thank you, church, for leading me to Christ, to the love you have shown people whom you never knew, and to me.

"I also want to thank the Spurgeon family. Thank you for allowing the community to put up a stone there on your property. We appreciate it very much," Mack said as he wiped a tear from his eye. Mack was weeping so much he could not continue.

The woman was the next to talk. "I am Beckie Jackson, Mack's daughter-in-law. My mother-in-law, Lizzie Jackson died eight years ago. She was a good

Christian woman who led us to Christ. Since her death, my father-in-law has wanted to find this place where he lived as a boy. Before he could find his home place, he first had to find a heart like Jesus, which he did. We are so glad your young people sent the article to the newspaper. Two young men changed the lives of this family forever, and we thank you.

"Also, we would love to stay here awhile, especially through the winter. If you know of a place we could rent or purchase, please let us know. Thank you again, for everything you have done."

Katherine and Mary talked with Beckie Jackson as soon as the meeting was dismissed. The men talked with Mack Jackson and his son, Jason.

Renie kept trying to interrupt the women to talk with Beckie. Finally, when she saw a pause she jumped in. "Was your mother-in-law Aunt Lizzie?"

Mary tried to help as she explained that Renie was looking for an Aunt Lizzie.

Katherine thought, well, why not, there are stranger coincidences. "I think what Renie is questioning is whether your mother-in-law could be the Aunt Lizzie who was related to Marie Stanel and Audie Bearden?"

Beckie made a hand motion to wait a minute and as soon as she could she asked Mack about family. "Mack, do you remember a Marie Stanel or an Audie Bearden?"

Mack thought for a minute and replied, "Sure, I remember Audie and Marie. They were sisters and belonged to Lizzie's brother. They are my nieces. They visited us often when they were little and Lizzie kept in touch with them by letters. They thought so much of Lizzie."

Katherine and Renie hugged because Renie's hunch had been correct. Katherine explained how they had been with Audie when she died and how they had found the letter. Sadly, Katherine explained how their letter was returned with the note on it.

Thomas, hearing the conversation introduced Mack Jackson to his nephew, Luke Bearden. He explained that Luke was the only child of Clyde and Audie Bearden.

Mack, Jason, and Beckie shook hands with Luke and gave him hugs. "Family," Thomas told Luke. "You have family, Luke!"

Thomas explained Luke had nowhere to go when his mother had passed, so he had come home with him and he was enjoying Luke's company. Thomas told the Jackson family about Luke's ability to play the piano. He also told them about Luke's knowledge of the scripture, how he could quote it so well.

Luke was quiet as Thomas and the others talked about him. He kept eyeing the food being put on the tables, which was far more interesting.

The church had the usual Sunday dinner with tables inside due to the inclement weather. Food was being put on the tables and the congregation was ready to say grace. The Cosby family encouraged the Jackson family to stay and eat with everyone. The Jacksons, glad to be asked, assured them they would like to stay and meet the gracious people of the community.

Lyssa and Ollie found Katherine and told her they wanted to keep Baby Loeta. She and Baby Oleta would be raised together along with Leah and Hobie's baby. Thankfully, Ms. Pearl was there to help both women with the children. She had been such a wonderful gift to them.

Pete and Andrea visited with the six Moore children. The Goodwins summoned Pastor Ship, Thomas, Katherine and Mary. Pete and Andrea told the group they had considered adopting the three school-age children. Pete explained that he and Andrea had prayed about adopting them when they heard the news.

Andrea motioned for her sister, Tammie Taylor and her husband, Donald to join them. "We would like to adopt the three youngest children, if possible," Tammie told the group that had gathered. "Losing our children was so difficult that we thought we would never allow ourselves to love children again. But, we feel God has given us this opportunity. We would like to adopt the three younger children. Since we live close to Andrea and Pete, the children will be able to see each other often."

The pastor made an announcement that the children were going to live with Pete and Andrea Goodwin and Donald and Tammy Taylor. The congregation was happy to hear the Goodwin family and the Taylor family had grown to include the precious children. Individuals gave the families words of encouragement and promises to help when and if they needed them.

———◆———

Monday morning, after the children had gone to school and the necessary chores were finished, Mary insisted Katherine work on her wedding dress. Katherine complained that she felt too sad to work on the dress. She still felt guilty and so shocked at the deaths of the Moore parents.

Mary would not allow Katherine to blame herself. "Katherine, look at those children. Baby Loeta has a wonderful home with a mom, dad, brother, and sister. Plus, she will have another family which includes a grandmother who will love her. Hobie and Leah and the new baby will love baby Loeta. And think of how much Pete and Andrea wanted a baby. Now they have three children whom they will love and care for. Also, the Taylor family have three children they will love and adore. I know it is not a good situation for the parents to die, but God provided homes for them. Now, don't worry. There wasn't anything you could do. But, you can get started on your dress so you will be a beautiful bride," Mary pleaded.

"Okay, I guess you are right. Those kids will be well cared for now." Katherine smiled and began to gather her things together.

The ladies worked on the dress most of the week. Tiny pearl beads were sewn around the high neckline, fitted bodice and the sleeves. The beautiful dress was finished by Thursday evening. Katherine slipped the dress on and danced around the cabin, dreaming of her wedding day.

The door slammed behind him as Thomas placed a basket of potatoes on the table. "Brought these from the cellar, thought you might want them."

"What do you think of my dress, Thomas?" Katherine asked as she could tell his mind was somewhere else.

"Yeah, like it,, pretty."

Mary chatted about the dress while she insisted Thomas sit for a cup of cold milk and a piece of molasses cake.

After taking off the wedding dress, Katherine put on her blue calico frock and returned to the kitchen. "Are we going to talk about it Thomas?"

"You know it is making me crazy not knowing. I've had a hundred different ideas about that letter. And you know, I felt like Judge Winston was saying that I should know."

Katherine sighed. "We probably should know. Yes, we should also have known enough about Johnny's friend David, someone he spent so much time with."

Thomas bowed his head at the table and cleared his throat. "Well, mom, I have an admission. I had heard more than once that Johnny was running around with a rascal, a boy that had been in trouble for stealing. Anyway, I told Johnny many times to stop running around with him, to not have anything to do with the young thief. Guess he didn't listen."

Feeling a bit sorry for her son, Katherine sat beside Thomas and patted his hand. As she did, she traced the coffee-stain birthmark on Thomas' left hand. "Thomas! I don't know why I didn't think of it before! Can you take me to see Bob right now? I can drive myself, but I think you will want to go with me."

Despite Thomas' efforts to get his mother to share her suspicions, Katherine would not give in. As the two walked into jail, Katherine gasped!

"Thomas, don't you see it?' Katherine shook hands with the young man and introduced herself. As she did she rubbed Bob's hand.

"There it is, Thomas!" Katherine said passionately.

"The coffee stain birthmark! All of my kids have it." Thomas looked at Bob for an explanation.

Bob looked down almost afraid to say anything.

"Rissa was right." Katherine said slowly as if deep in thought. "There were two babies."

"My...my name is Robert David Wright. My mother was a midwife." Bob said as he continued to look at the floor.

Katherine seemed to be bursting with excitement. "The midwife took Johnny's not identical, twin brother, away from us. Thomas, this is Johnny's friend David and Thomas...this is your son!"

———⋅———

Andrea took the children to school every day. They had their own lunch pail with plenty of food in them. The three younger children relished in the love and attention that the Taylor family gave them. Family and friends offered help to Andrea and Pete and Donald and Tammy with the children and everyone received a blessing from doing so. The community had a frequent scripture, *But Jesus said, Let the little children come to Me, and do not forbid them; for of such is the kingdom of heaven.*

Lyssa and Baby Loeta along with Baby Oleta were getting along fine, but Lyssa was not able to get much done between nursing both babies. Ms. Pearl was definitely a blessing for she was able to keep up with the cooking and cleaning, along with helping at the shop. Leah was due in a week or so, and although Leah tried to keep up, she was tired all the time. There were a few orders for winter hats which Leah had to work on. Lyssa also had a few orders to fill. The business had really taken off since opening day and the shop had sold many yards of muslin, silks, and calicos. The yarns and needles were beginning to sell since Leah had been giving free knitting and crocheting lessons. Lyssa had been designing and making a piece of women's clothing or a piece of children's clothing until Baby Loeta came along. Since then she had not had much time. However, she did not regret having Baby Loeta in their family.

The Jacksons decided they would move into the Bearden cabin, if okay with Luke. Luke was jubilant! He was quick to tell them he would go with them. When the four had settled in the home, Luke showed them where everything was, the cellar, the well, the attic, all the special hiding places. He split wood, brought it in, and took out the ashes.

Having been at the new home for only a couple of days, both men became sick. During the time, Luke was indispensable. Luke entertained the family by playing the old organ and repeating scripture. He never let the fire die down and was constantly taking out the ashes and cleaning around the stove. Luke went to the well and drew up water for the family and made sure there was always water on the stove warming. He helped with Mack, getting him up and down when he needed to go to the outhouse, even cleaning up after him.

After the illness had passed, Beckie told the Cosby family about how wonderful Luke had been to them. "You know, we took Luke into our family to help him, instead he has helped us. We could not have made it without him. Luke has a heart so loved by Our Lord. How hallowed he is, how we have been blessed by him! We are so glad we are here. Right up the creek is the Spurgeon place where Mack's family is buried, so we feel so close to Mack's family. We have been blessed by being led here. We will need to pray about our plans before we leave in March."

After their visit to the Jackson's, Katherine and Mary went to Upton to shop at Head to Toe. Mary checked in with the two babies while Katherine went to the post office. Lyssa was so proud of her baby girls. The shop looked great, fully stocked, and with customers. Mary was so happy for the girls and their families; she had made a good investment in more ways than one.

As Katherine looked at the envelope, she couldn't believe her eyes. It was a letter from Rebecca Boone, complete with a return address. Shaking, Katherine tore open the envelope and read.

Dec. 6, 1845

Dear Katherine,

    I hope that your wedding plans are going well. Wish I could be there. Thank you for your advice. I have not heard from my baby's father. However, I am looking forward to having my baby. I am living at my aunt's house by myself as she has gone for a while. I am working at a restaurant nearby. I know I have a lot to manage, but I keep thinking about my Grandmother and how she did it without any help, with ten children! Thank you for your encouragement. Best wishes to the Bride!

God Bless,
Rebecca

Katherine crossed the street to Head to Toe shop. She could hardly keep from shouting the news. Instead, Katherine greeted Lyssa and Leah and embraced Mary.

"Mary, I have the answer to our prayers," Katherine said as she handed Mary the envelope.

Mary spent the evening composing a letter to Rebecca. All she could do at that point was tell the truth, and hope that Rebecca understood. She poured her heart into the letter, praying as she wrote that she would choose the right words. When she had finished writing, Mary read the letter to Thomas. The couple held each other and prayed for the daughter who would soon receive the letter that could possibly change all their lives.

# Chapter 49

# Another Wedding

Wedding preparations were the focus of the week. Katherine's family had made plans to attend the wedding of the year. Some of the family would go home with Thomas and Mary while others would stay at Katherine's house. Dr. Larimore had only a couple of families coming from Lexington as it was simply too far, so they too, would stay in Katherine's house also.

Mary was making cakes and cookies which would last for the week. On the day of the wedding, Mary would take hams with biscuits and bread to Katherine's home. They would need plenty of food with all the people who were coming. She and the children were excited to see Thomas' sister and her family.

Dr. Larimore had hired a photographer to come take a picture of the bride and groom before the wedding. The photography was known as daguerreotype portraits and was something new for the area. Katherine wanted a photograph of the entire family after the wedding, so the family was coaxed to prepare for the photograph, to be in their best outfit complete with smiles.

Nellie was preparing some of her dried flowers as arrangements for the church using the flowers she had hung upside down to dry. Leah was very good at flower arrangements, so on Wednesday after school, Nellie and Mary rode to the shop to leave the flowers. The cock's comb which had dried beautifully and would add a lot of red to the arrangements. Included in the flower collection were hydrangeas, zinnias, wild coreopsis, and ironweed.

Leah sorted the flowers to be dipped in wax and a little mineral oil. The wax dipping would preserve them, keep them from shedding at church, and it would also make them shine. Leah made a large bouquet for the front of the church. She placed them in a porcelain pitcher and made a large bow of the silk that Katherine had selected for her dress. The rest of the flowers were used to decorate the end of the pews with a little of the silk ribbon. On Thursday, she and her mother would go to the church and finish the flower arrangements. Again, she thanked God for her mother. She and Lyssa agreed that they couldn't do without their mom.

Even the weather had responded to the wedding invitation as it appeared the most beautiful as a December day could be. The sun was warm, there was a gentle breeze and not a cloud in the skies. Katherine felt God had waved His hand to allow the answer to her prayers.

Mr. Martin began playing his violin, a signal for everyone to be quiet. Next, Katherine walked down the aisle on the arm of her son, Thomas. All the family sitting together gave gasps at how beautiful Katherine looked in her pink silk with the matching hat. Katherine had a radiance that made her look at least twenty years younger.

Dr. Larimore was up front waiting for his bride. He looked handsome in his black suit. Leah had made him a dark red silk tie and a matching flower to pin on his suit. Both of them were a beautiful couple as they stood before Pastor Ship.

Standing across from her, holding her hand, saying his vows to love, honor, and protect her for the rest of her life was the man that Katherine loved. Although they had known each other only a few months, Katherine felt this man was the love of her life. As they kissed, Katherine felt tingles from her head to her toes. She was so happy to be able to share her life with Keith.

As Katherine and Keith said their vows, Mike winked at Nellie. Nellie couldn't help but think that it meant something special.

As the newlywed Larimore couple walked down the aisle, the congregation clapped and cheered. "What a beautiful wedding," was repeated by all.

Handshakes and well wishes were extended, as friends and family greeted each other while the bridal party posed for a picture. The children became tired of standing and the adults were tired of smiling by the time the picture was actually made. Relieved, the family broke away and headed to Katherine's house for the reception.

Sallye and Andrea assured Dr. Larimore and Katherine they would get to the house first to welcome the guests. Buggies and horses were being taken care of by John, Pete, Ollie and Hobie. The men made sure that the horses were well cared for.

The evening was a night of merriment for the family. Dr. Larimore's friend, Louis, proposed a toast. "Ladies and Gentlemen, I want to propose a toast to this lovely young couple. They have taught me so much about the love of God because that is what it is all about. When we love God, we love others, and we let God be seen in us.

"On my last visit to this town, I tried to show Keith no community could be this good, people could not love God and their neighbors as much as they spoke of. Yet, I was proved dolefully wrong. This community loves each other, but more importantly they love the Lord their God.

"Therefore, I say to you this evening, rejoice because Keith and Katherine gave their hearts to each other. Praise God for bringing them together... and praise God for this community."

While family and friends ate wedding cake, many were talking about the sweet love story of Keith and Katherine. "Say, Doc! You and Ms. Katherine didn't court long, before'n you got hitched! How did you know that you wanted to spend yer life with her? Ollie asked.

The doctor wiped the cake crumbs from his mouth and smiled. "Well, that is a good story. In fact, I haven't told Katherine about this. You see I had a dream a few months before I came to Upton for the first visit. The dream was so real, I still remember it. I was hearing piano music, so I began looking where it was coming from. An angel appeared and was leading me somewhere, and she showed me a door. The door appeared to be to a doctor's office, but it wasn't mine. I looked at the door again, and it had my name on it. Going in the office I saw someone there. I couldn't tell anything about the person who was there, but I had this amazing feeling of love. I felt so good there around the person who was radiating love, but the angel didn't let me stay. She led me out until the piano stopped playing and I awoke."

Pete, obviously enjoying the story, wanted to know more. "What was the angel like? Was she pretty? Did she have wings?"

"I can't say she had wings, she was just able to move everywhere. She was beautiful. She looked a little like Renie, only an adult version, I guess." The doctor kept talking while the family looked at each other. "She was so filled with love, and I remember she was beautiful, and I wanted to go back where she had taken me, but I woke up."

The family and friends who knew Rissa, looked at each other with surprise. Mary, who had found a comfortable chair, became uncomfortable and kept changing positions in the chair. Suddenly, she jumped up claiming something had stuck her.

Katherine ran to the chair and looked to see if she had left a needle in the chair. "I am so sorry. Where was it?" Katherine apologized as she ran her hand around the cushion. Finding the needle, Katherine showed everyone. "A hat pin. I am so sorry, Mary. I don't know how this pin got here. Must have fallen out the last time I wore my hat." Katherine excused herself and went upstairs to her bedroom. The box for the hat pin was on her dresser.

Feeling the presence of someone else in the room, Katherine held the pin for a minute and thought about Keith's dream. "Thank you, Rissa. Thank you for bringing Keith into my life. I know you were the angel. And, my sweet Rissa, this hat pin, the pin that you gave me for my birthday, well, I had it safely in its box and put away. You certainly made your point! Thank you! You were the best daughter-in-law I could have ever had." Katherine felt she was now alone in the bedroom.

Doctor Larimore knocked on the bedroom door and called for Katherine. As he opened the door, he asked, "Katherine, are you okay? Come down with your guests. They are worried about you."

Katherine left the room, smiling. "I have never been better," she added as they walked downstairs together. Family members were talking among themselves, remembering good times, and enjoying being together.

Nellie introduced Mike to an older cousin, Dale Copelin. Dale was an adventurer, a traveler, and being single, had never settled down. Mike was fascinated as he listened to Dale tell tales about his adventures out west, past the Arkansas River and even the Oregon Territory trails.

Before long, the conversation was just between Dale and Mike. Mike was so enthralled with Dale's adventures, he couldn't stop asking questions. Dale realized Mike was much like him at his age. Dale shared his adventures with the explorer, John Fremont, along with Kit Carson, and how they were leading a group of explorers out west. He explained how the Indians were being pushed to the reservations. Although he knew Mike was part Cherokee, he did not seem sympathetic to the Indians.

"Yea, I just came from New York and I saw many Indians there." Dale moved from where he had been standing to a seat that had just been vacated.

"Since Jackson's treaty, all the Indians were supposed to move west of the Mississippi, but looks like many have stayed."

"Do you know where the Cherokee are? Where most of them are today?" Mike asked timidly.

"The Cherokee Nation is located in the south, around Georgia. There is a newspaper written by two Cherokee brothers. I think it's called the Cherokee Phoenix. The newspaper ran articles in Cherokee and English. Don't know, but I don't think it is in circulation now. I met one of the brothers a few years ago. His name was Stand Watie." Dale looked directly into Mike's eyes. "I was impressed with his political knowledge. Of course, President Polk has ideas of his own, with Texas becoming a state and problems from the Mexican War, he has not been focusing on the Indians."

Mike listened to how the west was being explored and how the Indians were being pushed aside. Somehow Dale had introduced him to a world he had not known existed. Mike felt a stirring in his soul which told him to move, to go find his Cherokee ancestors. His world was changing, and he had to tell Nellie. Mike felt he must help. He would wait until after Christmas to tell Nellie.

Finally alone, the married couple embraced. Sharing a long kiss, it was Katherine who finally brought an end to the magical moment.

"This has been a wonderful day, Doctor," Katherine said as she smiled at her husband.

"It has been one of the most wonderful days of my life, Katherine, my dear," Dr. Larimore said as he held her hand between his. "You know, I never thought that I would ever be this happy."

"I know what you mean; I thought I would not have the chance to share the rest of my life with a companion. Now, God has blessed me with bringing you into my life."

Katherine said, as she happened to remember, "So, we have a brother in Christ, Louis. No one talks about loving the Lord that much unless they have received salvation. Guess we could baptize him in the creek before he goes home," Katherine laughed. She figured it would be good payback.

As they headed to bed, nothing was more important than just the two of them being together. The love and passion that the couple shared was so special Katherine felt like the first time she had shared the marriage bed.

The family enjoyed the weekend together, sitting around the fire, telling stories on each other, playing games, eating all the snacks and goodies that had been prepared, and just enjoying being together for the wedding celebration. After the meal on Sunday, many of the family and friends started their journey back home. Although no one wanted to leave, many had their own families and friends waiting back home. Katherine made everyone promise they would get together the next summer. She would have everyone at her house for a large family reunion.

# Chapter 50

# Christmas

On Monday morning, Katherine and Keith woke early and had coffee together as they read the Bible. They had decided to not plan anything, but be with each other, no need to go anywhere or do anything but relax. Although the family had taken care of the dishes, and the house, Katherine was really tired from the weekend. She needed a day to rest and so did the doctor. For the newly married couple, being a new bride and groom had worn them out.

Hobie was at the door early Tuesday morning, Christmas Eve, "Mrs. Katherine, I think Leah is ready to have her baby. She started having pains about a couple hours ago. Can you and the doctor come?"

"We sure can. We will be there as soon as we can pack our things. You go ahead and we will bring our buggy," Katherine replied.

The medical emergency was the first time Dr. Larimore and Katherine would be working as a husband/wife team, and it felt quite natural to them. As they traveled to Leah, the couple talked about Leah's baby being born on Christmas Eve. "There is just something very special about a baby born on Christmas Eve or Christmas day. It will surely have a heart like Baby Jesus because of all the love surrounding it. Can't we go faster? We've got to get to Leah!" Katherine urged.

When the couple arrived at Hobie's house, Leah was having frequent contractions. Her contractions were coming every three minutes. Ms. Pearl had water on to boil and rags ready for them when they arrived.

Within the hour, Dr. Larimore and Katherine delivered a beautiful baby boy. Hobie and Leah held their son for the first time as they kissed the baby's head. They praised God for a beautiful baby boy and for an easy delivery for Leah.

"Do you have a name for your baby?" Katherine asked.

"Yes, ma'am, we do," Leah answered. "We are going to name him after my dad and Hobie's dad, Joseph Elijah Woodson."

"What a beautiful name for beautiful little boy, and you will call him, Elijah or Joseph, or maybe Joey?" Katherine asked.

"Since we just finished reading about Elijah in the Bible, we think we will call him Elijah. He was a blessing to many, and we hope for our Elijah to be a blessing," Hobie said.

"You know our tradition is that the newest baby is the one in the manger for the Christmas program. What do you think? Will you let Elijah be our baby Jesus?" Katherine asked.

Hobie and Leah looked at each other. "Well, what about the color of our baby? He is not a White baby Jesus, don't you think it might make a difference?"

Doctor Larimore was the first to answer. "Not at all. How do we really know what color Jesus was anyway? I think it would be wonderful for Baby Elijah to be Baby Jesus. Right, Katherine?"

"Absolutely," Katherine answered. "There couldn't be a more beautiful baby Jesus."

---

On Christmas Eve, the snow began to fall about noon. The roads, fields, homes, and trees were blanketed with beautiful sparkling snow. The snowfall was peaceful, almost a fat, lazy snow, with lovely, large flakes. Children were sticking out their tongues catching snowflakes, and their laughter filled the air along with a few snowballs. On that snowy evening at church, children, along with adults, had a sense of the Christmas excitement, the birth of Jesus.

Before the Christmas program started, Andrea had to see the Cosby family. Andrea found Thomas and Tommie to tell them the good news. "I hope you don't mind, but I sent one of Tommie's papers to a school up north. I received a letter back from them today. Tommie's paper won first place in the school's nationwide writing contest. They have a cash award and a possible scholarship for Tommie for next year. You can read this letter. It says they believe he has incredible potential, and they would love to have him at their school."

Tommie looked at his father in disbelief. Thomas took the letter and put it in his pocket. "We will talk about it. I am proud of Tommie. His mother would be especially proud today. Thank you for doing this for Tommie, Andrea. We have always known Tommie was exceptional."

With the activities beginning to start, Tommie had to take his place in the manger scene. Thomas joined Mary with the good news. He was so proud of his son.

The congregation saw a packed church as the families found seats and sat close together, keeping warm at the same time. Just before Nellie started the Christmas music, a young lady entered the church and found a seat in the back. Everyone focused on the program while Katherine went to the back seat.

Nellie, who had been playing Christmas music, changed to her Mary costume and took her place beside Mike, who was Joseph at the cattle stall. Baby Jesus had been placed in the crib and was peacefully asleep. As the children went through their parts, the parents strained to see their precious child say his or her part, while hearts overflowed with pride. The children sang their Christmas songs and said their parts of the manger scene. For the last song, the congregation stood and sang along. Baby Jesus lay swaddled in his crib without a sound, as though he had learned his parts well.

Hannah was one of the angels, and she was to end the program. The little angel said, "A Sav'er is born, He is born, He is..." As she looked at the baby, she was supposed to say, "He is born," instead, when she looked at the baby she said "He is brown?"

At first, the audience giggled. Eventually, they were roaring with laughter. From the innocence of a child, the fact was Baby Jesus in the cradle was brown. This baby, this child, was destined to a future which would lead to one of the most influential periods of the history of the community, the state, and the nation. However, tonight he represented the Savior of the World, the little King who would die to save all mankind.

As the children finished their program for the night, the congregation gathered around the pine tree which had been placed in the back of the church. The entire area had a heady scent of pine which made the church smell like Christmas. Fresh baked cookies gave a lovely smell of cinnamon and gingerbread. Homemade ornaments adorned the tree along with popcorn strings. Bags of candy and fresh fruit were presented to all the children. Thankful adults watched as all of the children were thrilled to be getting gifts. Every heart was lifted with the gift of Christmas.

Rebecca, who had slipped in the back of the church, held Katherine's hand. As soon as the Mack Jackson family saw Rebecca they came to her side. Anxious to learn about their niece's trip, the couple crowded around to their niece, as Jason and Beckie had many questions.

Mary was the most excited of all. As she introduced herself to Rebecca, Thomas approached the two. "Oh, Thomas, can you believe that she is here? This is a miracle."

"Well, yes, I can. See, I sent someone to pick her up and bring her home. Merry Christmas, my sweet Mary." Thomas said hardly able to keep his voice from breaking up.

Hugging his wife, Thomas felt better than he had since Rissa had died. "We have our prodigal children with us now. With David and Rebecca we will have even more to look forward to. I feel so blessed."

As the Cosby family prepared to leave, Nellie realized she should have worn her warm coat. Thomas noticed Nellie, with her thin coat. "Here Nellie, take my coat; I have my warm wool suit on and I don't need the coat."

Nellie nestled in the big warm coat, waving goodbye to friends and family. In an attempt to warm her hands, she plunged them in the pockets. Feeling a piece of paper, Nellie pulled it out and read aloud.

"Thomas, I saw you with Mary.
Paul."

As the families gathered outside the church, Pastor Ship gave each family a candle. "Take this candle out into the dark world and spread the gospel. Let your light shine, just as this candle shines to light the world."

For some reason Nellie felt compelled to burn the note with her candle. Quickly, the black ashes fell from the note into the soft, white snow, as though the black ashes had been made pure from the snow.

As families shared hugs and goodbyes, they left the church carrying their candles and the love of Christ, a newborn Savior, in their hearts. The snow was continuing to fall and accumulate to almost a foot in places, making it look like God had designed a special winter scene especially for them. What a beautiful landscape in the countryside as the families left in their buggies and wagons with their candle lights lighting the way. The people of the Roundstone and Upton community were spreading the hope of God's love with them wherever they went on Tuesday, December 24, 1845.

Many events would follow in the next few years; yet with God's people, there would always be love in the Hart of Roundstone.

# THE END

# Bibliography

Hunt, Rosalie Hall: We've a Story To Tell: 125 Years of WMU: Woman's Missionary Union, SBC, 2013

Printed in the United States
By Bookmasters